BRIAN MORRISON's first novel was *State of Resurrection*. *Blood Brother* is his second, and his third, to be published in Fontana in 1992, is *A Cause for Dying*. He has spent many years in Paris, but now lives with his wife and two daughters in Devon.

Reviews for *Blood Brother*:

'The author has a feel not only for the shifting loyalties and covert double-dealings which form the bloodied fabric of the Lebanon, but creates in Julia a believable central character ... Morrison writes with authority and a compelling sense of pace, creating a credible political thriller which is a disturbing reminder of the iniquitous acts of terrorism in the messy wars which plague the Middle East. Drawing in the wider political implications of hostage-taking and careerist manoeuvres in the White House, Morrison has come up with a gripping tale with a disquieting ring of accuracy.'
Time Out

'Excellent ... Fast-moving and pacy.'
Yorkshire Post

Available in Fontana by the same author

STATE OF RESURRECTION

BRIAN MORRISON

Blood Brother

FONTANA/Collins

*For Susan Shup an Claude Frankignoul
with thanks for all the help and encouragement*

First published by William Collins Sons & Co. Ltd 1990

This edition first published in 1991 by Fontana,
an imprint of HarperCollins Publishers,
77/85 Fulham Palace Road,
Hammersmith, London W6 8JB.

9 8 7 6 5 4 3 2 1

Copyright © 1990 by Brian Morrison

The Author asserts the moral right to be
identified as the author of this work

Printed and bound in Great Britain by
HarperCollins Manufacturing, Glasgow

CONDITIONS OF SALE

This book is sold subject to the condition
that it shall not, by way of trade or otherwise,
be lent, re-sold, hired out or otherwise circulated
without the publisher's prior consent in any form of
binding or cover other than that in which it is
published and without a similar condition
including this condition being imposed
on the subsequent purchaser

Prologue

'PAH-LAH-VI OUT! Down with the Shah!'

'Kho-mei-ni! Kho-mei-ni!'

The rhythmic chanting grew louder as the solid mass of bodies advanced up the broad avenue between the rows of shuttered shops. The wide pavements were deserted. Along each side of the eight-lane carriageway the ditches that served as drains ran a foot deep with the run-off from the last filthy remains of the snow that made the Tehran winter so harsh and ugly.

As the column advanced, filling the width of the road between the open drains, Julia felt touched by a strange certainty. There was something in the measured pace of their advance, the discipline, the orchestration of the slogans; for the first time she knew, absolutely, that these people would win. The days of the Pahlavis' preposterous attempt at a dynasty would soon be at a close.

The column drew nearer. Julia could make out individuals, their clenched fists raised, the men's faces contorted as they shouted the slogans, the women's hidden in the black folds of their chadors. She reached for one of the cameras that hung at her neck and began shooting, trying for shots of the turbanned mullahs at the head of the procession.

The sea of faces had drawn much closer, nearing the ornate mosque from the tower of which the address was to be made. On the balcony that encircled the slender tower, two-thirds up its height, robed figures busied themselves with last-minute adjustments to the huge speakers slung from the stuccoed tracery of the parapet. The square in front of the mosque was deserted. Julia turned to another photographer who stood close by her, intent on the procession.

'Strange, isn't it?'

The man kept his eye to his camera. 'What?'

'This.' She gestured to the empty square. 'No soldiers.'

The man glanced quickly in the direction of Julia's

gesture. He shrugged, returning to his photography. 'So what? The mullahs seem to have it under control.'

The procession was level with them now. Under the direction of a number of mullahs wearing distinctive yellow flashes pinned to the sleeves of their robes the crowd was deploying into the square.

Julia and the cluster of photographers began moving, keeping abreast of the leaders as they continued towards the mosque, concentrating on the small group of men at the centre of a knot of acolytes.

'Maybe the Shah's gone,' somebody shouted. 'There was a rumour he'd left for Switzerland.'

'No,' Julia rejoined. 'He's still here. Jean Fabre of *Le Monde* got an interview yesterday.'

'Lucky bastard,' a voice retorted. 'I've not been able to get near the palace for a week!'

'None of us has.' Julia spoke angrily at the man. 'Give the man a break. He's eaten up by cancer. Would you want to be photographed like that?'

Before the man could respond a roar rose from the crowd. The massed faces turned upwards. Julia and the others in the group turned quickly to stare up at the balcony. A small figure, black-robed, stood alone behind a row of microphones, his hands raised to quell the crowd.

Julia lifted the camera with the long snout of the telephoto to her eye and zoomed in on the lone figure. He stood stock-still for some seconds, waiting for the silence to become total. The only sound was the quiet whirr of the winding mechanisms of a dozen cameras as the group frantically snapped the diminutive figure. He dropped his arms and opened his mouth to speak.

Her eye pressed to the viewfinder, Julia kept squeezing the shutter release. She could see the mullah's Adam's apple bobbing below his short goatee. She saw with total clarity his head buck backwards and the man's frail body arch and then crumple, falling forward to hang across the stone parapet. A slash of vermilion drops appeared shockingly against the pristine white of the minaret. Only then did she hear the shot.

For a long moment it reverberated, the only sound in the silent square. Then, slowly, a ghastly noise, between a wail and a roar, rose from the throats of the crowd. As the volume of sound grew, so its quality altered until it became a gigantic bellow of rage.

At the same time Julia became aware of another sound, the deeper, ominous growl of motors. Letting the camera swing at her waist, she looked around the vast square.

'Holy shit!' she breathed softly.

From the wide avenue that stretched to the north and south of the square and from all the smaller entrances at the sides came the threatening bulks of tanks. Troops in full combat gear advanced between them. Some carried grenade-launchers, the bulbous shapes of tear-gas grenades already protruding from their wide barrels. Others carried rifles. All had long batons slung at their hips.

Julia spun at the roar of a motor behind her. A tank, its camouflage paint unblemished by warfare, had emerged from a side street not forty metres away and was rolling towards the spot where the photographers stood. Taking pictures all the while, Julia shouted to her colleagues. Cameras whirring, they began moving backwards into the square, away from the advancing tank.

The leaders of the procession began making for the sanctuary of the mosque. Julia followed them, still taking pictures. As she ran she was aware of the dull sound of the gas grenades being fired. Sudden clouds formed with deceptive prettiness among the running figures. People reeled away from the gas, clawing at their eyes.

A grenade exploded a few feet from Julia. She dropped to her knees, coughing and weeping. The group of mullahs had disappeared inside the mosque. All around her the soldiers were charging into the milling crowd, their batons flailing at the unprotected heads of the throng.

Julia's breath came more easily. As her vision cleared she stared in astonishment. Two tanks had drawn up facing the mosque. An officer in mirror sunglasses stood in the turret of one of them. He spoke into a padded microphone. A moment later both tanks recoiled in a squall of smoke and noise. Julia had only an instant to be surprised at the neatness of the two round holes that appeared, each the size of a dustbin lid, in the wall of the mosque. The next moment she was throwing herself flat as the heavy machine guns on the tanks began stuttering, sending a shower of masonry flying from the walls.

The tanks' turret guns continued firing, the sound of rapid fire merging into a continuous awesome crash. Julia lay motionless, watching as the breeze-block walls beneath the stucco began to crumble. Abruptly, a group of clerics burst from the building. Some of the men, older and feebler, leant heavily on the younger ones as they tried to flee.

A shout went up from the soldiers and a group of them charged into the fleeing group, lashing out viciously with their batons. The mullahs' efforts to defend themselves were ineffectual. Except for one man. Moving more nimbly than the others, he side-stepped and struck back at one of the soldiers, doubling him over with a blow under the ribs. The man sprang past the soldier and fled into the crowd.

Scrambling to her feet, Julia turned to follow the man. She had taken two steps when the world exploded in a flash of white lightning. She pitched onto the greasy tarmac.

Julia recovered her senses slowly. She pushed herself to her feet and put a hand to the spot on the side of her head that throbbed violently. She withdrew her hand. It was sticky with a coating of blood.

The tanks had stopped firing. The worst of the melee had moved some distance away. Slowly and unsteadily she began walking from the scene in search of somewhere to rest.

She walked on for two or three blocks, past the shops and cafés with their padlocked shutters. There were only a few soldiers now. They lounged, smoking, in small groups, watching with sullen curiosity as the bloodstained figure passed. The pain in her head was making her feel violently sick. She turned into a narrow cul-de-sac. Blank walls ran around three sides. She leant her head against a wall and vomited.

It helped. Her head felt clearer, though the throbbing still filled her skull. She turned to leave the alley.

At that instant a running figure burst from the street and sped past her. Julia could hear the man's breathing coming in great hoarse gasps as he came up short against the high featureless wall at the end.

For a moment the man stood looking up at the wall, his shoulders heaving. Then he turned and began running back towards the street. It was the man who had escaped from the mosque. As he passed Julia he stopped. A look of resignation entered his face. A soldier had appeared in the entrance of the alley.

The sweating soldier stood for a moment, weighing up the situation. Then, with a grim smile, he began moving slowly towards the cleric. The man gave ground before the soldier.

The two of them were almost level with Julia. The soldier was grinning blankly, his baton gripped in both hands. Without warning, he sprang forward and rammed the baton into the man's stomach. The young cleric pitched forward.

The soldier took a pace backward and settled himself on spread legs. He raised the baton high above his head.

Julia stared at the scene in growing horror. The cleric lifted his head and looked into the snarling face of the soldier. There was no fear as he helplessly watched the soldier set himself for the blow.

For an instant Julia seemed frozen to the spot. Then, with an intake of breath, she moved. Her left foot slid forward a pace. At the same time she used her right leg like a spring, pushing herself forward and upward. Her shoulders swivelled. Her right arm shot out like a piston. The heel of her open hand caught the soldier squarely under the nose.

There was a quite distinct, sickening crack as the bones of the man's face splintered. Without a cry he crumpled and lay still. Julia stared down at him, hardly believing what she saw. A thousand times, back in the gym in New York, in the anti-rape classes, she had simulated that blow. This was the first time ever she had needed to do it for real. The effects were awesome.

The cleric clambered slowly to his feet. Beneath his dark skin the blood had drained from his face.

'Thank you.' His English was confident, with a strong American accent.

Julia raised an eyebrow and smiled. 'My pleasure.' She dropped the smile. 'Shouldn't we get out of here?'

They ran for several blocks before stopping at a taxi rank where a solitary, battered taxi waited. The driver rose from his squatting position at their approach, pushing a sheaf of smudged documents into his pocket. Julia recognized the logo of the Khomeini newsletter that was being smuggled into the country for clandestine distribution.

The cleric turned to Julia. His expression was deadly earnest. 'Go straight to the airport. Go home. They won't forgive you for helping me.'

Julia looked at him, half amused. 'Are you that important?'

He shrugged. 'I may be,' he said, without false modesty, 'after the Revolution.' He gave a sudden smile, his first. 'You must come back then. What's your name?'

'Julia Colter.' She held out a hand. '*New York Times*.'

'Mehdi Bahrawi.' He flicked a hand at his beard. 'I'm a mullah.'

He caught her wry look. 'You Americans are wrong about the Revolution. You're wrong about Imam Khomeini. It's true he's a bitter man. He has a right to be. Your media don't talk about how he was forced to leave here in the trunk of a car. Or how the French humiliate him even now in that miserable house outside Paris.' He smiled again, a smile full of sudden warmth. 'We follow the Imam's teachings; we don't have to share all his views.'

Still smiling, he reached into his robes and withdrew a knife. The handle was encrusted with mother-of-pearl, its scabbard inlaid with silver. 'Please take this. As a souvenir of our meeting. It was made in Isfahan for my grandfather.'

She shook her head. 'I can't. Not a family thing.'

He folded her fingers over the knife. 'A token of your service to the Revolution,' he said, with gentle irony.

1

'IS THAT HIM?' The speaker handed the powerful binoculars to one of his two companions. The man put them quickly to his eyes. He tweaked the knurled wheel of the focus adjustment with a nicotine-yellowed thumb, a frown of concentration furrowing the tan brow above the binoculars. After perhaps five seconds he lowered the glasses and looked around at the other two men.

'That's him,' he said flatly. 'Let's go!'

Moving quickly, but without an appearance of hurry, the three men gathered their weapons and a plastic bag from where they lay on the bare cement floor.

Only the charred carcase of a sofa indicated that the flat had once been inhabited. Bright morning sunlight streamed into the room through two jagged holes in the masonry of one wall. Outside the French windows, from which they had observed the man, a few twisted strands of reinforcing bars showed where a balcony had once been. Now the windows opened onto a void.

The three men walked to the door. It was held closed with a length of charred wood jammed between the floor and the broken lock. The oldest of the men, the one with the nicotine-stained fingers, kicked away the wood and let the door swing open. They strode to the littered stairs, past the gaping door of the lift. The black tunnel of the shaft plunged several floors to where the lift had jammed on its last journey. The older man's nostrils twitched at the odour of corruption that wafted from the shaft. Somebody had been in it when it crashed. They were still there. It was not wise to use a lift in Beirut nowadays.

All three of the men were Arabs. The leader, around forty years old, tall and lean with receding sparse dark hair, was dressed in a khaki shirt with a lot of pockets, khaki cotton trousers with deep, buttoned pockets on the thighs and high lace-up boots. He looked like a soldier. The other two men, not more than twenty, wore similar military-style shirts, tight Levis, faded almost white at the knees, and dirty training shoes. The older man carried a small machine gun, the others the Kalashnikovs that were the standard weapon of all factions in the Lebanese maelstrom. They held the guns loosely at their sides, as familiarly as other men would have held briefcases.

They encountered no one on the stairs, although occasionally the noise of transistor radios reached them from flats now inhabited by some of Beirut's army of displaced.

On the pavement outside the broken block of flats a few hawkers squatted immobile alongside their impoverished displays of matches, razor blades and cheap soap. They showed no quickening of interest as the three armed men crossed the pavement to the scarred and battered Chevrolet which stood at the kerb, its windows left open in the heat.

The men climbed quickly into the car. The older man and one of the others sat in the dusty back seat. The other young man clambered into the driving seat and gunned the engine hard and needlessly. Then the car shot from the kerb with a scream of tyres, leaving a stench of burning rubber hanging in the oppressive air.

Michael Colter pushed his way through the heavy revolving doors of the American University building, feeling the heat as a sudden blow after the air-conditioned chill of the interior. He slipped on a pair of sunglasses and shrugged off the thin cotton jacket he wore to ward off the slight bite of the air inside, folding it over his arm. The forearms below the short sleeves of his shirt were thick and muscular. His hands were heavily knuckled and hard-looking, with tufts of black hair on the backs of the fingers, a striking contrast to the sensitive chiselled face.

Two more men emerged from the building behind him. One was elderly, silver-haired and elegantly dressed, with only the slightly yellowish tinge to his skin betraying his Arab origins. The other was young, athletic, dressed in jeans and a polo shirt. An American-made automatic rifle hung at his shoulder.

The older man smiled at Michael, said a few words, shook hands, his own lost in the younger man's huge fist, and turned to re-enter the building. Michael and his bodyguard began descending the steps, talking and laughing. They crossed the compound slowly, heading for the car park close by the big iron gates. In front of the gates two Lebanese Army sentries operated a red- and white-striped barrier.

They crossed the car park towards a small Honda. As they did so the bodyguard's constantly restless glance fell on a car pulling up at the open gates. Mechanically, one hand rose to begin slipping the gun from his shoulder. With the other he took Michael by the arm and pushed him roughly behind him. He watched as the sentries moved close to the car and spoke to the driver, the only occupant of the car. The sentries examined the driver's papers and then moved back, raising the striped pole and waving the car on.

The bodyguard relaxed, settled the gun back on his shoulder and mumbled an apology. Michael laughed away the apology and drew the car keys from his pocket.

The rusting Chevrolet drew into a slot a few spaces from the Honda. The driver got out, watched by the still wary bodyguard. He was empty-handed and had his back to Michael and his companion. At the car Michael and the bodyguard separated, Michael going to the driver's side, the other man walking around the bonnet to the far side of the car. At that moment a face covered by a white cloth hood appeared at the rear window of the Chevrolet. The bodyguard had time only to register the blankness of the hood before the barrel of a gun appeared and exploded into fire, cutting him down.

Horror and disbelief made Michael hesitate for just a second, his hand on the car door. It was a mistake it had been drummed into him to avoid. In that moment the driver of the Chevrolet was upon him. He warded off the first blow and threw a punch himself. The man's rush had thrown him off balance. The punch landed high on the man's head. Swearing, he pulled back, looking for room for another punch. The sunglasses hung awkwardly on his nose so that he only half saw the fist that flew towards him before the world fused into blackness.

The driver slipped the heavy brass knuckle-duster back into his pocket. With the help of the other young man who had sprung from the Chevrolet they dragged Michael's inert figure to the big car and pushed him into the rear. The third man stood by the car scanning the compound, the gun held in readiness. The only movement was from the two sentries who were fumbling desperately with the padlocked cables that held the gates.

At a word from the driver the three men leapt into the car. The car bucked forward into a fast slewing turn. One of the heavy gates was already closed. The sentries were still busy with the cable holding the second one when the car screamed to a halt before the barrier. The man with the machine gun, still hooded, leapt from the car and ran towards the two soldiers while the other passenger ran to raise the barrier.

The two sentries cringed under the threat of the machine gun, dropping to their knees in a pantomime of fear. The hooded man drew to within two paces of them. As he stood over them one of the soldiers looked quickly around. Seeing no one near, he gave a quick, conspiratorial grin, showing surprisingly good teeth.

'Not too realistic, comrade,' he said, leering. 'I promised the German girl at Mario's I'd go upstairs with her again tonight. I wouldn't want to plead a headache.' He giggled, obscenely collusive.

'Don't worry, comrade,' the gunman answered softly, the expression of the eyes unchanging behind the slits of the hood, 'you won't have that problem.'

He fired a short burst into the still-smiling heads of the two men.

2

JULIA SAT IN the high-backed leather chair, still trembling, her fingers digging deep into the upholstered arms. Tears streaked her face. Wet patches the size of her palms on the silk of her shirt above each breast showed where many had already fallen. On the desk in front of her stood a plastic cup, half full of cold black coffee. Empty cups lay on the desk-top.

Heaving with another huge sob, she picked up the strip of thin paper torn from the news agency tape. She dashed away tears as she read over the sparse text for the twentieth time since she had arrived.

'But why? For heaven's sake, why?' she asked, her eyes still fixed on the paper. 'Why Michael? Why my brother? He never hurt anybody in his life. He went there because he wanted to *help*. How could anyone do this to him?' Anger was growing in her, fusing with the pain.

The bulky man who sat with his rump hooked onto an edge of the desk straightened and walked round to stand beside her. He laid a beefy arm across her shoulders.

'That's right. Be angry. Don't let the bastards make you cry.' He squeezed her arm gently and walked to a cabinet against a wall. 'Want a drink?'

Julia nodded, biting hard at her lower lip. He took out a bottle of scotch and a stack of waxed-paper cups. He poured a couple of inches into a cup and handed it to Julia, signalling the other people who crowded the room to help themselves.

'Thanks, Harry.' Julia took a long draught of the whisky. 'What can I *do*? He's such a gentle man. There must be ways I can help.'

The big man took the paper from the desk, pushed a pair of glasses onto his nose and studied it again. He looked around the room. 'The Islamic Revolutionary Faction. Mean anything to anybody?'

The assembled journalists shook their heads. A crumpled-looking dark man spoke. 'It *almost* sounds like half a dozen of their groups. A new one appears every day in that snakepit. You wonder sometimes how *they* even remember what they're called.'

The editor smiled grimly. 'Yeah. Ron? Any ideas?'

Ron Watt was tall, dressed in tweeds, with the air of a successful academic. For many years he had been the paper's leading expert on the Middle East. He sucked on an empty pipe and gestured at the paper.

'That doesn't mention any demands that might give us some kind of clue. It just says they've got Julia's brother. It's typical of what we've been seeing for the past few years now. A splinter group, maybe no more than a few youngsters from a single family, kidnaps a foreigner, apparently just for the publicity. Then, quite often nothing more is heard of them. Nor, quite often, of the hostage.'

He looked uncomfortably at Julia. 'I'm sorry, but that's how it's been. There are at least a couple of dozen hostages out there. Some Americans, a few French. Some British. A Norwegian. Christ, even a couple of Iranians! Some of them have been held for years. We don't even know if most of them are still alive. None of it makes any sense, looked at through Western eyes.' He lowered his gaze. 'I'm afraid Beirut's not the West, whatever some Lebanese may like to think.'

Julia ran a hand through her short hair. 'But surely someone can't just disappear like that without *some* reason.'

The editor's voice was grave. 'Others have, Julia. Look at what's happening out there. It's a civil war where nobody knows what the sides are. The Shi-ites, Hezbollah, Palestinians, Christian militias, Druze militias, Lebanese Communists, even the Lebanese Army, for what that's worth.'

'Plus a whole lot more groups nobody could put a name to,' Ron Watt put in. 'Add to that the fact that every village in the place is a whirlpool of interlocking loyalties . . .' He broke off with a shrug.

Julia nodded and gulped. 'I know, Ron. You're right. But I

can't just sit and do nothing. I *have* to try and help. Isn't there some way to pressure the Government to do anything? *They* asked him to go out there,' she added, plaintively.

The editor tugged at his lip. 'We'll do all we can. We'll be running it as a lead story. So will every other paper in the country.' He paused, his look tinged with embarrassment. 'But it's no use kidding ourselves. The story won't last. Two days at most and it's the inside pages.' He shrugged and pursed his lips. 'That's the most I can promise you, Julia, you know that. The election's in less than two weeks. Nobody's going to be interested in anything else for more than forty-eight hours at a time.'

Julia nodded and smiled bleakly. 'I know. I appreciate all you're saying, Harry. But Jack Foreman's got a responsibility in this, election or not. Michael was there on a US Government contract. He only went into that vipers' nest in the first place because the Government asked him to.'

Harry touched her shoulder. 'Sure, he did. The problem is, the bastards down in Washington who got him into this read the polls, too. They've got their own preoccupations right now. Like looking for jobs.'

Very deliberately, Julia put her cup back down onto the desk. She sat slowly upright in her chair and smiled at the face above her. She reached out and touched the editor briefly on the arm.

'Fuck their jobs, Harry. Michael's my kid brother. The only family I've got. After twelve years on this paper I've got enough contacts in Washington. It's time to call in some favours. I'm going to go down there and *make* the bastards do something.'

Major Bradman did not wear a uniform. He wore a light-weight suit of crumpled cream cotton, brogues polished to a deep mahogany, and an open-necked, pale blue shirt. Even so, he began to perspire as soon as he stepped from the air-conditioned interior of the car into the baking afternoon heat. The tall, thin Negro in the marine camouflage uniform wiped away beads of sweat trickling from his unbuckled steel helmet. He grinned at Bradman.

'Afternoon, Major. Hot enough for you?'

Bradman smiled and rolled his eyes to show it was. He dropped the car keys into the black man's pale, upturned palm and stood watching, his hands in his pockets, as the marine opened the boot of the car.

He lifted the spare wheel and checked its housing. Satisfied, he closed the boot and moved around to check the interior. Last, he opened the hood and examined the engine compartment.

Despite the man's deceptively relaxed manner the search was painstaking. When he had been all over the interior he took a long-handled trolley with a mirror mounted on it and pushed it under the car, ensuring nothing was attached to its underside.

He turned his attention to Bradman. Unhurriedly he ran his hands over the Major's body, probing deep into pockets, armpits and the insides of his thighs. He ignored the bulk of the gun holstered beneath Bradman's left arm. He was not looking for conventional weapons; he was looking for bombs, which the Major might have been forced to carry under some kind of duress.

It was the third time that day Bradman had been subjected to this search. He accepted it with good grace, exchanging banter with the soldier as well as with the two others who looked on from the heavily sandbagged sentry post.

He had given the instruction himself: *everybody* was to be searched *every time* they entered the Embassy compound. There was to be no repeat of the recent bombing in which many marines had so needlessly died.

With an informal travesty of a salute the black marine stepped back. 'Okay, Major, you can proceed.'

His secretary was waiting for him at his office door, fretting visibly. 'Major Bradman, the Ambassador wants to see you immediately. In his office. It's very urgent. He's been looking for you for a half hour.' The last words were said in a tone of triumphant reproof. She was doing the Ambassador's dirty work for him and enjoying it.

He looked at her sourly. 'Thanks, Donna.' He turned and walked without hurry along the narrow corridor.

He entered the Ambassador's outer office without knocking. The Ambassador's secretary shot a warning look at the open door of the inner office. Bradman shrugged and strode towards the door. He could hear raised voices from inside.

'Major Bradman! At last!' the Ambassador shouted, his voice heavy with sarcasm. 'Kind of you to look by!'

Bradman shrugged again. 'I went to lunch. What's up?' he asked coldly.

'What's up?' the Ambassador almost shrieked. 'What's up is that while you've been out at lunch all sorts of shit has been hitting the fan. That boy Colter, at the university, has been kidnapped.'

'Oh shit,' said Bradman, softly, sinking into a chair. 'When did it happen?'

'Two hours ago.' The other man in the room spoke. He was the second secretary in the Commercial Section. That was what his visiting card said. His main job was CIA station chief. 'This was thrown at the gate from a car.' He handed a piece of paper to Bradman.

The note was on coarse yellow notepaper, written in a childish hand with a marker pen. Bradman read the short text aloud.

> 'We, the Islamic Revolutionary Faction, declare that the United States agent and spy Michael Colter has been arrested by us for his many crimes against the Revolution. He will be offered a chance to defend himself before a Revolutionary Tribunal.'

The note was signed with an equilateral triangle with two horizontal bars running through it.

Bradman groaned. 'Ah fuck,' he said softly. Ignoring the Ambassador he looked at the CIA man. 'Know them?'

The man shook his head. 'Never heard of them, until now. And you?'

'No. When did this come?'

'About forty minutes ago. Thrown at the gate wrapped around a rock.'

'Anyone see the messenger?'

The CIA chief shook his head again. 'Not really. Arabs. One of the guards got a shot at them. Thinks he might have hit the car, nothing more.'

Bradman turned to the Ambassador, who sat scowling at the two calmer men. 'Ambassador, in my opinion you should call the Secretary of State in person. Nobody else. He should inform the President personally.'

'But it's not even six-thirty in the morning over there!'

'Call him anyway. This has to be kept away from the press. If they get word of it it's going to put tremendous pressure on the President to trade with these animals.'

The CIA man concurred. 'The Major's right, Ambassador. We have to keep this under wraps for as long as we can. The President has enough problems without this. The press'll make a real meal of a thing like this just before the election. He could be forced into all sorts of trades. It could undermine everything we've been trying to do here. No American would be safe anywhere in the area.'

The Ambassador nodded vigorously. 'You're both right. I'll call the Secretary. Meanwhile I expect both of you to get this thing under control. Fast. Find out who's got the boy and get them negotiating. Understood?'

The CIA man had begun to respond when one of the telephones on the Ambassador's desk trilled softly. The Ambassador took up the phone. He listened for a few moments. The colour drained from his face, leaving a sickly, greyish tinge to his features.

'Hold them off,' he said at last, his voice hoarse. 'Just tell them no comment. Say nothing, nothing at all.' He replaced the receiver. The two other men looked expectantly into his face. He wiped a hand slowly across his slackened features. 'Oh, Christ,' he said miserably.

'What is it?' Bradman craned forward. 'Colter? He's not been killed?'

The Ambassador looked wearily from one to the other of the men. 'That was my secretary. The *New York Times* are on the line. They're asking for background on the Colter kidnapping. It's all over the wire services. The kidnappers must have given them the story before they even gave us the message.'

There was a moment of stunned silence. Major Bradman got to his feet. 'Sir, if you don't mind, I think Ted and I had better get to work. We had better start seeing if we can get any sort of a bearing on who might have grabbed Colter. If we can work fast we might be able to make contact before they make any public demands.'

The CIA man rose and followed Bradman to the door.

'Yes, Major,' said the Ambassador, an unpleasant whine in his voice, 'I think you'd better do that. You were the one supposed to be responsible for that young man's security.'

Bradman spun round. He kept his voice low and brittle. 'Perhaps I ought to remind *you*, Ambassador, that I was the one who opposed his being sent here. In case you've forgotten. Sir.' There was a weight of irony in the last word. 'It's all there on file.'

He turned and strode from the office, leaving the Ambassador looking as though he had just been whipped across the face.

3

MICHAEL WAS aware first of a searing pain that filled his senses, blotting out any other sensation. Gradually, the blinding red light behind his eyes subsided and the pain came into focus. The core of it came from his jaw. He clenched his teeth tentatively. The pain almost made him scream. He bit back the sound and opened his eyes.

The enveloping darkness brought him to the brink of panic, afraid he had been blinded. The panic ebbed away as he became aware of a faint filtering of light and felt the suffocating touch of cloth. His head was shrouded in a cloth or hood.

He lay awkwardly, his hands secured behind his back. The world vibrated. A sudden jarring motion sent the pain flaring again. He was in a moving vehicle. There was pressure on his ribcage. He flexed his body, seeking to ease the pressure. Instead of relief, a stabbing pain shot through him as a heel or rifle butt slammed down, driving the breath from him.

'Keep still!' The voice was angry, almost a snarl.

The same voice came again, just above him. 'How far now?'

A second voice responded, more muffled, from the front of the car. 'Fifteen minutes, God willing.'

Even through his pain Michael smiled at the last phrase. *Insha'allah*. God willing. Wherever Arabic was spoken, people might torture, maim, kill or kidnap but they always assumed Allah was on hand, keeping an eye on things.

A third voice, deeper and older than the others, spoke with soft, contained urgency. 'Look out. Checkpoint. Up ahead.'

Michael heard the chilling metallic sound of weapons being primed. The older voice muttered something, too low for him to catch. He felt his weight shift forward as the car slowed. Guttural sounds of shouting reached him through the open window of the car. He caught a demand for papers, for identification. Springs creaked as the men moved around, probably looking for their identification documents.

He lay motionless, sweat cooling on him. The group that had stopped them could be anybody. They could not have come far from Beirut. It could be any one of the dozens of groups fighting for a claim on power as the country entered its final stages of disintegration. It could even be one of the Christian militias or the Lebanese Army, acting as proxy for the Israelis.

Abruptly, Michael was aware of a movement of air that chilled his sweat-damp skin. The rear door had been opened.

A new voice shouted very close to him. The voice from within the car replied. Michael caught the word for traitor. The word was spoken with a leering emphasis that made him shudder, as though the speaker were sharing a lewd joke.

The voice outside spoke again. 'Patrice! *Hija o shuf!*'

The sound of the name Patrice made Michael's senses quiver. Christians, not Hezbollah or any of the other principal Fundamentalist factions that had been holding hostages. Heavy footsteps approached the car. Michael drew up his knees. With a violent bucking movement he thrust his head and shoulders out of the open door. 'Help!' he bellowed. 'Help me! I'm American. I'm . . .'

His last words were drowned in the clatter of automatic gunfire. Glass shattered. A wounded man screamed, a ghastly hyena sound, close to his head.

The car leapt forward. The open door smashed agonizingly against Michael's injured face. His shoulder burned as it dragged along the road. He tried to arch his body, to bring his shoulder clear of the ground.

'Help me, you bastards! Get me into the fucking car!' Pain and anger in about equal measure were making him bellow. His shouting was abruptly loud as the gunfire stopped. He was dragged roughly into the car and the door slammed shut.

'Fucking little bastard!' the voice screamed in English. He felt the gun barrel gouge his neck beneath the jawbone. The metal, still hot from the recent firing, drove against his windpipe, making him gag. 'I'll kill you now. I'll blow your face off, you fucker! I'll . . .'

'Stop it!' It was the older voice, peremptory and quiet. 'Be silent. You will not shoot him. You'll simply do as you're told. We all will. He can pay for his foolishness when the time comes. Until then you'll do him no more harm.'

The man above Michael continued muttering resentfully but the gun barrel was withdrawn.

They continued driving fast for another seven or eight

minutes. The men remained almost silent. The only sounds Michael heard were the words of the older man as he quietly gave directions to the driver. Without slowing, the car swung sharply and began bouncing and rocking over a rutted and winding route. He had the sensation they were rising, climbing a rough hillside. He was ready to be sick from the pain and the motion when the sump bottomed abruptly on the stony ground and they begun plunging headlong down a steep slope. When the car slid to a noisy halt he was running with sweat.

The door was thrown open. He was dragged roughly from where he lay. The sun beat on him briefly and then the air chilled again. He was inside a building. He felt hands fumble behind him, releasing his wrists. A blow to the small of his back sent him reeling. He lost his balance on the uneven floor and sprawled full length. A door closed behind him with a metallic crash.

Painfully, he pulled himself into a sitting position. He kneaded his fingers. They stung sharply as the blood forced its way back into the numb tips. He clawed the hood from his head, throwing it from him with a roar of relief. Blinking, he looked around at his cell.

Julia was preparing to dial the Washington number for perhaps the twentieth time when the phone rang under her hand. She snatched it up, almost sobbing in her frustration. Her exasperation melted at the sound of the familiar, warm, actor's voice.

'Rich! That's great! I've been trying to get you for over an hour.'

'I was at a meeting.' He spoke with a touch of irony, knowing her response.

She gave him an affectionate laugh. 'For a change. Look, Rich, can I come down and see you? It's about . . .'

'Michael's kidnapping,' he broke in.

'You've heard the news?'

His voice was low and weary. 'It's all over town. That's

what the meeting was about. I'm surprised it's not been on the TV news yet.'

'It will be. What have you heard?'

'The same as you, I guess. We got it off the wire services like everybody else.'

'What! You mean the wire services got it before the Embassy?'

Rich's voice was rueful. 'That's another of the things the meeting was about. The Department's going crazy. Christ, the State Department's just not supposed to find out things like this from Reuter's.'

'My God, neither are the victim's family!' She paused for a moment, fighting tears. When she continued her voice was gentle, pleading. 'What's happening, Rich? What's the Department going to do to get Michael out of this?'

'I don't know yet. We're meeting again in an hour. We're trying to talk to the Ambassador, find out if the kidnappers are making any demands. So far, all we know is he's been grabbed by a group nobody's even heard of. Believe me, Julia, we're all doing our best down here. A thing like this is going to put a lot of pressure on people, coming so close to the election.'

'Oh, fuck the election!'

'Huh?'

'I said, fuck the election, Rich. Michael used to be your brother-in-law, remember?'

'Now look, Julia,' he answered defensively, 'there's no point in making it personal. Things are as well in hand as they can be. We'll be putting out feelers, trying to negotiate, as soon as we can get a lead on this group that has Michael.'

'Don't any of the spooks at the Embassy know them?'

'Seems not. It's hard. You know that as well as I do. These groups appear out of nowhere; ask the impossible. There are limits to what we can expect of our people. I can tell you the President's taking a personal interest in this. He's making it top priority.'

'Oh, come on, Rich. Cut the bullshit,' she retorted softly. 'It's me, Julia. We used to be married!' She laughed. 'His top priority's getting himself re-elected. Forget the public relations stuff. Just tell me what they're doing to free Michael, please. He was supposed to be protected over there.'

'I know he was,' Rich answered, subdued. 'We're still trying to find out exactly what happened. Heads are going to roll if we find out somebody fucked up out there.'

Julia made a sound that was a mixture of a groan and a laugh. 'You're starting to bullshit me again. Of course somebody fucked up. If they hadn't, Michael wouldn't have been kidnapped.'

'It isn't that simple, Julia. It's . . .'

'It looks that simple from here. Look, are you in the office late this morning? I'm coming down there to see if I can't stir something up.'

'That's not necessary, Julia.' She smiled at the barely detectable edge of consternation in his voice. 'Why not wait to see what we can come up with here? I'll call you just as soon as . . .'

'Nice try, Rich,' she said, laughing. 'I'll get the noon shuttle. See you for lunch.' She hung up.

'The Islamic Revolutionary Faction,' the President repeated, slowly. 'Who the hell are they?' He looked around the room, blinking anxiously.

The Secretary of State glanced quickly at the other men in the room, the light glinting on his thick glasses. 'We don't know, Mr President. Nobody here's heard of them. Nor has anybody at the Embassy. I've just had the Ambassador on the line. They've never been heard of before.'

'And what do they want from us? Surely they're asking for something?' The President's voice had taken on a faint note of petulance.

'Not so far, Mr President.' The Secretary of State sat well back in the leather chair, his legs crossed, urbane and controlled. 'Perhaps they won't. It's happened before. To us, the French, even the Norwegians. People disappear. Sometimes they've been released, often years later. Sometimes they've turned up dead. A lot of them just disappear off the face of the earth.'

A short, thickset man in a plain grey suit that matched his close-cut hair spoke up from his casual perch on the arm of a big sofa. 'With respect, Mr President, I think it's probable that there will be demands, this time.'

All the faces turned to the solid-looking man. The President leaned forward. 'Why, Tom? What makes you say that?'

The man stood up and surveyed the room before speaking. 'Just this, Mr President.' He pushed his hands into his pockets and paced the room as he spoke. 'This is the first time in my experience that the news media have been given a story like this before the local embassy learned about it, right?' He looked questioningly at the Secretary of State, who nodded. 'And if you look at the timing, it's quite deliberate, right?' He paused. 'Whoever these people are, they *wanted* the media to get the story before we could smother it. They want the publicity. Now, *why* do they want it?' he went on rhetorically, his gaze swinging from the President to the men who sat around the room. 'They want it so that it will embarrass us into a deal. The Tehran hostages already cost Jimmy Carter an election. They think we'll be prepared to trade, to get our man back before the election.'

The other men were silent. Tom Jordan had been head of the National Security Council for a long time. They had all learned long ago to respect the power of his judgement. The President pulled pensively at his lower lip.

'You really think so, Tom? You know, it means a lot to me when I see an American citizen taken like this.'

Dean Sutcliffe, the Secretary of State, only just suppressed a smile. The President had slipped into the tone of practised sincerity he usually kept for television appearances. It was unusual for him to waste it on the group in the room. It was an indication of how rattled he was.

The President continued speaking. 'I feel for them; for their families.' He paused, appearing to remember something. 'By the way, Rich.' He turned to Rich Archer who sat in a straight chair close by the Secretary of State. 'I understand the boy's some sort of relative of yours?'

The President's tone had turned to one of tentative condolence.

Rich Archer nodded. 'Sort of, Mr President. He's the younger brother of my ex-wife, Julia Colter.'

'Oh shit!' The President was no longer sympathizing. 'That's going to be a terrific help. We'll have those vultures from the *Times* clambering all over the thing. Is it really too late to keep the press off our backs?' He looked pleadingly at the assembled men.

The Secretary of State shook his head. 'I'm afraid it is, Mr President.'

The President looked vexed, then suspicious, as a sudden thought struck him. He glowered at one of the gathering, a man who until then had remained silent. 'I suppose this boy Colter really was just teaching over there? He's nothing to do with your people? Somebody's not going off on a tangent?' Norm Clark, the man he spoke to, was the head of the CIA.

'No, sir, Mr President,' the man replied coolly. 'I've checked the file. He's known to us, of course. Been in some weird places what with the Peace Corps and one thing and another, but no, he's not working for us in any way at all. Never has. The original innocent abroad.' The man exchanged a wry grin with Rich Archer.

The President looked placated. 'So where do we go from here?' he asked. 'Your people in Beirut are on to it, I suppose?' The CIA man nodded. 'Good. Tell them, though, no deals. No trades for hostages. I want that absolutely clear.'

'Yes, Mr President.'

'Good. I want to know as soon as anything breaks. Any word at all, I want to hear about it at once, understand?'

The group murmured their assent. They stood, recognizing that the meeting was at an end. 'I want you all back here this afternoon at three. Meanwhile you'd better all stay available.' Again the men muttered their agreement as they filed from the room. Only the head of the National Security Council hung back.

'Mr President, may I have five minutes, sir?'

Faintly surprised, the President nodded.

Julia stepped from the lift and strode the few paces along the green-painted corridor to the door of Rich's office. The usher accompanying her knocked once and held the door open for her. She walked quickly into the office.

Rich's secretary greeted Julia with the affable hostility secretaries with their own designs on their bosses reserve for ex-wives.

'Julia! What a nice surprise. Is Rich expecting you?'

Julia smiled distractedly and nodded.

The secretary spoke briefly into a telephone. 'He'll be free in just a moment. Would you like to sit down?' She indicated a leather sofa. 'Horrible about your brother.'

Julia showed her teeth again in a smile that lasted less than a second and remained standing, pacing the office, looking at the familiar pictures without seeing them. It was two minutes before the door of the inner office burst open and Rich raced across the room to greet her. He embraced her and shepherded her into the office. The secretary watched them go, implanting a smile like an ice pick in the back of Julia's neck.

Julia sat in the generously upholstered chair Rich indicated. He touched her shoulder nervously and walked around the big desk to sit opposite. There was an unease mixed with his sympathy that puzzled her. A kind of embarrassment, at odds with his expansive style.

'What's happening about Michael? Has there been any news?'

Rich shook his head hard, causing his beefy, tanned jowls to quiver. 'Not a word. There's been nothing since the original message. We've got a line permanently open to the Embassy. If anything develops it'll be put right through. D'you want to go and get some lunch? We'll go upstairs. If anything comes in we can be reached.'

The conversation over lunch was desultory. Julia pushed food around on her plate, unable to find the appetite to swallow more than a mouthful or two. Rich, too, was preoccupied and strained, not at all the bluff and confident man Julia had always known.

'Rich,' Julia said, after a long silence, startling him from morose contemplation of a fruit salad, 'how bad do you think it is? I mean, d'you think we'll see Michael back with us? You've had experience with this sort of thing. You know the kind of people we're dealing with.'

He stared back at her for a long while before replying.

'I don't know, Julia, really I don't.' He gave a fleeting sour grin. 'You know as well as I do, we're only experts as far as the public's concerned. We can't tell them we don't know any more about it than they do. Christ, we've never even heard of the group that has Michael. There've been people held down there for seven years now and we've been totally helpless.'

The thought broke the last thread of Julia's composure. Tears came suddenly. When she spoke again her voice was a whisper, lumpy with sobs. 'I can't leave Michael to rot out there, Rich. I don't care if I have to personally kick every rear end in Washington. I want to see the United States Government doing something for once. I'll get to see the President himself, if necessary.'

'For Christ's sake,' Rich rejoined, sighing and reaching for her hand. 'I saw the President this morning. I'll be seeing him again this afternoon.' He glanced at his watch. 'In forty minutes. What can he do that he's not already doing? The election's almost on us. There's nothing he'd like more than to be able to wave a wand and get Michael back. The miracles in the Middle East all finished nearly two thousand years ago, Julia.'

She looked fiercely back at him, pawing at a tear. 'There must be things that could be tried. Hell, Rich, one minute they're telling us they have satellites that can examine the Kremlin cat's haemorrhoids, the next they're asking us to believe they're being outwitted by a bunch of teenagers who drive by the Embassy throwing rocks over the gate. I just won't accept that all we can do is sit around and wait for these people to name their terms. I can't. If I can't get anything moving here by tomorrow night I'm going out there myself.'

Rich had started to smile. Now the smile fell away. He sat bolt upright in his seat.

'You can't do that,' he said, aghast. 'You'd be mad to go out there. You'd end up the same way as Michael. Be sensible.' He shook himself and laughed weakly. 'Come on. You're kidding.'

Julia shook her head, her lips pursed tightly. 'Don't you believe it. And don't forget, I work for the *New York Times*. You'd be amazed how those lazy bastards in embassies start jumping around when they scent a reporter.'

Exasperation mingled with pity in Rich's face. 'You're mad. They're tearing each other to pieces over there. Those people couldn't give a shit whether you're a reporter for the *New York Times* or a reporter from the Holy fucking Bible. You'll just be another pawn in their crazy chess game. And a woman into the bargain, just to give the press something extra-juicy to bite on.' He stood up slowly. 'I'll buy you dinner. You want to stay at the house?'

It was shortly after eleven when they emerged from the restaurant. Neither of them spoke on the short drive back. They climbed the few steps to the front door. Rich flicked on the hall light.

'Sorry. That was lousy.'

'Don't mention it.' She laid a hand on his arm. 'It wasn't your fault. I'm so worried about Michael I can't think straight. It's been a very rough day.'

He nodded. 'D'you want a drink?'

'No. I think I'll go to bed.' She leaned and kissed him on the cheek. 'Goodnight. Thanks. You've been sweet.'

He watched as she began climbing the stairs. 'You know the way?' he said softly.

She turned, smiling gently. 'Mmm. I know the way.' She waggled her fingers in a tiny wave.

Julia took a long shower, and dried herself on the fresh rough towel. She reached down the terrycloth robe that hung on the wall. It was her size. The surprise lasted only a fraction of a second, until she realized it used to be hers.

She lay for a long time trying to coax sleep. An hour earlier she had been exhausted. Now, images of Michael milled and jostled in her mind, keeping sleep at bay. She saw him as a young man, just out of college, full of enthusiasm for his first Peace Corps assignment. And she saw him as he might be at that moment, blindfolded, hungry and degraded in some filthy hovel in the hills of the Lebanon. Despite her efforts not to, she found herself crying softly.

As she lay, her head turned into the pillow, she heard Rich's soft familiar footsteps. They paused for a moment outside her door, then receded as he walked gently to the room they had once shared.

She lay for a few minutes more, unable to stem the flood of images of Michael. At length, she slid silently from the bed and crossed the room. Her hair was damp from the shower and from the tears which still spilled down her cheeks. Soundlessly she padded to Rich's door. She listened for a moment and then gently pushed it open.

Across the room, through the open door of the bathroom, the sound of running water mingled with soft singing. She smiled at the sound. He never had been able to sing. Julia stood in the lighted bathroom doorway, naked and smiling, her cheeks still glistening with continuing tears. Rich hummed tunelessly as he stood, eyes closed, allowing the streaming jet of the shower to rinse the lather from his hair. He had grown thicker in the waist, the hair on his chest and shoulders had gone from brown to salt and pepper. The shower had plastered his hair flat, emphasizing the marked thinness that his expensive barbering camouflaged by day.

'Not bad, considering.'

Rich checked, his eyes still clenched shut against the

lather. Julia saw his belly flex as he briefly considered, then rejected, the idea of sucking it in. Slowly, he opened his eyes, so that he was looking at her through a curtain of water. He moved forward and wiped his eyes, clearing his vision. He had begun grinning the slow, familiar film-star grin, when he caught sight of the tears gleaming in her eyes. His grin dissolved in a look of sudden consternation. He took a quick step out of the shower cubicle and folded her in his arms.

She let herself be carried to the bed, her arms clasped tight around his neck and her muscular, almost boyish legs around his waist. He lowered her to the bed, their bodies pressed together. One arm was around her back and the other hand gripped hard around her tight-muscled buttock. Feeling her ready for him, he pushed into her with a tender, urgent ferocity she had not known since early in their marriage, in the years before he had let his career become so important to him, before he had let pompousness erode his sense of humour.

Julia groaned as he entered her, a primitive sound, expressing the relief that the unutterable blind need in her was about to be satisfied. She arched desperately towards him, urging him to drive deeper into her, to fill her body and her mind, leaving no space for the fear and apprehension that ate at her.

Rich understood her need. His mouth did not leave her flesh. It played over her eyes, his tongue flicking away the last vestiges of tears, and then roamed over her throat, to her armpits and to her tight, neat breasts. He pushed his mouth down over each breast, taking as much flesh as he could into his mouth while his tongue caressed the nipple.

Julia gasped and tightened her legs around him, pulling herself deeper onto his thrusts. Her fear had left her now. Her whole being was focused on the melting, surging waves that rose from deep inside her, spreading through her body, making every inch of her skin surface quiver with each touch, as though every nerve-end were directly linked to the place inside her where the feeling was generated.

The waves came stronger, invading her consciousness,

until she was aware of nothing else. Her breath began to come faster, a deep, hoarse sawing sound, as though she were in unbearable pain. Her hips began thrusting harder and stronger. Both Rich's arms locked around her, pinioning her own arms and crushing her chest. She ground her pelvis with rhythmic abandon against the powerful hips above her, matching her movements to theirs, until finally, arching so powerfully that she lifted him with her, she gave a long keening cry and fell back, spent, to the mattress.

Julia woke early. She opened her eyes slowly, smiling at the pillow next to hers. It was empty. She sat up and squinted at the disembodied red figures of the digital clock on the bedside table. It was not quite six o'clock. Light spilled from the bathroom as Rich emerged. He leaned down and kissed her lightly.

'I didn't expect you to be awake. I was planning to call you from the office.'

She shook her head and smiled wryly. 'Still the early bird, eh? I've got things on my mind, remember?'

He reached out and touched her hand. 'I know. Look, Julia, we've got another meeting with the President this morning. I'll tell him how you feel. I'll try to make it plain to him that the press, the *Times* in particular, will crucify him if anything happens to Michael. I'll try to convince him we should kick the shit out of those people at the Embassy; try and make him see he's got a major election issue on his hands.'

'You can also tell him that if we don't have anything by noon I'm on my way to Beirut. This evening.' Her voice was low and reasonable. Her eyes, on his, were unblinking.

He stiffened and jerked his hand from her arm, grimacing with exasperation. When he spoke his voice took on a wheedling note she recognized. And detested. 'Come on, Julia, you can't do that. What can you possibly achieve out there, the mess the place is in?'

'I can see some people. You're forgetting a few things, Rich, dear. I spent almost a year out there. I've got a lot of favours owed to me. And I intend to call some in. Like from Rachid Hamoun, for instance.'

Rich made a scoffing sound. 'Rachid? Come on, Julia. What do you think he's going to do for you? The man's got enough problems just trying to keep control of his own people.'

'He's still the Minister of the Interior.'

He laughed outright. 'Minister of nothing. Get it into your head, Julia, please, that nobody gives a shit for the government out there. It's all a charade. It's over. The mobs are the government now.'

'Yeah, well he still owes me. And so do a few other people.'

He shook his head. 'Come on. Admit the truth. There's *nothing* you can do out there, except maybe get yourself kidnapped. What good would *that* do Michael?' He waited a second or two for a response. Not getting one, he shrugged, stood up and walked to the door, pulling on his jacket.

He stood in the open doorway, looking back at her. 'Please forget it. It's a lousy idea. You'll get eaten alive in that jungle. If the CIA people can't even make contact with the people holding Michael, how do *you* expect to do it without getting into trouble? A woman, alone, out there!'

She waved at the closing door with the fingers of one hand. 'Fuck you, too, you chauvinist bastard,' she murmured, laughing.

4

MICHAEL WAS unsure if he had been woken by the pain that pounded in his head or by some exterior sound. He raised himself onto one elbow and lay listening. No sound came. Nor did any light filter through the single eight-inch-by-eight-inch grille set in the ceiling above him. Dawn had not yet broken.

He willed his stiffened limbs into life and pushed himself

upright. The slightest movement of his right arm provoked a painful burning sensation in the shoulder where he had been dragged along the road. He touched his left hand to his jaw. It was swollen like a football. The slightest pressure was excruciating, as though it might be broken.

Cursing the pain, his voice loud and angry, he felt his way around the walls of the room to the corner where he had placed the small light bulb. Still feeling his way, he found the short, frayed flex that hung from the middle of the ceiling and replaced the bulb in its socket. Someone had once painted the bulb a garish red, like an improvised Christmas tree decoration. It gave its light a nightmarish orange tinge.

He shuddered and folded his arms across his chest. There was no blanket in the room. There was nothing at all except the rotting mattress of thin foam rubber and an old bucket covered in chipped white enamel, its base and lip ravaged by rust, which he guessed was meant to serve as his toilet.

He let his jacket slip to the ground. Then he unbuttoned his shirt and eased it off his damaged shoulder. He stood under the dim light and examined the raw, torn flesh. He took a handkerchief from his pocket, spat saliva into it and, twisting awkwardly, began to squeeze the yellow and white filth from the spots where infection was trying to take a hold.

By the time he was satisfied the wounds were as clean as he could get them, grey light had begun filtering through the grating above him. Abruptly, a small panel in the door, the size of a postcard, slid open, revealing the upper part of a face. Dark eyes watched him for a moment. Then came a peremptory voice, heavily accented.

'Move away! Stand by the wall.'

Wordlessly, not moving, he stared back at the hostile eyes, which watched from the opening in the door. Without warning the door swung wide, revealing two figures, each holding an automatic rifle levelled at Michael. He stood his ground, resisting the overwhelming urge to look from their faces to the guns.

The two men stepped forward, each in the standard jeans, sneakers and military-style shirts. The lower parts of their faces were covered by coloured handkerchiefs. Blue berets hid their hair. They were three feet from him. Without any further word one of them jammed the barrel of his gun hard into Michael's stomach. He gasped and doubled over.

'Back. By the wall.'

Holding his stomach, his face creased in pain, Michael shot the man a look of pure hatred. But he stepped back against the wall.

A third man moved into the doorway. He wore a one-piece camouflage parachutist's overall and a hood similar to that worn by the kidnappers. He held a blue plastic airline bag in one hand. He spoke a soft command in Arabic to the young men, who each took a step to the side.

The hooded man withdrew a newspaper from his bag and tossed it to Michael. He made no attempt to catch it, letting it fall at his feet, his eyes defiantly on those of the newcomer. The tall man made no reaction. The gunman who had struck Michael made a clicking sound with his tongue and jabbed the gun barrel viciously, this time into Michael's groin. Michael grunted and sank to his knees.

'Pick it up.' The man emphasized his words with a movement of the gun. Painfully, he picked up the paper and pushed himself to his feet. He was still stooped from the sickening pain. The man made a further signal to him, indicating he should hold up the paper in front of his chest. Michael had made his point. Now he did as the man wanted.

Nodding satisfaction, the hooded man pulled a Polaroid camera from the bag and took four rapid shots. He dropped the camera back in the bag, holding the undeveloped pictures carefully apart between spread fingers. He signalled to Michael to return the newspaper. He gave another single-word command, turned and left the room. The two guards went with him, stepping carefully backwards.

As the two men reached the door he heard a voice speak softly in the outer room. One of the men reached around the door frame. An unseen hand passed him a plastic bottle which he set down just inside the door, and then a tin mug which he placed next to the bottle. The two men stepped from the room and the door slammed shut.

As soon as he heard the sound of the latch or bar being slipped into place Michael crossed the room and snatched up the plastic bottle. He drank thirstily, oblivious to the tepid, heavily chlorinated taste. His first thirst satisfied, he replaced the stopper in the bottle. He did not know when he would get more. Besides, he wanted water to clean his wound properly.

The battered metal mug held a mixture of rice and pieces of meat bound by a sticky gravy. With a grimace he carried it over to the mattress, sat down on the thin sheet of foam and plunged his fingers into the contents. He pulled out a wad of the mess, kneaded it in his fingers until it was a paste and pushed it carefully into his mouth.

As he ate, his mind tried to order the events of the last few hours. He recalled walking across the University compound, joking with his escort. He remembered the sudden crash of gunfire, and the look of total surprise on the face of the bodyguard just before he fell. After that he recalled waking in the car, his attempt to escape at the checkpoint, the brutal way his captors had restrained him, and then being almost thrown into this room.

His first reaction had been close to panic. A mixture of anger, fear and claustrophobia. It had been less than thirty minutes before he had learned what he supposed all prisoners learn, that all of those emotions pass very quickly. Within that time the futile hammering on the door, the useless shouted efforts to protest that there must be a mistake, the churning, irrational fear of suffocation, had all died down. They passed, leaving him with a choice. Anger or despair. He had determined to stay angry.

The room was about fifteen feet by ten and low, the ceiling about seven and a half feet from the bare cement floor. The walls were of rough plaster which in many places had crumbled to reveal the cinder block underneath. There were no windows. The only daylight came from the heavy iron grille set in the ceiling which appeared to give onto some kind of shaft, or chimney, and which therefore offered no view of the outside world, beyond a tiny square of sky. A shaft of daylight fell onto the floor beneath the grille, brighter than the dull light from the bulb. Apart from the mattress, the bucket, the light bulb and the food containers, the only object in the room was an old-fashioned sticky spiral of flypaper thumb-tacked into the mortared interstice between two of the ceiling blocks.

Sucking at another wad of food Michael patted his pockets. They were empty. At some point, probably as he lay unconscious in the car, they had been emptied. Nothing at all remained. No comb, no keys, no pen; nothing that could have provided a possible tool or weapon. They had left him his clothes, torn and filthy, but they had taken a first instalment on his dignity.

He had seen press photographs of other hostages, hollow-cheeked, bearded and ragged after years in captivity. He had seen the videos made by their captors and sent to television stations, seen them blankly reciting anti-capitalist texts written by their captors, their voices and their whole personalities drained of life. He wondered how much, or how little, time it took for a man to become like that. Even the thought made him sit a little straighter. He would make damn sure it took the bastards a long time to do it to him.

For the first time since his capture he was on the verge of a smile. He saw himself as a fastidious man. Before coming to the Lebanon, working in the field camps of Tanzania, he had always contrived, no matter how remote the camp, to have some kind of shower and to shave every morning. Now he was already reduced to cleaning himself with his own saliva and maybe, if his captors were generous, with a little of his precious drinking water.

He had been foolish even to listen to the offer that had brought him to the Lebanon. When the men had come to visit him in the bush, ridiculous in their pale tropical suits, he should have followed his instincts and sent them away. They had spent two days cajoling and persuading him that he would be more use in Beirut; that his experience fitted him uniquely to manage the programme designed to show the farmers they could make profits from something other than opium poppies.

They had persuaded him that his work could tip the balance in the power struggle that was going on, away from the Fundamentalists and towards a new stability.

They had promised he would find satisfaction. He had found only terror.

Despite everything, he really did smile now. The recollection of the men had made him think of Julia. She was eight years older than he was. Since the death of their parents, while he was still only in his teens, Julia had been the one person he had been able to turn to for advice. For ten years, despite their careers taking them far away from each other, they had stayed very close. When the offer had come up it was natural he should ask her opinion. She had spent a lot of time there until recently, knew everyone, was on first-name terms with half the factional leaders. She had told him he was nuts.

In the three months since his arrival he had found out what she meant. He had virtually never been out of the company of an armed guard. His initial fear had subsided into a thing he could live with. The irritation of being accompanied everywhere had also abated as the everyday reality of the danger had become clearer, giving way to grateful acceptance of the escort.

The danger was everywhere. Day and night, gunfire would erupt, often within a block or two. Car bombs were so common that passers-by crossed the road as a matter of habit as they passed any unattended vehicle. Michael had refused to do that, but he had never been able to stop his palms sweating, almost by reflex, until he was safely at a distance.

Fear, whether of the swaggering children, scarcely into

their teens, playing at soldiers with loaded Kalashnikovs, or of the unseen, disciplined killers of the rival militias and of the quicksilver political alliances, ruled the city.

As he finished the sticky, congealing food it was fear that Michael felt most. All his apparent defiance could not obscure the deep-seated, sickening knowledge that any one of the young men who held him could shoot him for nothing more than the pleasure of firing his gun, the way a child might pull apart a flower just to see the petals fall. He knew the people well enough now to know that death was immaterial to them. They simply did not consider it. Their satisfaction was in the feeling of the gun leaping in their hands, the noise and the instantaneous charge of power. It gave them no reason not to kill him.

With a shudder he stretched out on the stinking mattress and closed his eyes, trying to use the throbbing pain in his head to close out other thoughts.

Julia looked at her watch, as she had looked at it every two minutes for the last half-hour. Rich had promised to call her by twelve. It was three minutes past. The phone began to ring, a barely audible, trilling sound. Julia started and grabbed the handset.

'Julia?' Rich's voice was deep and solicitous.

'Yeah. What's the news? Have you heard anything?' Her voice was cracking with anxiety.

'Not yet, no. We're in constant touch with the people out there. If anything moves we'll know it immediately.'

'How about the kidnappers? Have they been in contact?'

'There's been nothing at all from them. Not a word. We've been working on trying to identify them. None of our contacts over there has been able to give us the faintest lead.' His voice was timid, apologetic.

'So nobody's claiming Michael's kidnapping? No one's asking for anything? No ransom? Not some kind of deal?'

'I'm afraid that's the way it looks. It's the worst kind of case, Julia. I'm sorry. It's not the first time we've seen this type of situation. You know that.' His sorrow was real, causing his voice to break slightly.

'And what did the Government do the other times?' Julia snapped, her frustration making her angry.

Rich sounded startled at her vehemence. 'What could we do, in circumstances like that, when people simply disappear? Be realistic,' he added, on a note of appeal. 'We . . .'

'Stop it!' she broke in. 'I'm sorry, Rich. I know it's not your fault. But I know exactly what you're going to tell me.' Her voice became sardonic. 'Everyone's very concerned. All the resources at the Government's disposal are being used. The full investigative skills of the CIA. The same CIA that was reassuring the Shah that it would all blow over while Khomeini's followers were already tearing down the palace gates.'

She paused, forcing herself to be calm. 'Come on, Rich, please. What did the President actually say?'

'He's very concerned about Michael,' he said stiffly, nettled by her derision. 'Christ, Julia, have you seen the papers this morning? They've gone to town on us. Especially,' he went on in a sourer tone, 'that shit of an editor of yours, Harry Moore. The *Times* has really gone for the President.'

'Good for Harry!' she said cheerfully. 'There'll be more of that, I hope. Personally, I won't be here to read it. I'll be in Beirut.'

'Julia!' He was almost shouting. 'Don't do that! Don't be stupid. You'll only make things worse. Shit, you'll probably end up kidnapped yourself.' He drew a loud breath. 'For Christ's sake, what are you trying to do to us? To me? The President? It's driving him nuts as it is. There's nothing more any of us can do. We're . . .'

'Rich,' Julia broke in sweetly, cutting him short, 'there's one thing you can do that I'd really appreciate.'

'Uh-huh. What's that?' he asked, mollified.

'You're a really sweet man. So please stop acting like a prick.' She put down the phone.

5

THE PHONE started ringing as Julia was pushing her few things into her soft leather flight bag. Glancing at her watch, she grabbed the receiver. Rich's voice, angry and insistent, came faintly from the handset, calling her name. Without putting it to her ear Julia stabbed a finger at the cradle, cutting the line. Immediately, before Rich could re-dial, she removed her finger and began dialling the *Times*.

'Miriam? It's Julia. Is Harry there?'

A few seconds later Harry's familiar bluff voice came on. 'Hello, Julia. How's it going?'

'It's not going anywhere. I'm wasting time down here. None of them can do anything. They're just sitting around waiting for the kidnappers to tell them their next move.'

'What does Rich say? Can't he help?'

'Poor old Rich.' She laughed, unable to keep the fondness from her voice. 'He's the worst of them. I'm a threat to his career. I think he'd prefer not to know me. I've become an embarrassment.'

'I can imagine,' Harry answered, wryly. 'Don't hold it against him. He's a nice man. Blame the State Department. Nobody gets as far as Rich in that outfit without taking care of his own ass.'

'Yeah,' Julia said, dismissively, 'I know. Look, Harry, I need your help. I'm going out there.'

'What do you mean?' he asked warily. 'Out where?'

'Beirut.'

'Julia, are you out of your mind? The place is falling to pieces. It's totally out of control. You could get killed.'

'That's what Rich told me,' she answered tartly. 'I'm going anyway, Harry. I'm going to see the people in the Embassy out there and make such a stink they'll *have* to do something. I'm just not going to sit here and let

Michael be forgotten like the others. I can't.'

'All right,' Harry replied, his voice resigned. 'So you're going. You'll need a visa. They aren't giving visas to Americans unless you can convince them you've got a good reason for wanting one.'

'Oh, come on, Harry,' she said, exasperated. 'This is the Middle East we're talking about. The hell with a visa. There are boats from Cyprus every night of the week. Can you have Miriam make a reservation for me? To Larnaca. And I'll need some money, cash and traveller's cheques. I'll reimburse the paper.'

'Forget it. It'll be an assignment. It'll be a hell of a story. If you ever get back.'

It was after four when Julia walked without knocking into Harry Moore's office. He sat in shirtsleeves, hunched forward in his chair, his big belly crumpled on the metal edge of the desk. He was deep in conversation with Ron Watt. He looked up in a flash of anger at the interruption, peering peevishly over half-moon glasses. Seeing Julia, his expression softened.

'Julia! Come in,' he said, unnecessarily. 'We were just talking about you. Ron and I were discussing tomorrow's lead.'

Julia and Ron nodded to each other. Julia did not sit down. 'Harry, did Miriam get my ticket?' He nodded towards a brown envelope that lay in a wire tray on a corner of his desk. 'Great. Can we talk?'

Without a word Ron Watt stood up and left the room, touching Julia lightly on the shoulder as he went. He pulled the door closed behind him.

More than an hour passed before Julia emerged from the office. Harry stood in the doorway and watched as she made her way across the crowded room to her desk. Colleagues looked up and smiled or spoke softly as she hurried past. She returned their encouragements with tight-lipped smiles of her own, not stopping to speak to anyone.

It took her less than ten minutes to gather a few things

from her desk. She strode out of the office, waving briefly to the people around her. In the elevator she fidgeted and twitched impatiently. Every couple of seconds she looked at her watch. Harry was a lovely, considerate man but he sure could be a windbag. Like everyone who was not going anywhere himself, Harry always felt you had plenty of time. It was going to be a tight-run thing to get packed and catch the plane.

Twenty minutes later she climbed the steps of the subway station and turned onto Broome Street, the familiar little worm of fear that she always felt in the subway withdrawing into her unconscious as she surfaced. She hurried past the restaurants and art galleries aligned beneath the fire-escapes and let herself into her building.

Across the street, two men sat watching from behind the window of an Italian bistro, inconspicuous among the rush-hour crowd. Cold cappuccinos stood untouched in front of them.

In her apartment, Julia changed quickly into drill slacks and a tan cotton shirt. Still cursing Harry's well-meant verbosity, she kicked off her shoes, pulled on soft suede ankle boots and began packing. She packed fast and expertly, pushing the few things she needed into the flight bag. She deliberately always kept her hair short. Like the clothes it was easy-care. No brush, no lacquer, no hair-dryer. She never carried deodorants. If she smelled she took a shower. If she could not get to a shower she went on smelling. Anybody reporting from a war zone who was not in the same boat had no business being there. She was closing the bag when the front door buzzer sounded.

'Damn!' She tossed her head, puzzled and annoyed.

Frowning, she walked quickly to the door and slid back the cover on the spyhole set in the armoured door. She squinted through the hole. Normally, anyone wanting to enter the building, unless they knew the five-digit code on the electronic lock, rang the bell on the street entrance and waited to be identified over the entryphone. Very occasionally, someone slipped in as another resident was leaving. They were assumed to be thieves, rapists or bores. The first two were often the easiest to put off.

A man stood outside, grinning foolishly at the spyhole. She threw open the door.

'Rich!' Her voice was a mixture of irritation and indulgence. 'What're you doing here?' She had already turned away from the door as she spoke, leaving him to enter and close it behind him. He conscientiously checked the door was locked and followed her towards the bedroom. He stood in the doorway and watched her finish closing the bag.

'You can't go out there, Julia. You can't do any good. *Nobody* wants you to go there.' Julia threw him an amused look but did not speak. 'Christ,' he went on, a note of desperation entering his voice, 'even the President doesn't want it. It can only make matters worse. What if you get hurt or kidnapped yourself?'

'Don't worry, Rich,' she answered, without looking at him. 'I won't expect *you* to come looking for *me*. It would be a black mark on your record. Your career might never recover.'

He took a step into the room, his slightly over-sculpted lips forming into the beginnings of a pout. 'Julia, look at me,' he said hoarsely. A new note in his voice made Julia turn towards him, her eyes narrowed.

She let him see her look again at her watch. 'Rich, I'm in a hell of a hurry.'

He swallowed and moved towards her. 'Julia, I'm begging you not to go. Be reasonable, please.' He moved another step closer and reached out, putting a hand on her shoulder. 'You don't appreciate how dangerous it is, believe me. If I thought you had a chance, even the smallest hope of getting Michael out, I'd say go. I wouldn't even try to talk you out of it. But the way it is, everything's just . . .' He shook his head as though shaking off a bad dream. '. . . hopeless. The whole place is a madhouse. They're killing people as if they were insects. Please stay here. Please let us handle it.' His voice had dropped so low Julia had to strain to hear him.

She stood for a moment, watching his face. He blinked and one cheek twitched. It was a tic she had never seen before. Beneath his tan the skin had blanched, making his face a sickly yellow. Moving fast, but with her irritation dissipated, she reached up and lifted his hand from her shoulder. She stooped to grab the flight bag. Straightening, she took one of Rich's hands in hers and squeezed it for just an instant, touched by his obviously genuine distress. She leaned forward and kissed him lightly.

'Bye, Rich. Thanks for trying.' She was already on her way past him, heading for the door.

He started, as though being aroused from a reverie. He hurried after her and wrested the bag from her hand. 'Here,' he said, suddenly busy, 'at least let me take you out to the airport. I was planning to drop off the car and get back to Washington tonight anyway.'

For some time they drove in silence. Rich's hands stayed clenched hard on the wheel as they edged through the late rush-hour traffic of the southern tip of Manhattan. Julia sat tight-lipped, staring silently at the traffic. Once in a while she looked at her watch. Rich's arrival had delayed her a little but not enough to upset her schedule. Like most regular travellers, she had long since honed getting to airports to a fine art. Airport lounges might excite the charter passengers scrambling for their duty-free allowances. It was a long time since she had found them entertaining. Without even looking around she could feel Rich shooting nervous little glances at her. Several times, he wet his lips and began to say something, only to tail off into an inarticulate mumble.

They skirted Chinatown and headed for the Manhattan Bridge. On the bridge the traffic loosened up a little, enabling Rich to pick up some speed. Julia relaxed a notch, even turning in her seat for the view. The lights were on in the cluster of skyscrapers of the financial district. It was one thing she could agree with the charter customers about. The view of that skyline still thrilled her as much as ever. Off to her right, beyond the Brooklyn Bridge, she could glimpse the

Statue of Liberty, resplendent since her facelift. That, too, could still make her shiver.

She settled in her seat. Suddenly, without any warning, images of Michael flooded her mind. One image in particular came to her: Michael, seven years old, cycling beside her from their parents' house on Long Island to the beach. He was just learning to ride no hands. And he had fallen off. She remembered his eyes glistening as he nursed his bloodied knee, determined not to let the tears show. And then she saw him as he might be at that moment, trussed, blindfolded, isolated. Tears wet the corners of her own eyes.

'Please, Julia, will you just *think* what you're doing?'

The sound of his voice startled her. 'Huh?'

He was staring straight ahead. 'Think about it, for Christ's sake.' There was a plea in his voice. He turned his head to her. 'It's worse than you remember it. The place is falling apart. Jesus, it's *fallen* apart. Every male over twelve is liable to be carrying a gun. You walk to the next block, you don't know whose hands it's going to be in. Which family's going to be at war with which other one over some imagined insult they can hardly even remember. They're shooting women out trying to buy milk for their babies. Blood brothers at breakfast are slitting each other's throats by sundown!'

'Shouldn't you keep your eyes on the road?'

He snapped his head back to face the front. Silent again, he turned his wrist and glanced at his watch. Julia studied him as he made the gesture. The fleshy cheeks had slackened. The twitch had grown more pronounced. His usually immaculate hair was all over the place. He looked sick.

'I'm serious, Julia.' His voice sounded hollow. 'It's all gone to hell. Half the people you knew are dead. The rest aren't going to talk to an American.'

'There's one that will. Rachid. He owes me.'

He snorted. 'Rachid? Sure! When you were Mrs Richard Archer, able to act as his direct line to the State Department. You think the duplicitous bastard's going to lift a finger for you now?'

She smiled and rested a hand on his arm. 'Look, I appreciate getting a ride from somebody so important, but would you mind driving a little faster? I've got a plane to catch.'

Miserably, he glanced again at his watch. Abruptly, he gave a soft grunt, tightened his grip on the wheel and slammed his foot down. Julia was driven hard against the back of the seat. Her half-laughing protest died as she registered the white knuckles on the wheel and the desperate, wild-eyed look that had come over his face.

He swung the car around the truck ahead of them, cutting into the outside lane. The chauffeur of the Lincoln that had been coming up fast behind them stamped on his brakes and let Rich have a four-second burst of headlights and horn. Rich did not appear to see or hear.

'I said, a little faster. I didn't ask you to get us killed.' Julia's eyes were fixed on Rich's face. He gave no sign of hearing her. His lips stayed closed in a grim line as he accelerated harder and wove to the right, passing within inches of the car ahead.

She sat pressed back in her seat while he jinked through the traffic as though he were at the wheel of a getaway car, closing on cars ahead and bullying them aside or weaving recklessly between lanes.

A huge truck pounded along ahead of them. It was moving fast but not fast enough for Rich. He swerved sickeningly, passing inside it. Fifty yards ahead of them a ramp joined the road. A yellow breakdown truck was coming off it, filtering into the right-hand lane. Instinctively, Julia's hands went out to grab the dashboard. Her legs stiffened, pressing her feet against the floor and her back hard against the seat. If Rich heard her gasp he ignored it.

She stared in fascinated horror at the rear of the yellow truck. To their left the monstrous bulk of the other truck boxed them in. Behind them the traffic rolled in a fast, unbroken stream. The gap was down to twenty-five metres. She turned to look at Rich. He was staring ahead, his eyes fixed on the breakdown truck. The tendons in his wrists stood out as his grip tightened on the wheel. She turned back to the front. They were bearing down hard on the truck. She had opened her mouth to let the scream come when he jerked the wheel hard to the right.

The gap between the truck and the crash barrier was too narrow. The nose of the car nudged the rear of the truck. Rich flicked the wheel further to the right. The front of the car ground obliquely into the crash barrier.

Julia was screaming abuse. It was not from fear but from anger at Rich's behaviour. Amid a cacophony of grinding metal and Julia's cries, the tail of the car skidded out into the path of the oncoming traffic. Something clipped their rear. The car spun through a half-circle and slammed to rest against the barrier.

For some moments Julia was aware only of a total calm. Then, from out of nowhere, faces appeared at the windows. A man yanked open her door. Two sets of hands pulled her out. She sank to her haunches, her back supported against the car. One of the men who had pulled her clear crouched in front of her. He put a hand under her chin and jerked her face up.

'She's okay.' He spoke over his shoulder to the other man. She stared up at him. There was frank disappointment in his voice. Other faces appeared over the man's shoulder, staring down at Julia. The man pushed himself to his feet. His companion was withdrawing from the car. 'How about him?'

The other man shrugged. 'Looks like a broken collarbone.' He glanced at the growing crowd. 'Let's get out of here.'

Julia struggled to her feet, ignoring the hands that reached out to help her. A siren began whining in the distance, drawing closer. She bent and thrust her head into the car.

Rich sat silent and immobile. His face was the colour of ashes. One arm hung loose in his lap. With the other he gripped the shoulder of the dangling arm. The men had been right. It did look like a broken collarbone.

'You okay?' Her face was inches from his as she spoke. He did not seem to have heard. He simply sat, staring ahead of him, his face contorted with pain. 'Rich!' She reached out and pulled his face around to face her. 'Rich. Are you all right. Is it just your shoulder?'

He stared into her face. He still did not speak. His pale blue eyes looked moist.

Exasperated, she began withdrawing from the car. 'Shit, Rich. Talk to me. If you're okay I have to leave you. I'm going to miss that damned plane.'

As she straightened the whooping siren died. A policeman dismounted from a motorcycle. She turned to him. 'He'll be okay, officer. He needs an ambulance.'

'Yes, ma'am. One's on its way.' He turned to the crowd. 'Anybody see what happened here?' Nobody spoke up. Julia looked for the two men who had pulled her out. They were nowhere in the crowd. 'Okay, folks. If nobody saw anything, on your way. Another minute and I'm going to be handing out tickets here.'

Reluctantly, people began drifting back to their cars. Julia dragged her bag from the car and stepped forward. 'Anybody here going out to the airport? I need a ride.'

A well-dressed couple in their thirties began to reply. The policeman held up a hand. 'Sorry, ma'am. I'm afraid I have to ask you a few questions here. You were a passenger in the car, weren't you?'

Even to Julia's own ears her story sounded stupid. It took her nearly twenty minutes to satisfy the policeman she was telling the truth. Several times he climbed into the car to try to obtain confirmation of the story from Rich. Rich did not utter a word. He simply sat, biting back the pain, hardly blinking.

An ambulance screeched to a stop. Two black paramedics sprang from it and unfolded a stretcher. It took them no more than a minute to haul Rich from the car and strap him onto the stretcher. Julia watched them slide the stretcher into the ambulance, the whole time shooting fretful glances at her watch. Rich did not once look at her. She frowned, shook her head, and turned to the officer. She waved her press card under his nose for the twentieth time.

'Look, officer, I've just got to get to JFK. I'm in a hell of a hurry. Can you help? Please?'

He pursed his lips and frowned at the damaged car. 'There's the wreck there, ma'am.'

She was almost weeping with frustration. 'Officer, I've told you, he's just a friend of mine. He was giving me a ride to the airport. The car's nothing to do with me. Jesus, it's *rented*. Hertz will take care of it. Please.'

Real tears formed at the corners of her eyes. He looked at her for a moment more and then stepped into the road. He flagged down a taxi with crumpled panels and a lady in the back with a suspicious look on her face. He explained the problem, emphasizing Julia's press credentials. The lady's suspicion turned to cooperation. She was still telling them how pleased she would be to help when Julia threw herself into the car and pushed two twenty-dollar bills at the driver. 'TWA terminal. Fast.'

At the airport she left the car at a run.

She tore across to the desk, leaving a trail of half-finished apologies as she jinked her way through the crowded concourse. She threw her ticket in front of the bored girl at the desk. The girl glanced automatically at the clock set high on the wall over the entrance.

'Sorry, ma'am. The flight closed some time ago.'

Julia's eyes watered with fury and frustration. She snatched up her ticket and ran through the concourse to the information desk. This time a clean-cut, slender young man with a mincing manner examined her ticket with an exorbitant show of interest before confirming that she was indeed too late. The flight had already boarded. He interrogated the machine in front of him. There was a British Airways flight to London departing in an hour. It would still get her into London in time for her Larnaca connection. With a brief smile of thanks, Julia set off, still at a run.

The paramedic squatted next to Rich's head. He watched

him with a look of puzzlement and concern on his face. The guy's face looked funny, as if he were shell-shocked or something. In the twenty minutes since they picked him up he had not said a word. On the face of it the guy had the kind of injuries you could get falling off a bike and yet he was lying there looking like he just found out he had liver cancer. It was weird.

Rich spoke for the first time at the hospital. His voice was hoarse and almost inaudible. He asked for a private room. As soon as he was alone he pulled the phone towards him and dialled a number. A voice answered immediately. It was a woman's voice, brisk and businesslike, not the sing-song incantation of a switchboard operator.

'Louise? Give me Tom.'

The woman sounded guarded. 'Who is this?'

'Rich Archer.'

'Oh, Rich! I'm sorry. I didn't recognize your voice. You okay?'

'Yeah. I guess so. Had a little road accident. Can I speak to Tom?'

'Sure. Mr Jordan's free. I'll pass you right over.'

Julia looked out of the window and gave an audible sigh of relief. They had dropped through the layer of cloud that had lain unbroken beneath them for the last two hours, and the curve of the Thames now lay below, snaking its way past the familiar landmarks of the City and Westminster. She consulted her watch. They were over an hour late. It would be another quarter of an hour before they were on the ground. After her panic at the airport they had been late boarding and then sat for nearly two hours in the plane before being cleared for take-off. Her irritation had been compounded by seeing the TWA aircraft leave, while she still sat fretting in the departure lounge. She would be hard-pressed to get her connection.

Julia was the third person off the plane. She strode quickly at the head of the crowd towards passport control. Going through customs and walking was the quickest way to change terminals. Provided they were not right behind a 747 from Bangladesh.

Something in the manner of the passport officer when he asked where she had come from made her stare hard at him for a moment. She shook off the faint feeling of unease and walked through customs.

The sight outside the customs hall stopped her in her tracks. A thin crowd stood waiting by the exit. Instead of watching the arriving passengers their eyes were turned to the arrivals board high over their heads. Many of them were sobbing. Some were close to hysteria. Couples and small family groups comforted each other. Julia followed their eyes to the indicator board. Against the TWA flight from New York no arrival time was posted, only the single word 'delayed'.

Julia turned cold. Her stomach churned. She had to fight down the need to vomit. She had watched the plane take off from the window of the departure lounge. She had been angry she was not on it. 'Oh,' she murmured softly to herself. 'Oh, my God.'

6

'FOR CHRIST'S SAKE, Dean! Are you telling me your people still haven't been able to pick up a *thing* on this outfit?' The President leaned forward, his forearms pressed onto the huge desk, glaring round the room.

The Secretary of State finished polishing his glasses and pushed them back onto his nose. He twitched them more comfortably into place before speaking, his tone low, measured. 'That's about the size of it, Mr President. Our people at the Embassy have turned up nothing. There are plenty of similar sounding groups that they're holding files on. But not that one, the Islamic Revolutionary Faction. They don't have a thing. Nobody has heard of them, even within Lebanon. Not until the last couple of days, that is.'

'Mind you, Mr President, that's not unusual,' Tom Jordan, the National Security Adviser, broke in. 'These people aren't necessarily organizations at all in the sense that they have any kind of structure. They might easily be just one family, a group of cousins with a grievance. A bunch of hoodlums.'

The President snatched up a piece of paper from his desk and tossed it peevishly from him. 'This is from a bunch of hoodlums?' he said incredulously. 'Don't make me laugh, Tom. This is from people who know exactly what they're after, not a bunch of kids threatening a Hallowe'en trick.'

Jordan sat impassive, showing no annoyance at the President's contemptuous tone. The Secretary of State spoke again.

'I think that's for sure, Mr President. Their timing's perfect. They think that with the election so close we're going to *have* to respond. Colter's picture's going to be all over tomorrow's papers. So is that message.'

The President picked up the sheet of paper and the blurred photograph, its definition lost in transmission. He looked musingly from one to the other, his eyes not really focused. 'Has anybody spoken to the Israelis?' he asked with sudden vigour.

The Secretary of State and Tom Jordan exchanged looks. Jordan answered. 'No, sir. Prime Minister Meyer's still in hospital. He was apparently operated on yesterday and was unable to speak last night.'

'Damn!' the President said, scowling. 'Isn't there anyone else?'

'Zimund, Mr President. He's acting head of government until Meyer recovers. To tell you the truth, we were holding off. Dean and I,' the Secretary of State nodded acknowledgment, 'would have preferred to wait and talk directly to Meyer.'

'You're right,' the President concurred. 'Zimund's a shifty bastard. When's Meyer going to be available?'

Dean Sutcliffe shrugged. 'A few more days. No more, I hope. We need him back in action damned fast. The coalition's falling to pieces anyway. Without him we're going to end up with elections there, too, before the month's out.'

The President nodded. 'We need another Begin. He was a ruthless little shit, but he certainly kept a hold on things.' He leant back and swung his gaze around the gathering. 'The question we have to answer right now is, how do we respond? What do we give the press?'

Jordan spoke up. 'In my view there's only one approach available. We publish their demands, which they'll be doing themselves, anyway, and refuse to give an inch. No withdrawal of the fleet, no representations to Israel to withdraw from Southern Lebanon or anywhere else. No change in policy towards the Gulf war. If we give anything at all to these people we can kiss goodbye to our whole policy.'

The President looked gloomy. 'You're right, of course, Tom. We *can't* be seen bowing to terrorists. At a time like this. But, ah, you're forgetting the boy, Tom. They're threatening to *dismember* him.'

Jordan leaned closer to the President. 'It's tough on the boy, sir, but he just had no business being there. We can't negotiate, period. Not before the election. The opposition would crucify us.' He looked hard into the President's face, letting his last words sink home.

The President blinked and fidgeted with the paper in front of him. 'You sure we couldn't try *something*, Tom? Send some men in and bring the boy out? That would really be something, if we could bring the boy out of there,' he added animatedly.

Jordan shook his head, still watching the President. 'We don't know where he's being held, Mr President.' He shot a fleeting look at Dean Sutcliffe. 'I have another suggestion, sir. I know Dean here disagrees with me, but I think perhaps we should let them have a response. Not the one they're looking for, though.'

'How do you mean?' the President asked, frowning.

'The same tactics that were used on Ghaddafi, sir. We've got the fleet on station in the Gulf. Let's use it. Surprise air strikes on Shi-ite bases, Palestinian camps, their ports, their supply routes, everything.'

'I disagree absolutely, Mr President,' Sutcliffe broke in. 'We've no idea yet who's holding Colter. For all we know it may be a group of freelancers! We have to hold off until we know more. Maybe the Israelis can come up with some information.'

'Hold off, Dean?' Jordan said, smiling patiently. 'That's what everybody wanted to do over Libya. It took the raids there to quiet Ghaddafi. If we'd been a little tougher in Lebanon before now we might never have seen the Embassy bombing.' He turned to the President. 'Of course we can hold off. We can wait while they send us pieces of Colter through the mail. Or we can hit them, show them who it is they're screwing around with.' He leaned back and made a sweeping gesture. 'I know which option the voters would prefer, sir.'

Julia strode past the smiling Cypriot customs officer and out to the taxi rank. She sank into the dusty back seat of the first cab.

'The Ledra Hotel.' The driver's smile faded. The clothes and the hotel marked Julia out as a correspondent. He might as well save his charm for the tourists.

Julia was still checking in when two figures appeared in the doorway of the bar, their arms around each other's shoulders, and began calling her name, pressing her with drunken insistence to join them.

In spite of the fatigue and grief, she smiled. Ray Walker and Byron Moody had not changed. They had kept her cheerful a hundred bad times in a dozen lousy, sometimes dangerous, places. At any other time she would have joined them at the bar and to hell with going up to her room. She gave them another smile and shook her head.

'Sorry, you guys. See you later, maybe.'

One of the men, medium height with powerful shoulders

and forearms, with red-blond hair and a trace of freckles under the tan, ducked out from his companion's grip and walked over to Julia. He was not laughing as he leant forward and placed a kiss on her cheek. Behind him Byron whooped enthusiastically.

'We all heard about your brother, Julia. I'm sorry.'

She nodded and blinked and squeezed his hand.

'If there's anything I can do . . .' The sentence tailed off.

She smiled. 'Thanks, Ray. I really appreciate it.' The lift door opened. She stepped inside.

'Anything at all. My room number's 435.'

She nodded and gave him a four-finger wave as the door slid shut. He stood looking at the closed door for a couple of seconds more, his face grave, and then turned and headed back to the bar. Byron gave another whoop, punched him on the bicep and handed him a fresh drink.

In her room Julia threw off her crumpled clothes and began unpacking. Without warning, her shoulders shook in a violent sob.

She fell face down on the bed, her whole body heaving uncontrollably. Throughout the flight from London she had held back, keeping her mind busy by compiling a background article on Michael for Harry. Now, alone in her room, the full impact of the shocks of the last seventy-two hours hit her for the first time. It was like a wall falling on her.

She lay naked and trembling, her face buried in the pillows. For a long time there was no coherent thought. She was conscious only of the strange, bitter mixture of relief and anguish that flooded her whole being. Relief at her escape, anguish at what was happening to Michael.

It was nearly an hour before the shaking abated. The sobs subsided into crying. Pushing the tears away with her palms, she rolled over and pressed the switch to turn on the television.

The news had just started. The crash was the third story. She did not need to speak Greek to follow it. The TWA flight had come down somewhere in the Atlantic. So far only an oil slick had been sighted. Two hundred and seventeen people had been on board. Abruptly, she pushed herself from the bed and ran into the bathroom. She vomited violently into the toilet bowl.

When it was over, she took a drink of water and stood for a moment, recovering. With another shudder she looked at herself in the mirror over the washbasin. But for Rich's sudden decision to play the clown there would have been two hundred and eighteen victims.

A bleak sensation of total, unbearable loneliness engulfed her. Mixed with it came a wave of guilt at her treatment of Rich. However exasperating he might be he was still the one person she could depend on absolutely, whatever kind of trouble she might be in. The one person apart from Michael who really cared for her. She looked at her watch. A few minutes after six. In Washington it would be just after nine in the morning. She reached across and picked up the phone.

'Richard Archer's office.' The voice of Rich's secretary was almost inaudible.

'Hello, Rosemary. It's Julia.'

'Oh, Julia. Hello.' Rosemary's voice rose, propelled on a note of strain. Before Julia had time to respond a deeper voice came on the line.

'Rich?' The voice was unfamiliar. Other voices murmured in the background.

'No. This is George Marks. A colleague of Rich's.'

'May I speak to Rich, please. It's Julia Colter.'

The man lowered his voice. 'I'm afraid not, Miss Colter.'

'Isn't he in? Is he at home?'

'No, Miss Colter. Rich isn't in. And he's not at home.'

'What? Did they keep him at the hospital? Can you give me his number, please. It's important. I have to speak to him.'

'I'm sorry, Miss Colter, I can't give you a number for him.'

'Mr Marks,' she exclaimed, irritated by his priestly tone. 'Will you please tell me what the hell you're talking about. Someone there must know where Rich is.'

'I do, Miss Colter. I'm afraid Rich Archer is dead.'

7

JULIA AWOKE SUDDENLY, dry-mouthed and unrefreshed. For the rest of the day and most of the night she had lain naked and weeping on the bed, unconscious of the chill of the air-conditioning. Finally, some time after three in the morning, she had fallen into an exhausted sleep, alive with haunted dreams.

She shivered and pushed herself from the bed. A glass of scotch stood unfinished at the bedside. She had tried it and it had not helped. With a shudder she took up the glass, carried it into the bathroom and emptied it down the toilet. The smell of the stale whisky made her recoil. Her face in the bathroom mirror was drawn and pallid, except for the dark stains beneath her eyes. She ran her fingers through her dishevelled hair and stepped into the bath.

She sat down in the bath and for twenty minutes let the powerful jet of the shower play on her head and shoulders, hoping the clean stream would bring some kind of relief. When, a few minutes later, dressed in fresh clothes, she stood at the door of room 435 she was crying again.

She brushed the tears away and knocked. It was not yet seven o'clock. She waited several seconds before knocking again, harder. After the third knock the bolt slid back noisily and the door opened six inches, revealing the dissipated and disgruntled face of Ray Walker. He squinted at Julia and looked at the place on his wrist where his watch would have been.

'I know. It's only five to seven,' she said, smiling wryly and pushing the door open. 'Sorry, Ray, but I need help badly.'

The man watched her walk past him into the room, his eyes screwed up against the light. He closed the door and followed her into the protective gloom of the room.

Julia sat on the edge of the bed. 'Shall I order some coffee?'

'Yeah,' he croaked, 'please.' He sat down beside her, tugging modestly at his crumpled undershorts. He buried his head in his hands for a moment, groaning softly, while she phoned room service. With an obvious effort, he looked up at Julia. 'Sorry,' he said grinning gauntly, 'I had a hard night.'

'Yeah. Me too.' She could not keep the sob from her voice.

He looked at her sharply, no longer grinning. 'Christ, Julia, you're crying.' He moved closer and put an arm around her shoulders.

She shook her head, angry with herself. 'I'm sorry, Ray. I didn't mean to do this.'

'Forget it. It's something to do with Michael, right?'

She nodded. 'Yeah, right.' She gulped back her tears and straightened, making a conscious effort to get a grip on herself. 'I want to help him, Ray.'

He grimaced. 'How do you expect to do that? He's in Beirut.'

'I'm on my way there.'

Very slowly, he straightened and turned to face her, his head cocked slightly on one side, examining her face for evidence she was joking. His hangover seemed to have dropped from him. His eyes were shrewd and alert. They scanned her face.

'You can't be serious. Return to that snake pit?' He did not even try to hide his incredulity. He stood up and took a couple of paces in silence. 'Are you sure you're up to date on how things are over there? Nobody in his right mind would go there now without a damned good reason.'

'I've got a good reason!' She found herself saying it angrily.

He held up a hand. 'Whoa. I know that. But no protection. Anyone going there without it would really have to be mad. That includes you, Julia. And your brother.'

'He went there to help.'

'Sorry, Julia, but you know my opinions about people who go to these places to help out. It's not factional skirmishing any more. It's all-out war. The Hezbollah and the Christians are tearing each other to pieces and the Palestinians and the Syrians are lying low, both hoping to pick up some of those pieces. It's conventional war *plus* every kind of treachery and double-cross in the book.'

He paused, waiting for Julia to react. She simply looked at him. Disconcerted, he continued. 'Christ, look, it's not just kids with Kalashnikovs any more. They've got artillery, mortars, even armour and aircraft. Amal are shooting women and kids for just trying to bring something to eat into the camps.'

Still Julia did not speak. She sat gravely, waiting for him to finish. At the sound of a knock he rose and collected the coffee tray from a waiter. He handed a cup to Julia. 'There's nothing you can do, Julia,' he went on, his voice more gentle. 'D'you have even the ghost of a notion who's holding your brother?'

'I'm going to find out!' Her voice began to choke with emotion. She swallowed hard, forcing her feelings back under control. When she spoke again her voice was soft and very distinct. 'Of course, what you say's true, Ray. But I don't care. Nobody else is doing anything. As far as the Government's concerned he can spend the rest of his life out there, chained up in some stinking hovel. Nobody's going to lift a finger, unless it's me.'

'So what do you want from me?'

'A name. Someone who'll get me into Beirut.'

He shook his head. 'It's too dangerous, Julia. I came out less than two weeks ago. You know why? Because I was scared shitless. I couldn't stand it any more. Cambodia, Vietnam, nowhere I've been's ever frightened me the way Beirut does.' He hesitated a second. 'Can't your husband help? He seems to be a pretty big wheel these days.'

He was perplexed to see the tears well up again in Julia's eyes.

'Rich died yesterday.' The words were almost inaudible.

He looked at her in stunned silence. 'Rich Archer?' he asked foolishly.

'Yeah. We were in a car smash. He died in hospital.' Her voice faltered. 'Poor, silly Rich. I thought he was faking.' Ray knelt in front of her. She threw her arms around him and held herself tightly against his chest. Her voice became fainter. 'You do see, don't you, Ray? Michael's all I've got left.'

He held her against him, looking at her hair. 'Yeah,' he said, in a hoarse whisper, 'I do.'

It was a few seconds before she unclasped her arms and pushed herself away from him. She looked up into his face. Her own face was wet and haggard. She smiled. 'Can I have the name?'

He looked at her for another moment, his face absolutely blank. Then he turned and grabbed a shabby leather address book from where it lay by a portable typewriter. He leafed through the book, found what he wanted and scribbled on a piece of paper.

'When do you plan to leave?'

She took the paper. 'Tonight, if I can.' She stood up and kissed him lightly on the cheek. 'Thanks, Ray. Thanks a lot. See you around.'

Julia stoically watched the distant purplish hills as the driver threw the car round the curves in the coast road. It was almost eleven. The telephone number Ray had given her had not answered until just before nine. She had then waited an hour and a half before the Jaguar and its monosyllabic driver had arrived in front of the hotel. The ride had taken them out beyond the crowded suburbs of ramshackle housing into the area of opulent stuccoed villas that clung to the coast. At a grunt from the driver she turned her attention from the hills to the road. They slowed and swung between two heavy iron gates into a drive leading up to a handsome pink house. The gates closed behind them, remote-controlled. Julia caught sight of men standing, alert but discreet, among the shrubs and pines that lined the drive.

The driver led her quickly up the three steps into the cool interior. On the far side of a marble-floored hall a door stood open. A man appeared in the doorway, as though their entry had been signalled to him.

'Miss Colter?' he said, amiably. 'Please, come in.' He stepped aside letting Julia precede him into the room.

Seated across the wide mahogany desk, Julia studied the man. He was around her own height, but probably weighed twice as much. Heavy gold jewellery glinted deep among the luxuriant hair at his throat and on his fingers and wrists. He wore expensive sports clothes that strove, unsuccessfully, to disguise his wrestler's physique. His colouring was Mediterranean, his accent soft and undistinguishable. It was an appearance characteristic of a type of Mediterranean entrepreneur. Only his age was surprising. The man could not have been more than twenty-eight.

'So you want to go to Lebanon?' he said, without preamble. Julia nodded. 'It's very dangerous.'

'I know. I'm told you offer a reliable service. I'll need accompanying to the American Embassy. Can you arrange it?'

The man raised an eyebrow and half smiled. 'Reliable? Honest, yes, but I can't really say reliable. That depends very much on the Israelis. Their gunboats have been very active. I've lost two boats in the last month. Together with all their cargo. Very unfortunate,' he said, matter-of-factly.

'Cargo? You mean people?'

He laughed. 'No, goods. Hardly any people want to go to Beirut these days. I mean real cargo. Import-export is my business. It's only rarely that I carry people now, and only if they can pay.' He laid some emphasis on the last words.

'I have money. How soon can you take me?'

He looked quizzically at Julia, as though her insistence amused him. 'Tonight, if you wish.'

'I do. How much?'

'Two thousand dollars.'

'Traveller's cheques?'

He gave a slight bow. 'Perfect.'

He watched, smiling, as she signed the cheques. He examined each one in turn before dropping them into a desk drawer. 'Yangis will collect you from the hotel at ten. Please be ready. We run to a very tight schedule.'

'That bastard Moore! That's three days running!' The President threw that morning's copy of the *New York Times* onto the massive oval table. He stood up and stalked to the window, cursing under his breath.

'We've got to get something under way with this Colter boy. Those shits on the *Times* are really going for us.'

'They aren't the only ones, Mr President.' His press secretary shuffled a pile of newspapers. 'They're all onto it. It looks like becoming an issue, sir.'

'You're telling me,' the President snapped. 'Hasn't anyone come up with anything? Don't we have *any* idea where they're keeping the boy? Norm, what are those pricks of yours in Beirut up to?' He stared at the head of the CIA.

Norm Clark was a dry-looking man with a wry sense of humour, well accustomed to the President's profanity. 'Well, so far there's nothing positive, Mr President. All our contacts within the Palestinian movement report nothing. We think it's reasonably certain he's not being held in the camps. As you know, our contacts within the Fundamentalist groups are not good. The Israelis' are better. We're in constant touch with Mossad.'

'And?'

'They're no wiser than we are.'

'Damn!' The President turned back to the window, his fists clenching in impotent rage. 'This is just what we didn't need. Why couldn't the boy stay away from the place?' He whirled back to face the window. 'Dean,' he said, chewing at his lip, 'don't your people have *any*thing for us? What's happening to this country that a bunch of ragheads can make us look ridiculous?'

The Secretary of State looked at the President's back for an instant before answering in a carefully measured tone. 'No, Mr President, there's nothing yet. These aren't the kind of people that go through diplomatic channels.'

The President looked around sharply, suspecting a hint of sarcasm in Sutcliffe's tone. He was about to speak when the door opened and Tom Jordan strode into the room carrying a green folder. With a brief apology he took his place at the table. His face was set.

'What is it, Tom? D'you have anything on the Colter situation?'

Jordan nodded. 'I'm afraid so, Mr President. First of all, we've just heard from the Embassy. They had a telex from Colter's sister. She's on her way there!'

'Oh, shit! How the hell . . . ?' The President broke off as Jordan held up a hand.

'There's worse, sir. The news agencies have just had a new message from the kidnappers.' He drew a sheaf of papers from the folder and passed a single sheet to each of the men in the room.

The President studied his copy for a few seconds, his brows knitted. 'The bastards! They must know we can't do this.'

Jordan shrugged. 'They're asking for it, Mr President. They want us to publicly call on Israel to withdraw support from the Christians. They want Israel out of Lebanon.'

Dean Sutcliffe spoke. 'Whoever they are they must know we could never agree to do that. Apart from anything else, if it weren't for the Israelis the Fundamentalists would overrun the place in days. It would be an outpost of Iran on the Mediterranean.'

Jordan turned to look levelly at the Secretary of State. 'That's what they're asking. That or they start sending us pieces of Colter as of tomorrow.'

'We can't do it,' Sutcliffe said flatly.

'I agree absolutely with Dean, Mr President. But I still say my own alternative is the way we should go. Hard surgical strikes. And if they don't give us Colter then we hit them some more.'

Dean Sutcliffe began to protest.

The President quelled him with a gesture. 'You really think it might work, Tom? We would need to be very careful. No civilian casualties.'

Jordan drew another paper from his folder and passed it to the President.

Dean Sutcliffe could not contain his anger. 'This is ridiculous. We can't just hit out blindly. We don't know who the kidnappers are. Or even where they are.'

'Dean,' Jordan said, with a patient smile, 'neither do the voters.'

8

THE JAGUAR drew up at a minute past ten. Before Julia had closed the door the car jerked forward, spitting gravel from beneath the tyres. Her bag contained a single change of clothes. Money, mostly in new one-hundred-dollar bills, traveller's cheques and passport were all stowed in the pockets of the waterproof camera bag slung across her chest.

Yangis drove in silence past the bright, open-fronted cafés. The men at the tables that spilled onto the streets scarcely looked up from their intense backgammon games at the speeding car. To the old men of this part of Larnaca expensive cars in a hurry were no longer a sight worthy of attention.

In a few minutes the cranes of the port became visible, towering over the new office buildings, built with the profits of Lebanese trade. The car raced along the seafront to a quay beyond the pale streetlights, on the very far edge of the commercial port. The quay was in darkness and, at first sight, deserted. Only as Julia clambered from the car, her eyes growing used to the darkness, did she make out figures hurrying in the shadows, their silhouettes oddly humped as they ran bent under the weight of bales.

'Miss Colter?' She started as a dark shape detached itself from the shadows.

'I'm Christian, the captain of the boat. Please follow me.' The speaker was a tall lean man around fifty, dressed in slacks and a roll-necked sweater, both of very dark material. He led her up a narrow gangplank onto the boat. It was a long, thin steel vessel on the lines of a wartime motor torpedo boat, plainly built for speed. As they boarded, the captain called out a few words in Greek. There was a last scurrying of the porters and somebody withdrew the gangplank. The motors came to life with a low coughing, settling quickly to a powerful throb. At another shout from Christian the boat began easing away from the quayside. The captain moved towards the wheelhouse. Julia made to follow him.

'Perhaps you would like to go below, miss.' She began to protest but he cut her short. 'Please do as I say, Miss Colter. There's always danger. From the Israelis. Even the Fundamentalists have boats now. They shoot very easily.'

'Why? You can trade, can't you?'

He gave a tired smile. 'They only ask what we are doing after they stop shooting. Please go below.' He pushed her towards a doorway.

Julia descended the narrow stairway carefully, made awkward by her bags. She found herself in a low cabin. A table ran down the middle with benches on each side wide enough to serve as bunks. The benches were piled with cartons. Prominent labels said they were Winston cigarettes.

'Hi there!' She whirled to face the sound. The crumpled figure of a man emerged, grinning, from a heap of cartons. He held a paper cup in one hand and a half-bottle of Teacher's in the other. 'Want one?'

She stood for a moment, surprise and exasperation in her face. 'Yes,' she said at length, laughing, 'I do.'

She let her bag fall to the floor and stood with her hands on her hips, watching with one eyebrow raised as he poured the drink. 'Okay, Ray, so what the hell are you *doing* here?'

He handed her the cup with a generous slug of whisky in it. 'Don't worry about the cup. I had the test when I came back from Zaire.' He grinned cheerfully. 'Professional pride. I thought if you could do it so could I. Besides, I thought you and your brother might make too good a story to leave it all to you.'

Julia laughed, shook her head and raised the cup to her lips.

Michael up-ended the bottle. He trembled so badly much of the remaining water ran down his chin and chest, mingling with the greasy film of perspiration. He threw the empty bottle aside and drew his knees up to his chest. He folded his arms around them, hugging them in a vain quest for warmth. He must have caught something from the water or the filthy food. For the whole of the previous day he had been shivering and alternately vomiting or emptying his bowels into the fouled bucket. Only late on the previous day had they changed the bucket, giving him some respite from the vile stench. They had allowed him a half-pail of water to clean himself and a fresh bottle of drinking water. At the same time they had taken away his clothes, leaving him naked.

The last humiliation had been that one of the guards had driven a steel eye into the wall and attached a chain from the eye to his ankle. He could no longer remove the light bulb in order to sleep. He was just able to manoeuvre beneath the shaft to find out if it was night or day.

Now, laboriously, he pushed himself to his knees and crawled beneath the shaft. Above him was blackness. It was still night, the fourth of his captivity. His throat was parched, the fever leaching the moisture from his body.

Exhausted, he sank back onto the mattress and lay face down, waiting for another bout of shivering to pass. He could feel despondency creeping over him again. He swore out loud, a twenty-second stream of filthy invective against his captors. It was a kind of mantra he had developed in the last forty-eight hours, a device to fuel his anger whenever he felt his spirits flag. He stopped as the sound of movement came to him from beyond the door. He was still struggling to rise when it was thrown open.

The tall, hooded man who had photographed him stood in the doorway. A second man, shorter, in a civilian suit, stood at his shoulder. He wore no hood to hide his narrow, nervous features. The hooded one stepped into the room. The civilian and two gunmen followed. The tall man spoke, very quietly, gesturing towards Michael.

One of the guards waved his gun barrel, motioning Michael to lie on his front. He did what they wanted. He had quickly decided that pointless resistance was a waste of energy. They had the guns. His best option was to cooperate until the time came when he could do himself some good.

The moment he turned over one of the men dropped with one knee planted in the small of Michael's back and, with casual force, applied a vicious choke-hold.

Someone grabbed one of Michael's arms and pinioned it straight out to the side. Retching from the choke Michael managed to twist his head far enough to the side to see the civilian approach.

Carefully, the man put down his bag and unzipped it, his movements precise and quick. Michael's eyes grew wider and a ghastly gargling sound emerged from his crushed throat. The fingers of the man's left hand clamped over Michael's wrist, holding the hand hard against the rough concrete floor. His right hand held a scalpel. Michael's terror gave him strength. He arched beneath the man above him, making the man loosen his hold. From deep in his throat Michael screamed. The scream died as he passed into unconsciousness.

The boat had been under way for several hours. Julia and Ray sat, slumped awkwardly in their cramped places, dozing fitfully. From the moment the boat had cleared the harbour it had been driven hard, vaulting the troughs of the moderate seas. Each new wave sent the bow bucking with a jolt that almost lifted them from their seats. They had fought seasickness with a second bottle of whisky. The bottle lay on the table, moving like a live thing with the vibration. Julia's head throbbed. She stirred and looked at her watch.

'How much longer?'

Ray opened his eyes reluctantly, chewing at the foul taste in his mouth. He retrieved his left hand from beneath his body and checked his own watch. 'Must be nearly there. Depends what the sea's been like. Feels as though we've been running flat out the whole way,' he added ruefully, rubbing at the back of his neck.

As he spoke, the noise and vibration abruptly stopped, leaving a silence so total Julia could hear the blood in her temples. She looked questioningly at Ray. 'Is this it?' She found herself whispering in the silence.

Before he could answer the light went out, plunging the windowless cabin into blackness. A moment later the door opened, showing a rectangle of paler darkness.

'Quickly,' a voice hissed. 'On deck.'

Instinctively grabbing her camera bag Julia followed Ray up the companionway.

On deck the only sound was of the waves slapping against the hull. Somebody led them into the wheelhouse. The captain spoke close by them.

'A boat.' His voice was so low it was beneath a whisper. 'Probably Israeli.'

Julia looked all around. The darkness was total. 'Where?'

He pointed ahead of them. 'Over there. About a mile. Without lights.'

They strained to see. Beyond the slight phosphorescence of the sea as it broke around the boat, everything blended into unrelieved blackness. With a suddenness that made Julia start, a searchlight beam split the night. It traversed slowly, sliding across the surface towards them.

Fifty yards away it stopped. Slowly, it began a return traverse. The captain slipped silently from the cabin. He returned after a few seconds and leaned close to them. A shadowy figure stood at the door. 'If anything happens, you must follow Paul.' He indicated the shadow. 'Do exactly as he says.'

The light began to move towards them again. As they watched, their attention riveted on the beam, Julia heard a faint splash behind them. The light came closer. The captain swallowed and slid his hands beneath the blanket that covered the faint glow of the controls.

'Go, now!' he said. 'Good luck.'

As they turned to go, the light struck the bow. Instantly, it twitched another fraction of a degree, dousing the whole length of the boat in its blinding glare.

'Go!' The captain was screaming the word now.

The crewman pulled them into the shadow of the wheelhouse, took one stride and leapt over the rail. Without even a look at each other they followed him over. Before her head slid below the surface Julia saw the first tracer bullets slicing through the sky above her.

She came up with the sound of shouting in her ears. The crewman, Paul, was screaming at her from six feet away. In the reflected light of the beam she saw that he was in a black inflatable boat, hacking at the rope that held it. Ray was already clambering aboard.

Julia had scarcely reached the dinghy when sudden gunfire filled the night. The light of the beam was abruptly doused. The next instant the boat's motors leapt to life. With a deafening roar, its bow bucked and it sped into the blackness, leaving a bright wake curving behind it.

The three of them lay sprawled in the inflatable, keeping well down and silent. Perhaps three seconds passed. A new searchlight sprang to life and began raking the sea. Twice the beam passed over them. There was no reaction from the Israeli boat, the dark inflatable probably almost invisible among the waves. As they lay watching, the beam fluttered and fastened onto the low outline of the speeding launch. Great silver spumes of foam curved from its bow as it raced through the water. A cry carried across the water from the Israeli boat and its own motors barked into life.

The launch began swerving in irregular short arcs, trying to throw off the beam. The light never wavered from it. A figure ran to the rear of the launch and immediately fire began to flash from the rail. The pursuing boat itself now began jinking, its wake a series of tight curves as it evaded the gunfire.

A voice boomed metallically through a loudhailer, in Arabic and then in English. It called on the boat to stop. The response was another long burst of machine-gun fire.

There followed a moment of dead silence and then a rapid series of flashes broke from the pursuers' boat. They chased each other through the darkness towards their target. The launch exploded in a gigantic, ragged hemisphere of flame. A sudden fierce wind slapped spray into their faces. The shock of the explosion struck them with a physical impact. The searchlight played on an empty sea.

The light turned down to sweep the area close around the spot. It was a formality. No-one could have survived such an explosion. After only a cursory search the searchlight was extinguished. The sound of the motors receded.

Ray pushed himself into a sitting position. He ran a hand over his face and turned to the crewman. 'As they say, cigarettes can seriously damage your health.'

The crewman grinned. 'Mortar shells,' he said laconically.

9

MAJOR BRADMAN climbed out of the car yawning. He put his hands behind his hips and stretched his spine, his chin thrust upwards. He let out his breath with a long sigh. 'Christ,' he said cheerfully to the sentry, 'how I hate these night-time calls. Why can't those bastards in Washington call us in the morning instead of at the end of their day when we should all be in bed? Try calling from here when it's three in the morning in Washington and see how many of those fat-assed civil servants would be there to answer.'

The sentry grunted agreement, his head under the dashboard. He checked the rear seat while another man did the outside of the car. Satisfied, he began patting the Major's clothing. As always, the search was meticulous and fruitless.

Major Bradman parked under the harsh floodlights of the compound and climbed the stairs. It was just after three. The call was scheduled to come through at three-fifteen. Instead of going directly to his office he headed for the bathroom. He examined himself wryly in the mirror, washed his face and hands, combed his hair and brushed a little red dust from his gleaming brogues. The phone was ringing as he walked through the door of his office.

'Bradman.'

'Good afternoon, Major.' Tom Jordan's voice was clipped and brisk.

'Good afternoon, sir.' He let the faintest ironic emphasis fall on the word 'afternoon'.

'Any news?' The voice held a gritty edge of irritation.

'No, but then I wouldn't expect to hear anything before morning.'

'Hmm. Has the woman arrived?'

'Not yet. Normally if they come in on the boats they arrive just before daybreak. It takes a while to get into town. If they don't run into trouble on the way.'

'Trouble?' Jordan said sharply. 'She's not to get into trouble, Major. The President's watching this closely. Understand that. We can't afford a second kidnapping.'

Bradman scowled. 'I do understand, sir,' he said stiffly. 'As you know, it was my opinion that she should have been dissuaded from coming here at all. I can't protect her until she shows up at the Embassy. Until then she's on her own out there and very vulnerable. I can't help that, sir.'

'That's okay, Jack,' Jordan said smoothly, switching to Bradman's first name. 'It's just that this really is very important to the President. He's very, ah, sensitive on the issue. He, ah, basically, he would prefer that the Colter woman left there as soon as possible. He's very, er, agitated about the prospect of her being snatched.'

'From the moment she shows up there's absolutely no problem. We'll take good care of her.'

'Yeah, well you just make damned sure you do. The President doesn't want her running around out of control out there. Do you understand what I'm telling you, Jack?'

'You can rely on me, sir,' Bradman answered. He said it as a simple piece of information, his voice empty of any note of pride. He understood perfectly the reasons that forced Jordan to adopt his elliptical, politician's style over the phone. Still, it pissed him off. It sat badly with his own straightforward military style. For Bradman it had always been simple. He knew his duty and did it to the best of his ability. Politics sickened him.

'I know I can. Bear it in mind, Jack, the President's taking a personal interest. He'll be very appreciative once the election's out of the way.'

The inflatable eased towards the cluster of lights. Beyond the lights a first hint of dawn outlined the distant hills. Julia and Ray sat wedged into the cramped well of the boat in an inch of sea water. Julia shivered violently.

'Where are we?'

'Shh. Voices travel on water,' Paul hissed, scanning the shadows of the dim shore. 'We're north of Beirut, about ten kilometres.'

'North?' Julia looked at Ray in surprise. 'Hezbollah country?'

He shrugged, laughing. 'Or Amal. Or Phalangist. Or Palestinian, or anyone else. You've been away too long. I've been out two weeks and *I* don't know. Get it into your head, fast, the whole place is crumbling. Not just breaking into two. Splintering into a thousand pieces.' He leant back easily against the rubber wall of the boat, nodding at the other man. 'Trust him.'

'Quiet!' Paul was leaning forward eagerly, straining to see into the near blackness. A dark shape slid into view. From the shape came a series of pale flashes, as though from a masked flashlight. He gave a quiet smile and set the boat towards the dark silhouette.

It was a boat like their own, but larger, with three men aboard. They drew alongside. Paul and the men held a brief conversation in Arabic. The three men became briefly animated, as though angry. Sharp words from Paul, who seemed to carry some authority, quickly quelled their anger. They took the smaller boat in tow and turned for the shore, casting curious looks back at Ray and Julia.

They landed at a tiny beach wedged between great broken slabs of rock. A group of some twenty armed men waited there. There was another whispered conversation. Again, a brief spasm of anger and disappointment ran through the group. It quickly subsided at a command from one of the men who had come out to meet them. He now took four of the men aside and spoke to them. As he did so the glances they turned on Ray and Julia were tinged with contempt.

After a short flurry of what seemed to be protest, the four men swaggered to where Ray and Julia sat on a rock, Ray sprawled easily, Julia upright and wary. The oldest was no more than twenty, the youngest perhaps fourteen. They looked down with hostile curiosity, unable to keep their gaze from focusing on Julia. Paul joined them.

'These men will take you into Beirut.' He put a hand on the shoulder of the youngest boy. 'Walid here speaks English.' The boy rolled his shoulders in a loutish acknowledgment, his sullen eyes not leaving Julia. 'Good luck.' He turned away as though he had already forgotten them.

They followed the four men as they scrambled up through a fissure in the steep cliff. At the top they were obliged to drop to their bellies and slither through a tunnel that led beneath a great rock. They emerged onto a stony flat place scattered with boulders as tall as a man. The men led the way, running surefootedly over the loose stones. They came to a place where several boulders lay in a close cluster. Between two of the boulders a dark van stood parked, its window spaces without glass. Two of the men sprang into the front, two jumped into the rear with Julia and Ray.

The van bounced wildly over the uneven surface. The rifles of the two men clattered and leapt around the floor of the van. Julia squatted on a wheel arch. Ray crouched beside her. Both of them watched mesmerized as the weapons jumped and slid around, apparently ignored by the two men, who crouched at the windows scanning the rapidly lightening landscape.

The bucking of the van stopped abruptly. Relieved, Julia turned and looked out. They were on a narrow road where scrubby grass pushed up among broken asphalt. In many spots the surface showed the scalloped imprint of tank tracks. Scattered across the narrow plain lay a sprinkling of buildings, the low, white-painted houses of farms. It was light enough now to see people moving in the fields.

The van slowed. As the wind noise and vibration subsided a new sound reached Julia. She looked around sharply and beckoned Ray to join her at the window. 'Listen.'

They both strained to hear. The two escorts were also listening intently. The sound came again, the low crumping thud of artillery. They drove slowly past the gutted remains of a villa. Its hedge of bougainvillea was immaculate behind a decorative wrought-iron grille. Beyond the hedge the villa stood jagged against the sky, its entire second floor blown off. Smoke still rose from the building. In front of the gates, half in the road, lay the lacerated, headless carcase of a horse. The van slowed further.

'Go down.' Walid was gesturing them furiously to lie on the floor. The Arabs crouched at the side windows. Outside, men were shouting, staccato sounds that conveyed nothing to Julia and Ray except suspicion, anger and fear.

Abruptly, the rear doors flew open. Three men carrying automatic rifles stood in the doorway. Julia and Ray watched dry-mouthed as the scowling men surveyed the interior. Their eyes narrowed at the sight of the two Americans. One of them spoke to the two youths. The younger one, Walid, began speaking rapidly to the newcomers. As he spoke he gestured often towards the prostrate passengers. Several times he made a bigger gesture, pointing to the road ahead. Julia caught the throaty local pronunciation of Beirut.

With a sudden leer the man who had asked the question appeared to stop listening. He swung himself into the van and moved over to Julia. Grabbing her wrist he jerked her into a sitting position. Ray started forward. The movement died as the man swung his gun barrel into Ray's face. He spoke to Julia in incomprehensible dialect, a lewd grin on his face. Julia stared back at him expressionlessly as the unshaven, streaked face with a cluster of boils on one cheekbone moved to within inches of hers. His foul breath forced her head back an inch. Abruptly, his grin growing wider, he released Julia's wrist and grabbed at a breast, fondling it obscenely. With a grimace of loathing, Julia slapped the man's hand aside. The hand flew back as though on a spring and dealt Julia a blow to the side of the head that made it ring.

Furious, the man grabbed a handful of Julia's shirt-front, pulled her to within a couple of inches of him and began screaming at her. Foam flecked his lips. Droplets of spittle spattered Julia's face. She recognized the word *sharmuta*, whore, repeated over and over in the tirade. Slowly, she became aware of another face close to hers. It was that of Walid. He, too, was shouting, but at the man, trying to penetrate his rage. He touched the man's arm tentatively, as though he were afraid of him. Then, as his own anger grew, he began to shake it, trying to loosen his grip on Julia.

Julia recognized nothing but obscenities in the man's Arabic and only the word 'Beirut' in Walid's. Gradually, as Walid's anger mounted, the other man's began to slacken. He released his grip so suddenly that Julia's head crashed back to the floor. He spat once at her, climbed to his feet and left the van. The van lurched forward. From the renewed vibration it was clear they had again left the road.

Struggling to a sitting position, Julia took the dampened handkerchief Ray proffered and wiped her face. She gave a shudder of disgust.

'Thanks. Who were they?' she asked the boy.

'Palestinians. Freedom fighters, like us. He is an important captain. He wanted to take you. Make with you, you know.' He made an obscene pumping gesture with a fist.

'Yeah, I noticed.' As she spoke she saw the boy's eyes roam

over her as though he were nursing ambitions of his own. She changed the subject. 'How long to Beirut?'

The boy shrugged. 'It depends. We cannot continue by the coast road. You saw it. They are shelling out there. We must go across country for a while. By small roads, through the suburbs.' His eyes shone. 'It's very dangerous.' The idea seemed to appeal to him.

Julia and Ray rose and crouched behind Walid, close to the window. They were following a rough dirt track that ran fairly straight through a patchwork of small fields. Many of them were untended. In several places they were blackened by fire or pitted with the ragged scars of shell craters. A few old women with skins like walnuts stooped in the fields or squatted by the trackside, offering for sale a few melons or a small pile of onions. There were no men to be seen.

They turned off the rough track onto an even worse one. The driver slowed down only as much as he needed to keep the suspension from collapsing. On each side of the track were the backs of villas, their high walls topped with coils of barbed wire or fearsome arrangements of spikes. One or two of the villas had miradors, steel boxes mounted on scaffold pole legs from which armed guards surveyed the surrounding area. They were entering one of the wealthier suburbs to the north of the city. Julia remembered the area as having been Christian dominated. Now, it was anybody's guess.

The track ran parallel to a paved road at a distance of three hundred metres. Between the villas they caught glimpses of traffic moving on the road. Many of the trucks and even some of the private cars had weapon-carrying guards very much in evidence.

After several minutes of the bone-jolting ride the van first slowed abruptly and then accelerated hard and slewed to one side. From the window Julia saw a rough pole laid on trestles across the track. Next to it stood a roughly built hut made of old pieces of packing case and roofed over with rusting corrugated iron. As they careered past, lurching wildly over the pitted ground, two young men wearing only dirty boxer shorts scrambled from the hut shouting instructions to each other. It took them a second to bring the weapons they carried to their shoulders. With a shout that was almost a laugh Walid thrust his own weapon out of the window. Julia gasped and flinched as a row of holes stitched itself into the metal above Walid's head. Then the van was filled with a head-shattering noise as Walid, screaming triumphantly, emptied the magazine of his gun.

Silence returned. The van was back on asphalt. The choking smell of cordite made Julia retch. Ray crouched over her. 'Better get used to it.' He nodded at the window. 'This is Beirut.'

Walid grinned. 'Yes. Very soon you'll be at your Embassy. If we have no problems.'

Julia looked wryly at Ray. 'What kind of problems does he have in mind now?'

He grimaced. 'Don't ask.' He pulled her back to the window. 'Take a look. See if you still recognize the place.'

The crowd was as thick as ever, spilling from the pavements. The traffic was much thinner than she remembered, but not that much quieter. Impossibly overloaded trucks honked continuously as they forced their way among the battered Hondas, the dusty, out-of-date American monsters and the donkeys that kept obstinately to the middle of the road. The entrances to private offices and public buildings were still protected by chicanes of sandbags. Adhesive tape crisscrossed their windows. Armed men were everywhere, in and out of uniform.

They came to the river. At the eastern end of the bridge a concrete dug-out stood abandoned. Next to it children played among a heap of discarded ammunition boxes. They drove fast across the bridge, the only vehicle on it.

'What's happened to the checkpoints?' Ray questioned Walid.

The boy, crouched at the window, ran his tongue nervously over his lips. 'This one finished.' He nodded towards the far end of the bridge. 'Yesterday, over there was clear also.

I hope today.' He gripped his rifle hard, a new magazine in place.

'I hope so, too,' Ray said, dryly.

They drew level with the checkpoint. It, too, was deserted. Walid's breath left him with a long hissing sound. 'Still okay. Thanks be to God.'

'Yeah. *Alhamdulillah*,' Ray said tonelessly.

They wound through narrow streets unfamiliar to Julia. They were in the predominantly Christian area of East Beirut. The two men's eyes flickered nervously as they scanned the streets for hostile forces. Their gun barrels rested on the sills of the windows, their fingers tight around the triggers. At every turn the van slowed almost to a halt as the driver inspected the street ahead before venturing into it. Julia crouched behind Walid. He was tense and perspiring freely, despite the relative chill of the morning. The smell of body odour was powerful.

They turned a corner and suddenly Julia knew where they were. They were approaching the Rue de Damas, part of the Green Line that sliced from north to south through Beirut, marking the demarcation line between Christian and Moslem sectors. If they were going to see trouble this was the most likely place.

The van rolled slowly forward. A few people walked the street, passing quickly in front of the boarded-up storefronts, hardly noticing the van and its armed passengers. They slowed almost to a walk and emerged onto a broad avenue. From the window they could not see directly ahead of them. Away to their left, at the end of the block, stood a concrete blockhouse, stacked about with sandbags. Two uniformed men lounged on the sandbags, smoking. Over the blockhouse a torn flag hung limp in the still air. It was impossible to discern whose flag it was.

Julia became aware that her fingernails were biting into her palms. She turned to Walid. 'Do you have passes to get us through here?' Her voice came out hoarse. He did not appear to hear her. He remained motionless, pressed close to the window. His hair was lank with the sweat that coursed from his hairline to his chin and dropped in a rhythmic trickle onto his thin chest. The van stopped.

Low voices came indistinctly to them. One of the voices rose suddenly, as though protesting. There was another low exchange and the van lurched forward, almost pitching Julia to the floor. She recovered and pressed herself against the wall, waiting for the bullets to come. Not until they turned a corner and slowed did she speak, or even breathe.

'How did you do that?' she gasped, at length. '*Did* you have passes?'

Walid glanced up at her, an obscene look of triumph on his young face. He gestured with his right hand, rubbing the thumb and first two fingers together. 'Dollars,' he said succinctly.

They continued for another twenty minutes, the driver making better time now they were in the Moslem part of the city. Without warning they swung between two scarred buildings into a deserted yard.

Walid grinned, an unpleasant hint of cunning in the grin. 'The Embassy is two or three blocks away, over there.' He gestured to the east.

'Thanks,' Ray said affably, holding out a hand. 'We'll do the rest on foot. Anyone stepping out of a closed van in front of the Embassy could very easily get shot. Those marines are very jumpy.'

Walid ignored Ray's hand. Ray shrugged and made as though to move to the door. With an almost imperceptible movement Walid's companion barred the way. He, too, was grinning wolfishly.

'We brought you here,' Walid said pointedly.

'Sure. Thanks. That was the deal.' Ray was still smiling, but only just.

'It was very dangerous for us.' Walid's eyes were on Julia. His tone was a troubling mixture of sulkiness and aggression.

'You were terrific, both of you,' Ray told them, manufacturing some enthusiasm. Smiling amiably, he let his glance drift from one to the other. The two men stood well apart, both fully alert.

'The man back there,' Walid said, addressing Julia, 'wanted to keep you there, make a lot of . . .' Again he made the obscene gesture with his pumping fist. Some residual prudery prevented him from actually uttering the word, which he certainly knew. It was prominent in the vocabulary of any Lebanese with even the slightest smattering of English. He stepped closer to Julia, leering nastily.

Gooseflesh crept on her arms. He was close enough for her to see every hair in the wispy beginnings of his adolescent moustache. 'I want something. For me and my friend.' She felt sick, hardly able to listen. The boy ran his tongue over his lips and spoke again. 'You have money?'

She almost laughed aloud with relief. 'Money? Of course, Walid. How stupid.' She grabbed at her bag and produced two one-hundred-dollar traveller's cheques. With a hand that she could hardly keep from trembling with the shock of the reprieve, she signed them. Walid held them out in front of him, examining the signatures with shrewd expertise. Smirking, he pushed them into a pocket. 'And my other two friends?'

Ray opened his mouth to protest. Julia laid a hand on his arm and reached into her bag. A couple of minutes later they hurried side by side from the yard. On the street Julia let out a long sigh.

'Welcome to Beirut,' Ray said, softly.

In another five minutes they were on the wide boulevard where the American Embassy stood. The sea glinted off to their left, dazzling under the now risen sun. They walked quickly towards the sandbagged emplacements that marked the entrance. A short way ahead a child, no more than six years old, emerged from an alley and trotted in front of them. Drawing level with the entrance he suddenly ran close to the barricade and tried to throw a package over the sandbags. It hit the top row of bags and fell back into the dust.

A tall marine gave a shout and began scrambling out from the bunker. By the time he reached the pavement the child was already disappearing into another alley. The guard gave up the pursuit with a curse and began gingerly examining the package.

10

'WITH WALKER?' the Ambassador shouted. 'What the hell is *he* doing here?'

'I don't know, sir,' the marine answered levelly, his voice distorted by the speaker phone. 'Shall I send them in?'

The Ambassador's glare swung accusingly to the other two men in the room, Major Bradman and Ted Gower, the CIA station head.

'Walker's with her!' He said it as though he expected them to explain themselves.

Both the men had been surprised by the guard's announcement. Neither of them wasted time staying surprised.

'Better get them up here right away, sir. The sooner we know what they're up to, the sooner we can stop it,' Gower said, calmly. Bradman nodded.

The Ambassador gave them another, intensified glare, as though he'd counted on them for a better idea, and turned back to the intercom on his desk. 'Have them brought up here, Corporal.'

'And get the package to security for testing,' Bradman called. 'Then get that up here, too, if it doesn't explode. Let's see what they've brought us this time.'

Three minutes later Julia and Ray were shown into the Ambassador's office. Their clothes were stained with salt and grime. Crystals of dried salt glinted in their eyebrows. Julia's short dark hair and Ray's reddish curls had dried spiky and wild in the wind after the boat journey. Their boots showed tidemarks of greyish deposits. The Ambassador stood to greet them, his eyes cold, his lips pursed in distaste.

'You made it, then, Miss Colter,' he said, superfluously. 'Your telex never mentioned that you'd be accompanied.'

Ray raised a hand in cheerful acknowledgment to the scowling men.

'I wasn't told.' She smiled at Ray. 'But that's not the point. I'm here, and I intend to stay until we can get my brother released.'

'And how do you intend to achieve that?' the Ambassador asked, superciliously.

She shrugged. 'For a start, I was hoping to get some advice from you, Ambassador.' She looked around at the others, including them in her challenge.

'Our advice to you, Miss Colter, is to leave Lebanon immediately. There's nothing you can do to help. Nothing whatever. That goes for both of you,' he added pointedly.

'You mean I should get out and leave everything in the hands of the experts?' Julia said, derisively. 'The experts who should have been protecting Michael in the first place! Please don't let anyone misunderstand me. I'm staying, and I'm going to do everything possible to free Michael. Raise ransom money if necessary. If none of you knows where to start I'll do it on my own. I've got plenty of contacts here. Ray has more.' Ray inclined his head. 'I'll buy information, if necessary. You people should already have been doing that.'

'I'm sorry, Miss Colter,' the Ambassador broke in, 'but we aren't here to treat with terrorists in any way. Speaking as the Ambassador of the United States, I can't permit any such dealings, even through private initiatives, by United States' citizens.'

Julia gave a soft laugh. 'Speaking as the sister of the victim, Ambassador, that's bullshit!'

The Ambassador's face became pinched, as though acid had been dashed in it. He was gathering himself for a reply when a marine entered carrying a box file. He placed it on the desk in front of the Ambassador. 'The package the kid brought, sir. It's okay to handle. Shall I open it?'

'No, Sergeant. Thanks. That'll be all.'

The soldier left the room, throwing a curious look at the dishevelled pair in front of the desk. The group waited in silence until he had left the room. The Ambassador was still preparing to reply to Julia. Ted Gower intervened.

'Excuse me, sir, but shouldn't we take a look at the package? It's probably connected to the Colter boy.'

The Ambassador looked at him sharply, still smarting. 'Go ahead!' He shoved the file towards the CIA man.

Gower flipped open the box file and withdrew a thick envelope, folded over and sealed with brown adhesive tape. The others watched in silence as he picked up a paperknife and gouged at the package.

With a grunt he tore off the last piece of tape and unfolded the envelope. He up-ended it over the desk.

A sheet of paper fluttered to the desk followed by two small objects that fell with a tiny thud onto the inlaid leather.

A shriek from Julia sliced through the stillness of the room. The two pale objects that lay on the desk were human fingers, cut off at the second joint.

11

JULIA STARED OUT through the slats of the blind. Between the buildings opposite, one of them an ugly, angular concrete church topped by a cross of stainless steel that threw the sun's rays directly back into her eyes, she looked down on the port. Only two ships lay there, both sleazy, rust-streaked tramps, both apparently deserted. Behind her, Major Bradman had been speaking for some minutes. She turned to face him. Her eyes were red-rimmed and the lids puffy, but her crying was over. Her mouth was set grimly.

'That's just crap, Major.' Bradman stopped in mid-sentence. 'I don't give a shit about all that. I didn't come to Beirut to help the President get re-elected. I just want to find Michael, that's all. Can you please try to understand that?'

'But, damn it, Miss Colter,' Bradman pleaded angrily, taking a step closer to her, 'we're already doing absolutely everything possible. I've told you already, myself and my colleagues have got every contact we have in this town, in the whole of Lebanon, working to come up with some kind of lead. You aren't supposed to know this, but we've got the cooperation of the Israelis' local command *and* of the Syrians. The plain fact is that *nobody* knows who's holding your brother.' He took a further pace forward and touched Julia's arm tentatively. 'I'm sorry, Miss Colter, really, but if Michael's in the hands of a breakaway group of Fundamentalists, which is how it looks, then it's bleak. We just don't know who to talk to.'

She looked into his eyes, grateful for the sympathy she saw there. 'You're probably right, Major. I appreciate all you're doing. I still have to try, though. I'm sure you understand that.'

He nodded and gave her a tired smile. 'I guess I do.' He looked from Julia to Ray, who sat comfortably in one of the bamboo armchairs. 'Look,' he went on, 'there's something you both ought to know. If it were up to me, I'd damn well *make* you stay right here in this apartment. I'd put a man right outside the door and neither of you would move out of here until I said so.' He looked around at each of them, making sure they understood.

'Fuck that, Major,' Ray said, easily. 'You don't have any right to do that. We're not in your army.'

'Yeah, well, fuck you, too. And your civil rights. I'd do it for your own good. And for the good of the United States. The only problem I have is the Ambassador won't stand for it. He insists I play it by the book. If you ask me he's an asshole.'

'It's nice to know there's something we can agree on, Major.'

Bradman ignored Ray's remark. He turned to Julia, smiling a rueful little smile. 'I'll do it the Ambassador's way on one condition. I need an undertaking from both of you, especially from you, Miss Colter.' They both looked at him. 'I want you both to agree to use this apartment so long as you're here. It's safe. The security guards are reliable, not the teenage jokers you'll find on most buildings. Also I ask you please not to go out alone.'

'We'll stick together like glue,' said Ray, with a mock salute.

'That's not quite what I meant, Mr Walker,' Bradman replied, coolly. 'I mean use the car. It's at your disposal.' He looked hard at them both. 'I don't mean use it if you want to. I mean *use* it. Don't set foot on the street without it. The driver and guard are good men. If you put a toe out there on your own, I swear I'll have you both shipped out of here in crates!' He gave Julia a smile that managed to be both an apology for and a reinforcement of the threat. 'Oh, and please feel free to use the phone here.' He gestured at the telephone that stood on a low table. He nodded. 'I guess that's all.' He took a card from his breast pocket and laid it by the telephone. 'Please call me if you need anything, day or night.' He turned to leave. 'Goodbye, Miss Colter.' He nodded at Ray.

'Is it okay if I call my paper?' Ray called after him. 'The taxpayer will never know.'

'Go ahead,' Bradman answered, dryly. 'It'll cost the taxpayer less than trying to get you back from kidnappers. Not that I think they ought to try too hard in your case.'

'Shithead,' Ray murmured as the door closed.

'No, he's not,' Julia said. 'He's being helpful, in his way.'

'Huh,' Ray grunted. He rose to his feet and moved to a cabinet by a wall. He looked inside and gave a small cheer. He took out a bottle and two glasses. 'Want one?' he asked, brandishing the bottle.

Julia shook her head. 'No thanks.' She gave a yawn that made her whole body tremble. 'I need to get a little sleep. Then I'm going after Michael. Will you wake me in a couple of hours?'

Michael retched and spat bile into the bucket. The flies that had somehow got into the room rose in a brief droning circuit of protest and settled again on the caked rim. Michael dropped back onto the mattress. He lay staring up at the ceiling. Several of the flies alighted on the spot where the manacle had broken the flesh above his ankle and on the bloodied stumps of the severed fingers, where they stood, unnoticed, drinking the fluids.

Sweat stood out all over his begrimed, blood-smeared body. Abruptly, a spasm contracted his limbs and pinched his face. He groaned.

Ths spasm passed. He fell back, half off the mattress, shivering violently. He lay for a few moments groaning half-formed, delirious phrases, until another spasm shook him, stronger than the last one.

Voices rose outside the room. With a crash the door was thrown open. The sharp-faced civilian entered, brushing aside the attempts of the two guards to restrain him. Speaking angrily to the two men he knelt by the still figure of Michael and laid a hand on his forehead.

His face darkened with rage. Opening his bag, he shook two tablets from a plastic box. He threw the empty water bottle to one of the guards, snapping an instruction at him. The guard caught the bottle and ran from the room.

He returned a few seconds later and handed the bottle back to the man. The man dropped the tablets between Michael's lips and forced water after them. Michael coughed and swallowed. The man waited for perhaps a minute, his fingers pressed to Michael's wrist, before turning his attention to the wounds.

Pulling cotton wool and alcohol from his bag he began carefully cleaning the damaged flesh. When he was satisfied, he poured antiseptic onto a wad of lint and roughly dressed the severed fingers.

He left the room, speaking to one of the guards as he passed. The man immediately ran to carry the pail of filth from the room. The civilian turned to the other guard, his voice sibilant with anger. 'Vicious fools. I told you what to do. Begin doing it. Otherwise we may lose him. Your stupidity could cost us everything.' He left the room pursued by the guard's sullen stare.

The other guard returned with the emptied bucket. An inch of liquid in the bottom gave off a powerful odour of bleach. He also carried a fresh bottle of water and a mug of food. He set them down noisily, as a mark of his resentment, and left the room.

Almost twelve hundred kilometres away the head waiter in charge of the Kuwait Sheraton's lunch buffet watched in mute horror as a big olive-skinned man in a straining beige tropical suit dropped his spoon, pushed back his plate and belched audibly.

The man pushed himself to his feet and walked from the room with the ponderous step of a big man carrying a full belly with care. In the lift the knot of Europeans holding briefcases with combination locks and the robed Arabs fingering worry beads all moved closer to the walls of the lift, instinctively giving ground to the big man.

The top-floor suite was immense, on the scale of the man himself. He looked at his watch, a big gold affair like a navigation aid, with a wide strap that sank deep into the flesh of the wrist. It was not quite two-thirty. The meeting was scheduled for two-forty-five. But this was Arabia. He had plenty of time for a leisurely shower.

Twenty minutes later he emerged from the bathroom. In place of the suit with its suspicion of sweat stains at the armpits he wore an immaculate white dish-dash and, over it, a dark blue robe of fine woollen material, its edges heavily embroidered with gold and red thread. A headdress of Swiss voile, held in place with a double rope of blue silk, completed the transformation. In place of the bulky, faintly sleazy businessman who had entered the bathroom there now stood a desert prince, his six feet three, two hundred and fifty pound bulk made magnificent by the flattering lines of the robes.

He strolled out to the terrace to await his guests and stood surveying the rooftops of Kuwait. He did not wish to sit, for fear of creasing the robes. It was important to impress these people. A faint contemptuous smile pulled at his lips as he looked out on the scene below. The huge villas with their ridiculous antennae, enough for a small television station, the gimcrack high-rise office buildings with the roofs that began leaking the day the contractors moved out, the wide avenues that led nowhere. And, beyond it all, on the one hand the desert, waiting to return, always testing, reaching out exploratory fingers of sand to reclaim the preposterous streets, and on the other the waters of Kuwait Bay with, beyond that, Iran. He chuckled. Khomeini was dead, but it was still the Iran he had created. The unpredictable wild card that cast its shadow over the whole area, from Afghanistan to the Nile and through the whole of North Africa, and was frightening the region's rulers out of their wits. Frightening them so that they were investing all they could move in Los Angeles, London, the Riviera and Zürich. Counting, very often, on reliable, efficient go-betweens. Like himself. He moistened his lips with his tongue and turned to answer the insistent ring of the doorbell.

It was twenty past three before the last man arrived. Most of his face was concealed by opaque sunglasses. He was serenely indifferent to the fact that he had kept seven people waiting. He went to each of the gathering in turn, embracing them and kissing them on both cheeks. The big man proffered Monte Cristo cigars and proposed drinks. Two took Coca-Cola, five took whisky. He took the bottle of Chivas Regal from the brown bag in which alcohol journeys around Kuwait and poured generously. When everyone was served and settled in the big white sofas, he spoke.

'Gentlemen, my friends.' He easily subordinated his own natural Lebanese accent in favour of the purer forms of Gulf Arabic. 'You have seen the newspapers?' He picked up a sheaf of papers and magazines, mostly American, from a low table and brandished them theatrically. The listeners nodded. 'It is exactly as I promised, is it not? President Foreman will be compelled to act. No American President could afford to ignore the pressure. It would be virtually impossible at any time. Just at this moment, so close to an election, he'll be *forced* to do something.'

'But how can we be certain just *what* it will be?' The speaker was the latecomer. His voice was scarcely more than a murmur. It made people listen. He bore himself with the easy assurance of a man who knew they would. 'He can be a very stupid man.'

The big man's smile was sweet and ingratiating. A whore's smile. 'We are rather relying on that, Your Highness.'

The meeting was very short. Discussion was mostly between the latecomer and the big man. The latecomer posed questions, the big man responded. It was the latecomer who decided the meeting should end. Apparently satisfied with the big man's answers, he stood up, bowing briefly to the assembly.

'I must return to Riyadh, before my absence raises questions.'

The big man embraced the last guest and closed the door behind him. He stood behind the door for some seconds, in silent contemplation. Then with a chuckle he moved to the phone.

'Hello?' At the sound of the voice the big man smiled to himself. He still drew a lot of satisfaction from the thought that he, a boy who had been shoeless in the streets of Sidon, had access to the private number of a man so powerful.

'It is I, Ali.' He felt faintly foolish. His real name was Georges. Ali had been Tom Jordan's choice of pseudonym.

'How did it go?' Jordan's voice was harsh and impatient.

'Beautifully,' he answered silkily. 'The others follow the Prince. He had some reservations. I was able to win him over.'

Jordan did not proffer any congratulations. 'When will everything be ready?'

'Tomorrow.'

'Good. I'm counting on it.' Jordan rang off.

The day had begun even earlier than usual for the Secretary of State. He had risen at five and been at his desk before six, studying the blurred facsimile copy of the kidnappers' message. His call to Beirut had found the Ambassador still in his office. He had been waiting all afternoon, knowing that the message he had transmitted would oblige the Secretary of State to call him.

By seven-thirty he was at the White House conferring in low, urgent tones with several other men as they waited for the President's Chief of Staff to usher them into the Oval Office.

The President was not alone. His press secretary and his campaign manager were already in the office. All three men were grim-faced. The President greeted the newcomers without his customary show of warmth, watching with a resentful glare as they took up their usual places around the room. The last man was not yet seated when the President began speaking.

'I'm afraid things are looking grim, gentlemen. Gerry and Marcus here,' the two men sitting closest to the President each nodded at their names, 'and I, have just been going through the latest stuff from Lou Harris.' He stood up and paced the space behind the desk. 'We're looking at a disaster, gentlemen, a regular fucking disaster.' There was an instant of silence. Nobody volunteered to fill it. The President glared around the room. 'I'm running three full points behind Wilton. And you know why? Because he's out campaigning and I'm stuck here in the White House. I'm afraid to show my face because if I do the first thing that happens is that some smart-ass little reporter wants to know what I'm doing about this Colter kid.' His voice had risen now, taking on the truculent whine that was familiar to all of them. The President had started looking for a scapegoat. 'And what do I have to tell them? Not a damned thing, because,' he continued, sneering unpleasantly, 'we don't even know who's got him.'

The President's gaze ranged over the seated men.

'It's worse than that, Mr President,' Dean Sutcliffe said, his quiet manner in stark contrast to the President's. 'There was a new message overnight.' He pulled out a sheaf of papers from a document case and passed one to the President before distributing others to each of the men in the room.

There was a pause of perhaps a minute while the men studied the documents. Each of them held in his hand two sheets of paper stapled at one corner. The top sheet was a photocopy of the facsimile message, crudely handwritten and bearing the symbol of the triangle and the two bars cutting through it. The bottom sheet was also taken from the fax that had come in from the Embassy in the early hours. It was a blurred image of a Polaroid photograph. The photograph showed, about twice life-size, the first two segments of the first and second fingers of a pale-skinned right hand. Shocked protests ran around the room. The President's own face worked angrily. A voice called from Sutcliffe's left.

'Hold it, Dean. How do we know these belong to the boy?'

Sutcliffe turned to face the speaker. 'His sister identified them.'

'Two pieces of finger!' It was Tom Jordan. His rugged face was creased in a look of half-amused doubt. 'Could you recognize anyone just from a couple of pieces of finger?' He tapped the photograph. 'From something like this I wouldn't recognize my wife.'

'Yes,' the President joined in, his gloom lifting slightly. 'How can we be sure, Dean? Those bastards could be fooling us.'

Sutcliffe sighed. 'Look closely at the photograph. It's hard to see, but just between the joints of the first finger there's a small scar. It was made by a potato peeler. Apparently she did it, when they were kids.'

There was a short silence while they considered the news. The next question came from Marcus Springer, the campaign manager. As so often in his association with Jack Foreman he was anticipating him, saving him from expressing the thought that might be embarrassing. 'Have the press got this?'

Sutcliffe shrugged. 'Not from us. The photograph was taken at the Embassy and put through on a secure line. There was nothing in this morning's papers.'

'But there might be in tomorrow's?' Tom Jordan said. It was not really a question.

'Huh?' Sutcliffe said sharply, blinking at Jordan. 'What's that supposed to mean, Tom? You think there's a leak in the Department? Or in this room?' he added sourly.

Jordan gave him a faintly patronizing smile. 'No, Dean, neither of those. I'm sure the Department's watertight. It just seems to me the kidnappers have been outsmarting us. They know how to use the press. That's why they announced the kidnapping to the papers. To throw us off balance. I just don't feel they'd be about to miss the chance to use photos like that, of their own. And their claims will be right there alongside the picture.'

The President winced. 'You think so? Jesus. What the hell do we say then? I can't go public and ask Israel to pull out of South Lebanon. Not with the election damned near on us! Christ,' he went on, plaintively, 'we've *been* asking the bastards privately for months. The shits ignore us. They know until the election's over they can laugh at me.'

'Mmm. Well, if pieces of the Colter boy start showing up in the TV stations' mail, that'll lose us a few votes too.'

The President glowered. 'Thanks, Dean, I needed that.' A sudden thought made him change tack. 'How about the kid's sister and the other asshole? What are we doing about them?'

Sutcliffe shrugged. 'I talked to the Ambassador about that. The man out there that takes care of Embassy security is dealing with them.'

'I hope he's getting them out of there.'

Sutcliffe shot a look at Tom Jordan. 'That's difficult. We have no right to do that. They're free to do as they wish. Let's say he's keeping them under control. Everybody understands the last thing we need right now is more American hostages.'

Jordan nodded. 'Dean's right. Strictly speaking they're free agents. But I think I can speak for Major Bradman. He's a good man. Better than that. He's the best. I wouldn't worry about it.'

The President rolled his shoulders. 'Mmm. Yeah. I'll try. Let's get back to this business of the press. Tom's probably right. These people are shrewd bastards. They know how to use what they've got.'

'Perhaps we should learn to do the same, Mr President,' Jordan said softly.

All eyes in the room turned in his direction. The President squinted suspiciously at him. 'How's that?'

'Use the Gulf task force to hit every place on that list I gave you yesterday.'

'Great idea, Tom,' Sutcliffe said tartly, his eyes flashing behind the thick spectacles. 'Let's inflate a cheap little crime into a major confrontation. Christ, we've been through it a dozen times. The Navy's using bases in the Gulf. If we get those ships to hit Lebanon there'll be hell to pay.'

He paused for an instant, struggling to control his anger. When he went on he spoke with quiet emphasis, only the brittleness in his voice betraying the fury below the surface. 'Look, if we want to hit the Palestinians it means hitting the camps. They're full of women and children. They're the ones who'll be pictured dead in the world's press. Maybe you prefer to try hitting Hezbollah? If we do, then Bahrain, Kuwait, the whole Gulf, will be shitting in its pants waiting to see how their local Shi-ite populations react. They've already blown up a couple of Kuwait's refineries. We'd probably lose what little help they do give us.'

'So what's the State Department's view, Dean?' Jordan asked with a sarcastic smile. 'We wait until they send us the boy's head?'

'Don't personalize this, Tom. We've got objectives out there. We can't lose sight of them for Colter.'

'So you think we should just wait, do nothing and let them do their worst to the boy?'

'Indiscriminate strikes won't do him any good,' Sutcliffe retorted, his anger rising again. 'They're as likely to get him killed. What I'm saying is we don't upset the balance in the whole area for a single hostage.' He turned to the President. In a lower voice he said, 'Our interests there are just too important, Mr President.'

The President sat looking from one to the other. He smoothed the wings of hair that skirted his baldness. 'I don't know, Dean,' he said slowly. 'A lot of people were saying the same thing when Ronald Reagan wanted to bomb Libya.'

Sutcliffe bit back his exasperation. 'I'm afraid there was a lot of confusion there, too, Mr President. Before and since. All the signs are that Ghaddafi's gone on with business as usual. It seems to me it was a similar case to what we have here. Everyone wants something *done*. Nobody wants to try to understand the issues.'

'Jimmy Carter understood the issues with the Tehran hostages,' Jordan intervened. 'Better than anyone. So he did nothing. And lost the election.'

'Look, Tom, in terms of its effects on terrorism, the Libyan raid achieved absolutely nothing.'

Jordan smiled at Dean Sutcliffe and then at the President. 'Ronald Reagan's rating rose a full eight points,' he said softly.

12

JULIA AWOKE to a cocktail of sounds that could only have been Lebanon. Against a faint background rumble of distant artillery, small arms crackled with the quick ragged sound of firecrackers. Over it all, drifting on the gentle westerly breeze, came the plaintive, far-off call of a muezzin. She sat up abruptly. It was five o'clock, the hour of the Al-Asr evening prayer.

She walked quickly into the bathroom and splashed cold water on her face. Using the set of toilet items Major Bradman had provided she brushed out her perspiration-damp hair and freshened her mouth.

The lounge was empty.

She felt a momentary flash of panic. 'Ray!'

'Yeah.' She pushed through the gently moving curtains onto the balcony. Ray was installed in a canvas chair with an open beer can in his hand. His chin rested on the wrought-iron rail. He looked up at Julia, grinning.

She scowled. 'Do you know the time? I asked you to wake me in two hours!'

'You needed the sleep. Anyway, you weren't going to do anything with your afternoon.' He turned his attention back to the street below.

'Not do ...?' She broke off in exasperation. 'Of course I was. I have a whole lot of calls to make. You do, too, if you really plan to help me look for Michael instead of lounging around here drinking beer.'

He held the can at arm's length and looked at it reproachfully. He shrugged and stood up. 'You wouldn't have made your calls. The post office doesn't open till six.'

She jerked a thumb over her shoulder. 'What's that thing on the table in there?'

'A phone.' He took her hand and drew her gently to the rail. 'Look.'

She followed his gaze down to the street below. Two uniformed men loafed against a long black car, their rifles cradled in the crooks of their arms. The men were watchful, scanning the street as the crowds re-emerged after the long afternoon break. Julia looked oddly at Ray.

'So what? Bradman told us they'd wait for us.'

'Not them.' He kept his eyes fixed on the two marines. 'Don't make it obvious, but take a look across the street to the left, about thirty yards. You see the café?'

Julia looked to the right, as though viewing the distant mountains, and then let her gaze roam slowly over the port in front of them and the street below, until she was squinting into the westerly sun.

'Well?'

'Well what?' she answered, still looking to her left as though admiring the view over the minarets of West Beirut.

'The two backgammon players. Just inside the window.'

'What about them?'

'Several things. First, they've been playing a hell of a long game. Second, they have a car waiting in the alley. Third, they came along just as two others left. Exactly at four. Fourth, when their car passed, the marines down there didn't even look at them. Nobody else on the street and yet they didn't even turn their heads.'

Julia chewed at her lip. 'You mean they knew them?'

'You're damned right. Look at them now. They're jumpy as hell. Yet when a car passes them on an empty street they don't so much as give them the once-over.'

'You think they're watching us?'

'I'm sure of it. Look, Julia, you don't know Bradman, do you? You'd gone before he came. He's a good soldier.' He smiled an ironic little smile. 'He was responsible for Michael. Now he's responsible for you. Whether you like it or not he'll be sticking to you. Like shit to a blanket.' Julia smiled at the expression. 'I'm serious. He'll have had the *strictest* instructions not to fuck up the President's chances by allowing a second kidnapping.'

Julia nodded towards the phone. 'And you think they have that tapped?'

'Of *course* they do. Bradman wants Michael back. I don't have to tell you how lousy American spooks' contacts with the Shi-ites are. There just aren't that many Fundamentalists who care enough about America to risk waking up with their balls in their mouths.'

Julia smiled. 'So he's hoping to learn from us?'

He was suddenly serious. 'That's right. He wants to know who we talk to, who we see. If we can get a lead to Michael he wants it, too.'

'So he could step in ahead of us!'

'He could keep you out of trouble and save his career.'

'Sure. And the way it works is, we persuade someone to risk his life by talking to us and Bradman's apes decide to interfere. So the two of us end up distrusted or dead. The people talking to us'll be dead for sure.'

She stood looking down at the two marines for several seconds before she spoke again. 'Is there a back way out of here?'

The thick crepe of their soles made no sound on the marble stairs. They had encountered no-one. In more peaceful times there would have been no chance of a Lebanese choosing the stairs rather than the lift. Nowadays many people preferred the climb to the chance of being trapped in a power cut or a bombardment. One flight up from the vestibule Ray signalled Julia to wait. He crept to the next landing and peered carefully down the last stairs.

The entry was in deep shadow, contrasting sharply with the sunlight that slanted through the double glass doors. He scanned the shadows for the security guards. Every building in Beirut had guards drawn from one or the other of the kaleidoscope factions, depending where it was situated. He saw none. He moved down two more steps. He was on the point of calling Julia when a movement made him freeze. A fat man in his fifties emerged from behind the open door of the concierge's booth and stood staring out through the glass doors at the street. Before Ray could move the man swung to look right at him. The muzzle of the man's rifle seemed to point directly at his chest. Ray could read the slogan on his tee-shirt. It recommended a restaurant. Judging by the size of his belly the man would know what he was talking about. The man walked back into the booth. Ray let out a long, silent breath and eased back out of sight. As the man had turned from the brightness outside, the stairwell would have seemed in total darkness.

Julia looked questioning.

'Security,' he hissed. 'Right inside the door. We can't reach the service door without walking past them.'

'Would they take a bribe?'

'They almost certainly have. From Bradman.'

Julia grimaced. 'Okay,' she whispered. 'Let's try another way.' She turned and padded up the stairs. At the landing she stopped and looked around. Four numbered doors led off from the landing. She leaned close to Ray. 'We'll try one of these.'

'Try what?'

'To get out to the back. These two must give onto the rear.'

Ray shook his head. He jabbed a finger at the floor, indicating the guards. 'The noise. Have you ever tried kicking in a door?' Julia shook her head. 'It makes a hell of a noise. Also, it's not as easy as it looks in the movies. If they have any kind of a decent lock it doesn't work but it hurts like hell. We have to . . .' He broke off at the sound of voices from the hallway below. 'Oh shit,' he breathed. 'Bradman!'

He pressed himself against the wall beside the nearer door. 'Ring the bell,' he hissed.

She rang, a long ring. Bradman's voice rose clearly from the lobby, mixed with Arabic voices as someone interpreted for him. She was about to turn to the opposite flat when the door swung abruptly open.

A thickset, olive-skinned woman with powerful black eyes stood in the doorway. Her hair was hidden by a white towel knotted into a turban. Her face, which was still handsome and had certainly been beautiful, was pearled with perspiration. Moisture clung to her faint black moustache. She held a silk dressing gown tightly closed over a grandiose bosom. She frowned.

'*Qui êtes-vous?*' The French was spoken with a haughty, disdainful tone, as though Julia had come for an interview as a maid and arrived unacceptably late.

Julia improvised, not knowing what Ray expected. Her voice was indistinct, hardly above a whisper. 'Good afternoon. I wonder, do you speak English? I'm a reporter from the *New York Times*.'

She had said the wrong thing. The woman shrank back and began closing the door. 'No, no. Not reporters.'

Ray spun away from the wall and drove his fist at her stomach. The woman's movement threw his aim so that his blow shook her but did not hurt her. She opened her mouth to scream. Ray threw himself on her, clamping a hand to her mouth. They fell to the floor in a tangle. Ray groaned as his own head cracked on the marble floor. Julia stepped inside, closing the door quickly behind her. She snatched a heavy glass ashtray from a low table and knelt by the woman, threatening her, her finger to her lips for silence.

The woman's eyes flashed but her struggling subsided. She lay still, the open kimono revealing surprisingly slender legs and heavy breasts. Ray got to his feet, holding his hand to a cut over his eye. Blood pumped from between his fingers.

Before either of them could decide on their next move they heard an exclamation from the end of the hallway. A youth, no more than fifteen years old, stood in a doorway, gaping at them. He was naked, his body starkly white against the dark tan of his face and arms. He moved a hand instinctively to cover the ruins of an erection. Then, recovering himself, he turned back into the room.

Ray sprinted after him. By the time he reached the door the boy was sprawled across a big double bed, reaching for something. He was coming up with a rifle when Ray landed on top of him. The boy's breath left him with a hiss.

Ray grabbed at the snout of the gun and tried to tear it from the boy's grasp. The teenager clung to it with an unexpected wiry strength. They spilled from the musky-smelling bed to the floor. Ray could hardly see for the blood that filled his eyes. He groped for the boy's throat. The boy lowered his chin and sank his teeth deep into Ray's wrist.

With a bellow of outrage Ray let go of the gun barrel and, before the boy could react, drove his fist into the side of his skull. The boy gave a sound like a sob and went momentarily limp. Ray pushed himself off and hit the boy again as he tried to raise his head. This time he went out cold.

Ray got up, nursing his fist. It felt as though it might be broken. He picked up the gun and from the doorway motioned Julia to bring the woman into the bedroom. Seeing the boy covered in blood the woman gave a cry and dropped to her knees.

'Shit,' Ray murmured resentfully, sitting down heavily on the bed, 'it's *my* blood. See if you can find something to tie them with.'

After a few moments Julia returned with a roll of adhesive tape. Ray had to jab the woman hard with the gun before she would let herself be bound. Julia quickly taped their hands and feet and placed a piece of tape across each of their mouths. She stood up.

'I'm sorry,' she told the woman. '*Je suis vraiment désolée.* But this really is an emergency.' They withdrew to the living room.

Ray walked to the window, wiping the blood from his eyes. The balcony overlooked a cemetery. The cemetery was bounded by a wall topped by corroded iron spikes. Between the wall and the balcony a service alley gave access to the rear of the buildings. The drop was no more than ten feet.

They looked around at the other balconies. There was nobody in sight. Ray tossed the rifle over the cemetery wall into a tangle of prickly pear and went over the rail. He straddled the gap between the balcony and the wall. Holding the balcony rail for support he kicked with all his might at the rusted spikes. They bent as though they were putty. When he had cleared a space of eighteen inches he handed Julia over onto the wall. He pushed off from the balcony and stood poised alongside her. He checked, caught his balance and jumped. He cursed sharply as he stumbled into a clump of prickly pear, and turned to look up at Julia. She stood on the wall, hesitating.

'Jump,' he hissed. 'Quick! Bradman'll already be looking for us.'

She gulped and leapt. She landed with her hands on his shoulders and his on her waist. For a very brief instant they remained like that. Then, with the faintest suggestion of a smile Ray turned and led the way into the tangle of undergrowth.

The cemetery was a shambles of broken headstones and vandalized mausolea. The mausolea varied from simple structures the size of telephone booths to extravagant edifices as big as houses. The broken doors hung from their hinges. Inside, fragments of smashed urns lay among dusty plastic flowers and torn photographs.

They reached a path and began running. They had run perhaps fifty metres when they came to a patch of ground where the tombs had been completely destroyed, leaving a clearing the size of a tennis court, surrounded by rubble. A triple row of wooden crosses ran alongside the path. The fresh flowers that lay on many of the graves had not yet had time to shrivel in the sun.

A sudden noise chilled Julia. To her left, a half-dozen dogs, their grey coats matted and torn, squabbled viciously. As she watched, one of them gave a snarl and tossed its head, jerking an object into the air. Julia's diaphragm contracted and the sour taste of vomit flooded her palate. The dogs were disputing a human forearm. Despite her heaving stomach she hesitated.

Ray grabbed her arm and hurried her on. 'Come on! They're dead anyway. Keep running.'

She shuddered as she followed him. 'Do they just dig them up?'

'I guess so. These were most likely killed in the big bombardment last week. Probably not more than a foot under.'

'Jesus. Don't they even bury their dead properly?'

'Julia, the people who did the burying were exhausted. They'd been under bombardment for three days and nights. It's a credit to them they didn't just leave the dead out on the streets where the dogs could get right at them.'

She shook, as though she felt the touch of something loathsome, and ran harder. Thirty metres further on Ray stopped suddenly, a finger pressed to his lips. The sound of low voices reached them from somewhere near at hand. They continued warily, their pace now a careful walk.

They spun at a sudden burst of tinny, keening Arab music coming from one of the narrow side alleys. A group of people had colonized a cluster of the larger tombs. Women squatted in the open, chattering stridently as they prepared food. The music came from a radio suspended from a stunted olive tree. Bedding hung over other branches. The conversation stopped short as the women caught sight of Julia and Ray. One of them called softly. A man emerged from one of the tombs. He was naked but for a pair of shorts and a bandolier of ammunition worn, Mexican bandit style, across his chest. He carried the inevitable Kalashnikov.

Ray and Julia continued walking slowly, trying to keep their eyes straight ahead. The tomb dwellers were silent. For a while the radio music was the only sound. Then there came a double snicking sound of metal striking metal. Both of them knew the unmistakable sound of a weapon being primed.

As one, they bent forward and broke into a crouching, swerving run. A rifle cracked. Julia heard the ricochet whine into the distance. Both of them were still running. They continued at full tilt for another fifteen seconds. There were no more shots.

Straightening, Julia saw a small iron gate set in the wall of the cemetery just ahead of them. Breathless, she urged Ray towards it. A damaged padlock lay on the ground close to the gate. Relieved, Julia pulled the gate open and burst out into another narrow alley. Ray followed her.

Julia pulled the gate shut and turned to speak to Ray. She let out a soft exclamation. Ray had sunk to his haunches against the wall. He held a hand pressed to his wounded eye. He looked about to faint. Julia dropped to her knees beside him and examined the cut.

'That's bad. We have to get it looked at.'

He shook his head. '*I* have to get it looked at. You need to get to the post office.'

She started to protest. 'Shut up!' he said, smiling and waving a hand. 'Get going. I'll see you at Habib's as soon as you can.'

She looked at him for a moment longer and stood up. 'Okay. Take care.' She drew a hand from a pocket. 'This might be helpful. I don't have a handkerchief.' She threw him a tiny package.

'Yeah. You take care too. See you later.'

He watched her go. As she disappeared around the corner, giving him a final wave, he smiled and examined the package. His smile widened. He unpeeled the wrapping of the tampon and pressed it to his eye.

13

THE STREET teemed with people. Traders crouched by wares set out on blankets on the ground or on makeshift stalls set up against the walls. Others stood in the open fronts of their shops touting passers-by. Julia paused to catch her breath, leaning against the wall of a store. After an initial curious glance the stall-holder nearest her got down to serious matters. He began trying to interest her in a dark wood Syrian coffee table inlaid with an intricate pattern of mother-of-pearl, which might have been genuine.

She smiled a gentle refusal and started off down the street. The crowd, largely women, paid her only scant attention. A foreigner on the streets of Beirut nowadays, even in the Christian sector, would always be in a hurry.

Turning out of the comparative anonymity of the market, she headed west along a narrow street that ran parallel to the Rue du Fleuve and the port. It was still busy, though less so than the market. Most of the people on the street were shopping single-mindedly, plainly anxious to get back to the protection of their homes. The café tables were still placed optimistically on the pavements. Only an obstinate handful of old men used them, sitting with their hands clasped over the butts of smooth walking sticks and sipping strong black coffee as though they acknowledged no change in the city since the French had left, more than a generation earlier. The rumbling passage of a tank, which sent Julia stepping quickly into a pastry shop and most other people closer to the buildings, did nothing to change the stately rhythm of the old men's conversations.

The crowd thinned as she approached the twin avenues that marked the last stretch of the Green Line before the port. People looked at her with more curiosity now, as she made her way towards the stretch of no-man's-land that separated the two sectors.

She stayed close in the shadows of the buildings, pausing at sandbagged doorways under the wary gaze of edgy security men to check the scene ahead of her. Beyond the four-foot wall of sandbags that ran across the end of the street she could see no sign of any Moslem militia.

Among the line of squat palms that lined the road, many of them severed or stripped of their fronds by blast, nothing moved. Carefully, she moved up to the sandbag barrier and crouched, scanning the wide street.

Dry-mouthed, she swung herself over the barrier and began running for the grassy central reservation. She threw herself down on the grass in the scanty shelter of a torn hibiscus bush and lay pressed to the dirt, waiting for a challenge. It was several seconds before she let herself believe there would not be one.

She examined the next stretch of road. Away towards the port, men in red-and-white headcloths clustered around a lorry. The men were far enough away for their shouts to be very faint. She took a deep breath, clambered to her feet and sprinted over the last exposed stretch and into the shelter of the narrow streets.

The streets were poorer looking than in the eastern sector of the city. Much of the damage the Israelis had wrought in 1982 remained unrepaired. Several of the buildings she passed were windowless or had tarpaulins hung in place of doors. Noise from transistor radios spilled from every aperture, filling the streets with a nerve-jangling cacophony.

Many of the women, far more than Julia remembered, were swathed in voluminous black chadors, held tightly closed so that only an eye was left visible. She felt more uncomfortable under the sinister one-eyed gaze of these women than under that of the many men who turned unashamedly to watch her as she passed, with stares that were at once curious and lewd.

She reached the wide square in front of the main post office. The palms that stood among the benches of the square were scorched by blast. The square was almost deserted, a stark contrast to the teeming melee that Julia remembered. Almost running in her anxiety to be off the street she hurried up the broad monumental steps.

Inside was chaos. Dense knots of people milled and struggled at the few manned counters. The marble interior magnified the noise as everyone shouted his business and his family history to the sullen counter clerks, each hoping to find a distant cousin among the staff who would promote him to the front of the queue.

Julia fought her way to the desk where a fat, ill-shaven clerk reluctantly distributed wooden discs with numbers branded into them. She found a space on the littered floor and sat down to wait, leaning against the wall and watching the frantic crowd.

It was almost an hour before a second clerk called her number in Arabic and French. She squeezed into the cabin he indicated, leaving the door ajar to allow the pungent evidence of previous occupation to escape. She propped her address book on the inadequate shelf and began dialling.

'*Allo! Monsieur Hamoun, Rachid, s'il vous plaît.*' She paused, listening. It was the ninth call she had made. The voice at the other end asked her name. 'Julia Colter.' There was a brief acknowledgment and then a long silence. She fidgeted with the wooden plaque as she waited. Nobody was speaking to Americans. It was understandable. But surely not Rachid?

She had known Rachid Hamoun for eight years. Since her first visit to Lebanon. He had been a struggling factional leader then. Through Rich she had been able to help him get a direct line to the American Government. She knew he had received a lot of very discreet help since then. Arms had been supplied. Rivals had died mysteriously, one in a Paris hotel, one in Vienna. There had never been any admission that the Americans had been involved, but in journalistic circles it was common knowledge. In the meantime Rachid had become a minister. He owed her a lot. Only he knew just how much. The voice was back on the line. It spoke for a long time.

'*Bon*,' she broke in wearily. '*Dîtes à Monsieur Hamoun que Julia Colter voudrait lui parler. Je serai ce soir chez Habib. Merci.*'

She put down the phone, rubbed her eyes and sighed. It looked as though Rachid was turning out like the rest of them. Suddenly she was taboo. She made another half-dozen calls before she struck lucky.

'Abu Bashar, please.'

'This is Abu Bashar.' The voice was wary.

'Abu Bashar! This is Julia Colter.'

'Ah, Miss Julia. Hello, my dear. From where are you speaking?' The wariness was still there, not quite hidden by the warmth.

'The post office. A public phone.'

'Ah! That's good. I've been expecting you to call.' The wariness had gone but the warmth was still tempered.

'You knew I was here?'

'Not exactly. But I thought it was very likely to be you. I heard that a lady had come in from Cyprus. And then I heard that this same lady had entered the American Embassy. The description made me think of you. And then there's this business of your brother, is there not?'

Julia laughed. 'Your spies are still everywhere, huh? You're right about my brother. I'm here to look for him. I need help.'

'Ah, yes,' he said delicately, 'you certainly will. It promises to be a very difficult task. It's a very fine thing that you have come to help him. Sadly, it's not common in your Western societies to care so much for family. But I fear it might be a very dangerous business. And you are a woman,' he added mournfully.

'I know that, Abu Bashar. I was a woman before, too. It didn't stop you accepting my help.' She paused, letting his memory work. Abu Bashar was another of those who had been happy to accept favours from somebody with good connections into the State Department. 'Now I'm the one who needs help. Can I see you?'

'Ah, my dear Julia, I would love to be able to help you. Unfortunately, things have changed in Beirut. It's not easy for me to be seen with Americans. These Fundamentalists are very ruthless people. I don't say they're wrong, but one must be very, very cautious.'

'Abu Bashar,' Julia said in a very low voice, 'I'm *begging* for your help, at least to find out who are the people who are holding my brother.'

He clucked his tongue. 'It hurts me to hear you beg, Miss Julia. It pains me to see somebody dear to you in trouble. In fact, when I learned it was your brother who had disappeared, I had my people ask questions. As you know, I have dealings with many of the groups here in the city. Nevertheless, I was able to learn nothing. Nobody knows these people who contacted the newspapers. They must be a very small group. There are more and more of them nowadays. The only thing of which I *think* I can assure you is that they aren't Palestinians. The Palestinians are more disciplined than that. If your brother were in their hands the leadership would know. I would know.' He said the last words without a hint of boastfulness, a simple fact. 'You must look among the groups supported by Iran. I wish you much luck.'

'Thank you for your kindness, Abu Bashar. I treasure your help.'

'I wish I could do more to help someone I admire so deeply, to whom also I owe so much. Alas. God be with you, Miss Julia.'

'God be with you, Abu Bashar.' She put down the receiver. 'Asshole!' She made three more fruitless calls before pushing her way through the crowd to pay the dead-eyed clerk.

Habib's was situated in a down-at-heel backstreet, a block north of Hamra, and it was not called Habib's. The name over the door, in a florid neon lettering that had given up flickering, even intermittently, well before the war, was the 'Rotary'. Habib had acquired an unexpected enthusiasm for the Rotarian movement during a brief spell as a retail pharmacist in England. This period had come to an end for reasons he left obscure but which were widely believed to be connected to the over-liberal dispensing of certain restricted substances. Habib had retreated to Beirut, considerably wealthier than when he had left, and taken over a run-down bar and restaurant that had quickly become a favoured hangout for foreign journalists. It had enjoyed a moment of relative respectability when the St George Hotel had been destroyed and the assorted diplomats and spooks that had made its bar their headquarters temporarily adopted Habib's. Since the division of the city they had moved on to safer havens, abandoning the place once again to the few journalists and hard-drinking drifters on the fringes of the arms trade still prepared to run the risks of the sector.

When Julia entered, Habib was just in the act of shepherding Ray to a seat at the far end of the bar, beaming and pounding him on the back in enthusiastic welcome. At the sight of Julia he seemed to swell, as though the accumulation of pleasure would make him explode. He raced towards her, dragging Ray in his wake, and folded her in his short fleshy arms. He kissed her several times on each cheek, dropped her, and in his excitement did the same to Ray. He took a pace back and looked Julia up and down, beaming.

'Julia! You look wonderful. More beautiful than ever.

What a surprise.' He pounded Ray on the shoulder with a fist like a boulder, rocking him. Ray winced and put a hand to the bulbous dressing over his eye. 'You see, Raymond. You aren't the only one who comes back to see me. Julia, too, thinks of old Habib.' He reached for Julia again.

Laughing, Ray drew him towards the end of the bar, away from a lone dice player and the two other customers who sat grinning at Habib's showmanship. 'Hands off, Habib, she's here to meet *me*.' They reached the end of the bar. Ray lowered his voice, dropping the bantering tone. 'Any messages?'

Habib frowned and shook his head. 'No. You expecting some?' He walked around the end of the bar. 'What can I get you?' He reached for a Johnnie Walker bottle, his face turned to Ray, who nodded. He poured an inch and a half into a glass and placed it on the bar. Ray took an appraising sip.

'Mmm,' he said appreciatively, 'the Bulgarians are improving.'

Habib gave a pout. 'How can you say that? I have a man who brings it in direct from Cyprus.'

Ray leaned across and took up the bottle. He pointed out the fault in the label. 'He's screwing you. How about a drink for Julia? Getting over here has probably been a little nerve-racking.' He raised an eyebrow at Julia. She nodded and made a wry face.

The indignation left Habib's face. 'Of course. I'm so sorry. What will you have, Julia?'

'The same.'

Habib looked faintly embarrassed. He pointed vaguely to a spot beneath the counter. 'A real one?' he urged.

'No, thanks. The Bulgarian will do fine, as long as you've got some ice. Do you know anything about my brother, Habib?'

Habib started, dropping an ice cube. He glanced around the bar and stepped closer. Julia waited for him to speak, not allowing her hopes to rise. Habib was the kind of man who checked out a room from force of habit, even if he were going to tell you nothing more confidential than the time. 'Is that why you're here?'

'Of course it is. I'm trying to find him. Have you heard anything? Gossip? A rumour? Anything at all?'

Habib shook his head so hard his chins quivered. 'Nothing at all, Julia. It looks very bad. With the war, you know, things have changed here. It's so much worse than it was. Ask Ray.' He looked at Ray for confirmation.

'Sure, Habib, I already told her. Don't worry, we're not asking you to get involved. We would like to sit here and wait for any calls, though. That be okay?'

He shook his head, shrugged and gave a deep chuckle. He placed a hand on Julia's. Although fat it was wide and powerful, enveloping hers. Huge gold signet rings tortured the flesh of the fingers. 'Of course it would. Only, please,' he added, his eyes clouding,' be discreet. I'll tell you frankly, those people make me afraid. Before, I had many friends everywhere. I was as safe as anyone could be here. Now, I try to be very careful. You should do the same. Do you understand what I'm telling you?'

They nodded and tipped their glasses. 'Cheers, Habib.'

His watery-eyed look evaporated. Grinning, he took up a glass and splashed some of the Bulgarian into it. 'Cheers.'

Major Bradman sat, white-faced, staring stonily out through the softly waving curtains of the French windows. He held the phone stiffly, two inches from his ear, as though it carried a contagion.

'How can that be, Major? Your instructions were absolutely explicit.' Tom Jordan spoke with steely lack of emotion.

'I know, sir. The security guards claim they were there the whole time. Right outside the door. The Ambassador refused to let me restrain them further, sir.'

'He's an asshole. Were both guards Lebanese?' Jordan's voice held a sneer.

'There were marines there, too, sir. They confirm their story. I'm sure they're telling the truth.'

'It doesn't matter. The important thing now is to find them. They *must* not be taken as hostages. Is that clear, Major?'

'Yes, sir.'

'Good. And furthermore, we want them out of there. We may be having to move others out, too. The Secretary of State will be talking to that dickhead the Ambassador about that just now. If we do, you'll be in overall charge, Major. Make sure it's done properly. You'll be getting full instructions over the wire.'

'Sir, when might this be for?'

'Very soon, Major. You'll get it all on telex. You'll be getting all the necessary authority, through the Ambassador, of course.'

The Major's eyes glinted. 'Sir, does that mean the President accepts . . . ?'

'Is this a secure line, Major?' Jordan snapped. Then, in a milder tone, 'You'll get all the instructions you need. Call me from the Embassy if you need anything further.' He rang off.

Major Bradman looked at the silent telephone for a moment before slamming it back onto its cradle. As he stood up the tentative beginnings of a smile flickered at his mouth.

14

BY NINE O'CLOCK every seat at the bar was taken. Julia was still the only woman. The drinkers were mostly of European appearance, studiedly unkempt men in suede boots. The collection of ends snipped from ties, that hung among the Lion's club pennants behind the bar, had not been added to for some months.

Four times Ray had been sent by Habib into the tiny back office to take telephone calls in private. Julia had been called twice. Both of them had drawn blanks. Their activity attracted no attention. Habib's served as an unofficial office to half the men there and some among them had also been called, either retiring to the back room or crouching low over the phone at the counter, a hand cupped close around the mouthpiece.

Julia twitched a finger over their glasses, calling for their fourth refill. Habib leant close as he poured the drinks.

'It's not going well? Nobody has anything for you?' His concern was sincere. 'Perhaps the American Government will do something. Make a bargain, maybe. Like the French.'

Julia snorted. 'Forget it, Habib. Foreman's not going to risk publicly asking Israel to back off. Not just before the election.'

With a grimace of commiseration Habib turned to serve a customer at the far end of the bar. The dice player in the dirty suit finished a phone call and replaced the receiver. The phone instantly rang again.

Habib picked it up with one hand while pouring arak with the other. He spoke into the phone, shouting over the background noise. At once his eyes narrowed, almost disappearing among the folds of flesh. He caught Julia's eye and jerked his head towards the back room. He waited just long enough to hear Julia's voice on the extension and gently replaced the handset. He caught sight of Ray staring at him and spread his hands in a gesture that expressed his ignorance. Ray slumped lower over his drink. He was a little drunk. Habib reached and took a slip of paper from a sheaf pushed behind a corner of a mirror.

Smiling sweetly he strolled along the bar to Ray and slid the paper across the bar. Ray squinted warily at it, having a little difficulty focusing. 'Raymond,' Habib began. The use of his full name confirmed Ray's growing suspicion. 'Can you pay me now, please? It's more than three months.' He shook his head as though asking made him unutterably sad. 'Times have changed. My suppliers all demand cash. I'm sorry, Raymond.' He gave Ray a smile that was equal parts commiseration and obstinacy.

Ray began tapping his pockets. It took him a while to track

down the current whereabouts of his cash. Unbuttoning a breast pocket of his safari jacket he drew out a fistful of crumpled banknotes. He peered learnedly at them and gave them a speculative prod. 'Sorry, Habib, I've got no Lebanese notes. I'll take care of it tomorrow, okay?' He grinned winningly at the other man.

Habib reached a hand into the pile and withdrew a screw of paper. 'Dollars are better these days, Raymond.' He smoothed out the note. It was fifty dollars. He took another, picked at it to open it out and ran the back of a hand over it. He gave a grunt and pocketed the two notes. Scrupulously, he counted out thirteen Lebanese pounds and some piastres and handed them to Ray. 'Thank you, Raymond. Have a drink with me, please.' He sloshed whisky into Ray's glass. Ray looked morosely at the nearly worthless Lebanese money for a moment then pushed it, together with the remaining American currency, back into his pocket. He began to lift his glass.

'Ray!' Julia emerged from the back room, her face alight with excitement. 'I think I've got something.' She took him by the arm and almost dragged him off his stool. 'We've got to go!'

He took a last hurried gulp of the scotch and put the glass unsteadily back on the bar, spilling whisky on his jacket. He gave it a last regretful look and waved a hand at Habib. 'Goodnight, Habib. Put those on the tab, will you?' Habib bowed, smiling ruefully at Ray's retreating back, and reached for the sheaf of paper.

The street was very dark. The nearest working street lamp was at the corner a hundred metres from them. They hurried towards it, alone on the broken pavement. They were almost at the corner when the grinding of gears and the whine of a motor signalled the approach of a vehicle being driven hard. Automatically, they pressed themselves into the shadows of an entry. The light from the corner lamp slanted across the entrance, half illuminating Ray.

A jeep took the corner in a scream of tyres and rushed past

them. They had an impression of men with their heads swathed in headcloths and the sinister silhouettes of weapons. The jeep mounted the pavement and slewed to a stop outside Habib's. Four figures leapt from the vehicle and piled into the bar.

Julia was the first away, with Ray, suddenly sober, half a step behind. They ran hard for the corner. Julia glanced back to see light cascade from the open door and people spill onto the pavement.

They ran on, twisting through the darkest back streets for several minutes. Finally, Julia stopped, leaning against a wall, a hand to her heaving chest. Ray bent over on wide-planted feet, his hands gripping his thighs. He retched whisky.

'Jesus,' he gasped, 'am I out of shape.'

'How would you know,' she panted, 'if you've never been *in* shape? Do you think they were looking for us?'

He straightened, still breathing hard. 'Search me. You'd have to think so, though. Until now Habib's place has always been kind of neutral territory. I don't think he's been paying protection to any of them.'

'Maybe someone decided he should.'

'Maybe. Let's not kid ourselves. A lot of dangerous people knew we were at Habib's tonight. Maybe the kidnappers found out and wanted you for a family reunion. Where the hell do we go now?'

'To see Rachid Hamoun.'

Ray drew back. His surprise was genuine. 'Wow! Rachid? Is that who called you just now?'

Julia nodded. 'He's sending his car to pick us up. At nine-thirty, in front of the Zitouni Bank building.'

Ray looked at his watch. 'We're going to be late.'

They set off, walking quickly and in single file, staying close to buildings and taking all the advantage they could of the shadows left by broken streetlights. There was virtually no traffic. Whenever they did hear an approaching motor they withdrew into doorways and waited, the blood throbbing in their temples, until it passed out of earshot. Several times they heard the sudden crack of a rifle and once a machine gun rattled a short tattoo no more than a block to their left.

Julia checked her watch. It was already past nine-thirty. She hurried on, three paces ahead of Ray. From somewhere up ahead she heard the low-pitched snarl of a heavy armoured vehicle. They began scanning the street for a place to hide. The building in front of which they were passing was long and low, marble-fronted, with heavy grilles fixed over its windows and entrance. There was nowhere within fifty metres that could conceal them. They began running.

They were still only level with the sealed-off entrance when the tank came into view. It swung ponderously around the corner to face them. Its big gun trailed scraps of camouflage netting. Julia ran harder. Ray came panting up behind.

'Come on,' she urged, 'over there!' She pointed to a wall of sandbags shielding the entrance of the next building. They ran side by side for a few steps. A yellow tongue of flame spat from the slit that housed the tank's machine gun. Before she even heard the barking rattle of the gun, something tore at Julia's cheek. She cried out, clapped a hand to her face and kept running. There was another flash of flame from the tank. Again, she heard the impact and saw debris shower from the wall above her head. Ray was screaming in her ear, urging her to lie down. Without slowing she turned to him, her own voice a fear-filled scream. 'No! Keep running! We've got to get off the street!'

He never heard her. Her words were drowned in a tremendous crash that shook the pavement under their feet. A huge sunburst of flame engulfed the tank. The air hit them like a falling wall, bowling them both over. Julia was back on her feet before her ears had stopped ringing. Blood ran from the nick in her cheek. She helped Ray up and bullied him, still dazed, back into a run. They covered the last twenty metres and threw themselves headlong into the sandbagged emplacement.

Julia lay for a moment, gasping for breath. She opened her mouth to speak to Ray when an arm clamped painfully around her throat, choking off her words.

Three men crouched over them. Their eyes shone wildly in the light from the blazing tank. Their faces were streaked with grime. One clutched a rocket-launcher, another a rifle which he pointed at Ray's head. The one who held Julia pushed a revolver against her temple. He spoke to her in deliberately slow Arabic.

She mimed incomprehension, rolling her eyes and trying to spread her hands in a shrug. The one with the rocket-launcher spoke sharply. The grip on her throat eased. She swallowed and spoke. '*Bah-kish Arabi. Nihna Amrikiyin.* We're Americans. Journalists.'

The grip on her throat tightened, making her gargle. The three men conferred in low, rapid Arabic. Julia strained to identify any word from her limited Arabic vocabulary, anything that might give her a clue about how to handle these men. They were young, in their early twenties, but hard-faced, with the pared-down, hollowed appearance of men in war who have not slept well for many nights. They had the look of real soldiers, with none of the swagger of the teen-aged militiamen. She wondered as the men debated whether she had been right to tell them she and Ray were Americans. People with the mentality that allowed them to drive a truck stuffed with explosives into a marine barracks were capable of shooting them out of hand.

The three men seemed to be disagreeing. The one with the rocket-launcher gesticulated angrily, apparently taking a different stance to his companions. Quite suddenly, he lashed out with a foot, catching Ray squarely in the face. Ray clutched at his face and fell back, groaning. The man went on arguing. The gesture chilled Julia, for it seemed strangely devoid of malice, as though the man were just thoughtlessly emphasizing a point.

She cast around for something to say, something to offer the men. They wore no identifying insignia. There was no way of knowing whether anything she said would reassure them or provoke them to murder. The grip on her throat slackened a fraction. She swallowed and spoke up. 'We are meeting Rachid Hamoun,' she said, as distinctly as the hold on her throat allowed.

The three men stopped speaking instantly. They stared down at Julia, hostile and mistrustful, the hollows of their faces thrown into nightmarish relief by the flickering light of the burning tank. Without taking his eyes from Julia the man with the anti-tank weapon spoke again. She heard the name Rachid mentioned several times and the sneer of disbelief that thickened the man's voice. She was about to repeat her words when the sound of an approaching vehicle caused the men to turn sharply around, lifting their weapons.

The tension in their faces ebbed as the vehicle drew nearer. A car door slammed and soft footsteps approached the bunker. There was an exchange of greetings and some brief conversation as the men apparently explained what had happened. The word *Amrikiyin* was repeated several times with venom. The newcomer spoke to the men, silencing them. Julia found herself looking up into a man's face as he leaned forward across the barrier. The man smiled broadly.

'Miss Colter? Mr Walker? Good evening. Please could you accompany me. I'm to take you to Rachid.'

The car was a big Mercedes. Unlike the scaling, battered paint job that characterized most of Beirut's cars, this one had an unblemished dark finish that gleamed richly in the light of the smouldering hulk of the tank. It sat low on its suspension, weighed down by its armour-plating. The driver wore a pressed uniform with a green beret. A guard sat in the front passenger seat, also in crisp khaki and festooned with ammunition belts.

Ray and Julia slid into the rear seat followed by their escort. The car hurtled from the kerb and drove at speed away from the scene. Julia touched the blood that oozed from the scratch on her cheek.

'You're hurt, Miss Colter. Did our men do this?'

She shook her head. 'The tank. They shot at us. I think I got hit by a chip of masonry.'

The officer looked regretful. 'You were very lucky!' He shook his head. 'These Christians! They are crazy. Their tanks come almost every night now. Nobody's safe from them now they know we have no tanks left here to fight them. Ours have all been called to the front. They act like savages.' His voice was sad and bitter.

'Your men didn't seem to be impersonating Sunday school teachers,' Ray said sourly, rubbing the side of his face where the kick had landed.

The man looked at Ray, the beginnings of surprise in his face. 'They hurt you?' He tried to be indignant but could not sustain it. 'Ah, yes,' he said, almost to himself. 'It's got very dirty. Very bad.'

A checkpoint barred their way, a makeshift arrangement of cars parked to form a chicane, lit by a single floodlight and manned by a group of rough-looking men with the same honed, exhausted faces as the ones who had destroyed the tank. They examined the driver's pass minutely and came forward to peer into the car, their ravaged faces pressed close to the glass. Their eyes lingered on Julia long enough to make her squirm. Satisfied, they waved the car on.

There were two more checkpoints before they drew up in front of a pair of solid iron gates set in a high wall. The driver pressed the horn three times. Instantly a small judas opened. Behind it, eyes glinted in the headlights. The gates opened a foot and a uniformed man slipped out. He went through the same routine as the checkpoint personnel, checking passes and faces. Before slipping back through the gates he examined the road carefully, looking hard in each direction several times.

The gates swung open and the car slid between them. Short palm trees with cigar-shaped trunks stood among beautifully groomed areas of shrubbery. As they stepped out of the car they heard the soft tinkling of water from a fountain. And, in the distance, the continuing rumble of artillery.

Their escort led the way up the five floodlit steps to the entrance of the imposing villa. A tall, burly figure in a kaftan stood waiting. He spread his arms and embraced Julia.

He broke away with a nod to Ray and walked ahead of them through a high-ceilinged hall and into a spacious sitting room. The room was beautifully decorated in shades of beige. He indicated a huge sofa that could have seated five, upholstered in nubbly beige silk, and lowered himself into a matching armchair facing them.

'Can I offer you a drink?' Rachid smiled, deepening the crow's-feet that fissured the flesh around his tired eyes. 'Coffee? Tea?'

'Coffee, please,' Julia responded, returning his smile.

He looked at Ray. Ray looked back at him, a little ill at ease. He cleared his throat. 'Er, I, they, er, keep me awake. The caffeine. I wonder, er . . . ?'

Rachid shook his head, smiling gravely. 'I'm sorry, Mr Walker. We Sunnis don't have the ardour of the Fundamentalists, but there are still a few of us who try to be good Moslems. I'm afraid I can't offer you alcohol.'

Ray laughed. 'A Coke?'

Rachid nodded and clapped his hands once, making a surprisingly resounding sound. At once a door opened behind him and a small, neatly-built servant, very dark-skinned, entered and stood waiting.

'Two coffees, and a Coca-Cola for Mr Walker.' Rachid nodded to the waiter, dismissing him. He turned back to them. 'Julia,' he said earnestly, 'what have you done to your face? Is it bad? You look awful.'

She grinned, wincing slightly. 'It's nothing, a chip of cement. Somebody took a few shots at us.'

His face filled with consternation. 'Who? Close to here? My men?'

'No, Rachid. Near the Zitouni building. A tank.'

'Thank God it was not worse then.' As he invoked the name of Allah he made the gesture, touching his hand lightly to his chest. 'Maronites?'

Julia shrugged. 'Christians anyway, your men said. They took good care of them.'

'They pretty nearly took good care of us, too,' Ray added, grimly.

Rachid leaned forward in his seat. 'I'm sorry, Mr Walker. This is no time for foreigners to be in Beirut, especially on the streets at night. We have our own problems,' he said, looking suddenly careworn, 'and we have to resolve them in our own way. Foreigners, all foreigners, should stay out of it.'

Julia nodded. 'We aren't trying to get involved, Rachid. We just want to find my brother and get out of here.'

He looked up suddenly at the mention of Michael, as though he had forgotten the purpose of their visit. 'Yes, of course,' he said briskly, pushing himself up from the chair. 'That's why I invited you to come here.' He pushed his hands into the folds of his kaftan and walked across the room, his head bowed in thought. Julia felt a tinge of pity. She had known him as a big-framed man with a solid belly and well filled-out face that had bordered on fatness. Now, although he still carried a paunch, it hung on him like the potbelly of an old man, thrusting out against clothes that, although beautifully cut, hung too loosely. His eyes were underlined by deep-purplish bruises. White flecked his luxuriant moustache. Despite the opulent surroundings, there was an air about him that was deeply saddening.

'Do your people have Michael?' Julia asked the question, directly, without a trace of anger or embarrassment.

He answered her with the same simplicity. 'No. I'm quite certain of that.'

'But you know who has?' She was unable to keep the eagerness from her voice.

He looked into her eyes, frowning, and continued pacing the floor. 'Both of you know a great deal about me, about my past . . .'

'And your present, I guess,' Ray said. He spoke softly, having sensed the sadness in the man. 'You're still Minister, aren't you? Nothing's happened?'

'No, Mr Walker, nothing has happened. I'm still the Minister of the Interior. Only the Government is no longer really a government.' He gave a grim smile and shook himself. 'But that's my problem. The important thing is that I have held the portfolio for a long time, since well before this filthy war began. I pride myself on having contacts second to nobody here.' He smiled again, less grimly. 'Perhaps not even to yourselves.' His face became grave again. 'We Sunnis are going to be wiped off the face of the map here in Lebanon. We and the Palestinians. It's inevitable now. I know that *we* are not holding your brother. There have been hostages in the past, taken by wild elements we could not control. It's different now. For us and for the Palestinians, Arafat's Palestinians, anyway.'

'So you also don't think it's the PLO?' Julia broke in.

'The situation's too serious. We no longer have anything to gain from such nonsense. We're fighting literally for our lives.' He shook his head. 'No, we must look at who would gain advantage from such an action. I have my theory.' He drew closer. 'I think, Julia . . .' Rachid broke off at the sound of a soft rapping at the door. He clapped his hands. The servant entered bearing a tray with two tiny cups, a long-handled copper coffee pot and a frosted glass of Coca-Cola. As he placed the tray on a low table it jarred loudly. Some coffee spilled onto the tray. Rachid looked sharply at the servant. The man's eyes were moist. He was trembling.

Puzzled, Rachid opened his mouth to admonish the servant. Before he could speak the man threw himself to his knees at his feet. He clutched at Rachid's hands, sobbing openly. 'Forgive me, sir. Please forgive me.' The man's voice came only half intelligibly through his sobs.

A flash of anger passed over Rachid's face. 'What is it, Mohand? What's the . . . ?'

He got no further. As Rachid stooped to question the servant a man had stepped silently into the doorway. He held one arm stretched out in front of him. At the end of it was an immense black revolver, made more monstrous by the four-inch cylinder of a silencer.

The gun emitted three soft, consumptive coughs. Rachid's mouth contorted in surprise and indignation and he sank soundlessly to the floor, crumpling across the kneeling servant. Scarlet stains appeared on the pale carpet.

Julia and Ray did not see Rachid fall. The moment the man appeared in the doorway they had moved in unison, scrambling over and around the sofa towards the tall French windows behind them. Holding onto each other and almost falling in their haste, they half stumbled, half dived for the windows. They smashed through them in a crash of splintering wood and glass, protected from the showering glass by the heavy curtains.

They landed on a small raised terrace, surrounded by a stone balustrade. Julia recovered herself first. She threw her weight against Ray, sending them both spilling sideways over the balustrade to the spiky grass of the lawn. As they fell they heard the slapping sound of two bullets kicking up broken glass behind them.

Bent double, they sprinted headlong across the small lawn and threw themselves into the shadow of a clump of shrubbery. They lay utterly motionless, watching the lighted window. For perhaps three seconds nothing moved. The house and garden were silent. Then, very faintly, they heard another soft cough from inside the room.

The man appeared at the window. He paused for just an instant, scanning the shadows around the lawn. In that moment, framed in the lighted windows, Julia got her first real look at him. She gasped. 'Habib's!' she whispered. 'The man at the bar! The dice player!'

The man reached into a pocket of his stained jacket and brought out a handful of ammunition. He quickly reloaded the weapon. With a glance behind him, he vaulted the balustrade and began walking warily towards them.

Julia felt Ray's hand take hers and draw her deeper into the blackness of the shrubbery. They stood pressed together in the deepest shadow, breathing silently through open mouths. The patch of bushes was an island of darkness in the pale light that flowed from the window, lighting the surrounding lawn. They would have to cross several metres of open ground to reach the dense greenery that bordered the lawn, several metres during which the gunman would be no more than ten metres from them.

The man kept moving carefully towards them, walking with his feet spaced wide apart for balance. Suddenly, the man seemed to be struck by a thought. He lowered himself to his hands and knees and spread them so that he was close to the ground, almost lying, his head turned to one side.

Julia gave a sharp intake of breath as she realized what he was doing. At ground level the bushes where they stood were bare. He was looking for their feet.

Julia was preparing to scream to Ray to run for it when a shout from the house cut her short. The man twisted to look back. Three men stood on the terrace, gesticulating. Without hesitating, the gunman pushed himself up and set off at a run as though out of starting blocks, loosing off a couple of shots at the terrace as he went. Rifles cracked. The man ran for the cover of the clump of shrubs. As he ran into shadow he passed within two feet of where they stood. With the courage afforded by his rank fear Ray took a step forward and swung a fist into the running man's abdomen, hoping to hit something soft. He felt his fist sink deep into the unguarded stomach. The man hit the grass face-first and lay twitching. Julia snatched up the fallen gun. The two of them moved quickly around the shrubbery, keeping it between them and Rachid's men, who were now running across the grass. The men reached the fallen man and began kicking him, shouting furiously to each other in Arabic. With the entire area of shrubbery shielding them from sight, Ray and Julia broke from the shadows and sprinted across the lawn to the thick vegetation that lined the wall of the property.

The wall was of smooth cement and at least nine feet high.

They groped their way along it in a total darkness that was not penetrated by the light from the house. The darker twisted shape of a pine stood out against the sky above their heads. They felt their way to its trunk. Ray went up first. Standing on a branch at the height of the wall, he whispered to Julia to follow.

She began clambering after Ray. He balanced himself on the branch, rocked gently to test it, and leapt for the wall. He landed on the top of it as light exploded around them. Ray, Julia, every branch of the tree, was bathed in a white glare from floodlights set on pylons along the wall. For an instant they both froze, horrified. A rifle cracked again, and then another.

'Jump!' Julia screamed, scrambling for the high branch. A bullet rang past Ray's ear, so close that it stung him. He jumped. Julia launched herself for the wall. She landed, stumbled, regained her balance and jumped again. She landed heavily, sprawling, on the asphalt pavement. She gathered herself into a kneeling position and looked around for Ray. He stood with his back to the wall, clutching his stomach. In front of him a man in a green beret and neatly pressed uniform had stopped hitting Ray with his gun barrel to gape at Julia. They looked at each other for a moment in blank incomprehension and then the soldier began swinging his gun at Julia. With a whimper of fear and disgust, hardly aware of what she was doing, she raised the pistol and shot him.

15

JACK FOREMAN stood in the private toilet, right off the Oval Office, peeing and looking at himself in the mirror. He had come a long way.

His prowess as an oarsman had taken him from a very small town in Idaho, a state where, as he liked to joke, all towns were small towns, to a good college in the east. He had returned a minor hero, a significant performer in an insignificant sport, except in a town too small to be choosy.

He had joined a local law practice and begun making himself useful to the farmers. They had liked his hard-swearing, down-to-earth manner. And he was a good lawyer. He was soon sought after by the organizers of local charities, and his abundant energy and presence saw him quickly to the chairs of many of the committees on which he was asked to serve.

It was not long before some of his local cronies began to suggest politics as his logical next step. He had modestly laughed off their suggestions, and then went home to lie awake half the night considering them.

He had hesitated for a long time. Not from diffidence, but because he knew he was vulnerable. A confident, good-looking man, prominent in local affairs, had a lot of opportunities to screw around. He had been taking them just as fast as he could fit them in, and he liked it a lot. One of those nights lying awake in bed he decided to stop.

Within six months of his decision he had married, at thirty-three, the pretty and intelligent daughter of a prominent local farmer. They made a handsome couple. Foreman had grinned, back-slapped and cheek-kissed his way among the three hundred guests, consoling himself with the thought that he had made love to probably fifteen of the prettiest of the women under forty. He put out of his mind the pang of regret that he felt about the remainder.

Two years later he was in Washington, sitting in Congress.

For twenty years his progress had been unstoppable. He was an energetic representative, considerate of his constituents' interests, and a master of horse-trading, the give and take required to get them taken good care of. He was in his element. He entered the Senate young and served well on committees that got a lot of exposure in the media.

The huge next step, to the presidency, had seemed almost natural, practically a formality, as though everyone agreed the Senate was no longer big enough to hold him. In short, everything in Jack Foreman's life had gone wonderfully for him.

And now everything was fucking up, fast.

Marcus Springer had just left his office. The campaign was falling apart. Wilton was running away with it. His television performances were electric. He was coming across as younger, with more vitality and a detailed mastery of the issues.

Christ, just how fucking detailed could you get? In a television debate between the two men ten days previously Wilton had talked for minutes at a time in answer to every question put to him, elaborately building his case. Foreman had relied on his usual bluff style, counting on his record and his skill with a cutting put-down. The polls the next morning had shown Wilton's approval rating fifteen points above his.

He stared at himself in the mirror. The thinning hair that had given him a rather distinguished, academic appearance, contrasting nicely with his country boy manner, had mostly gone, leaving sparse wings of white hair that the slightest disarrangement transformed into nutty professor spikes. The big shoulders had begun to round in the beginnings of a stoop. He swore once, dried his hands and strode back to the huge polished desk. He picked up one of the phones and pressed a button. The voice of the President's Chief of Staff came over the line.

'What was I doing at two?'

There was a pause of a second. 'Boy Scouts of America, Mr President. On the lawn. I have the speech here now if you'd like to look it over. The photographers will be . . .'

'Cancel it,' the President cut in.

'Sir?'

'Cancel it.'

'But, Mr President, some of those boys have travelled across the country. We've got kids, and their parents, from Seattle, Chicago, Texas, all over. The photographers are all set. It's only scheduled for twenty minutes, Mr President, then you have the Soviet Ambassador.'

'I know. That's why I need to be free at two. Get the Vice-President to handle the kids.'

'He's in Detroit, Mr President.'

'For Christ's sake! Get my *wife* to do it, then. But get the Secretary of State and have him come over here right away.' He put down the phone.

When Dean Sutcliffe reached the Oval Office he was still angry. He had been obliged to break off his meeting with the Italian Foreign Minister and hurry over to the White House, leaving the Italian with an apology. The visitor had been understanding. He knew about these things. They had elections in Italy, too. They also had hostages in Lebanon. Nonetheless, Sutcliffe felt humiliated and he intended to let the President know it.

He stalked into the office, exchanging stiff greetings with the Chief of Staff, who was just emerging from the Oval Office. He found the President slumped in the deep, blue-leather upholstery of the enormous swivel chair. His eyes were undershadowed by great pouches of dark flesh. The President waved him to a chair. The Secretary of State sat down, surprised to find himself the only other person in the room.

'Good of you to come over, Dean.'

Sutcliffe nodded, muttering a reply. The technique could still take him by surprise. Foreman *ordered* him out of a vital meeting, giving him no option whatever, and then thanked him for coming, for all the world as if he meant it.

'Have you seen these?' The President gestured to the newspapers that littered the desk, which normally held nothing more than an untouched blotter and a single document. Sutcliffe pulled the papers towards him.

They were all that morning's. They all told the same story. The President was not going to win the election. Foreman remained silent as Sutcliffe glanced over the main items. Most of them he had already seen in his office first thing that morning. With a shrug he sat back and looked into the President's face. Without a word Foreman took some documents from a drawer and tossed them onto the desk. Sutcliffe reached for them, recognizing the brittle, slightly glossy paper of facsimile copies.

A few seconds later he dropped them on the desk and sat back heavily in his chair. 'Shit,' he said, almost inaudibly.

'I couldn't have phrased it better myself,' the President said with grim humour.

Sutcliffe picked up the sheets and sifted through them a second time. 'Are we absolutely sure they're authentic?'

The President gave an ironic little laugh. 'I wish we weren't. They were picked up by a CIA monitoring station in Turkey and relayed straight over here. What you're looking at there was shown on the Soviet evening news a few hours ago.'

Sutcliffe looked morosely at the pictures, his lips pursed. They were grainy but entirely recognizable shots of a man, taken from the waist up. The man's torso was naked and he was unshaven. He looked exhausted. His hands were extended to the camera. The first two fingers of the right hand were missing. Sutcliffe sat quietly, pondering the implications.

The President rose and walked around to the front of the desk. He hitched his rump onto a corner of it. 'Dean,' he said, in a tone of simplicity he had not used to the Secretary of State for years, 'will you *please* give me again the reasons why I shouldn't agree to Tom's proposition and just send in the Navy planes.'

16

WHEN MICHAEL AWOKE no light filtered from the grille above him. He lay for some minutes, listening to the messages he was getting from his body. The shivering and the excruciating headache were gone, along with the nausea. He worked his jaw. It no longer hurt. The pain from his hand was insistent. He concentrated on it, turning his mind to the rhythm of its ebb and flow. Once he had done so, once he was able to predict each new peak of pain, it became tolerable. He contrived a smile. It was something Julia used to tease him for when he was still a teenager, his theories about the body, how it could handle pain. Well, he thought ruefully, now he could prove it to her. If he ever saw her again.

He moved his legs. The metal of the manacle bit into the bone. That, too, could be made bearable.

He was hungry.

Sitting up, he looked around for the food pail. At the same time he saw the full water bottle and the empty, disinfected slop bucket. For an instant the sight of those things filled him with real pleasure. Then, immediately, he became angry with himself. Angry at catching himself beginning to fall into the prisoner mentality; being thankful at being offered food, grateful to his captors for the opportunity to wash, for not hurting him more. It was crucial to his survival to stay angry.

He swore, clambered to his feet and began improvising a set of exercises. He worked out hard, loosening the stiffened joints, coaxing life back into his cramped muscles.

By the time he had finished he could feel the energy flooding back into his body and brain, giving him new reserves. He drank off a long draught of water and ate a little food. Then he began a careful examination of every inch of the cell.

Nothing he saw encouraged him. The door was roughly made, but of massive planks held by iron rivets that he had no hope of prying loose. The crude ceiling or the grating set in it may have offered weaknesses. Without something more substantial to stand on than the rotten pail they would stay beyond his reach.

He began examining the wall. In many places the rough stucco crumbled and pulled away easily. The cinder blocks behind it, though, were sound, and the interstices well mortared. He would make no impact on the wall without a tool.

He hobbled over to the latrine bucket, holding his chain so as to minimize the friction of the manacle against his ankle. He picked up the bucket. Although the pail itself was badly corroded, the handle of thick wire, the diameter of a coat hanger, was in good condition. It was attached through holes in the rim of the bucket, around which it was bent into eyelets. They were tightly closed. He sat down by the bucket and began working at it.

A quarter of an hour later he threw the bucket aside. The handle was still firmly attached to it. His wounded fingers bled. Raging at himself and the obstinacy of the bucket, he stood up and looked again around the cell. With an exclamation he stepped quickly across to the spike set in the wall to which the chain was fastened. The chain dragged at his ankle. In his excitement he was oblivious of any pain.

He took as firm a hold on the spike as he could and tried working it, using all the force of his powerful hands and arms. It did not budge. He leaned on it with all his weight, first forward then back. He sat on the floor and pushed up against it. Then he held onto it and raised his weight from the floor, swinging on it. Sweat began prickling in his hairline and spilling down his forehead. He could smell the staleness of himself. He kept on pushing at the spike.

It was at least half an hour before he thought he detected just the minutest suspicion of give. He let himself slide to the mattress to rest. His heart pounded with jubilation and hope. He lay still for a few minutes, took a long drink and attacked the spike with renewed energy.

In another half-hour he could move it a quarter-turn in its hole.

He was bathed in sweat. He let himself rest for only a minute, forcing himself to be calm, before again getting to his feet. He crouched close to the wall and brushed some of the crumbled plaster and dust that lay there into a small heap. He spat on the pile and kneaded the mixture into mud. Reaching for the food pail he took a fistful of the food he had saved and began mixing it, awkwardly, using just his left hand, into a tacky, binding mess.

He stood up and took a firm hold of the spike in his left hand. He began twisting the metal rapidly backwards and forwards, at the same time pulling it back with controlled force. Slowly at first, and then more easily, it slid clear of its hole. He replaced it and re-examined the spot where it entered the wall. The hole was not enlarged. No casual glance would detect that it had been extracted.

He drew the spike from the wall once again. With his heart pounding he set to work, laboriously scratching the mortar from the exposed joint between two cinder blocks.

He guessed he had been working for a couple of hours when he heard sounds in the room beyond the door. Startled, he pushed the spike back into its hole. He snatched a handful of the food and mud mixture and smeared the malleable paste into the cavity he had made in the mortar. It was no more than two inches long. The mortar was hard, full of tiny shiny pebbles, and his tool was primitive. The dirty paste was hardly distinguishable from the colour of the wall.

When he fell, perspiring but elated, back onto the mattress he had no need to feign exhaustion. He had just closed his eyes when the door opened.

Michael opened his eyes reluctantly, as though awakening from a deep sleep. Slowly, he turned his head to face the door. The way he recoiled was real. He only just choked down an urge to cry out. The guards and the tall man in the hood stood in the doorway. Behind them were two more guards. Between them, his face twitching nervously, was the man with the bag, the one who had severed his fingers.

The men stepped into the room. The hooded man murmured something to the one with the bag and moved aside. He began unconcernedly pulling his camera from his own zippered bag, ignoring the five men who advanced on Michael.

Michael's first instinct was to begin scrambling on all

fours away from them. He stopped, calling on an enormous effort of will, when he saw the chain start to tighten and realized it would pull the spike from the wall. He moved defiantly forward, letting the chain slacken, and tried to push himself upright. One of the men threw himself onto his legs, pinioning them. Two others sprang at him and knelt on his arms.

The man with the bag set it down and took out a scalpel. Michael's face was deathly white. Fully knowing it was useless, he writhed and bucked under the weight of the guards. Instinctively, he clenched his fists into tight balls, protecting his remaining fingers. One of the guards snatched a handful of hair, and yanked Michael's head sideways. Pressing his other palm flat onto his temple he pushed his head hard against the concrete of the floor.

The man with the knife knelt behind Michael's head. Michael strained to look around, his eyes rolling wildly to the side. The man spoke low to him in heavily accented English.

'Try to be still. I will hurt you as little as possible.'

Michael felt the man take his ear between finger and thumb and pull it, stretching the skin tightly away from his skull.

They pulled Michael to his feet. Blood coursed from the wound. His chest was already a sticky mess of crimson. He felt the warmth of it on his leg. He looked straight ahead, refusing them the satisfaction of seeing him look at the blood.

The tall man stepped forward and took a series of Polaroid close-ups. Michael stared at him. For just an instant the other man's gaze seemed to rest on his. Michael looked back at him, trying to read something in the eyes opposite. He saw no pity, only the maniac glint of the fanatic serving the cause. The man turned on his heel and left without another word.

Michael sat motionless for a long time, slumped against the cell wall. His knees were drawn up. His face rested in his hands. The sounds beyond the door finally ceased. He thought he heard the noise of engines coming to him faintly from beyond the ventilation shaft. Long after the sound had faded into the stillness he did not move.

Strangely, the new wound gave him very little pain. He half remembered hearing somewhere that there were very few nerves in the gristly part of the ear. Perhaps it was true. Or perhaps the pain would come later, when the shock subsided.

It had been a shock. More horrifying in a way than the fingers. There had been some sense in the fingers. Fingerprints would serve to identify him, to prove that any group asking for a ransom or a deal actually held him. The ear was pure terrorism. It was a message to whomever they sent it that there would be more. That they held him. Controlled him. Owned him. That they had the power over him that a butcher has over a carcass.

Slowly, he withdrew his face from his hands. His face was set. Very gingerly, he dabbed at the wound with his hand. The bleeding had finally stopped. That, at least, was a relief. For some minutes he had bled like a stuck pig. His whole body was daubed with it. Taking care to make no sound with the chain, he pushed himself to his feet. Carefully, he poured water into a cupped hand and washed his hands and arms. Satisfied he would make no telltale smears he silently withdrew the spike and resumed the laborious scraping.

He worked for several hours, taking time every few minutes to brush the fresh, pale mortar dust into the flakes of plaster and dirt that lay along the wall, never allowing a telltale accumulation to gather beneath the hole. At one point he felt a surge of jubilation. He was sure he had felt the point of the spike break through to the outside. He contained his urge to enlarge the hole. He only wanted a reading on the wall's thickness. It would be dangerous to make a hole that could be seen from the outside before he was ready to attempt a break-out.

He stopped work, almost overwhelmed by fatigue, when

there was no more food left to make the dummy mortar. The vertical joint between the two blocks was cleared. In addition, he had completed about half of the horizontal joint beneath one block. The makeshift mortar of rice and dirt was detectable only on the closest examination. He smeared a last handful of dust on the joints and brushed away the remaining mortar dust from the floor.

Standing, he replaced the spike in the wall, drove it firmly home with the heel of his hand, and lay down on the mattress. A tentative pale light was filtering into the cell, dimming the orange light from the bulb. Sleep came within seconds.

17

RAY CAME OUT of his shallow sleep confused and afraid. He lay staring around him, trying to recollect where he was.

'Julia?' he called huskily. There was no answer.

He dragged himself to a sitting position. In the pre-dawn greyness he could just make out his surroundings. He was in the cab of a burned-out truck. The passenger seat in which he sat was a skeletal affair of blackened metal and bare springs. The windscreen, surprisingly still in place, was crazed with tiny cracks, making it completely opaque. Holes gaped in the dashboard where instruments would once have been. The steering wheel had been removed from its column.

The hulk of the truck lay in a rubble-filled depression that must once have been the cellar of a building. It was more or less concealed from the avenue by a tangle of prickly pear and bougainvillea. The occasional growl of a truck or the roar of a badly-driven car reached him from the road. The sound of distant artillery had stopped.

He called Julia's name again, as loud as he dared. Julia had gone. He felt sick to his stomach. He sank his head into his hands, groaning with despondency and fear for Julia.

A sound from the passenger side made him whirl around, his face breaking into a grin of relief. The outline of a chador-swathed woman appeared in the doorway.

With a choking sound of fright and disappointment he lunged across the seat and caught the woman by the cloth of her chador, dragging her into the cab. 'Quiet,' he hissed, 'or I'll kill you!' He held a clenched fist close to her face.

'Yeah? Fuck you!'

He gaped at the black shape. His fist fell to his side.

'Julia!'

'Expecting somebody else?' she asked, pushing herself upright and throwing back the chador.

'Jesus! You scared the shit out of me. Where did you get the outfit?'

'*I* scared *you*, you bastard? I thought you were going to brain me. I stole it. That, too.' She produced a small bundle.

'What is it?'

'Camouflage uniform. For you.' She held up a blue-and-white-checked headcloth.

Grinning, he draped the cloth over his head, throwing one end across the lower half of his face. 'How's that?'

'Perfect. A born freedom fighter. I got this, too.' She pulled two flat loaves and a can of Fanta from her clothes.

They ate and drank in silence for a moment or two. Ray spoke first.

'Julia, I think we ought to get out of here.'

'Me, too. Another hour and there'll be people all over.'

'No, I don't just mean out of this spot. I mean out of the country. Go home.'

She looked at him in disbelief. 'Stop looking for Michael?'

He nodded. 'Rachid was like a god to a lot of the Sunnis here. If they get their hands on us we're dead. They can't help but think we had a hand in Rachid's killing.' He reached out and put an arm around her shoulders as she blinked back tears. 'We've done all we can expect to do. Rachid practically guaranteed no Sunni or Palestinian group has Michael.'

'Then it's Shi-ites.' She spoke defiantly.

He grimaced. 'That's right. And the Shi-ites are fighting a war against Israel. To them that means America, too. No Shi-ite in his right mind is going to risk helping us.'

She stared at the ground, biting hard at her lower lip. He moved closer and held her tighter. 'Let's find a phone and call Bradman. He can come in here with some marines and get us. He'd be only too pleased to send us off home.'

They sat for a full minute. Julia cried silently while Ray held her, his face against her hair. Finally she straightened and wiped her face with a corner of the chador. 'Call him if you want, Ray. I'm going on looking for Michael.'

Ray went first up the steep slope to the rim of the depression. He crouched in a clump of bougainvillea close to the edge of the pavement and scanned the street. He beckoned Julia to join him.

'Okay,' he muttered, 'I'm going.' He stepped clear of the foliage, pretending to button his fly, and walked briskly across the wide road. He walked a few paces and halted, loitering by the display of cheap shoes which a merchant was setting up outside his store. The merchant stepped towards him, ready to start his day. Ray waved a forefinger in the quick rocking motion that was the definitive way of saying no to an Arab, and turned his back. The merchant looked heartbroken and re-entered his shop.

Ray looked idly up and down the street. Fifty metres away, two women were waddling towards him, their great hips, half as wide as their height, thrusting at the voluminous folds of the chadors. They might see Julia emerge, but nobody else would. The longer they waited, the more people would fill the street. He made a discreet beckoning gesture. A black-shrouded figure emerged like a great bird from the bougainvillea and began walking sedately down the street.

Ray drifted along on the opposite side of the road, sometimes hanging back, sometimes getting ahead, but always staying within twenty or so metres of Julia, and always watching the street. Increasing numbers of people passed them. Discreetly, he watched the faces, studying them for signs of any unusual reaction. Most of the passers-by at this hour were men walking to their work. Their eyes mostly stayed on the pavement directly ahead of them. Beirut was no longer a city where it was prudent to allow oneself to catch another person's eye. Trouble could come too suddenly, for too little reason.

In the thin stream of people Ray himself passed unnoticed. The headcloth partly masked his face and covered the cut on his eye. He had removed the dressing as too conspicuous. The growth of coppery stubble and the reddish hair on his arms were unimportant. A surprising number of local people had red or even blond hair. His clothes, bush jacket and khaki cotton slacks, were common enough to pass muster. The smudges of dirt and the few small tears collected in the events of the night were also nothing unusual in the suffering and destruction of the city.

For Julia it was the same. The chador swathed her head and fell in an unbroken sweep to brush the pavement, covering even her shoes. A single eye looked out from the shadows behind the one tiny opening.

Ray walked on to where the avenue intersected another broad street and turned out of sight. Julia drifted after him. She stopped short.

A group of men were herding passers-by into line. Three cars and a donkey cart were drawn up at the edge of the road. The men, in uniforms and shiny, calf-length laced boots, looked like an elite militia force, not at all the usual rabble. They were demanding documents and searching the vehicles. They looked tough and angry. Ray was already caught up in their net. He stood, sixth in a line being checked by one of the soldiers.

Her pulse racing, Julia turned and pretended to examine the display of plastic washing bowls, nylon broomheads and galvanized buckets crowding the pavement outside a hardware store. Her mind raced, searching desperately for a solution. From thirty metres away she could see the silent, desperate plea in Ray's eyes.

She studied the scene for a moment longer, turned away and strode into the store. She grabbed a long-handled straw basket, threw down a handful of money in front of the surprised merchant and headed back towards the street.

Shielding her moves from the view of the still chattering shopkeeper, she plunged a hand into the chador. When she emerged onto the street the hand was pushed deep into the basket. Someone called sharply to her. One of the militia was ordering her to join the line. She gestured weakly and strolled towards the back of the line. Ray was now third from the front.

As she passed close to the donkey cart she was racked by a sudden cough. The cough covered the soft plop as the hand hidden in the basket squeezed the trigger of the silenced gun. The donkey gave an extraordinary braying scream, tried to rear up in the shafts of the cart, and bolted forward.

It tried to run between the cars and the queue of pedestrians. The wheel of the cart caught one of the cars and it spilled onto its side. A loathsome mass of severed chicken heads cascaded at the feet of the queue. The militiaman and the waiting people scrambled aside. Julia was among them. Stumbling, she upset a stall on which plastic sandals were heaped in a crude display. The sandals spilled among the chicken heads.

The donkey's owner swung on its rope bridle and flailed with a thick stick as the maddened beast reared and snorted, trying to throw off its shafts. The owner of the shop, a grotesquely fat, smooth-faced man, lumbered from the interior and began screaming at them. Recovering herself, Julia stepped behind the owner, took Ray by the arm and drew him gently into the doorway. Nobody called after them.

They sprinted through a door to the rear. They were in a storeroom with a big casement window looking out onto the sidestreet behind the shop. Iron bars an inch thick, like the bars of a mediaeval dungeon, crisscrossed it. Julia wrenched open a door. Inside was a Turkish-style toilet. And it was blocked. High in the wall was a small window, fastened by a simple catch. Ray pushed past Julia, reached up and tore it open. She hurled the basket from her. Ray grabbed the silenced gun from her hand and shoved it into his belt.

Ray went through head-first, landing in a heap in the alley. Two old men sitting with their backs to the alley wall listening to a tinny radio scratched ruminatively at their grizzled eight-day stubble as he turned back to the window to help Julia through. The men's heads swivelled on scrawny turtle necks as they watched the strange pair pick themselves up and dash out of the alley.

At the first corner they stopped running. Once again they split up, Julia on one side of the street and Ray alternately trailing and leading on the other.

Julia walked positively, trying not to give the appearance of too much hurry. Unless there were an air raid or a bombardment it was unusual to see an Arab woman walk fast. Three times she stepped into doorways while a jeep or a lorry full of soldiers passed. Once, a group of young men came along the street at a trot, weapons held at their sides, supervised by some kind of officer. They bothered nobody but ran, looking blank-eyed straight ahead of them. Several had bloodied bandages on their heads or limbs.

The sun had fully risen now. Beneath the black cloth of the chador Julia's clothes were clinging to her. Her hair was plastered to her scalp. Her eyes were gritty from lack of sleep. She was tired, scared and angry. And she stank. She was very glad to see the white-marble exterior of the building that was their destination.

She made for the entrance. An elderly man in improbable Ray-Ban aviator sunglasses and a youth who might have been his grandson sat outside the door on two plain wooden kitchen chairs brewing tea on a small butane-gas stove. They wore yellow armbands with a text hand-printed in red.

As Julia approached, the old man got to his feet. He lifted a device somewhat like a table-tennis bat from the ground and, with a smile of equal parts apology and prurience, he ran the metal detector over her body. He waved her into the building.

She waited in the shadowy hallway. It was over a minute before Ray sauntered up to the security guard. She watched, dry-mouthed, as he was submitted to the same routine. He was waved into the hallway. She let out a long breath.

'What happened to the gun?'

He grinned. 'I buried it. Let's go up.'

By the time they reached the sixth floor Ray was blowing like a whale. He leaned against a wall of the landing and put a hand on his breast, feeling his heart pounding. He wiped the perspiration from his face with an end of the headcloth. Julia had let the chador fall from her face. She held her thumb to the bellpush.

Habib's eyes were only just visible beneath the puffy folds of his lids. They flicked from Julia to Ray. They stayed on Ray. For an instant Julia did not understand the fear that flooded the fleshy face. Then, with a quick laugh, she reached out and pulled the headcloth from Ray's head. Habib's fear gave way to an exhausted smile.

'Come in,' he said, standing to one side.

Julia dragged off the chador and threw it aside. Habib stood watching them, kneading his hands like a shopkeeper. 'You both look terrible. Can I get you something?'

'Coffee,' Julia said in a mock croak. 'This big. Black. Not the Turkish mud, please.'

He gave a *moue* of mock offence and turned to Ray.

'D'you have a beer?'

'Help yourself. You too.' He smiled to include Julia and pointed to the kitchen. 'Excuse me for just a moment.' As they walked to the kitchen Habib slipped into the bedroom.

Julia could not find the coffee beans. She walked to the door. 'Habib! Where do you keep the coffee . . . ?' She broke off. Habib was padding across the room towards the hallway. One big arm was around the shoulders of a willowy youth of around fifteen in a Lacoste polo shirt and a lot of heavy gold jewellery. Habib was pushing money into the boy's hand.

He closed the door behind the boy. He started as he saw Julia watching him. He recovered himself and walked into the kitchen, spreading his hands. 'The girls have left Beirut, Julia. One moves with the times. The coffee's in the freezer. Now tell me why you're here.'

They told him. He listened in total silence. By the time they finished Habib seemed to have aged ten years. 'Rachid's dead?' He seemed to be talking to himself, absorbing the shock. He shook himself. 'And his people think you're mixed up in it?'

They nodded.

'You've got to leave Beirut,' he said flatly.

Ray slammed down his beer. 'Christ, that's exactly what I've been telling her!' He turned to Julia. 'Let's call Bradman, and have him get us out of this.'

She shook her head. 'I'm here to find Michael.'

Ray snorted and looked appealingly at Habib. 'Look, they're trying to *kill* us out there. We can't compete. We're journalists not fucking spooks.'

'I want to talk to Hezbollah. If it's not Sunnis and it's not Palestinians that have Michael, then it has to be Shi-ites. Hezbollah are the likeliest group among the Shi-ites. They're the ones that hate Americans most.'

'That is a fucking brilliant idea,' Ray groaned. He looked appealingly at Habib.

'My dear Julia,' Habib said softly, anxious not to give offence. 'Nobody from Hezbollah is going to talk to Americans.'

'They'd talk to the Iranians, though.'

Ray laughed out loud. 'You want to call up Tehran and ask if a minister or two could help us out? Help a couple of deserving Americans? Be sensible, Julia.'

'Just one minister. Bahrawi.'

He laughed some more. Gradually the laugh died. 'The Minister of Defence? You're kidding.' He watched her face for several seconds. 'No, you're not,' he said, speaking slowly. 'You really know him.'

She nodded. 'And he owes me one.' Her eyes moved to Habib. 'Are the lines to Tehran working?'

He shrugged, still incredulous. 'Maybe. Frankly it's not somewhere I've ever needed to call. Some days you can call anywhere in the world. Some days you can't call the people downstairs.'

She walked into the living room, heading for the phone. 'Let's hope it's a good day.'

18

'BARBARIANS! The whole damn bunch of them!' Harry Moore's voice was thick with contempt. 'The Islamic Revolutionary Faction? They've got to be kidding!' He let his eye roam once again over the paper in his hand. 'Nobody saw who left this?'

Ron Watts shook his head. He took the empty pipe from his mouth, making a soft sucking sound. 'No, Harry. One of the girls found it lying on the desk down in the lobby. Nobody really saw who put it there. One of the doormen thinks he might remember a dark-skinned guy coming in, maybe Mexican, he thought, but could've been an Arab. That's all.'

Harry Moore nodded, his eyes still on the document. 'The bastards are really torturing that boy.' He glanced at his watch. 'We've still got time. You want to do the piece, Ron?'

Ron nodded. 'How much?' At this late hour a greyish stubble made his narrow face look older, more used. The controlled academic had given way to the family doctor in the last stage before alcoholism. It happened every night.

'Say, seven hundred words?'

Ron's eyebrows rose. 'You going to have that much room? With the Gallup results and all?'

Harry Moore massaged his face with the heels of his hands. 'What's the difference? It tells the same story as all the others. Jack Foreman's blown it.' He flipped the paper onto his desk. 'And this won't help him a bit.'

Ron Watts tapped his pipe deliberately against his teeth. 'Harry, are you sure about this? I mean, I know it's Julia's brother, and we all want to help, and, Christ knows, I'd like to see the back of Jack Foreman as much as anyone around here. But just what does anyone expect him to do? Nuke the place?'

Moore massaged the back of his neck. 'He's had four lousy years, Ron. This wouldn't be happening if he'd had any kind of policy. All we've done all that time is react. Every miserable little group out there thinks they can push us around. Ever since the Tehran Embassy fiasco. Every time some crummy little faction wants something from us they think all they have to do is grab a couple of citizens. They know damn well they don't have to worry. We make the right noises, threaten them with the might of America, and then quietly offer to trade.' He stood up and turned abruptly to stare out over the city, trying to control his anger. 'Jesus, Ron,' he said, still facing the window, 'the bastards just can't lose.'

The other man watched him, frowning. 'It didn't start with Jack Foreman, Harry,' he said softly.

Harry turned from the window and gave him a tired smile. 'Nobody asked him to be president. Do you want to do the piece?'

'In my view, Mr President, it's time we took the initiative. Every time we let someone kick us around once, they come back and do it again. When the Tehran Embassy was invaded Jimmy Carter should have wiped out the Abadan oil installations instead of pussyfooting around. If Reagan hadn't let them use hostages to screw arms out of us this wouldn't be happening. They'd have learned that hostages were more grief than they were worth.'

The President looked alarmed. 'You're not proposing we hit Iran?'

Tom Jordan shook his head and gave the President a steely smile. 'No, sir. Lebanon. I'm suggesting we send in the Navy planes and bomb the shit out of them. And we tell them that if we don't get Colter back right away, and the other people they're holding, we'll be back and bomb them some more.'

The President blinked at Jordan, studying the craggy face. Lack of sleep had left Foreman gritty-eyed and resentful. A few years ago he would have eaten a man like Jordan alive. Now he could feel the man manipulating him.

It had been apparent to Foreman before he ever became President that foreign affairs was not going to be his strong suit. He was a flesh-pressing, deal-making politician with a natural feel for his rivals' weaknesses. The intricacies of foreign affairs bored him. The Japanese over-awed him a little. The Europeans, with their impressive ease in English and their grasp of geography, he suspected patronized him. Latin America confused him. The Middle East he held in contempt. He regarded Arabs as basically shifty, either some kind of lazy camel drivers, or terrorists. The exception in the area was Israel, which was more or less reliable, although crammed full of Jews.

The Lebanese situation had slipped beyond his comprehension years ago, and with it the quicksilver alliances of its neighbours, Iraq and Syria, Syria and Israel, Palestinians and Shi-ites. Maybe the Palestinians *were* Shi-ites. It was the sort of thing he relied on his aides for, on Dean Sutcliffe and Tom Jordan. They had the factions at their fingertips and frequently explained everything to him. But it was complicated.

'It's the only way we're going to turn this thing into votes, Mr President.'

Jordan had been talking about something the President had not really been hearing. Now he was talking about something he could focus on. He leaned forward. 'How's that, Tom?'

Jordan's features showed no sign of irritation. He repeated himself. 'We ought to hit the targets on that list I gave you without delay, sir. If you agree, that is, Mr President, that they're all appropriate.' He watched the President's eyes, saw the blankness that flitted there, and pulled a typed sheet from his document case. 'This is a further copy.'

The President took the document and leaned back, squinting at it. He ran his eye slowly down the list, looking for a name he recognized. Realizing with a stirring of disquiet that he was not going to have any luck, he laid the paper deliberately on the desk and made his fingers into a steeple.

'I, er, haven't had the opportunity to study it in detail yet, Tom, but I suppose you're suggesting terrorist training camps, Palestinians, that kind of thing?'

Jordan nodded. 'That's the kind of thing, Mr President. Some of them are Palestinian training camps, some are Shiite strongholds.' His eyes on the President's face, he added, 'Mostly supported by the Iranians.'

Foreman's eyes flickered with interest. 'Mmm. Civilians?'

'There are women and children in the Palestinian camps. As often as not they're training with the men. It's difficult not to have at least some casualties among them.'

Foreman looked pensive. 'I don't know. It seems to me that whenever anything like this happens all those bastards at the newspapers print is pictures of injured civilians.'

'Once the picture of Colter that came in this afternoon goes out in the morning editions, Mr President, I don't think we're going to have to worry about that.'

The President got up from his chair and began prowling the room, his hands pushed deep into his pockets. Two deep clefts formed a shallow V-shape superimposed on the rubbery corrugations of his brow.

'You know Dean's absolutely opposed to anything like this?' he said. His voice held a tentative note, an invitation to argument.

'Dean has excellent judgment, Mr President, and I respect it. But,' he continued, timing his pause with an actor's skill, 'I have to say I think his views sometimes belong in a different age to ours. He sometimes seems to me, I don't know, too European.'

'He's concerned about the repercussions. Around the Gulf, and with the Saudis. And he seems very worried it might encourage the, er, the Fundamentalists in Egypt.' There was a hollowness to the President's tone, as though he were trying out phrases in a foreign language he had only just begun to master, unsure if he was making sense.

Jordan kept his voice even. Nevertheless, it quivered with contained rage. 'Dean's concerned about encouraging the Fundamentalists in Egypt, he's concerned about what those sheepshit-eating assholes in the Gulf will think of us. He's probably concerned about helping old ladies across the road. And *I'm* concerned with the concrete fact that there are some bastards out there torturing American boys and we aren't doing a damned thing to stop them. I'm also concerned to see you win this election, Mr President.'

'Now, Tom, we can't let electoral considerations enter into this,' the President chided, mechanically.

'Okay, let's leave them aside. We've still got a bunch of terrorists sending us pieces of one of our citizens. So far they send us fingers and ears. What if tomorrow they send us his head? How will that look staring at us from the front page of the *Washington Post*?' He stood up and moved close to the President. 'They need a lesson, Mr President, the way Ghaddafi needed one.'

'That was a while ago, Tom. And Reagan got a lot of flak over that Libyan thing.'

'From the *Washington Post*, maybe. Not from the voters. They *want* something done. They're tired of hearing why we have to negotiate and never offend anybody. They can't understand how we have so much power and allow ourselves to be pushed around by a backstreet gang from a fleapit like Beirut. It doesn't make sense to them.'

The President sighed. 'To tell you the truth it doesn't

make sense to me either, Tom. The shitty part is we don't even know who's holding the kid, or where. We can make a lot of enemies in something like this.'

'Are we making friends this way?' Jordan jabbed a finger towards the window. 'The people out there just don't see the difference. The way they see it, is that none of these groups could exist without a lot of support from the local people. They see a dead American, an innocent boy, on the front page of their newspapers. They aren't about to enrol on a political science course. They want revenge! And they'll vote for the person who gives it to them.' He spoke the last words very softly and distinctly.

Jack Foreman did not speak for several seconds. Jordan remained immobile. His face was as expressionless as a stone, except for the light-blue eyes riveted on the President's face. The President pushed aimlessly at the paper on his desk, picking it up and letting it flutter back. His big shoulders were hunched forward as though under a weight. He drew a long, noisy breath. He raised his head and met Jordan's eyes.

'We'd have to move any Americans out beforehand. Close down the Embassy.'

Tom Jordan was a very controlled man. Even so, he had to bite his lip in the effort to keep the triumph from showing in his face. 'Quite right, Mr President.'

He pulled two sheets, stapled together, from his document case and handed them to the President. 'I took the liberty of sketching out a scenario, sir. Perhaps, we could look it over right now, to see if it's the kind of thing you had in mind.'

Jordan stood at the window, silently contemplating the lights of Washington. Outwardly, he was absolutely calm. Behind the immobile planes of his face his brain was tinglingly alert. He felt the exhilaration, the sense of being in control of events that he had first known in Korea and then, years later, in the inky, wet darkness of night-time operations in Vietnam and Cambodia. He had not realized until now how much he had missed that sense of manipulating things. The intervening years, even so close to the seat of power, had offered no satisfactory substitute for the thrill of action. The open fire crackled loud in the silence. The President looked up. His voice was a murmur.

'Let's do it, Tom.'

Jordan remained at the window a second longer, long enough to drive the jubilation from his expression. By the time he turned and walked to his seat his face was as closed as usual.

'Very good, Mr President. I'll set the ball rolling tonight.' He looked at his watch. 'It's mid-morning over there. There's no reason they can't start making evacuation arrangements today.'

'Right, Tom. There's no sense delaying. We want to hit them fast, before they kill the boy.' His decision made, the President's manner had taken on a fresh air of resolution. 'And we'd better get Dean over here.'

A flicker of a frown crossed Tom Jordan's face. 'Are you certain about that, Mr President? This is going to be a very delicate operation, sir. I thought probably it would be advantageous if not too many people were informed. That perhaps, er, as far as possible, *I* should handle things.'

The President looked at him in some surprise. 'But, Tom, we're talking about closing down the Embassy. That's State Department business.'

'Well, yes, I see that, Mr President. It's just that, well, I feel our own lines of communication over at the NSC might be more secure. This isn't something we'd like to see on the front page of the *Post* before it happens.'

The reference was not lost on the President. He had set up a committee only two months previously to look into leaks that hurt his campaign. 'Do you think you could handle it, Tom? Without upsetting State?'

'There are only a handful of Americans left over there, sir. Apart from the marines, the Embassy staff is no more than a dozen people. They mostly live on the compound. Apart from that there probably aren't more than twenty US citizens out there.'

'Including hostages?'

Jordan gave a wry grimace. 'There are four hostages, other than the Colter boy. However, we don't know if they're alive or dead, or even if they're still in Lebanon. They could have been moved out, to Syria, maybe, or even Iran.'

'What am I going to tell the relatives if they're all delivered to us, dead, right after we hit?'

Jordan grimaced again and shrugged. 'The election'll be over by then, sir.'

The President gave him a long, hard look. 'What about Colter's sister, and the bastard with her?'

'Walker.' He looked grave. 'If the news from there is accurate, they're probably dead anyway, by now. The rumour's out that they were mixed up in the assassination of Rachid. If it's so, they're probably in a ditch somewhere with holes for eyes. Major Bradman's trying to locate them. Frankly, I'm planning to instruct him to concentrate on the others. Those two went looking for trouble.'

The President nodded, frowning. 'Bradman's your man over there. Is he capable?'

'The best there is. He was with me in Vietnam. He'll handle it well, sir.'

The President nodded, his face still shadowed by doubt. 'He'd better! You've sketched out a very nice operation. I'd hate it to go wrong because a few Americans were foolish enough to be in the way, or because we weren't smart enough to get them out in time.'

Jordan drew his document case towards him. 'Count on Major Bradman, sir. I vouch for him.'

The President smiled and rose, extending a hand to Jordan. 'I'm glad to hear you say it, Tom. Let's get to it.' He shook Jordan's hand vigorously. 'I'll make a few calls.'

Jordan turned and walked towards the door. After three steps he turned around. The smile had already gone from Foreman's face. 'Oh, Mr President, just one other thing.'

The President looked up sharply, as though he had already forgotten his presence. 'Mmm? What, Tom?'

'I think it would be a good idea if you could make the Ambassador the first of those calls, sir. If it could be done immediately it would be very helpful. Then I can give Major Bradman the green light without risk of any, er, crossed wires.' He gave a conspiratorial smile.

The President nodded brusquely, and glanced mechanically at his watch. He made a faint pursing of his lips as though tasting something mildly sour. 'Don't worry about it, Tom. I'll do it right away. Goodnight.'

'Goodnight, Mr President.' Jordan left the room. A marine sat alert in the outer office. He gave a snappy salute.

Jordan returned it with a flourish. 'Goodnight,' he said cheerfully. 'Beautiful night.'

The marine nodded and watched him disappear through the door. In six months of service it was the first time Tom Jordan had given him more than a nod.

19

IN THE OFFICES of the National Security Council, deep in the White House basement, night and day could be distinguished only by reference to the big, clear-faced electric clocks that were everywhere on the walls. In its work, too, there was no differentiation. Night in Washington was the broad light of day in Turkey or Cyprus from where the mountain-top listening posts beamed back a constant stream of intelligence gleaned from radio communications within the Soviet Union.

The night staff showed no surprise at seeing their chief step from the lift and stride to his office at such an hour. He did it often, always with the immaculate clothes and perfect military bearing of a man fresh from eight hours' sound sleep.

He returned the greetings of the gritty-eyed staffers with curt, wordless nods and entered his office. He pressed a button on the squawk box on his desk, called for coffee and stripped off his jacket.

As he sat at his desk turning the cuffs of his shirt back two meticulous turns, a young woman in army uniform brought in a tray on which sat a white porcelain coffee pot and a matching cup and saucer. She placed it carefully on the desk at his elbow and smiled. To her surprise he smiled back.

'Anything else, sir?'

He shook his head. 'Thanks, Mary. Close the door as you leave, would you. I don't want to be disturbed for a while.'

She left the room, pulling the doors to after her. The two doors were arranged so that when they were closed a layer of air the thickness of the wall was trapped between their padded surfaces. It was very effective soundproofing.

Jordan poured himself a cup of coffee, sipped it appreciatively and reached for one of the telephones. It was a landline, not a microwave transmission, and was regularly and often swept for listening devices.

His first call woke a man who had been sleeping on a daybed two miles away, across the Potomac, in an office high up in the Pentagon building. The man listened attentively for maybe two minutes, before emitting a low sound that fell just short of being a whistle.

'The President's behind you on this, Tom?' he asked warily.

'Absolutely. I've just left him. He accepts the plan entirely. He's asked me to oversee the whole programme. He wants it just as we talked about it.'

'Er, will I be getting something from you? You know, well, a memo, some kind of confirmation?'

'You'll be getting the President's handwritten confirmation delivered to you before breakfast.' Jordan's voice had turned wintry. 'Meanwhile, would you please make a start with those calls, Greg. We're in a hurry.' He hung up without waiting for the other man to speak again.

He took another gulp of coffee and expelled breath angrily. They all wanted to be covered by a memo. All of them were the same; bureaucrats who had been lent uniforms by the Government so that they could impersonate soldiers. He still felt oddly out of place among them; a soldier impersonating a bureaucrat.

His next call was to the town of Newport, Virginia, just north of the huge Naval base of Norfolk. The telephone rang aboard a thirty-two-foot sloop moored in the marina. A short wiry man with close-clipped, prematurely grey hair and deeply etched sun-wrinkles around his eyes retrieved an arm from beneath the overweight divorcee next to him and rolled over, grumbling, to take the call.

The voice at the other end of the line brought him fully awake instantly. 'Tom? Hold on a second.' He eased himself quickly from the bunk and padded softly into the saloon. He took the extension off the hook and pressed it to his ear. 'Tom?' he said, keeping his voice low. He got a grunt of confirmation. 'Another second.' Silently, he returned to the bedroom and replaced the phone gently on its cradle. He slipped back into the saloon, closing the connecting door carefully behind him. 'Okay,' he said, his voice low but distinct. 'Go ahead.'

Jordan wasted no time on greetings. Their relationship, developed years before when they had both been prisoners in the same Viet Cong camp, until they had escaped together, did not need niceties. 'What can I do for you, Tom?'

'D'you have any plans for the next few days, Gerry?'

The wiry man smiled. 'Same as I've had for most of the last few years. Some fishing, some fucking, some sailing.'

'Some flying appeal to you?'

Gerry glanced at the door, checking he was alone. He was no longer smiling. 'What's up, Tom? You have something for me?'

'Yeah. Can you get up here today?'

Gerry's eyes opened wider. 'If you like. What do I do about baggage? I mean, hot or cold? How many days?'

'Hot. Three or four days, maybe.'

'Do I come there?'

'No. Check into the Four Highways Motel. Across from the Holiday Inn at the airport.'

'I'll find it. What do I do when I get there?'

'Whatever. More fucking if you want. But be free and packed by ten tonight. I'll be by to get you. Look out for me. I won't want to be enquiring at the desk.'

'I'll be there. Any chance of your telling me what it's about?'

'After I pick you up. 'Bye, Gerry.' The line went dead.

Gerry stared into the mouthpiece for a moment, grinned, and set it down. He walked back through to the bedroom, throwing the door aside hard, careless now of the noise. The woman still slept. He flipped on the light and gave her shoulder a shove. She rocked under the impact. He shook her again, sitting down on the edge of the bunk. She stirred and opened her eyes, blinking in the light. She smiled sleepily and placed a hand on his thigh.

'What are you doing?'

'I'm leaving. Sorry. Business. Something just came up.'

She struggled up onto one elbow. She leaned over and looked at her watch where it lay beside the bunk. 'Christ,' she protested, her voice hoarse with sleep, 'it's still the middle of the *night*. Come back to bed. You can't be going anywhere at this hour.' As she spoke she ran her palm up the inside of his thigh.

He watched her, smiling quietly, the corners of his eyes crinkling along the lines of the sun-wrinkles. He, too, looked at his watch, the only thing he was wearing. He did a quick calculation. He only need be in DC by ten. And at his age any chance might be your last. He slid down beside the woman.

Jordan made several more calls. Each conversation was short and to the point. Mostly, he issued terse instructions while other people listened. To the few questions he gave even terser answers.

At length he put down the phone and leaned back, humming to himself. His eyes fell on the coloured map which covered one wall of the spacious office. Clusters of coloured pins crowded the area stretching in a broad band from Kabul to Cairo. The tiny, apple-green flecks that signified Fundamentalist activity had, in the last few months, broken out from the concentrations in Iran and Lebanon and now speckled the Gulf States and the whole Arabian Peninsula. Cairo and Alexandria bristled with thickets of pins.

Jordan drank off the last of the coffee and looked at one of the clocks over the door. It was noon in Saudi Arabia. He took up a different phone and began dialling. The phone was connected to the outside world by a series of relays, the number ostensibly belonging to a run-down Ford dealership that had been going broke in a shabby section of Washington for the last few years. No record was available of numbers dialled on it. The number he dialled now was in Riyadh, Saudi Arabia.

The big, sallow-skinned man lounged on a sofa. Although designed for three people, his huge spadelike feet still protruded beyond one of its arms. He wore an embroidered kaftan that could have cloaked a camel. He was reading his seventh paperback of the week. Empty Coca-Cola and Schweppes cans lay on the thick woollen carpet. The corner of an ashtray showed from under a heap of ash and ringpulls. He had just been beginning to wonder if he did not feel hungry when the phone rang.

'*Aywa?*' The faint pinging echo told him he was being called via a satellite. Moving lazily, he clamped the tiny microphone of a portable tape recorder to the handset.

'Saïd? It's me,' the voice was abrupt, without warmth.

The big man smiled, multiplying his chins. 'Good morning, my dear friend. I had been wondering whether you had forgotten me. I had hoped to hear from you earlier. My good friends here were beginning to lose a little of their faith in me.'

'You're hearing from me now. You can inform your friends, our friends, that our contract has been concluded. Our chairman has given complete approval.' Jordan felt curiously childish at using such oblique language. A satellite line, open to anyone who wanted to eavesdrop, imposed its own disciplines. 'I'll be overseeing the work personally.'

'That's excellent, my friend, really excellent.' The big man chuckled from deep beyond the flesh of his chins. 'Their Highnesses will be delighted. They think very highly of you.'

Jordan grunted. 'It's mutual. You can tell them that,' he added, without a lot of conviction. 'You can tell them I'm planning to leave tonight. You'll get a telex confirming my exact arrival time from the usual source. Be there with the materials.'

The big man smirked. 'The materials are already in place, my friend. They have been for some days. We were waiting for the chairman's approval and, of course, your own arrival.'

'So now you have both. You've done well,' Jordan said sourly. He hated doing business with middlemen. They were always ingratiating, duplicitous and arrogant. Being forced to use them made Jordan dislike himself. 'I'll see you this evening.'

The big man put down the phone and switched off the tape machine. It was important to have insurance.

He turned to look out over the gleaming white architecture of the palace, the elegant forms of the university and the rooftops of the extravagant villas. It was easy to admire the glinting white of the surfaces and ignore the decay beneath. As most of the Saudis were doing.

His smile curdled into a sardonic grin. Recent events had shaken them, the disturbances in Jeddah and M'dina, the scattered outbreaks of Fundamentalist terrorism from Kuwait down to Oman. Most of all the disintegration of the Syrian regime, torn by internal conflict and preoccupied with the situation on its eastern frontier. No longer able to play its role of area policeman, to act as their frontier guard against Israel.

He turned away from the window and walked into the bathroom, throwing off the kaftan. He pinched a handful of flesh at his waist and smiled at himself in the mirror. Life had been good to him since he had discovered how useful he could be to these people. It would soon become even better, with the Americans, too, so deeply in his debt. He began preparing for his appointment with the Prince. His Highness was a man worth preparing for. One of the very shrewdest and one of the most powerful of men.

The Ambassador glared at Bradman. He was so angry he could hardly speak. He made two tries before he was able to articulate anything. 'This is a fucking outrage! What the hell's going on? I'm a career man, not a goddamned sportswear manufacturer, given Paris to pay me off for campaign contributions. I should be handling a thing like this. What the hell do they suddenly want to close us down for?'

Bradman shrugged. 'No offence, Ambassador. Maybe the President has his reasons. He did mention to you that it had to be kept very confidential. The way things are over at State . . .' He let the sentence die, leaving the Ambassador to pick up the implication.

'But for Christ's sake, it's ridiculous. Closing down an embassy without even informing the State Department! It just can't be done that way.'

'It won't be. Things will carry on as normal here until we get every American we can assembled and ready to leave. When everything's set we'll inform State. Until then I'm sure you'll appreciate that you should hold off. After all, if the President called you personally you have to assume he would really value your cooperation.'

The Ambassador had already had the same idea himself; it was just that he could not stand Major Bradman. The Ambassador was a bureaucrat and liked it. As long as you had hierarchies everyone knew where they stood. Bradman unsettled him. He was too familiar with the marines, too relaxed with the staff, and too damned effective.

'And the Colter boy? What happens to him after we move out?'

'I'm doing all I can to get word of him before we pull out,' Bradman answered, his jaw muscles tightening. 'So is Norm. We've got every contact we have working on it.' He stood up. 'With your permission, Ambassador, I have to get this evacuation under way.' He gave a brusque nod and turned to the door. As he reached it, the Ambassador called after him.

'And what about the other hostages? What's going to happen to them after we pack our bags and leave, Major? Tell me that.'

Bradman turned, one hand gripping the door handle. 'That'll be up to the State Department, sir.' He walked out.

In his office he tossed his jacket over a chair and pulled at his tie. For half the morning they had been on emergency electrical supply, no air-conditioning. It was happening all the time now. The whole town was falling apart. What was left looked like being *blown* apart.

Before he had even finished his thought, the first crump of an explosion rattled the windows. The dirty cup on his desk tinkled musically as the rest of the bomb cluster hit in a rapid thump-thump-thump. He began counting. Right on cue, the aircraft barrelled past, climbing out over the sea, leaving its banshee scream behind it. Before the sound had died he felt the air vibrate from the explosion of the second plane's load. There was no need to take shelter.

Six planes in all, dumping their loads on Burj al Barajinah, and turning for home again. The whole mission taking no more than fifteen minutes from take-off in Israel to home again. He shook his head. All but the first load were a waste of time. From the time the first bomb exploded it took no more than fifteen seconds for the population of any one of the camps to be under cover. Everything after the first cluster was psychological warfare. It would cause further damage to the miserable homes and sad possessions but do nothing more, except to inflame the Palestinians further. It was not a kind of warfare Bradman understood. To him, if you used armaments you struck at targets they could damage. Otherwise you might as well drop leaflets and economize on the ordnance.

Blowing from the heat, he walked across to the refrigerator and pulled out a beer. It was tepid. A sudden thought made him exclaim. He thrust a hand into the freezer, pulled out a plastic bag and looked inside. The bag held the two pieces of finger and the portion of ear which they had received a few hours earlier. They were soft.

With an expression of loathing he threw the bag back into the freezer and slammed the door. That Ambassador really was an asshole. He had insisted on keeping the pieces to give them back to the sister in case the boy was never found. His mortal remains: two fingertips and a piece of ear. For Christ's sake. He took a long swig of beer and set it down on his desk.

He dragged a tired-looking pink folder from a drawer and tossed it onto the desk. Inside were a half-dozen sheets of paper, each bearing a handful of typed names and addresses. He flicked through the sheets. Over a third of the names were crossed through. Next to each deleted name was a comment, mostly 'Gone Away'. Several bore the word 'Dead'. Four of them were accompanied by a question mark. They were the four still presumed held hostage somewhere. He thumbed through the pages. Finding the name of Michael Colter he made a soft sniffing sound and reached for a felt-tipped pen. Very deliberately, he drew a line through the name. Next to it he put a careful question mark.

Twenty-two names remained. He knew all of them. Nineteen men and three women. Mostly journalists and teachers. A couple were elderly Arabists, scholars, more Lebanese by now than American. These two would never agree to leave. After fifty years they were not about to let themselves be run out of town over a detail like a civil war. In a way, he admired them, but they still had to go. He considered, looking for the lies that would get them onto the compound. A message from the President? Dinner with the Ambassador? Once on the compound he could *make* them go. Trouble was, neither of them gave a shit for the President, even less for the Ambassador. He would probably have to send a squad of marines for them. He was not going to be responsible for any spare-parts surgery on American citizens, however unwilling they were.

He began phoning.

20

HABIB'S SHIRT clung to him, showing the black coils of hair across his belly. He set a carton of beer down on the carpet and flicked sweat from his brow. He looked anxiously at Julia who stood by the wide-open window gnawing at a fingernail.

'Any news?'

She shook her head hard. 'They're trying,' she said bitterly. 'They've been trying for four hours!'

He shrugged. 'Be patient, Julia. It can take longer than that to call the airport.' He looked at his watch. 'I have to leave you. It's nearly opening time.' He slipped on a blazer and buttoned it absurdly tight across his paunch.

'Maybe you'll have better luck after two, when people take their afternoon rest.'

Habib had been gone more than two hours before the phone rang. Julia sprang to pick it up. The operator's voice was almost drowned in a cacophony of static. Through the clamour she heard the distant soft burr of the phone ringing in Tehran. Her mouth was quite dry. It was after two. It was quite possible the ministry would have closed for the day, war or no war.

A voice spoke incomprehensibly into her ear. She shouted, making each word utterly distinct. 'May I speak to Minister Bahrawi, please?'

A short silence and the voice came again, still indecipherable.

'Minister Bahrawi, please.' She was close to tears.

Another silence. Another voice, clearer, speaking English. 'Who are you calling?'

'Minister Bahrawi, Mehdi Bahrawi.' She did her best to imitate the Iranian pronunciation. More noise on the line was followed by yet a third voice. 'Who are you?'

'Julia Colter.' She was bellowing. 'The Minister knows me.'

Voices broke in on a crossed line, speaking French startlingly close, and faded again just as suddenly.

'Hello?'

'Mehdi!' She almost screamed the name. 'I'm so . . .'

He cut her off without ceremony. 'I can't speak.'

'But you must. I . . .'

'Where are you?'

'Beirut.'

The news did not seem to incline him to be warmer. 'Give me the number and wait there.'

Ray looked on in dismay as she gave the number and rang off.

'Jesus! You shouldn't have done that. You don't know *who* might have heard.'

She shrugged. 'He's our last hope of finding Michael.'

Ray stood at the window watching the street. The power cut continued. The street was in deep shadow now and it was almost impossible to make out the people below. Ray was jumpy. The phone call, Habib's taxi boy, or even Habib himself could all have betrayed them. The ringing of the phone made him start.

Julia snatched it up. At the sound of Bahrawi's voice she sank into a chair, sighing.

He lost no time in greetings. 'It's about your brother, I suppose.'

'You know about Michael?' Her voice was vibrant with hope.

'From the American papers. You've got good friends.'

'But do you *know* anything?'

'No, I don't,' he said flatly. He left her nothing to hope for.

Her voice began to crack. 'But can you help? Mehdi, you must. You're our last hope. At least help me meet the Hezbollah people.'

'Julia, the situation there's very delicate. If I could do anything to help get your brother released I would already have done it.'

'A meeting, Mehdi, please. It's the only thing I'll ever ask of you.' She did not even notice herself pleading.

He paused for so long she thought she had lost the line. 'You ask me to take an enormous risk. Things are very volatile here, too.'

'A meeting,' she insisted. 'Nothing more.'

Another long pause. 'I would have to tell people where to contact you. It could be very dangerous for you, after last night.'

'We can explain about Rachid.'

'You wouldn't get the opportunity. Where are you?' She gave him the address. 'Don't move from there. Goodbye, Julia.'

Ray grimaced. 'So?'

'There's something wrong. I'm sure there is. He sounded so reluctant to talk.'

'He's got a lot to be reluctant about. An Iranian minister helping free an American hostage?'

'It was more than that. He seemed almost afraid.'

Ray lifted a beer to his lips. 'Me, too.'

By eight o'clock the street below was in total darkness. Julia sat by the open window in the unlit room watching the occasional noisy passage of a jeep or group of hurrying armed figures. From away to her right the low booming of the artillery came much more clearly than during the chaos of the day, with its traffic and the insistent horns. Against this background there were frequent sharp splashes of a much clearer, higher-pitched sound, the sound of hand-held weapons, fired in single shots, or, more often, in undisciplined bursts. Some of them were very close at hand.

A short distance away, behind the building opposite where she sat, an explosion had been followed by the glow of a fire. Sirens had wailed briefly, cut short by gunfire. Since then the glow had grown brighter as the fire raged unchecked. It may have been part of the war. It may have been someone burning down a rival's property in a vendetta over some trivial insult. Or both. In Beirut the lines were blurred.

In the deeper shadow between two buildings a few yards down the street something moved. She strained to see it. Light glinted on something. Very faintly, she made out the outline of a vehicle. Figures flitted around the cab.

Keeping her voice down to little more than a hiss, she called to Ray. He came out of the bathroom at a run, lather on his face and Habib's razor in his hand. He stared down at the spot to which she pointed.

A figure detached itself from the shadows and ran across the road, losing itself again in the darkness at the bottom of their building. Two more followed. They could make out further silhouettes, deeper black against the shadow around the truck.

They craned forward, trying to see the base of the building below them. Julia thought she caught the sound of a low voice and then a brief gargling cry.

Neither of them doubted the men were coming for them. They would already be on their way up the stairs. The throb of the artillery had died away, to be replaced by the pounding in their own temples.

At the rasp of the doorbell Julia gave a single convulsive shudder. She turned from the window.

'I'll go. If it's Mehdi's men they'll be expecting a woman. If it's Rachid's people it won't matter.'

She put a hand on the door latch. Hesitating, she looked back at Ray. He stood in the middle of the living room, watching her, his hands slack at his sides. The lather provoked in her an incongruous urge to laugh. Another ring at the doorbell quelled it. She turned the latch.

The door flew open under the weight of the two men. One

pinioned Julia to the wall. His breath made her wince. The other ran to where Ray stood motionless, his hands spread to show they were empty. The men frisked them. Julia tried not to flinch at the lubricious thoroughness of the search. Reluctantly, the man withdrew his hands and stepped away from her. Only his eyes were visible above the headcloth wrapped tightly around his face. They were very dark, almost black, with deposits of grit in the corners, at each side of the very narrow bridge of his nose. The feel of his gaze on her was as unpleasant as the feel of his hands.

Ray came into the hallway propelled by the snout of the other man's rifle. He was pushed into position alongside Julia. The two men wore uniforms of camouflage material and good boots. Each carried insignia at the shoulder, one of them a single rectangle of yellow felt, roughly sewn on; the other, two pieces of the same material. Taking it that the extra piece of felt was a badge of authority, Julia spoke to the second man.

'Who are you?' she asked. His eyes showed no understanding. 'Are you from Hezbollah? *Etes-vous* Hezbollah?' The man's stare did not change. '*Vous*,' she said, pointing at both of them. 'Hezbollah? Sunnite?' Maybe it was her accent. The officer looked back at her blankly for another moment and then spoke a single word. His own accent was so thick it took her a while to recognize her own name.

'Come.' He pulled open the door and signalled her to leave. Ray made to follow her. The man next to him said something sharply to him in Arabic and pushed him back. Julia spun around at Ray's protest. Striding back into the hallway she took his arm.

'We go together.'

The officer looked at her blankly for a moment and then gave a sharp command. A third man came in from the landing. The officer spoke again. Without a word the newcomer stepped across to Ray and drove stiffened fingers into his abdomen. Ray made a soft squealing sound and folded to the floor. The two men took Julia's arms and dragged her out of the door. She twisted to look back. Ray lay on his side, silently vomiting beer.

By the time they reached the bottom of the stairs Julia had stopped protesting. As they hurried through the dark lobby she saw a figure sprawled inside the door. It was the older security guard. His face wore his most lascivious grin. A dark crescent beneath his chin mimicked the grin. A stain, gleaming wetly, spread across the pale marble of the floor.

The leading man examined the street. He waited, drawing back into the shadow of a pair of ornamental orange trees beside the entrance, until a patrol of three men had passed. With a brusque movement of his head he urged them forward. The two gunmen hustled Julia out of the building. As they passed the shrub behind which the third man stood she caught sight of the younger security guard. He sat against the wall with his knees drawn up and his gun across them. His head rested on his chest. The dark patch at the crutch of his khaki fatigues, where he had soiled himself in death, was the only sign he was not asleep.

They ran hard across the deserted road to where the truck waited, surrounded by hard-faced young soldiers. Julia's escort pushed her into the back of the truck and piled in beside her, together with two other uniformed men. The sound of another engine starting came out of the darkness.

The engine of their own truck started up. A dim light came on inside. Julia glanced quickly around her. From outside, the van looked like any of the city's dilapidated vans. Inside, it was different. Benches ran across the front and along the sides. The windows in the sides and the back doors were hinged so that they could be opened up completely. Rocket-launchers and heavy machine guns stood in racks against the walls. To anybody stopping them at a roadblock it was an ordinary delivery van. They would get a very nasty surprise.

One of the soldiers stood and motioned her to the front. Like the others, he wore a cloth wound tightly over his face. His eyes glinted with hostility.

'Your papers,' he said harshly, in English.

She pulled her passport from a pocket and handed it to him. He examined it shrewdly, holding it close to the light. Apparently satisfied, he grunted and shoved it back into her hand.

'Look,' Julia said, standing up and moving closer to him. 'Who are you? Hezbollah? Rachid Hamoun's people? Where are you taking me?' The man stared wordlessly back at her. 'Speak, for Christ's sake!' she said. Almost sobbing with frustration, she raised a hand as though to strike him on the chest. The man raised his own hand, placed spread fingers on Julia's shirt front and shoved her sharply back into her seat. As he did so, he spoke negligently over his shoulder to the other men. One of them sprang forward carrying a soft canvas bag with drawstring fastenings. Not speaking, he pushed the bag over her head and tied the drawstrings.

Julia wept soundlessly.

Michael's frustration was bitter. The progress he had made in the early stages had given him false hope. The crumbling mortar at the spot where he had begun had given way to sound material embedded with tiny flints, which resisted his crude tool.

Throughout the day he had not dared to dig. He had spent most of the time on the mattress. Much of the time he dozed. During the waking periods he fought the boredom by devising isometric exercises. His existence had quickly divided into two separate parts. On the one hand was his determination to be free. On the other the need to confront the probability of indefinite confinement, possibly for years. The exercises, designed to keep him in shape with a minimum expenditure of energy, were a part of facing up to the latter.

His constant fear was of another visit from the hooded man. The fear above all that they would damage his good hand. If they did so it would be impossible to dig any more. Already, the injured hand had begun hurting again, sending white-hot barbs of pain deep into his brain whenever he tried to use it.

Some time during the day, not long after he had woken from the exhausted sleep that had followed his previous night's efforts, he had been aware of a disturbance beyond the cell door. He had thought he heard the faint ringing of a telephone and voices raised in angry altercation. For a while, then, he had been very frightened. But the sound had died away and no-one had come until the evening, when they had brought him food and fresh water.

He attacked the wall with fresh vigour, gouging at the stone-hard mortar. He forced himself to keep his hopes in check, to regard each minute stone or tiny cascade of greyish powder, not as evidence of the daunting task that remained, but as a small stepping stone to be laid beside the ones before, on the path to escape.

He was able to dig for only a few minutes at a time. After that, violent trembling and perspiration forced him to rest until the sensation passed. He wondered if it were a result of his wounds or if it were connected to the cluster of painful, angry, red bumps low on his back which he had discovered when he had awakened that day. They looked like insect bites, with pus-filled heads that oozed and bled from scratching. He promised himself that before going to sleep that night he would scour every inch of the cell in an effort to unearth the culprit.

The trembling fit passed. He went on sitting for a few moments longer, fighting to prevent despair taking hold. Briefly, he allowed himself to wonder again what purpose he was serving for his captors; what demands they were making of whom. He thought, too, of Julia. She was the only family he had. Certainly, she would be trying to mobilize people. He smiled at the thought. The Congressman or bureaucrat who tried to put Julia off with platitudes would be in for a major shock.

The smile turned to a sour little laugh. The other hostages held in Lebanon probably had their leverage, too. Families to bombard their Congressmen with letters; wives and children to appear, distraught, on nationwide television. None of it had ever done any good. They kept up the pressure for a while, but people got tired. They became immersed in their own problems. The families stopped writing. The wives, obliged to feed the children, found jobs. The hostages remained hostages. Julia would not tire of trying. But the power structure would tire of her. Laboriously, he pushed himself to his knees again.

21

THEY DROVE for what she estimated to be half an hour, travelling slowly. Once, the firecracker sound of an automatic weapon made her duck instinctively. There was no response from the van. It was probably just someone in the street letting off steam. The smell of gunsmoke made her feel faintly sick. Mostly, though, she just felt scared and lonely. A hood makes you feel terribly lonely.

The van stopped abruptly amid a sudden clamour of voices. She was pulled roughly from her seat and out of the van. A hand groped between her thighs. Spitting abuse she lashed out with her foot. She had the satisfaction of hearing a cry and feeling the hand snatched away as her foot raked a shin-bone. A fist to her stomach folded her over.

She braced herself for more blows when a voice called sharply. Voices close to her grumbled and the hood was pulled off. Blinking, she was pushed into a jeep. In almost pitch-blackness she could just distinguish the outline of several vehicles.

'I apologize for all that.' The voice came from her right. She turned to face the speaker. Her eyes were growing used to the starlight. She saw a tall, middle-aged man with thick glasses smiling at her. 'I'm afraid Americans are not permitted to learn our routes out of the city.'

She shrugged. 'Who are you?'

'Hassan did not tell you?'

'If he's the one who had my friend beaten up he told me nothing. He didn't speak at all.'

The man pursed his lips. 'Hmm, I'm sorry. He's one of those who despise Americans. There are many here who feel the same. In fact, you should be very careful, Miss Colter. In your place I would go away as soon as possible, out of Lebanon.'

'I appreciate the advice. You still haven't told me who you are.'

'Hezbollah. Fighters of the Integrationist Alliance. We're followers of Sheik Mukhtar Hussein. That's who we're taking you to see. Didn't you know?'

'Not exactly. I'm honoured.' She meant it. Mukhtar Hussein was the most important of the Shi-ite warlords who controlled the north of the country. He had managed to unite, however temporarily, the major players among the splintered factions of the Shi-ite Moslems, just as Rachid had done, before his death, with the Sunnis. With the help of Iran he had become a major force in the Lebanese power game. 'Mehdi didn't say who I'd be meeting.'

The man's eyes narrowed. 'Mehdi? Bahrawi.'

'That's right.'

The man's manner became deferential. 'We're on our way to Bcharré, Miss Colter. To Mukhtar Hussein's base.'

She raised her eyebrows and waved a hand, indicating the surrounding countryside. 'Is that safe?'

'Not on the highway.'

Almost as he spoke the jeep lurched off the road onto a rock-strewn track.

The wild bucking of the jeep grew worse. They were moving further inland, climbing the first slopes that spread like ribs from the spine of mountains that ran the length of the country, dividing the fertile coastal strip from the Bequaa Valley.

They covered several kilometres without incident. In the

villages they passed through, the only signs of life were the incongruous blue flicker of televisions and the quick shapes of rats. It was a comment on the discipline of her escort that nobody fired at the rats. Most of the country's armed rabbles would have been unable to resist.

They pulled out of maybe the fourth village in a roar of gears and began a steeper climb into the hills. A violent red light outlined the mountains ahead. It was some seconds before she realized it was not a fire but the moon rising. She was gazing, riveted, at the perfection of it when the first mortar bomb struck. It landed just in front and to one side of the leading jeep, flipping it onto its back.

The years of covering combat had left Julia with good instincts. Before the noise of the blast had died she was over the side of the jeep and running, zigzag, for shelter. Even as she ran she changed her mind about moonrises. The light made her feel very conspicuous.

She threw herself down close to a boulder as another explosion shook the ground. Beyond the line of jeeps, she could see men fanned out, prone, in a semicircle, taking expert advantage of the long shadows cast by the low moon.

She heard the thump of a fourth bomb being launched. It was accompanied by a brief lightening in a stand of pines two hundred metres away. The soldiers had seen it too. A dozen dark silhouettes were on their feet and running for the spot.

A deafening exchange of fire, the rattle of machine guns, the whoosh of rockets and the dry crackle of rifles lasted no more than four seconds. As Julia's senses cleared she saw two men with their hands behind their heads being driven towards them. She got to her feet and joined the group converging on the undamaged jeeps.

The officer stood surveying the overturned jeep. Two men lay pinioned in the wreckage. Three more lay brokenly around it. Only one of them moved. His face was a bloodied pulp. The officer turned to confront the two captives.

They were very young, perhaps thirteen or fourteen. Their faces held no fear, only a kind of fanatic defiance. The officer punched the taller one, very hard, in the face. The smaller boy flinched as the officer made to do the same to him. Instead, the man feinted and then brought his knee smashing into the the boy's groin. The youth collapsed next to his companion and lay inert. The officer pulled out his pistol from its holster and shot them both through the head.

The convoy pulled away leaving the wreck and the dead men where they lay. It was ten minutes before Julia was sick, suddenly and violently, over the side of the jeep.

'Are you not well, Miss Colter?' The officer asked as Julia, ashen-faced, pulled herself upright.

She looked at him in blank amazement. 'You just shot those two men down in cold blood. It was horrible.'

He frowned, not understanding. 'But they were Druze,' he said reasonably.

She covered her eyes and hung her head. She knew what he meant. She knew that the Druze, though Moslem, were bitter enemies of Hezbollah. She knew so much about it all; the origins of the Druze sect through the prophets Hamza and Darrazi, sent out by the Caliph of Cairo eight hundred years ago to spread the new doctrine; their belief that each newborn Druze housed the soul of a predecessor. She was familiar with the Shi-ites' hostility to the other forms of Islam. She knew all this. It was just that none of it made the slightest sense. She sobbed softly.

The jeeps roared on, pitching wildly over stream beds and broken ground. They stopped after half an hour in a plantation of conifers. Lights crawled on a road ahead of them.

The four men sent to investigate returned cheerful. The traffic was a detachment of the *official* Lebanese Army. The officer smiled and gave an order. The convoy plunged across the road, knowing the Army would not dare interfere.

They crossed the almost-dry bed of the Nahr el Kelb, one of the rivers that watered the coastal plain, and picked up speed. Over Julia's right shoulder the seven-thousand-feet peaks of Mount Lebanon glinted in the moonlight. Incongruously, silhouetted against the skyline, stood the angular outline of a ski-lift. It would be a long time before the tourists returned to ski on Lebanon's slopes.

The convoy followed the contour of the mountainside, confident of the territory. They crossed the Zahle road and shortly afterwards hit the highway from Baalbek to the coast. They swung onto the road. Here, Shi-ite control was total.

They sped over the crumbling asphalt through deserted villages, dilapidated places of low houses with rusting corrugated roofs.

The names of the villages were daubed in Arabic and sometimes in English on boards or oil drums. Julia recognized none of them until they reached Afqa. That one made her shudder. Less than a year earlier two German journalists had been kidnapped there. They had been found three days later in Beirut, alive but partially flayed.

Beyond Afqa the road wound along the shoulder of the mountain for a couple of kilometres before merging with a better, metalled one. The metalling ran out just across the Ibrahim river bridge at the approach to Aaquora. A bullet-scarred sign exhorted tourists to take advantage of the skiing and visit the Roman ruins. It made no mention of the chance to get flayed alive.

After a few more kilometres the majestic shelving cedar trees gave way to pines. A sign indicated Bcharré to be eleven kilometres further. The road rose steeply through a series of hair-raising bends until they reached a checkpoint. The makeshift barrier would have stopped a runaway train.

Her escort exchanged loud banter with the soldiers on the checkpoint. One by one the soldiers found an excuse to pass close by the jeep to peer, sniggering, at Julia. The barrier rose to let them through. As they passed under the steel bar one of the guards pointed at Julia and pawed at his groin, provoking his companions to a paroxysm of laughter.

The road ran clear of the trees and widened out into a large square. Military vehicles of all types were parked there. Uniformed men stood or squatted in clusters, smoking and talking, their weapons held carelessly at their sides. They stopped talking and stared as the convoy passed.

Around the square the buildings were low, two- or three-storey, mostly of a sturdy wooden construction. Behind the buildings a swathe had been cleared in the trees and an idle ski-lift stretched away towards the snowcap. They drew up in front of the biggest of the buildings. It was a substantial stone-built hotel with a shingled roof, designed to impersonate an alpine chalet. Most of the shutters were tightly closed.

The officer accompanied Julia up the steps. Two surly guards went through the routine of examining her papers, yawning ostentatiously.

The reception area of the hotel looked like the aftermath of an earthquake. All over the floor men slept, wrapped in blankets and snoring violently. Gear and weapons lay in haphazard heaps beside them. Close by the reception desk a group of four men crouched over a spirit stove, brewing tea and laughing softly as they passed around a loosely rolled cigarette. Julia smiled gently to herself as she caught the sweet smell of the smoke.

The officer picked a path among the prostrate bodies and mounted the broad stairs to the first floor. As they turned into the corridor three alert guards stopped them. Once again she showed her passport. The officer was made to show his papers, too. The two of them were thoroughly searched. The search included removing their footwear, which was carefully examined for concealed weapons. With courteous smiles and bows the men handed them back their boots and spoke to the officer. Nodding, he led the way into a room.

Two men sat cross-legged in the middle of the dimly lit room, facing each other and talking animatedly. They stopped talking and rose. One wore the dark gown and turban of a mullah. The other was in military fatigues with a sports jacket thrown over his shoulders. Both wore the customary thick black fuzz which was more than stubble but not yet a beard. Each of them embraced the officer, holding him to them for several seconds and clapping him repeatedly on the spine as though he were a long-lost son returning to the family home. They bowed solemnly to Julia. With a muttered word of excuse the older of the men, the mullah, left the room, his slippers making a soft swishing sound on the carpet. The remaining man nodded at the officer. The officer made as though to speak, thought better of it under the other's powerful gaze, turned, and left the room.

'So you are Miss Colter,' he said civilly. 'I am Sheik Mukhtar Hussein.' He held out a hand to Julia. 'You're here to seek help for your brother?'

Julia nodded eagerly. 'Yes.'

He sighed. 'Then I'm afraid, Miss Colter, you're wasting your time.'

22

GERRY GREELEY checked into the motel wearing stained overalls, a Texaco baseball cap and steel-rimmed glasses. He signed the register, using the name of a man he had once known, and handed over twenty-five dollars in exchange for the key. The woman at the desk examined the money furtively. She had long ago learned to distrust anyone who spent the night at her motel.

In the room he threw off the glasses and cap and changed into a pair of crisp dark-blue linen slacks, a fresh white shirt and a cotton sports jacket. He hoped Tom Jordan would not want to talk walking around the block. The clothes were wrong for a Washington November. He pulled a half-empty bottle of scotch from his bag and poured some into the plastic toothglass. He drank off a slug and grimaced, not at the taste of the whisky but at the taste of the plastic. His watch showed nine-thirty. He flicked on the television and settled down to wait.

He was on his second scotch and a woman on the television was becoming hysterical at the prospect of owning a food blender when a black car turned into the forecourt. The headlights flashed once as they were killed, as though by accident. Nobody got out of the car. He put down his glass, grabbed his bag and left the room. The lady on the television was sobbing, unable to cope with success.

Tom Jordan sat at the wheel of the darkened car. 'Hi, Gerry. Do you have your car here?' Nothing in Jordan's manner indicated they were old friends who had not seen each other in over a year. Gerry jerked a thumb at the Honda. 'Follow me, then. You can leave it at a lot down the road.'

He drove out past the hissing signs that gave a hint of reptilian menace to the neon promises of free coffee and colour TV in every room, and followed the big car to the parking lot of a shopping mall. He locked up the pick-up and climbed in next to Jordan.

'What's new, Tom?'

'I've got some flying for you.'

'Flying what?'

'An F16.'

Greeley whistled softly. 'Where?'

'Lebanon.'

Greeley's eyes widened. 'Wouldn't it make more sense to use the Israelis?'

'They're not being told about it.'

Greeley frowned. 'In their backyard? Who is?'

'You. Me. Maybe five good friends in the Middle East.'

'State? The CIA?'

Jordan shook his head. 'Just the people I mentioned.'

'The President?' He waited for Jordan's answer. He did not get one. He gave himself a few seconds to grasp the implications. 'Jesus.'

'He *approves*, Gerry. Trust me.'

Trusting in Tom Jordan had saved Gerry Greeley's life. Twice. Nevertheless, this thing gave him the shivers. 'Don't you think you ought to tell me what the fuck's going on here?'

'Let's start with the Saudi F16 that disappeared last week. You saw the story?'

'Yeah. The pilot was some Fundamentalist nut. Defected to Iran. Took the machine over with him.'

Jordan grinned. 'That was the story. We've got a better one. Try this. It wasn't the Fundamentalists that got the plane but a bunch of *Israeli* nuts. The back-to-the-Old-Testament longhairs. Divide their time between studying the Talmud and torching Arab villages.' He grinned at Greeley.

'I don't get it.'

'They wanted the plane to hit a Shi-ite base in Lebanon. They hired a pilot, a mercenary.' He grinned again at Greeley. His eyes did not take part in the fun.

'Shit,' Greeley said slowly. 'That's me. Where's the base?'

'I doubt if you've heard of it. Some dump called Bcharré.'

23

THE MOON had gone. The only light now was from the stars and the many tiny fires that studded the square. Julia shuddered and drew the blanket closer around her. The faint light gleamed on the wetness of her cheeks. She had been crying for a long time.

It was impossible. She had not allowed herself even to entertain the possibility that Mukhtar Hussein would know nothing. He was the man the whole Shi-ite alliance regarded as their leader, outside of Iran. Hezbollah, Islamic Jihad, even Amal, whose natural allies were the Syrians, all looked to him for guidance. Between them all, they had spies and informers in every village, every town. On every block, on every street, every alley, in the parts of the country they controlled. If Michael were being held by anybody in Mukhtar's area he would absolutely *certainly* have heard something. A rumour. A whisper. And anything would have been better than the flat denial he had given her.

She pictured his face as he had spoken, scrutinizing the image in her mind, hearing the voice in her head, looking for some sign that the man had been concealing something.

She knew that *taquiya*, the form of institutionalized duplicity that was so much a part of the Shi-ite creed, and so difficult for Westerners to comprehend, would have allowed him to lie to her without the slightest qualm, if the lie served his own purpose. Even allowing for that, he had seemed quite sincere.

If he had made any attempt to pretend to care one way or the other about Michael's fate, or to sympathize with her, she would have suspected his sincerity. As it was, he had plainly not given a damn. Like so many of the Shi-ites she had met over the years he regarded everything Western with contempt. Western people, Western morals, Western values, Western goods. They were just not worth the bother of lying.

No. Mukhtar simply did not know. The plain, unbearable truth was that he had been her last hope. And now it was gone.

She had tried. She had contacted all the principal groupings. None of them could help her. For the first time in her life she had to admit that her brother was beyond her help. All his life, through his childhood, through college and into his manhood, Michael had always turned first to her. They had trusted each other, been closer than either of them had ever been to their parents. Julia had taught him so much. She thought of the uncountable hours she had spent helping him, an eager four-year-old, to read. She had taught him to swim, in those summers at the beach close to the house. She had been the one who had given him his interest in the larger world outside America. That same interest that had led him to Lebanon! She dabbed the tears away and got up from the bed. Pulling the blanket closer around her she moved to the big window. She slid the glass aside and stepped out onto the balcony.

Below her, most of the fires had died to red smudges. The dark shapes of tents and the smaller patches of shadow where men slept rolled in blankets almost filled the square. A few of the fires still burned brightly. Around those, men clustered, playing dice or backgammon and talking in loud, argumentative gutturals. Always, near the players, lay guns.

Without warning, she was swept by a wave of blackest despair. Tears welled, spilling unchecked down her cheeks. She was sick and tired of the guns, of the mindless violence, the adolescent machismo. Suddenly, everything to do with the country made her nerves jangle. The language, coming to her in indecipherable, hacking rasps from below, the quickness to take offence, the swaggering, misplaced pride. The whole culture seemed suddenly hostile and alien.

A sense of overwhelming loneliness flooded her. She thought of Ray and the way they had hurt him. The thought of him brought with it a sudden pang. It came as a shock to find how desperately she was wishing he were with her. It came to her for the first time, with a blinding impact, that he had not come to Lebanon for the story. The realization made her laugh through her tears. Blinking, she turned from the balcony and stepped back into the room.

She woke with a start. She was spread-eagled on the bed, the blanket still around her shoulders. It was still dark. A glance at her watch told her it was three-thirty. With a groan, she got to her feet and began to undress. As she did so she was aware of a commotion in the square outside. It must have been that which had woken her. Over the shouting came a tremendous clattering roar. She recognized the sound of a helicopter and crossed quickly to the window.

Lights were on in the square, picking out a patch of ground thirty metres square. A helicopter was just settling to rest in the illuminated space.

She watched as armed men ran to take up positions, forming an avenue from the helicopter to the steps of the hotel. Mukhtar bounded down the steps and strode to the machine. The door of the helicopter was on the far side, hidden from Julia's sight. She saw Mukhtar throw his arms wide and enfold the slight figure that emerged from behind the machine. They kissed each other several times on each cheek. The visitor withdrew from the embrace a fraction earlier than Mukhtar.

Julia started. She leaned forward, gripping the rail of the balcony, hardly able to believe her eyes. The visitor turned towards the building. His face was perfectly clear in the light. Unable to contain herself she waved an arm above her head. Her voice was cracking with excitement.

'Mehdi!'

24

JULIA WAS already halfway along the corridor when the robed figure strode into sight with two guards scurrying at his heels. She made as though to throw her arms around him. He stopped her with a frown and a shake of his head. She offered her hand. He shook it decorously.

He nodded towards her door. 'Let's go to your room, Julia. We need to talk quietly.'

She led the way into the room. He followed her, motioning to the guards to remain outside. He left the door ajar. Immediately he was out of sight of the two guards his severe expression melted into a grin. With a glance at the door she threw her arms around him and planted a long kiss on his cheek. He returned her embrace and then, slowly, he disengaged himself. His grin had gone. His face was grave again.

'How are you, Julia?'

She shrugged and gave a little, breathy laugh. 'Well, it's *great* to see you, anyway. I can hardly believe it. Why didn't you *say* you were going to be here?'

He sighed, no longer smiling. 'On the phone, Julia, from there?' He shook his head. 'Since the Imam's death one must be very careful. Very careful indeed. There's so much happening there. More than anybody outside realizes.'

'How do you mean? What sort of thing?'

Bahrawi hesitated, glancing towards the door. When he spoke his voice was almost a whisper. 'There must be changes there, Julia. It's become completely crazy. We have no friends left in the world. We're at war, or on the brink of war, with half our neighbours. We've lost thousands, hundreds of thousands, of our children. The economy's ruined. Somebody has to act. A few of us think we can carry the country with us.'

She stared at him. 'A coup? You plan to take over the place?'

He nodded. 'Not just me. There are others.'

'Ready to stage a coup? Against Khomeini's heirs?'

'That's right. It's time. Imam Khomeini did very many good things for Iran.' He held up a hand at her attempt to interject. 'I know it's difficult for an American to appreciate, but it's true. Without him we would never have been rid of that posturing imbecile of a Shah. As well as the materialistic society he had imported from you.' He laughed at Julia's new effort to protest. 'I mean it. People were praying for someone to restore our religious traditions. He did that. It's what the people wanted.'

'Did your women want to be forced back into purdah?'

He spread his hands. 'It all went further than I would personally feel was right. You shouldn't forget, though, a lot of our women *welcome* the return of the veil.'

'How about the return to hostage-taking?'

He ignored the vehemence in her voice. 'You know very well, Julia, that's also an old Islamic tradition. It's typical Western arrogance for your people to come here and expect to impose their own rules, as though you were the British running their empire. Our traditions apply here. Out here taking hostages has always been a legitimate form of warfare. We don't have to apologize for it.'

'Even if it's the brother of a friend?'

He was finally stung. 'We don't have Michael! Understand that.' He lowered his voice again. 'Sheik Mukhtar gave me his word. Your brother's not being held by any group we control.'

'How about Shi-ites who aren't part of the alliance? Would he know?'

'Probably. His network's very good, all over Lebanon. Even down in the south, among Haddad's militia, right to the Israeli frontier, he has his people. He knows virtually everything that goes on.' He placed an arm gently around Julia's shoulders. 'No, Julia. I'm afraid the most likely explanation is the one that it's appeared to be all along, that Michael has been taken by a small group of renegades with no real allegiance to anyone. They'll be totally unpredictable. I'm sorry.'

'But, do you *really* believe Mukhtar?' she said desperately, unwilling to see her last hopes fade. 'Would he have any reason to tell you the truth? He detests Americans.'

He smiled. 'It's nothing personal. He has no reason *not* to hate Americans. Mukhtar's family used to be big farmers in Palestine. Next to the British he blames America for all that's happened since. He understands the Israelis. It's the West he hates, for betraying Palestine. As to why he'd tell me the truth, it's very simple. We pay him.' He paused, smiling at the surprise in her face. 'That's right. Without the support we give Mukhtar the whole alliance, the entire Shi-ite effort here, would just fade away.' His voice dropped still lower. 'But all that's irrelevant.'

'How's that?'

'Because whatever he may think of Americans, kidnapping one right now would be absolutely against his own interests. His people have the *strictest* instructions not to get involved in anything like that.'

She stared at him. 'Mehdi,' she said slowly, 'you didn't come here just to see me. What the hell's going on? What are you *doing* here?'

'I can't tell you. Not yet. What I can tell you is there's almost certainly nothing more you can do to help your brother. Whoever it is that's holding him will choose to release him, keep him, or perhaps kill him, and there's nothing at all you can do about it.'

Julia lowered herself heavily onto the bed and sank her head in her hands. She began alternately crying and cursing. Bahrawi came close and stooped to comfort her, only to shy away, flushing, as his eyes fell on the flesh exposed by her unbuttoned shirt. He turned and took a few steps around the room, silently stroking his beard, waiting for the crying to pass.

'Look, Julia,' he said as her sobbing subsided, 'there may be one thing you could do that might just *improve* Michael's chances.'

She looked up at him, her face streaked with tears. 'What? I'll do *anything* that might help.'

Bahrawi hesitated as though reluctant to speak. Then, seeming to reach a decision, he pulled a chair close to her and sat down.

'Look, I have to explain some things to you. If my friends and I are going to succeed in what we are trying to do we've got to carry the people with us. If we don't we'll have a virtual civil war on our hands. None of us wants that. Personally, if I thought that would be the price of our actions I'd leave things as they are.'

'Wouldn't that be better anyway? Wait until things really fall apart, then try to be the ones to pick up the pieces?'

'Of course we could do that. We could sit it out and await a better opportunity. Only, if we wait, thousands more of our young men will join those who have already died in the war. We want to act now. It's crucial, though, that the people see us as patriots. Heroes, if you like. Of course, we cannot seek to be respected as the Imam Khomeini was,' he added in a conditioned reflex of respect. 'But we must be at least, well, credible. You follow me?'

'I guess so. How does your being in Lebanon fit into this?'

'I can't tell you that, Julia, I'm sorry. In another day or two you'll know anyway.'

'Look, I appreciate what you're trying to do, but what does

it have to do with Michael? You said I could do something that might help him.'

He nodded gravely. 'I think you can.' He lowered his voice to little more than a whisper. 'As you know,' he said with a quick flash of humour in his eyes, 'we are not as traditional in all matters as these clothes sometimes lead people to expect. One area where we're quite sophisticated is intelligence gathering, both electronically and by buying information.' He smiled ironically. 'Another old Middle-Eastern custom. Baksheesh. We have good reason to believe the United States is preparing some kind of action in the Gulf. We think it can only be directed against Iran, or our supporters. And it's imminent.'

'Why would we be doing that? What kind of action?'

He snorted softly. 'Why? Because in a few days from now your country goes to the polls. What other reason do you need? Hurting us would be very popular. It could only help Mr Foreman's cause.' He paused and studied her face. 'Whatever they're planning it *must not* take place. It would rally people to the current leaders just at the moment they're beginning to question. It *must* be prevented.'

'What do you imagine I can do?' Julia asked, genuinely puzzled. 'Ask the *Times* to publish a story telling the Government to be nice to Iran so you can carry out a coup?'

'Hardly, Julia,' he said sardonically. 'I want you to return to Beirut. You know Major Bradman, at your embassy?'

She snorted and nodded.

'Well, we know he's the man with the best connections to the White House.'

'Bradman? He's the security man. Makes sure the windows are locked.'

'He's more than that, Julia, believe me. If you could persuade him that it would be a mistake, really convince him, I don't think the raid, or whatever it is, would happen.'

'How does this help Michael?' Julia asked.

Bahrawi grimaced. 'Julia, even if I don't know who's holding your brother, it's only realistic to assume it's people sympathetic to us. For God's sake, nobody else *takes* hostages now,' he added with sudden candour. 'If we're right about that, then any attack on us only increases the chances of Michael turning up in a gutter somewhere.' He looked squarely at Julia, his eyes sorrowful. 'It's happened many, many times before.'

She stared back at him, her face quite blank. Moisture gathered in the corners of her eyes. Then, without warning she sprang at him, clawing at his face. 'You asshole!' she screamed. 'You double-dealing fucking bastard!' He fell backwards onto the carpet with Julia on top of him, trying to protect himself from the raking nails. 'You lying, unscrupulous asshole!' She continued screaming epithets and clawing at his face.

Recovering, he managed to snatch her wrists. He forced her hands away from his face, obliged to use every ounce of his strength to contain her rage. The door swung open. One of the guards stared into the room. With a shout, he began to run at them. A word from Bahrawi stopped him in his tracks. The man stared at them for several seconds, totally bewildered, before backing reluctantly out of the room.

It was some seconds before her anger subsided. Slowly she climbed off him and sat down on the bed, sobbing and shaking. Bahrawi climbed shakily to his feet, dabbing at the blood which welled from three parallel scratches on his cheek.

Julia looked up at him. Her face was smeared with tears. 'I'm sorry. Why didn't you let the guards handle me?'

He shrugged and turned to the window, dabbing at the scratches with a handkerchief. He stood for several seconds contemplating the scene outside, the bustle of preparations for the newly dawned day. Very slowly, as though he were suddenly terribly tired, he turned to face Julia. He did not smile or try to explain himself. He spoke in a voice that was low and oddly gentle.

'Will you talk to Major Bradman?'

Julia looked up at him. For a second she was ready to be

angry again. Realizing the futility of it, she put the anger aside. 'You leave me no choice, do you?'

He sighed. 'I suppose not, Julia. I'll arrange an escort for tonight. For today, please stay in this room.' With a short inclination of his head, he left the room.

Michael was surprised to find grey light from the grating casting its chequered pattern on the floor, so absorbed was he. The frustration of the previous night had given way to elation. After two or three hours of painstaking, almost fruitless, scraping, his progress had suddenly accelerated as he had struck another patch of rotting mortar. In a matter of a couple of hours or so during the middle part of the night he had almost cleared a complete block. There had been a moment of pure jubilation when he had felt a tiny draught of cool air flutter through the crack and cool his face, despite his efforts not to penetrate the last quarter of an inch. He had no idea what lay on the other side of the wall. Any gap visible from outside could easily betray him.

The debris was becoming a problem. Some he distributed around the cell, treading it into the floor, masking its fresh colour. Some he used to mix with the food to make his dummy mortar. He pushed the small stones deep into slits in the mattress.

As soon as he became aware of the dawn light he began hurriedly plugging the last three inches or so of the cavity with the malleable fake mortar. Over the last nights he had been filling the gap as he went. In the event of an unexpected visit, the slightest sound beyond the door, it took only seconds to fill the remaining aperture and replace the spike in the wall.

He crossed the room and scattered the last palmful of dust, shuffling his feet to obliterate all trace of it. He walked, almost jauntily, back to the mattress, pushed the spike into its place in the wall, and knelt down. He had left a half-inch of the cavity unfilled. He bent his eye to the spot. It was the place where earlier in the night he had felt the cold air-current. He almost cried out in excitement. A few inches from his eye, daylight streamed in, momentarily dazzling him. As his eye became accustomed to the light he was able to make out a patch of wall across what he decided must be a street. He straightened and began filling the hole. It was what he had needed to know, that the cell adjoined a street, not another room in which more gunmen might be waiting.

He yawned mightily. The depression of the last days had given way to an extraordinary feeling of euphoria. Once again he felt in control of his life. He stretched out on the mattress and closed his eyes. As he fell asleep, he was half aware, as though already dreaming, of sounds from the outer room.

Beyond the door the guards looked up expectantly at the tall man. One of them lifted the camouflage suit and hood from where it hung on a nail close by the door. The man brushed it aside.

'You want to see him?' one of the guards asked.

'No,' the man snapped. 'There's no need. I only came to tell you that tomorrow night you will get rid of him.'

'Release him?' The older guard looked surprised.

'Get rid of him. The doctor will be here to help. Perhaps his body will be found in the port, for example. I leave it to you and the doctor. Goodbye.' He turned sharply on his heel and walked out.

25

GERRY GREELEY rolled over, reaching for his watch. He had set it to Saudi Arabian time before going to sleep. It showed four-thirty in the afternoon. He turned to the window and looked down, blinking in the fierce glare. The ground was an almost uniform tan colour, relieved only by the occasional green flecks that revealed the presence of a well. Far off to his left he could make out the arrow-straight trace of the pipeline and road that ran from Dhahran to the Mediterranean, slicing through the hostile terrain of the vast emptiness of northern Saudi Arabia.

He spent ten minutes in the big shower cubicle. When he stepped out, a towel tight around his waist, a trim, green-eyed young woman brought coffee and fresh orange juice. They exchanged appraising smiles. It was his first experience of the kind of flying available to senior members of the administration. It beat flying on a 747 with three hundred and fifty sweating tourists.

The plane flew under the livery of a private charter company registered in the Cayman Islands. The personnel had all recently been members of the US Air Force. It explained why they referred to seven foot by five beds with feather pillows and goosedown duvets as 'bunks'.

The airline was used on occasions when a member of the US Government had to be where he had no business being. After his long talk with Jordan after take-off he understood why this was one of those occasions.

'We'll be landing in Dhahran in thirty minutes, sir.'

A quarter of an hour later they sat, strapped into the soft leather armchairs, and watched Dhahran rise to meet them. The neat chequerboard pattern of Dhahran itself, small-town America transposed to the Arabian desert, contrasted sharply with the tangled sprawl of the neighbouring Saudi town of Al Khobar. The first was an orderly, neatly laid-out town of prefabricated, white-painted houses surrounded by low picket fences. The drunken, disorderly rednecks and their overweight wives did not show up in an aerial view. The second was a typical Saudi town where the oil boom had seen most of the mud-brick houses torn down to make way for marble-faced office blocks and the showrooms of air-conditioning distributors. Of the original character of the town only the cavalier disdain for any kind of planning had survived.

The plane rolled to the very end of the runway. Instead of

turning and taxiing back to the airport building the pilot killed the engines where they stood. Greeley watched a mobile staircase being manoeuvred into position.

They stepped out into a fierce dry heat that rose out of the baked tarmac and blasted their mouths dry. At the foot of the steps a group of men in Arab robes awaited them. One was very tall, fleshy-faced, and imposing beneath the copious robe. Greeley surmised that in Western clothes he would be just plain fat. Next to the big man, standing very still, his sharp features immobile behind impenetrable sunglasses, was a much smaller figure in a simple brown woollen robe and white headdress. Jordan strode forward to greet them. Greeley was mildly surprised to see he shook hands first with the smaller man.

'Good evening, Your Highness. This is Mr Greeley. He's the pilot I spoke of.'

The man nodded and extended a hand at an angle that seemed to offer the option of kissing it or shaking it. Greeley shook it, briefly.

'Saïd,' Jordan was saying, taking the other man's upholstered paw. 'How are you?' He turned to Greeley. 'Gerry, this is Saïd Hassan. He's been very useful in helping get this thing organized. He'll be giving you any help you need before you leave.' To a careful listener Jordan's voice carried a distant echo of disdain. The big man was a very careful listener. Although he continued smiling down on them from among the flesh of his chins, the light in his eyes altered subtly. Deep beneath the flesh a tendon tightened.

'You're too kind, Mr Jordan,' he said sweetly.

Jordan turned to Greeley. He gave his hand a single firm shake. 'So long, Gerry. Good luck. I'll be in touch. I have to get right out to the carrier. I'd hate to have to land on one of those bitches in the dark.' He punched Greeley once on the shoulder and climbed into a waiting black Mercedes, accompanied by the prince and two wary-eyed men who had been hovering in the background. The car sped away towards a waiting helicopter.

'Shall we go, Mr Greeley? Or may I call you Gerry?' Saïd purred.

Gerry grinned and shrugged. 'Sure. Let's get moving.' He hefted his bag and followed Saïd to a second Mercedes.

They drove for twenty minutes along a single ribbon of asphalt, not seeing any other car on the way. At the end of that time they turned off the road and started along a track that was marked only by the ruts of previous vehicles. It appeared to head straight into the desert. The desert was not sand. On either side of them the land spread absolutely flat, except for a few scattered outcrops of sandstone boulders glowing orange in the sinking sun. The surface was earth, baked to the hardness of stone and covered with a chaotic tumble of stones like axeheads. In a few places a colourless scrub battled its way through the stones and looked as though it had worn itself out in the effort. The only obviously living things they saw were a group of eight or ten camels that crossed the track ahead of them, and their owner. The camels walked indolently in front of the car with their peculiar lounging gait. The owner leant stock-still on a staff and watched through slitted eyes as the Mercedes sped by.

The ride was uncomfortable. Gerry clung to the grab handle and wished they would turn off the air-conditioning. The blast was chilling him through his light clothes. He did not want to insist, though. Saïd was pumping out sweat like a man in a horror cheapie being threatened with a chain saw.

'Is it much further? This is worse than a chopper in a thunderstorm in Vietnam.'

Saïd shook his head, spotting Gerry's shirt front with a few beads of sweat. 'Five minutes. My apologies for the discomfort.' He pursed his lips in a smirk. 'I'm afraid Mr Jordan and I judged privacy to be more important.'

A few minutes later a cluster of buildings rose from the flat landscape. Several long, low huts stood a foot and a half off the ground on cement blocks. Beyond them rose a much bigger structure, open at one end. All the buildings had roofs and walls of dark roofing felt. They looked as though the temperature inside would be about two hundred degrees.

A double fence of razor wire, over ten feet high and topped with coils of the same vicious wire, enclosed the area. Double gates were set across the track. As they drew closer two guards emerged from beneath a makeshift tent inside the gates. Greeley noticed more men at intervals along the fence. They were dug into shallow foxholes shaded by well-camouflaged tarpaulins.

The guards waved the car through, exchanging greetings with the soldier beside the driver. He was relieved to see they carried themselves like real soldiers. On most of the missions he had carried out for Jordan the swaggering, half-trained, half-witted adolescents he had to deal with were more dangerous than the enemy. These were Yemeni mercenaries, the disciplined fighting core of the Saudi Army.

Saïd preceded him into one of the huts. In fact, the temperature was only about a hundred and fifty. Greeley threw his bag down on one of the several single beds and walked around the room throwing open windows. Apart from the beds the room contained a suite of lounge furniture, a massive television with video and a heap of cassettes, and a monstrous radio and tape deck with more controls than the plane he would be flying tomorrow.

He walked into a kitchen. The refrigerator was crammed. He ripped the ring-pull off a beer and took a long, grateful swallow.

'I hope you find everything to your liking, Gerry.' He looked around to see Saïd lounging against the door frame, his bulk almost filling the doorway. He brandished the can and smacked his lips.

'I didn't expect this.'

'We try to look after our guests. You'll find whisky in the bag there.' He pointed to a crumpled brown-paper bag standing on the refrigerator. 'We would appreciate it if you'd try not to let the guards see the alcohol.' He straightened. 'Would you like to see the plane now?'

Greeley tossed back another long draught, put down the can and followed Saïd from the hut.

The sight of the silvery machine made him catch his breath. The thrill, even just seeing one of the machines close to, had hardly diminished. Not since the time, over thirty years earlier, at Inchon, when he had first flown a plane into combat.

A handful of technicians stood around the plane, naked beneath their greasy overalls. They smiled at him, shy and proud, waiting for him to approve their work. He swung himself onto a set of steps and scrambled into the cockpit. He let his fingers play caressingly over the controls. It felt good. He grinned at the waiting technicians and gave them a thumbs-up sign. They burst into relieved laughter. He climbed down to rejoin Saïd.

'I understand, although I'm far from being an expert in matters of armaments, that extra fuel capacity has been added. You'll have plenty of range, in case you have need of evasive action anywhere on your route,' Saïd told him in a low voice, as though he were sharing a confidence. 'Those men are some of the best technicians in the country. All trained by the manufacturers.'

Greeley glanced at the men. Two of them were holding hands. 'Glad to hear it,' he said drily. They began walking back to the hut. 'What do I do until flight time?'

'Stay in the hut. I'm sorry there's no air conditioning. These Saudis.' He gestured and rolled his eyes, impressing on Gerry that he should not make the mistake of taking him, Saïd, for one.

Gerry shrugged. 'I've put up with worse. Is there any chance of female company?'

Saïd guffawed. 'In Saudi Arabia? In Dhahran, maybe, among the wives whose husbands are away in the desert.' He grinned lewdly. 'In the rest of this country I'm afraid things are a little strict. Unless,' he added, as a cheerful afterthought, 'you would be interested in a young boy?'

'I'll stick to the video,' Gerry replied acidly.

They had reached the steps of the hut. Saïd held out a hand. 'I'll be back tomorrow afternoon, in good time for your departure. Enjoy yourself.'

Gerry watched the Mercedes sag as Saïd eased himself into it. He responded to the big man's wave with a tilt of his head and stood looking on as the car moved away. He got himself a fresh beer and carried it out to the step. This would probably be his last desert sunset, and his last chance to fly a machine like that. With the money from this one he would call it a day. Maybe even marry Donna. If only she would lose a little weight. He drank off some beer and lay back against the wall of the hut.

26

JULIA AWOKE with a start. The room was in total darkness. There was another knock, louder. She clambered from the bed, pulling on her shirt. It was eleven-thirty. The officer who had brought her from Beirut stood at the door. He invited her to follow him.

Bahrawi waited in the hall which was lit only by a feeble petrol lantern. He waved the officer outside and took Julia's hand.

'I'm sorry for everything, Julia. In case we never meet again, please believe me when I tell you I know nothing about your brother.'

She shrugged and nodded, not speaking.

'I'll keep trying to help you, but you must understand the pressures. What we're trying to do is more important than any individual. My position is very delicate. Being seen taking too great an interest in helping an American hostage could destroy me. Remember Shapour Bakhtiar? One moment he was prime minister and the Imam's most trusted associate, the next he was reduced to skulking in Paris issuing communiqués nobody reads. I don't intend that to happen to me, Julia.' He squeezed her hand. 'Please see Bradman. Goodbye.'

Two jeeps waited in front of the hotel. She climbed in beside the officer. Tears stung her eyes as she turned for a last glance back. Bahrawi stood on the hotel steps, one hand raised in farewell. She felt sorry for him. He was trying hard to bridge two cultures. He was in serious danger of falling into the chasm between the two. The fall would very probably kill him.

The jeeps retraced the route of the previous night. The Baalbek road was thick with military traffic. Jeeps and armoured vehicles sped past them, bursting with armed men. They shouted and gesticulated to Julia's escort, twisting dangerously in their seats to prolong the conversations. Julia could feel an excitement in the air that had not been there the previous night.

They crossed the Zahlé road and struck across country. On the road where they had encountered the Lebanese Army there was no military traffic. Instead, there was a stream of refugees. Some drove cars, belongings lashed in swaying heaps on straining roof racks. Others pushed bicycles or urged on donkeys, all of them piled high with bedding, kitchen equipment and furniture. Huge transistor stereo sets sat in every pile. Among the chattels, children perched, their faces blank around dark, feverish eyes, numb from excitement and fatigue.

The jeeps bullied their way through the fleeing column, sending a donkey laden with a heap of possessions as tall as itself and with a small girl astride its neck shying into a roadside ditch. The driver of their jeep gave a whoop of imbecilic laughter as the beast lay terrified, on its side, with the little girl lying beside it sobbing. The donkey's owner had run to the girl's side and was screaming a stream of bitter invective after the jeep, flailing his stick angrily. As they drew away from the scene only Julia bothered to glance back. The man was on his knees beside the girl, crying bitterly.

The jeeps plunged on, bucking over the rocks and ruts of

the barren hillsides. It was nearly forty minutes before they came to the place at which they had been mortar-bombed. The bodies of the two boys who had attacked them had gone. The two of their own men who had been killed lay by the overturned jeep. Their heads had been severed. Heads, bodies and jeep were a grisly, twisted, blackened mass, calcined almost beyond recognition.

Julia clutched her hands to her face, covering her eyes. Her stomach heaved. She wished more desperately than ever that Ray was with her. The senseless savagery was overwhelming. Even the officer and the other men in their escort could find nothing in the scene to smirk at. Instead they stared edgily into the darkness, swallowing hard, their weapons nervously at the ready.

A few minutes later they halted at the village through which they had passed just before the attack. The escort began talking animatedly, obviously delighted. Julia stared in disbelief. Where only a few hours earlier had been a village housing a functioning community, there was now only rubble. The narrow, rutted street was pitted with craters big enough to engulf one of the jeeps. On either side of the road was rubble. No building stood intact. Bricks, sandstone and corrugated iron lay in jumbled heaps. Here and there a mattress or a broken chair-back protruded from the debris. The place seemed at first to be utterly still. Then, gradually, they became aware of the soft mewing and the sinister bustle of rats. They had survived and now ferreted among the wreckage. They gathered in obscene scrabbling clusters wherever they found anything soft enough to eat. Julia closed her eyes, trying to shut out the repulsive images that came to mind, of victims lying trapped and helpless, prey to the gruesome creatures.

The jeeps picked their way carefully among the shell craters. Although still watchful, the men seemed cheered by the destruction of the village. The officer gestured around at the devastation.

'You see,' he said, proudly, 'our people control the area

now. This is a message to the Druze who don't want to join us. They can leave, or they can be destroyed. We will give them the choice,' he added, generously. Julia could not think of an answer that would have meant anything to him.

The jeeps, clear of the village now, speeded up a little. It seemed that they were taking a different path down through the foothills, perhaps more worried than they would admit about reprisals from the Druze, many of whom had surely remained stubbornly in the inaccessible villages scattered over the broken, rugged terrain.

They rounded a shoulder of the hill, bringing the lights of Beirut suddenly into view. The curve of lights around St George's Bay lay like a broken necklace, the gaps revealing where the years of war had destroyed streetlighting and buildings. With their approach to Beirut, their escort had become increasingly edgy. Too many maverick and unpredictable groups of gunmen infested these hills close to the city. Even for these trained and disciplined men, moving through this area meant dry mouths and damp palms.

They moved from the rough ground onto a track which led down into a narrow ravine. At the bottom lay a dry river bed, overgrown with a thick tangle of scrub. Dotted among the scrub, broken walls and heaps of stone marked where rough huts, probably shelters for sheep and herdsmen, had once stood. One of the huts, deep in the undergrowth, was still complete.

The officer motioned Julia out of the jeep. Perplexed, she climbed down.

'We can take you no further,' the officer said. 'You must wait here.'

Julia looked around. In the silver glow of moonlight it looked like the arid surface of another planet. 'What for?'

'Your guide. Selim.' The officer looked at his watch. 'You will not wait too long. He has instructions to rendezvous with you at dawn. Wait for him. Make sure he sees you clearly. If you surprise him,' he added, grinning, 'he will probably shoot you. He will be very sorry. Afterwards.' The officer was still laughing as the jeeps roared away, shrouding Julia in dust.

Dawn was a long time arriving. She had tried to enter the ruined hut, looking for shelter from the chill breeze. A quick scurrying movement that had turned out to be a four-inch scorpion had changed her mind. She had spent the intervening hours sitting against a rock, hugging her knees.

She clambered painfully to her feet, cramped and cold, and made her way up the side of the ravine. In the distance the artillery batteries had opened up. From the top of the slope the ground fell away towards the distant glint of the sea. On the other three sides the scrubby ground rose in rugged folds. Any of those folds could be concealing a village full of hostile gunmen. She gave a violent shiver, a mixture of cold, fear and loneliness. She felt very vulnerable.

It was nearly six-thirty and had been full daylight for more than half an hour when she saw a wisp of smoke or dust far off to the south. It grew nearer, veering through long arcs as it followed the contours. It was fifteen minutes before she caught the first glint of metalwork.

The car was a beaten-up American Ford, painted a violent turquoise that had never been in the maker's catalogue. A taxi sign, unreadable under its coating of dust, was bolted to a bar on the roof. Julia stood with her hands held open in front of her, waiting for the cloud of choking red dust to disperse. She wiped her eyes and walked to the car.

Selim was a dark-skinned man in his late twenties. He wore a Cardin polo shirt, jeans, tasselled moccasins and several ounces of gold. He also wore a bandolier of Kalashnikov ammunition across his chest. Smiling, he held open the rear door and bowed ceremoniously.

'Please get in.'

Julia discovered she was sharing the rear seat with a sackful of Christian Dior shirts and a half-dozen Louis Vuitton handbags that were almost genuine. The front passenger seat housed more shirts, a Kalashnikov and a huge revolver. Selim threw the car into a wild turn and set off back the way he had come. The soft suspension made Julia feel she might be glad of the thick film of transparent plastic that protected the upholstery.

He looked at Julia in the mirror for a while, as though he were sizing up her need for a handbag. He must have decided she was as well off without one.

'It's very bad.' He was still smiling.

'What?'

'For you. There's fighting between Rachid's people and the Shi-ites. Rachid's men are offering a big reward for you.'

'Oh shit.' She dropped her head into her hands for a moment. Then a thought struck her. 'What are you?'

He grinned. 'Whatever I want to be.' He reached into the glove box and held up a sheaf of identity documents. 'Sunni, Shi-ite. Syrian, sometimes.'

'But what *are* you, really?'

The smile left his face. 'Palestinian. Shi-ite. I was born in a refugee camp.' He caught the sudden pallor in Julia's face. He laughed. 'Don't worry, please. I work for Mehdi Bahrawi. He instructed me to take care of you. You're like my sister.'

She inclined her head. 'How long to Beirut?'

His shoulders rose and fell. 'An hour, if we are lucky. If we aren't lucky, maybe never.' He drew a finger across his throat, laughing. 'You want to go to your Embassy, yes?'

'I guess so. But I want to pick up someone first.' She gave him Habib's address. He frowned but said nothing. She knew they were both thinking something neither of them wanted to talk about. Habib's flat was in an area where Rachid's people were very strong.

They drove in silence for some time, sweltering in the growing heat. The only ventilation came from the two-inch gap at the top of the driver's window. All other windows were firmly closed and the winding handles long since disappeared. Abruptly, they swung off the faint track, bucked down a stony bank and hit an asphalt road. Almost immediately, they were into the squalor, stray dogs and gangs of street urchins of the outskirts of Beirut.

Julia did not recognize the streets. The chadors of the women told her it was a Moslem sector. She did not wait for Selim's murmured instruction before sitting well down in her seat, making herself as unobtrusive as possible. She was grateful for the dust that caked the glass.

The car slowed almost to a standstill. Ahead of them, cars, laden donkeys, trucks and handcarts milled at an intersection. In the centre of the confusion a policeman gestured hopelessly and blew continuously on a whistle. The whistle was almost drowned by the cacophony of car horns. Not wanting to be conspicuous, Selim jammed his thumb on the horn.

Julia dropped her head into her hands. The lack of sleep, the strain and the noise had brought her to breaking point. Something rapped on the window. She looked up to see a pair of dark eyes, shaded by a uniform cap, looking in at her. Her sobbing cry made Selim spin around. He paled and cursed softly. Then he donned an obsequious smile, opened the door and swung himself out of the car.

Julia stared straight ahead of her, chewing at a thumbnail. Abruptly, the rear door swung open, making her start. She managed to suppress a cry as she realized the figure bending across her was Selim. He hooked two shirts from the sack next to her and withdrew. She heard angry voices. Selim bent again into the car, his face drained. He reached beneath the driver's seat and pulled out a carton of Camel cigarettes. She saw him push them into the hands of the policeman.

Neither of them spoke until they were clear of the intersection. Finally, Selim let out his breath in a long noisy sigh. 'You see. An American life is not worth much in Beirut now.'

She gave him a thin grin. It was not the kind of joke she needed.

They stayed on the busier avenues, feeling less conspicuous than in the teeming backstreets. Despite the intense militia activity they were not molested again. Twice they were diverted, at spots where the militia had cordoned off parked cars as a prelude to blowing them up as suspected car bombs. Beirut was the only city in the world where you had more chance of being killed by a stationary car than by a moving one.

They turned a corner. Five hundred yards ahead of them Julia caught sight of a cross incongruously outlined in neon. They were at the edge of the Christian sector. She leaned forward, gesturing ahead. 'Selim, you're not planning to go through there? You could get torn to pieces.'

He reached into the glove box again. 'Not Selim, now. Joseph.' He waved a document under Julia's nose. It was a baptism certificate in the name of Joseph Houry. 'For you it will be much safer. We won't have to worry about Rachid's men for a while.'

The traffic had thinned to a trickle. They drove on slowly, approaching the makeshift sentry post. The dug-out on the Moslem side was deserted. The Christian guards watched them warily.

The sight of Julia both puzzled and reassured them. A guard studied their documents. Julia had an uneasy feeling his attention quickened when he saw the name in her passport. As they pulled away from the guard post she saw him huddle in conversation with a colleague, staring and pointing after the car.

They drove north, moving faster now that Selim knew his American passenger was safe. They were several blocks from the checkpoint when Julia called him to stop. Puzzled, he drew into the kerb. They were in front of a big open-fronted café. With a word to Selim to wait she ran into the café.

Watched by curious men who sat over coffee and mint tea she ran to the rear of the room. She spoke rapidly to the owner who sat presiding at his cash register. He reached down and lifted a telephone onto the scarred counter.

It took a dozen attempts before she got through. The sound of her voice shook Habib completely awake.

'Julia! My God! Where are you? Are you all right?'

'I'm fine. Is Ray still there?'

'Of course.' There was a tinge of disappointment in his voice. 'I'll get him.' She heard muffled calling. Five seconds later Ray came on. His voice was cracking. 'Julia? Oh, shit! Are you okay? Where are you? Where have you . . . ?' She cut him short, laughing and at the same time almost sobbing at the sound of his voice. 'Ray, we should be there in a quarter of an hour, if Rachid's people don't turn me into hamburger on the way.' She described the car. 'Watch for us. We won't want to hang around.'

They were close to the port before they again turned left, heading west towards the Green Line. Instead of making for one of the principal crossing points Selim swung into the network of narrow streets clustered around the port. He wove through the trucks that choked the streets in front of wholesalers' depots, his hand not leaving the horn as he nudged the throng of porters and merchants aside.

He turned into a yard. It was a depot for one of the private bus lines that had flourished since the public services had broken down. Bright painted buses with lame suspensions were parked haphazardly around them. Selim dragged out a carton of cigarettes and jumped from the car.

He hammered at the door of a peeling yellow hut. A man in soiled shorts opened the door. He and Selim embraced and kissed each other several times on the cheek. Selim muttered a few words and handed over the cigarettes. The man nodded, tossed the carton behind him into the hut and crossed the yard. He kicked aside the litter of discarded oil containers, drink cans and greasy paper and took the heavy bar from the gate.

Selim gunned the motor hard. With a wave to the man he sent the car leaping through the gate, across a wide street and into the alley opposite, running across the hindquarters of an indolent mongrel dog. A single rifle shot snapped out, almost drowned by Selim's whoop of triumph. They had crossed the Green Line. They were in West Beirut.

They wove through narrow streets for another ten minutes. Julia was utterly lost until they took a corner and she recognized Habib's street.

Ray was already emerging from the building by the time they came to a halt. He sprinted across the street and almost fell into the car. Their arms were around each other before either of them could say a word. They were still locked together when they turned onto the corniche and drew up in front of the sandbagged entrance to the Embassy. Holding tight to each other's hands they jumped from the car and dashed into the compound.

Windows and doors stood open. Curtains blew gently. A shutter banged as the air stirred. The building was deserted.

27

TOGETHER, they sprinted into the building and through the deserted corridors. In the offices filing cabinets stood open, their contents spilling onto the floor. Taking the steps four at a time they ran down into the basement. It was the last place that would be abandoned, the place where the shredders would be installed, where the marines that worked for Bradman would be busy until the last moment destroying documents.

Beside the bank of shredders a makeshift incinerator contained a deep litter of black paper ash. Not a single scrap would have been readable. The ash was still warm.

They hurried back up the stairs, anxious now to be out of the place before the looting started. As they ran across the deserted lobby an object clanged onto the marble floor and rolled noisily beneath a chair. Ray stared at it for a fraction of a second. He gave a single sharp curse, bundled Julia under one arm, almost lifting her off her feet, and half ran, half dived for the door.

The scorching blast sent them rolling in the dust of the compound. They staggered to their feet, stunned. Two uniformed men stood staring at them with frightened, hostile eyes. They looked bewildered and panicky, out of their depth. One of them held a rifle trained on Ray. Ray grinned.

'Shit, Vern, put that thing down.'

The hostility drained slowly from the marine's face, to be replaced by open-mouthed astonishment. The second marine spoke. 'Walker! What the fuck are you doing here?'

He shrugged. 'Looking for Bradman.'

'He's not here. Everyone's cleared out. Matter of fact the Ambassador was going nuts over you two. Right, Vern?' Vern nodded, his frightened eyes back on the windows of the building, as though he expected shooting to start at any moment.

'Where are they?' Julia asked urgently.

The marine pulled the pin from another incendiary grenade, as casual as if he were opening a can of Coke, and lobbed it into the cloud of smoke that already billowed from the open door. They shielded their faces as the blast sent another wave of heat sweeping over them. 'Over at the port, waiting to be taken off. Seems like something's about to break loose.' He tossed a third grenade into the blazing lobby. 'We're the only chumps left here, Vern and me. And Lonnie.' He nodded to an Embassy car parked facing the entrance. A black marine sat at the wheel. He twitched an index finger in acknowledgment. The marine who was speaking nodded at the burning building. 'Bradman made us come back and take care of this. Seems sort of drastic to me.'

'Is that where Bradman is? Over at the port?' Julia asked.

The marine snorted. 'Bradman? He was supposed to do this himself. Then, suddenly, it's a big panic. He has to leave. So we get stuck with it.' He jerked a thumb towards the west. 'He left going that way. Said he had to get out to the airport.'

'How long ago?' Julia pressed eagerly.

The marine shrugged. 'Five minutes? He left us here and took off. He's got a couple of his rag-heads, his Arabs, with him. His local army, eh, Vern? Trusts them better'n he trusts us.' Vern sniggered, still watching the building. Ray and Julia were already running back to the car.

They sped along the curve of the corniche past the shuttered and barricaded British Embassy. The sea to their right was studded with the small tramp steamers that waited to enter the port for discharge. Offshore they were less vulnerable to the mortars.

Tension in the car grew as they swayed through the curves in the road where it skirted the district of Ras Beirut. Scattered groups of young men turned to watch sullenly as they passed. Silently, Selim reached over and picked up the handgun that lay on the seat beside him. He handed it over his shoulder to Julia. Without taking his eyes from the road he leaned and felt in the glove compartment for the document he wanted.

'We may be stopped,' he said, matter-of-factly. 'If we are, keep the gun out of sight until I tell you. If I have to ask you to use it, shoot to kill.'

They drove on for another kilometre. Taking the last curve before the long straight stretch that led to the airport they all saw the barricade at once. Two burned-out buses stood at an angle across the highway. They could see the silhouettes of men in headcloths in a sandbagged dug-out.

Selim slowed the car. His fingers kneaded the wheel. 'Be ready,' he murmured through immobile lips. They drew closer to the barricade. A man stepped from behind it into the road and raised a hand.

Selim slowed further. Close to, they could distinguish the shoulder flashes of Rachid's private army. The car stopped three feet from the man. He stepped forward to the driver's door and stooped to look inside. His eyes met Julia's. Instead of the hostility she expected the eyes held a look of fear and pleading. As he opened his mouth to speak the last spark of expression left his eyes. He took a small step and fell facedownward in the road. The back of his tunic was covered in blood. Selim snatched up his rifle and rolled out of the car into the road. He crouched in the cover of the car waiting for the other sentries to start firing. They remained utterly still. Frowning, Selim eased himself gingerly from the shelter of the car and approached the dug-out.

One of the men stared at him, still not moving. Selim moved closer to the barricade, placed his gun beneath the man's chin and shoved. The man crumpled out of sight. The other soldier did not move as Selim leapt the barrier. The men's clothes were dark with blood. A third man lay beneath them, his face blown away. Selim leaned down and touched the man's flesh. It was warm, and flies had not yet begun to gather.

They looked inquiringly at him as he slid back behind the wheel. He shrugged. 'I think perhaps your friend is not far ahead of us,' he said, in a voice without expression.

They reached the northern extremity of the airport perimeter without incident. The road ran arrow-straight through the dunes for several kilometres. Far ahead of them a vehicle moved, going in the same direction. Julia craned forward beside the driver, pointing excitedly.

'That's an Embassy limo! It's him.'

Major Bradman shifted peevishly in the rear of the limousine, cursing again the styling that lavished space on the outside and left the interior too cramped to suit anyone but a pygmy. He extracted his legs from the well behind the front passenger seat and stretched them with a sigh along the rear seat. Until recently he had refused to use the Embassy cars at all. For this trip, though, he had liked the idea of the quarter-inch armoured panels and the other anti-terrorist accessories. Since Rachid's assassination things had been getting out of hand.

He finished reloading the ammunition clip and rammed it into the pistol. He would have preferred not to have had to kill the men at the roadblock. But their own intentions, as soon as it became clear he was American, had left him no choice.

His racing mind turned back to the evacuation. Everything had gone absolutely smoothly. Every United States citizen in the city had been assembled. As he had expected, a couple of the old hands had needed the persuasion of an armed escort, but they had finally come around. The boat would be in at noon. The Embassy would be in ashes by now. He would not be responsible for a repeat of the Saigon fiasco, where the fools from the CIA had abandoned the building leaving cabinets of card files intact. Thousands of Vietnamese, all good friends of America, who had served her well, had perished as a result of that piece of incompetence.

He sighed. There were two problems he could have done without. He had not been able to locate the Colter woman and that drunk Walker. And the call he had received at the Embassy less than half an hour earlier. The call that had almost had him panicking. The call that could ruin everything. He addressed the two Arabs who sat in the front, raising his voice to make himself heard around the half-closed glass partition.

'Pull off by that building. Get the car out of sight.' The lazy authority in his voice gave no hint of the anger and fear that churned in his mind.

The driver pulled the car across the road onto the stony shoulder. The hut the Major had mentioned was a ruined cinder-block structure. Faded posters promoting defunct nightclubs hung in fronds from the walls, swaying in the slight breeze. The vestige of a track led from the road around behind the building to end among a growth of vicious-looking prickly pear.

He stepped out of the car, grimacing at the litter of cans, wrappers and human excrement. He glanced up at the steep escarpment, covered with loose rock, that rose sharply above him. He made a quick, wry face, reached into the car and pulled a bag from the parcel shelf.

Treading carefully among the filth, he stripped off his polished brogues and light cotton suit, exchanging them for combat boots and overalls. He shrugged the shoulder holster into place and slammed the door. Nodding to the two men to follow, he walked out of the thicket and led the way to the foot of the trackless, treacherous slope. Spread three-abreast to avoid the danger from dislodged rock, they began climbing.

Julia sat hunched over the front seat, squinting through the windscreen. The caked dirt made it almost opaque as they drove into the sun. She was oblivious to the squalid shacks that nestled among the dunes, the miserable broken-down businesses that made a living selling overpriced necessities to the beleaguered inhabitants of Burj al Barajinah.

Under Julia's urging Selim pushed the car to its limit, disregarding the potholes that sent sickening impacts pounding through the tired fabric of the car. On the long straight past the airport they gained noticeably on the car ahead of them. Julia's excitement grew as the characteristic low outline of the car, caused by the weight of its armour, confirmed her belief that it was an Embassy limousine.

Beyond the airport, where the road was joined by the road from the eastern suburbs, the highway curved gently away to the east, hugging the sweep of the coastline. The black car swept into the curve and out of sight. By the time they emerged from the curve themselves the road ahead was empty.

Julia was the first to recover. 'Selim,' she cried, almost angrily, 'are there side roads? Anywhere they could have turned off?'

Selim shook his head and gestured at their surroundings. 'On the right there are only dunes and the sea. Only a jeep could drive in them. Over there are the hills. There's no road before Khaldeh.'

Ray pointed eagerly beyond Selim's shoulder. 'Look!'

No more than a kilometre away, a faint dustcloud hung over the hillside. Selim stamped on the accelerator. Forty seconds later they slewed to a stop by the ruined shack.

Julia was out of the car and running before the car had

fully stopped. She followed the wheel tracks into the thicket. The big black car stood empty. She turned and raced back to the others. They squinted up the slope. At their feet lay a pile of jagged rocks. A thin smoke of dust still rose from the heap.

'It's a fresh rock-slide,' Ray said. 'He must have gone up there. D'you want to try it?'

The climb was hard and dangerous. They soon learned to stay in a line abreast, spread well apart. The slightest misstep sent stones the size of a man's head cartwheeling down the mountainside, gathering more rocks as they went. They inched upwards on all fours, keeping their bodies close to the slope. Once, Julia's footing gave way, sending her sliding twenty feet down the treacherous scree. She managed to halt her slide, digging toes and hands into the sharp rocks, and lay for a full ten seconds of stark terror as rocks cannoned around her head. Miraculously, her only injury was a blow to an elbow. It hurt like hell but it would not stop her.

They reached the top and looked over the ridge. Beyond them the land fell away in a gentle slope into a shallow wooded valley with more hills rising beyond it. Immediately in front of them lay neglected orange groves intersected by tracks just wide enough for a donkey cart. Underbrush had pushed up between the trees and overhung the paths. Directly in front of them a path ran straight down the hill to a collection of low single-storey farm buildings, five or six hundred metres distant. Nothing moved.

They pulled themselves over the crest and set off down the path towards the farm. Ray carried Selim's pistol at his side. The area south of Beirut was in a state of total chaos and anarchy. A wooded, isolated area like this could conceal anything. A Palestinian training camp as easily as an Israeli commando patrol. Even with the gun for comfort Ray's mouth was parched. Blood pounded in his head.

Tendrils of thick undergrowth snatched at their clothing as they passed, leaving spines lodged in the fabric. Around them the silence was total. No bird sang. The long and cruel tradition of 'hunting' that meant blasting any bird that moved, however inedible, had ensured that only shrewd and silent ones survived.

A sound in the undergrowth off to their left made them wheel and crouch down, each seeking cover in the edges of the underbrush. Selim put a finger to his lips and motioned them to be still. He unslung the Kalashnikov and lowered himself to the ground, supporting his weight on his elbows and knees. Making no sound, he slid out of their sight.

The scuffling noise came again, very faint but very close. Julia and Ray exchanged looks. Ray wriggled closer to Julia so that they touched. He held the big handgun tightly in his right hand. His left arm lay lightly across Julia's shoulder. Neither of them was breathing. They listened intently for the slightest sound. The silence was total.

Selim's shout made them gasp and recoil momentarily, closer into the cover of the bushes. Then, they sprang to their feet, moving towards the sound. As they plunged into the thorny scrub, Selim erupted awkwardly to his feet three yards from them. He held the Kalashnikov in a firing position, trained at something on the ground. They pushed their way through to join him, ignoring the thorns. A figure lay stretched in the dust, staring up at them.

Julia dropped to her knees with a sound between a scream and a sob. 'Michael!'

Michael stared at her. For a moment the shared shock made both of them speechless. Then, everybody moved at once. Michael tried to scramble to his feet, disregarding the muzzle of the gun which the perplexed Selim still held two feet from his head. Julia threw her arms around her brother, her head resting on his shoulder. Tears of pure joy ran down her cheeks onto his dirt-caked skin. Selim took a step back. The gun barrel wavered. He looked at Ray for some clue as to what was happening.

Ray reached out and gently pushed the gun barrel aside.

'Jesus,' he said, half to Selim and half to himself. 'It's her brother.'

It was perhaps half a minute before Ray leaned down and drew Julia's arms from around Michael's neck. He spoke with a gentle urgency. 'Come on, both of you. Let's find Bradman and get out of here.'

Julia nodded, still gazing unbelievingly into her brother's eyes. 'Yeah. Right. Come on.' As she spoke she took Michael by the hand. He winced and snatched it away, shouting an involuntary protest.

She looked at his hand. For the first time she noticed the mutilation. 'Oh, my God!' She leaned away from him, looking him over. The damaged hand was a mess of caked blood. Beneath the matted hair the missing ear was a scabbed stump of gristle. The naked body was coated with grey dust. From the dozens of fresh lacerations, where he had crawled through the thorns, tiny rivulets of blood carved tracks through the grime. Several insect bites on his back and shoulders were turning to festering sores.

She stood up, helping Michael to his feet. Inside her, along with the pity and concern that showed in her face, she could feel her anger congealing into a cold, steely rage.

Surprisingly, Michael laughed. 'Hey,' he said gently. 'Don't cry.' He grinned at the other two. 'Give me five minutes in a shower, I won't look half so bad.'

Ray smiled back. 'Yeah. First, let's just get out of here.' He turned to lead the way back to the path. As he broke clear of the undergrowth a commotion broke out below them. He pulled back into cover. A door opened in the biggest of the scattering of buildings. Four men emerged. The one in the camouflage overalls stood head and shoulders above the other three. Ray recognized Bradman. Stepping onto the path, he cupped his hands around his mouth and shouted.

'Hey! Major! Up here! Fast!'

Bradman spun to face the sound. For a moment he stared, immobile, at Ray and the group emerging behind him. Then, he broke away from the others and was sprinting towards them.

Ray was grinning at his eagerness when he heard Michael cry out behind him. He turned.

Michael was pointing down the slope, confusion stamped on his face. He had met Bradman many times during his time in Beirut. There was no mistaking his face. But the overalls, the man's height, his presence there. . . . The horror of the realization flooded his face.

'It's him, Julia! Bradman was the guy in the hood. He's the one that was keeping me prisoner!'

28

FOR JUST a split second stupefaction froze them. Then all of them were racing up the slope for the ridge.

They heard two sharp slapping sounds in the trees to the side of them and saw sudden white scars as bark flew. The sound of the shots reached them a split second later. They swerved off the path and began crashing through the undergrowth.

With a word to the others to continue, Ray turned, moved to the very edge of the trees and dropped to his knees. He clasped the gun tight in both hands and loosed off a shot at the running figure of Bradman. He had the satisfaction of seeing the man duck sharply and leap for the cover of the trees. He had not seriously expected to hit him. Just knowing his quarry were armed would be enough to slow him. Ray ran on to catch the others, bending low.

They reached the ridge. Bullets ripped through the foliage dangerously close to them. Ray and Julia each grabbed the barefoot, naked Michael by an arm and plunged at a run onto the sharp, unstable scree. They went down, half on their haunches, taking as much of Michael's weight as they could. Around them rocks big enough to crush their skulls bounced and spun, gathering deadly momentum. Screaming instructions to each other, they gouged their heels into the loose rock, slowing their descent. At the same time they tried to slither crabwise, going down in a diagonal line to try to avoid the gathering mayhem behind them. Selim passed them going face first, blood pouring from a cut over his eye and a stream of vile curses pouring from his mouth.

They hit the bottom tobogganing on a stream of moving rock, and were off it at a run for the protection of the prickly-pear thicket. Ray scooped the dazed Selim to his feet and dragged him with them.

Bradman's face appeared on the skyline. He had learned his lesson. He did not intend going down the slope without knowing what weapons they might be carrying. Not, at least, until the other men caught up with him.

Pushing the others towards their own car Ray ran to the black limousine. Taking deliberate aim, he fired bullets into two of the tyres. Turning to join the others he caught sight of the pale-coloured suit and the pair of brown brogues on the seat. He snatched them up and ran to their own car. The crack of gunshots made him flinch. Emerging from the undergrowth he smiled grimly to see that it was Selim, recovered from his fall, chuckling to himself as he loosed off shots from the Kalashnikov at anything that showed above the rim of the hill.

Ray leapt into the car, thrusting the clothes at Michael. 'Here! Put these on. Beirut's a mess but naked men still attract attention.'

Michael grinned. 'Yeah. It'd be hard to melt into the background.' He began struggling into the suit. Selim let off one last shot and swung himself into the car. He shoved his gun at Ray in the seat next to him, slammed the car into gear and stamped on the throttle. They screamed off the hard shoulder straight into a hundred-and-eighty-degree turn. The tyres squealed and the passengers pitched to their left. By the time Julia and Michael got themselves straightened out they were sixty yards from the spot and accelerating hard. A bullet bit a piece the size of a fist from the road ahead of them. Selim muttered to himself and began zigzagging erratically, using the full width of the deserted highway. He seemed to be having a good time.

They were a hundred yards away before the firing stopped. Behind them four men were scrambling headlong down the slope. Michael finished manoeuvring himself into Bradman's jacket. He leaned back in the seat and closed his eyes. He sat like that for several seconds, breathing deeply, as though the air in the car were nectar. When he finally opened his eyes he was smiling. Turning to Julia he spread his hands. The cuffs of the jacket reached his knuckles.

'How do I look?'

With the filthy, matted hair, bloodied ear, growth of stubble and the coating of dirt, he looked like a beggar. Julia leaned over, threw her arms around him and planted a kiss on his cheek.

'Wonderful!' Tears were in her eyes again.

The speedometer needle hovered at the hundred-and-forty-kilometre mark. It quivered as they hit a pothole that lifted them off the seats. Ray touched Selim's arm.

'You can ease up a little. I fixed the limo.'

Selim grunted and jerked his head at the rear-view mirror. The three of them twisted in their seats.

Julia shot a glance at Ray. 'You fixed the limo.'

Ray stared through the rear window. The big black car was closing on them. 'Shit,' he said, incredulously, 'I shot two tyres out.'

Julia groaned. 'You should have put a bullet through the gas tank. That's an Embassy car. The goddamned tyres are standard anti-terrorist equipment. You need a bazooka to take the damned things out.'

'Oh, Jesus,' he murmured, almost inaudibly.

The limousine had drawn closer. A bullet whanged off their metalwork. Selim threw the car into a swerve. Julia sat on the edge of her seat. One hand was on Ray's shoulder. 'Can you get any more speed out of this thing? Can we outrun them as far as the city? In town we might be able to lose them.'

Selim shook his head. 'The car will go no faster,' he said flatly.

'So what the hell do we do?' Ray gestured at the expanse of dunes to both sides of them. To their left, beyond the dunes, any hope of escape was cut off by the sea. To their right were more dunes. Beyond them they caught glimpses of the barbed-wire-topped wall of the Burj al Barajinah refugee camp. Beyond it lay the low houses and minarets of the Shi-ite dominated suburbs. Their narrow streets teemed with hostile armed men.

There was a silence of several seconds. They winced as another bullet slammed into the car. Michael pushed himself forward. 'I may have one idea.'

Ray turned to glance once more through the rear window before looking at Michael. 'Yeah? It'd better be good. Another five minutes and those sons-of-bitches are going to be on us.'

'We could try the camp.'

They stared at him.

'Burj al Barajinah?' Julia asked incredulously.

Michael glanced back again at the black car. His face was gaunt. 'It's a better deal than letting those bastards get us.' He addressed Selim. 'I don't know what you are. Would you be safe in there?'

'Safer than you. I was born in there. That's not the problem.'

'Yeah,' Ray broke in. 'Amal have the place blockaded. Nobody gets in or out without their say-so.'

'There's a way.'

As Michael spoke, the rear of the car yawed wildly. Selim snatched at the wheel, struggling to straighten it.

'*Sharmuta!* The tyre.'

All of them could feel the slapping of the stricken tyre.

'Okay! Stop! By the booth up ahead.' Michael spoke sharply, galvanized by the threat. He pointed to a ravaged, abandoned drink kiosk at the roadside fifty yards ahead of them. Selim shot a glance at Ray. Ray raised his eyebrows and gave an almost imperceptible shrug.

'Shit, Michael,' he said softly, 'I sure hope you know what you're doing.' He looked back. The black car was much nearer. 'Because if you don't, we're dead.'

The car slewed to a stop. Before it had even come fully to a halt they were spilling out of the doors. Michael ran around the car and led the way into the dunes. Two more bullets gouged splinters off the rotting kiosk.

They stumbled through the soft sand, running directly away from the road. Michael led the way. His breath was coming in raucous, whooping gasps. Until then he had not known how weak his fever had left him. Behind them they heard the limousine screech to a stop. Doors slammed. For the moment they were out of sight of the road, hidden by a fold in the dunes. They ran on for some seconds, throwing glances over their shoulders. Selim shouted a warning. At the same instant a plume of sand leapt up inches from Michael's feet. He sidestepped and fell on his face.

As Michael staggered to his feet, spitting sand, Selim turned, dropped to one knee and fired two single, closely-spaced shots. The pursuer who had fired dropped out of sight behind the rim of a dune. Selim was on his feet and running again.

With Julia and Ray supporting him by his arms, Michael led them around the shoulder of another dune. Ray scrambled to the top, gouged an indentation in the crest and waited. A moment later a figure rose over a crest and tried to take aim at Selim's back. Ray fired. The sound of his shot made the other gunman drop again to his knees before he could get off his shot at Selim.

They continued in that way for two hundred yards, Selim and Ray covering each other in turn from the shelter of the dunes. Julia and Michael drew further away from them. Each time the pursuers appeared they were a little nearer.

Ahead of them Michael was keeping going on sheer adrenaline. His legs buckled at each step. Julia held tightly to his arm, frantically urging him on. She looked back. Ray was running towards her, bent low and weaving as he ran. Selim was nestled in the sand, his rifle to his shoulder. Abruptly, not thirty yards away from Selim, to his left, she saw Bradman rise from cover.

She screamed. Selim looked around, saw Bradman and twisted his body in an effort to roll out of the line of fire. Selim bucked as though he had been hit. He continued rolling to the foot of the dune. Julia hesitated, torn by the instinct to return for Selim. Then, to her relief, she saw him rise and start running towards her, one arm loose at his side.

She turned back to Michael. 'Where are you taking us? A few more seconds and they'll have us cold.'

As she spoke they emerged from the coastal dunes onto a flat expanse of barren, rocky ground covered with chest-high scrub. Shacks built from packing cases and driftwood dotted the area. Beyond it, two hundred yards from them, stood the cinder block and razor wire of Burj al Barajinah. To their left smoke spiralled upward from a campfire of the Amal militia that were blockading the camp.

Julia turned to Michael. She was almost sobbing with frustration and fear. 'What are you doing? We'll never make it across this.'

He shook his head and pointed to one of the shacks that stood about twenty yards from them. 'Over there. Come on.'

He set off, brushing away Julia's support. She turned quickly, ensuring the others could see her, indicated the hut and began running after Michael.

The thorns ripped at her clothes and skin. In her sheer fright she did not even feel them. A few paces ahead of her Michael reached the hut. He threw himself inside. Julia looked around. Ray and Selim were together, just breaking from the cover of the last dune. They raced towards her. She crouched in the underbrush, scanning the sand behind them. Almost at the moment Ray and Selim sprinted up to her Bradman and one of his followers appeared at the edge of the sand. They fired off a volley. The three of them ducked lower and hurled themselves into the flimsy shelter.

•

At the edge of the dunes Major Bradman halted. He smiled to himself. He could feel the old feeling, elation tinged with regret, that he had known often, many years before, in the soaking jungles of South-East Asia. One particular time came to mind. On a mission in Viet-Cong-held territory he had peered into a hut of grass and bamboo and seen the men he had come to kill squatting by a tiny stove, eating rice and talking in the high, staccato tones of their impossible language. They had been very young men, almost boys. Through the crack in the wall he had watched them laugh and been struck by how ordinary, how harmless they looked. For just a fraction of an instant he had allowed himself to regret the power he held over them. A fraction of an instant before he threw the primed grenade into their midst.

It was the same now. He watched his quarry sprint across the open ground to the hut. Watched them hurl themselves inside, deluding themselves that it would offer protection. He gestured to his men, orchestrating their movements as they surrounded the shack. Two or three times shots came from within the hut. It was poorly directed fire, intended only to remind him they were not completely helpless.

When the men were in position he raised a hand and dropped it again. The three men and Bradman stormed the hut, raking the tumbledown structure with a hail of fire.

The whole building seemed to tremble under the force of the bullets. Slivers of wood the size of pineapples flew from the far side as the bullets, tumbling from the impact of entry, ripped their way through the far wall. The firing continued for perhaps thirty seconds, until Bradman again held up a hand. In the total, numbed silence of the aftermath of gunfire, Bradman and his men stood ten feet from the shack, listening intently. There was no sound from inside. Gesturing to the other men to wait, Bradman approached the riddled door. It hung open, still swinging gently from the blows of the bullets. He stood stock-still, counting to ten, and then hurled himself into the hut, moving to the side as he passed through the door. He held the handgun two-handed in front of him. He stared around at the hut. Light from the bullet holes dappled the earth floor. Except for a jumble of blackened stones it was empty.

When Ray, Julia and Selim dived into the hut Michael was on his knees in a corner of the gloomy interior. With his good hand he was tearing at a circle of sooty stones that had apparently served as a makeshift hearth. Ray crawled quickly across to help. Michael moved aside to give him room.

'The stones. We have to move them.'

Ray did not take the time to ask questions. He began tearing the stones aside, hurling them away from him. Within seconds they had cleared a space of darkened earth. Michael scrabbled with his fingers in the earth. He gave a grunt of satisfaction and tugged at something. Under Ray's astonished gaze, an area of earth about two feet square swung upward.

'Holy shit!' Ray whispered. 'A tunnel.'

Michael nodded. 'The poor bastards in the camp use them to run the blockade. For medical supplies, mostly.'

As he spoke bullets tore through the fabric of the shack, so close they heard the crack of the sonic boom as they passed. Julia, Ray and Michael pressed themselves into the dirt floor. Using his elbows, Michael propelled himself over the edge and spilled into the tunnel mouth, calling Julia to follow him.

Selim, using only his good arm, had thrust the rifle through a gap in the wall. He fired a couple of times at random, unable to see what he was shooting at.

'Selim!' Ray's voice was an urgent whisper. 'Leave them be. We're getting out of here.'

Selim fired twice more without looking, withdrew his gun from the aperture and snaked across the floor, dragging his injured arm. Showing no surprise at seeing the tunnel, he slithered head first into the hole. Ray put a hand on each side of the opening and lowered himself in after him, pulling the trapdoor shut above his head.

29

CLAUSTROPHOBIA clawed at Julia's stomach. She concentrated on each breath, fighting down the panic that threatened to engulf her. She was on all fours, crawling on a dry earth floor with many loose stones. Her hair brushed the roof, which touch told her was of rough planking. The darkness was absolute.

They scrambled along for some time in silence, putting distance between themselves and the entrance. Ray, at the rear, turned constantly to look back, watching for the paler light that would tell them the trapdoor had been opened. He had no fear of enclosed spaces. He had a serious fear of hand grenades. A single grenade, rolled into the tunnel behind them, would probably bring the roof down, entombing them. Only when he judged they were far enough from the entrance to be safe did he speak.

'Michael,' he hissed, 'do you want to tell us something? How the hell did you know about this?'

Ahead of him in the pitch darkness he heard Michael make a sound between a laugh and a grunt. 'Some guys at the University. They're from Burj al Barajinah. They brought me through here. They wanted me to know how things really were. What conditions were like since the blockade started.' He gave a derisive snort of laughter. 'The poor bastards trusted me. They thought I'd be able to tell the American people how it was. They thought I could do some good.'

'Did you?' Julia panted.

He laughed again. 'Sure! I went to the Embassy. I told Major Bradman about it!'

They crawled on for another minute in silence before Michael called softly, 'This is it. We're there.'

Ahead of him he had felt the end of the tunnel. Rough wooden steps led up a shaft. Selim whispered from behind,

'Let me go first. The entrance will be guarded. I will speak to them.'

He groped his way past them to the front. Feeling his way, impeded by his injured arm, he pulled himself up the first rungs of the ladder. Wedging himself in the narrow shaft, he reached above his head. The exit was a foot above him. He rapped sharply on the planks of the trapdoor. There was a pause of several seconds during which they heard sounds of movement from beyond the door. Abruptly, the trap opened. Light flooded into the gap, blinding Selim. The muzzle of a gun was thrust into the aperture. A voice called harshly in Arabic. Blinking, he hauled himself up the last few rungs.

Three men stood around the entrance to the shaft. Two held rifles. The other, standing back behind the trapdoor, out of immediate sight, carried a light machine gun. Nothing could have come out of the tunnel that they could not have cut to pieces.

Selim stood on the last rung. At a shout from one of the men with rifles, another man came in from an adjoining room, moving at a run. He was completely bald, around forty, with a smoothly shaven double chin. He began firing questions at Selim. From beneath, crouching in the tunnel, Ray, Julia and Michael gazed up at the silhouette of Selim as he answered, gesturing excitedly with his intact hand. They heard him pronounce the word Bahrawi several times. Not much else of what he said, in a rapid, corrupt dialect, was clear to them. Finally, the bald man signalled Selim to step clear of the ladder. Speaking English, he called them to come up.

One by one they dragged themselves out. They were in a room fifteen feet square with walls of undecorated cinder block. Four wooden chairs stood around the room. A pair of canvas camp beds stood along one wall, each with a single ravaged blanket left in a tangle on top of it. An aperture in one wall, without a door, led to the alcove from which the bald man had emerged.

'Against the wall.' The bald man indicated the spot with a

flick of his gun barrel. The four of them did as he said. 'Turn around.' They turned to face the wall. One of the rifle carriers put down his weapon and frisked them. When he came to Julia he searched her as thoroughly as the others. He kept it brisker and more businesslike than she had feared. Nevertheless, when he finished he was flushing violently beneath his tan. He took away the gun Ray carried, pushing it into his belt. He tried to take Selim's gun. Selim protested, turning to the bald man to arbitrate. The man clicked his tongue at Selim and gave a single shake of his head. Selim let the gun go without further protest. It was an entrance fee.

'You cannot stay here,' the bald man said, without ceremony.

Julia protested. 'You can't send us back out there! You . . .'

The man cut her off. 'We can. We shall. We are not interested in your problems. Rachid's people are very angry. They will stop at nothing to get revenge for what you did.'

'But we did nothing.' She glanced desperately at Ray. 'We didn't kill Rachid. Christ, he wanted to *help* us. What do you . . . ? He was a *friend* of mine! Hell, we aren't killers.'

He looked from one to the other of the three Americans. 'No, you are not.' It was not a compliment. He shook his head. 'What you did is of no importance. What matters to me is the safety of our people. Already those madmen of Amal are blockading the camp. Our women are allowed out to buy a little food, when they permit it. Babies are dying for lack of medicines and milk.' He shook his head again. 'We cannot allow our people to suffer Rachid's mortars in addition to everything else.'

'Look,' Julia said, desperately, gesturing at Michael and Selim. 'We have two people wounded. Can't you at least help them?'

The man made a wry face. 'Selim is our brother. He may stay here, if he chooses. This one,' he pointed negligently at Michael, 'will be treated. Then you will leave.' He murmured to one of the gunmen. 'Follow him,' he said brusquely, addressing Michael and Selim.

Julia watched them pass through the door that gave directly onto a narrow alley. She turned again to the bald man. 'Please. We need one more thing. We're reporters. We must speak to our newspapers. Is it possible to have access to a telephone?'

The man looked at her pityingly. 'Access to a telephone,' he mimicked with savage irony. He moved closer to her, his fists clenching angrily. Julia stood her ground as he moved his face close to hers. Ray shuffled closer, his own fists bunching. 'Children here collect weeds to make soup. Babies die of measles because we have no vaccines. The cats and dogs were eaten long ago. And you think they left us *telephones*?' He turned away, trembling with rage and disgust.

When she spoke again Julia's voice was barely more than a whisper. 'I'm sorry,' she murmured. 'Please excuse me. May we go and join my brother and Selim? Maybe we can help?'

The man nodded to the remaining youth. He managed a smile. 'Hassan will show you to the hospital.'

When Major Bradman looked down at the bare floor where he had expected to see bodies he had stood for a moment, utterly numbed by surprise. The surprise turned quickly to rage. Swearing violently, he strode over to the spot where the movement of the trapdoor had spilled the earth from on top of it, leaving the bare planks exposed. He let out a roar of pure, uncontrolled anger. The three men who now stood inside the door recoiled, looking at him with awe and fear in their eyes.

'It's a tunnel to Burj al Barajinah, Major.'

Bradman turned a venomous look on the man. 'I know, you fucking imbecile. We've lost them,' he said icily.

The man made to move to the trapdoor.

'Come away, you idiot,' Bradman told him, turning abruptly away. 'We'd be picked off like clay pigeons.' He left the hut and began striding back towards the road, obliging the other men to run to keep up with him.

Bradman addressed the oldest of the men, speaking with

rough authority. 'I want all the camp exits covered. Can you do it? Do you have enough decent men?'

'Not our own men. I can organize it, though, Major. I have many cousins among Rachid's people. They will help us.'

Bradman looked at him sharply. 'Will they keep it discreet? We want those dickheads out of the camp where we can deal with them. They won't dare move with Rachid's mob trying to kick down the gates.'

The man looked sulky. 'My cousins aren't a mob. They are very good people.'

'Sorry, Bashaar,' Bradman said, with a distracted smile of apology. 'I didn't mean it like that. I'm sure your family will understand just what we need. You always do a first-class job for us.' A thought seemed to strike him. Abruptly, he stopped and turned to face Bashaar. 'Do we have somebody who can get inside?'

'Maybe,' Bashaar replied, mollified, and eager once again to please. 'The husband of a girl cousin. He goes inside very often. He takes in hashish. They like to use it. When a person is very hungry it's a good friend.' He jabbed a thumb back towards the camp. 'In there they're always very hungry. Starving,' he added, with a smirk.

'Is this cousin reliable?'

Bashaar looked up shrewdly at Bradman. 'That depends.'

'On what?'

The Lebanese shrugged and gave an apologetic laugh. 'On how much he is paid.'

Bradman glanced down at the man, his lips forming a faint, contemptuous smile. 'Good. We'll get along very well.' They had arrived at the car. Bradman threw himself onto the rear seat. 'Get Rachid's men into place. Then take me to this cousin.'

30

JULIA AND RAY followed the young man, Hassan, between the cinder block and corrugated-iron houses that crowded on both sides of the teeming street. Most of the houses were single-storey, a few had a second floor grafted onto them. Often, the second storey covered only a part of the building, ending in a gap-toothed line where the building blocks had run out.

Many of the buildings had canvas or tarpaulin awnings rigged on poles, which covered almost the full width of the street, shading it completely from the sun. The shade, the teeming children, the women crouched in front of the houses, hunched over cooking stoves and fires, their belongings arrayed on the ground behind them, gave the street a faintly festive air, like a souk in Marrakesh or Cairo.

A close look at the faces dispelled the illusion. All the women looked old. Their faces were seamed, their cheekbones prominent under hooded eyes. Here were none of the padded, indulged faces of the women of the Gulf or North Africa. Only the hollowed, weary stamp of deprivation and hunger. As they moved, slack, arid breasts flapped beneath the loose robes.

Even the children had the shrewd, shadowed faces of people too hungry even to sleep properly. Their play had a lethargic, joyless quality. As Ray and Julia passed, the children swarmed around them, tugging silently at their clothes and holding out soiled little palms in mute, hopeless appeal.

Hassan barked a command, officiously urging the children away, angry and ashamed at their behaviour. They fell back and followed at a distance of a couple of paces, staring up at the strangers.

Hassan turned off into a narrow alley. A group of half a dozen men in stained shirts and slacks squatted on their heels around a burbling hubble-bubble pipe. Each of them in turn inhaled a deep draught of the smoke before passing the soft looping tube of the pipe to his neighbour. Julia smiled wryly at Ray as the characteristic sweetish smell of the hashish smoke reached them. Hassan spoke to the men, admonishing them. The men responded with soft derisive chuckles.

Hassan led them through several more beaten earth alleys where astonishing cleanliness belied the unbelievable density of the population. The explanation for the cleanliness became clear when they passed a group of boys and girls of eleven or twelve, each with an old plastic bag, meticulously collecting even the tiniest piece of litter under the vigilant supervision of a uniformed teenager.

They emerged from the tangle of alleys into a space the size of a tennis court. Along the far side of the square ran a long single-storey building with two huge red crosses plainly visible on the black tarpaper of the roof. Hassan pointed to the building and left them alone.

They made their way across the square, picking a path between the men and women who sat or lay on blankets on the trampled earth, with limbs, heads or torsos heavily bandaged. An awning ran along the front of the hospital. Beneath it, more patients lay packed close together. For beds they lay on broken wooden pallets.

The lobby was stiflingly hot and very clean. A young Arab girl in an improbably crisp white tunic sat at a small table making notes in a dog-eared exercise book. Her smile was gaunt with fatigue. 'Yes?'

'We're looking for my brother and our friend. They were brought in a few minutes ago.'

'At the end of the corridor. The last cubicle on the left.'

They started up the corridor, almost at a run. Each of the open-fronted cubicles contained two beds end to end. There was just room for a person to squeeze between the wall and the beds. All the beds were full. Many of the patients were in obvious agony. One young man, his head swathed in gauze so that only his mouth and nostrils showed, screamed a continuous heart-rending scream.

They found Selim sitting on a bed contemplating the thick bandages on his arm and the bloodstains on his designer polo shirt with about equal dismay. Michael lay stretched out on his back on the other bed, naked and snoring loudly. His wounds had been washed and dressed and his body was a patchwork of vermilion stains of Mercurochrome.

'Selim, are you okay?'

He smiled and shrugged, lifting his arm and letting it fall back. 'I have often been worse.'

Julia smiled. The smile faded quickly. She turned anxiously to Michael. 'How's my brother?'

'A great deal better than anybody else in here.' The words came from behind Julia's shoulder. The Scottish accent was almost impenetrable.

A woman of around fifty stood in the doorway. The top of her grey-tinged hair came up to Julia's shoulder. Very clear blue eyes gleamed among a shoal of freckles. Dark crescents stained the skin beneath her eyes down as far as her cheekbones. She wore a button-through overall of white cotton with smears of blood, still wet, spattering the front of it.

'Is he anaesthetized?'

The woman shook her head. 'Not really. A mild shot, more to get him off to sleep than anything. His wounds are not serious.'

Julia bridled at the woman's words. 'Not serious? What the hell do you mean? They chopped off two of his fingers and an ear!'

The woman gave her a tired smile. 'That's right. As I said, nothing serious. I can't speak for any psychological scars, although he seemed perfectly okay, but his physical wounds are nothing serious.' She saw Julia gather herself to protest. 'Would you like me to show you some of our other patients?' she asked quietly. 'Pregnant women with shrapnel wounds in their stomachs?' She jerked her head at the partition separating them from the next cubicle. 'Your brother's neighbour there lost a leg yesterday, on an anti-personnel mine. She'll be dead this evening. She has five children.' She let the words sink in as Julia stood silent. She held out a hand and gave a sudden bright smile. 'Alice Carnegie.'

Julia took the hand in hers. It was dry and firm. 'Julia Colter. This is Ray Walker. Selim you've met. And that's Michael, my brother.'

'Michael Colter?' She looked down at the sleeping Michael. 'Hmm.'

'You've heard about him?'

'He's the one that was kidnapped?' She looked again at Michael. 'They released him? He was lucky.'

'No, they didn't. He escaped.' Julia looked into the candid blue eyes. Alice Carnegie looked back at her, her gaze calm and steady, the curiosity only a faint light, far back. 'Tell us, Alice, is there any rumour around the camp as to *who* has been holding Michael?'

Alice shook her head. 'What I've been hearing is that *nobody* knew.'

Julia took her by the arm and drew her into the cubicle with Ray following. 'Alice,' she said softly, 'it's possible we may not come through this whole thing. Do you mind if we tell you something?'

When Julia finished speaking Alice's face was set. Her skin had grown quite white, heightening the colour of her freckles and the dark patches under her eyes. 'It makes sense, in a lunatic way. You're on the brink of an election, aren't you?' They nodded. 'And I suppose Mr Foreman's not doing well. So he sends aircraft to bomb us here and show the voters he isn't a man you can play around with. And if a few dozen, or a few hundred Palestinians get killed, so what? They're all a bunch of terrorists anyway, Hmmm?' Her eyes flashed angrily.

Ray held up a hand. 'Hold it, Alice. They're trying to knock us off, too, remember.' He smiled, and watched her anger slip a couple of notches. 'Anyway, from what Bahrawi told Julia, it's Iran they're shaping up to attack, not Lebanon.'

She shrugged. 'Maybe he's right. I only know the rumours here in the camp. It's going to be the Lebanon.'

Julia looked sceptical. 'Bahrawi seemed to have a pretty good idea what he was talking about. D'you really think the Palestinians have access to better intelligence than the Iranians?'

She gave them both a long, peculiar look. 'That's another thing that's strange about this whole business. The word among people in here who usually know is that the information came from a most reliable source.'

Ray smiled. 'Alice, I know you're maybe biased in their favour, but what passes for a reliable source in this country?'

She ignored his flippancy. 'The same thing that passes with your own intelligence services. The Israelis!'

They looked at each other, dumbfounded. 'Are you saying the *Israelis* are giving intelligence to the Fatah?' Julia said incredulously.

Alice laughed and shook her head. 'No, I'm not saying that. I said the rumour is that the information *came* from the Israelis. I didn't say they *gave it away*.' She paused, half smiling, as the others stared in disbelief, turning over the implications of what she had just said. She continued speaking in the very soft, tired voice of someone explaining the obvious to obtuse children. 'Israel's the Middle East, too, remember. Fatah, the Palestinians generally, may be eclipsed by the Fundamentalists just now, but don't imagine they're finished. If anything, more money's being pumped in here than ever, now that the Saudis and the Gulf sheiks are getting in a twist over Shi-ism. Believe me, they've money enough to buy information anywhere it's available. Including Tel Aviv. The pity is,' she added, gesturing around her, 'that they don't put the money to better use.' She rose to leave.

Julia leapt to her feet. 'Alice, we have to get to a phone. We *must* get the truth about Michael's kidnapping out, to our papers. Don't you see? If those crazy swine *are* planning a raid it's the best chance we have of stopping them. You have to help us.'

Alice turned back from the doorway. She stood silently for a moment, contemplating them. Then her eyes drifted to the sleeping figure of Michael. 'Do you want to take him with you?'

Julia put an involuntary hand on Michael's shoulder. 'There's no way we're leaving here without him, Alice. I know Michael. He'll want to get out of this and screw the bastards that've done this to him.'

Alice pursed her lips. 'I'll be back in ninety minutes. I hope we'll be able to rouse him by then. The shot I gave him will keep him out like a light for a while. There's a water tap down the corridor. Don't drink from it if you can help it, the supply's scarce. The toilet's outside. Don't use that, either, if you can possibly help it.' With another of the sudden smiles that were in such dazzling contrast to her brusque manner, she wheeled and left them.

Bradman watched through the dark-tinted glass of the limousine window as Bashaar stood hunched by the open-fronted booth making his calls. The booth, which advertised prices for two dozen different drinks, could actually supply black coffee or warm Pepsi-Cola. Milk would have been too vulnerable to the vagaries of the electricity supply, as Bashaar's cousin, a wry, laconically humorous man, had explained to him. At least, it would have been if he had been able to get the milk in the first place. And the fridge was broken anyway, since last year.

Bradman sipped coffee from the thick glass and grimaced. In a few minutes Rachid's men would be converging on Burj al Barajinah. Their job was to keep track of the Colters and hold them until Bradman could speak to them. He chuckled. In the mood they were in they would probably shoot them out of hand and tell him they had tried to escape. He would prefer to talk to them first. He wanted to know whom else they had talked to, who might also need to be attended to. If he could silence Colter and his sister and that troublemaker Walker, dealing with a few Lebanese would be easy. By Friday the election would be over. If the raid produced the right result some powerful people would be in his debt, starting with the President. Three more citizens lost in the Lebanese turmoil would not be an issue for long. They had no business there in the first place.

Bashaar threw himself into the car, grinning triumphantly. 'It's all done, Major. Men from my cousin's section, trustworthy men,' he added, proudly, 'are on their way now. All the gates will be watched, discreetly.'

'Yeah, they better be discreet,' Bradman said, sourly. 'If the Amal boys find a bunch of Rachid's Sunnis drifting into the area they'll wind up tearing each other to pieces.'

Bashaar clicked his tongue. 'Please, Major.' He laughed self-deprecatingly. 'These men know how to do it.' He laid a hand lightly on his chest. 'Believe me, Major. I swear on the heads of my children, all the exits will be watched.'

Bradman grimaced. 'Yeah. How about the tunnels?'

Bashaar frowned. 'They can be a problem. I told them to watch all streets for a block away from the camp. Tunnels would not go further. The airport road too. In half an hour the camp will be completely sealed off. We have them trapped in there.'

'You've done well, Bashaar.' He turned to the driver. 'Take us to the abattoir.'

The abattoir stood close to the shore near the Beirut river, opposite a long promontory of land that enclosed an oily lagoon. A thick scum of rubbish heaved slowly in the swell. A rust-streaked ship rode eighty metres offshore, its engines turning.

On the littered quayside a group of people, some holding suitcases, two of them nursing pet cats, clustered nervously inside a defensive ring of frightened marines. The marines, who were armed, kept uneasy eyes on the surrounding warehouses. A blunt-nosed launch built of weathered timber chugged noisily towards the ship. Aboard it stood a further contingent of civilians and two more marines.

As Bradman's limousine drew up the Ambassador stepped busily from the crowd, ostentatiously examining his watch. He strode officiously to the car. Ted Gower, the CIA station chief, strolled in his wake, smiling thinly at the Ambassador's back.

'About time, Bradman,' the Ambassador called, loud enough for the group behind him to hear. 'Do you realize how long you've kept everybody waiting? How *vulnerable* we've been?' He lowered his voice. 'And where the hell did you acquire that ridiculous outfit? This isn't Vietnam.'

Bradman glanced down at the camouflage overalls. He shrugged. 'It's been one of those mornings, Ambassador. You're going to have to leave without me.' He drew the Ambassador closer to the huddle of evacuees. He spoke conversationally but clearly. Most of the group recognized him. They stared with frank curiosity at his clothes. 'I think I may have a lead to Julia Colter and Walker. Maybe even to her brother. I'm staying to follow it through.'

The Ambassador made a peevish face. 'Don't be absurd. You can't stay here alone. I can't allow it.' His voice rose petulantly. 'I *order* you to leave with us.'

Bradman lowered his own voice, but not so low the crowd could not hear him. 'I'm sorry, Ambassador,' he said, sincerely, 'but I can't do that. There are Americans in danger back there. I need to try.'

He held out his hand for the Ambassador to shake. The Ambassador's shoulders heaved under the pressure of his anger. His eyes flashed bitter resentment at Bradman. He shot a quick glance over his shoulder. The crowd were watching the scene in fascinated silence. When the Ambassador turned back to face Bradman his mouth was fixed in a smile. He grasped the outstretched hand and pumped it in both of his. 'Good luck, then, Major,' he said heartily. He spun and left him alone.

Bradman settled back against the upholstery. Behind the protection of the dark-tinted windows he allowed himself a soft chuckle. Whatever happened next, he had done what he could to protect himself. The Ambassador was a halfwit. The evacuees had witnessed his own self-sacrifice.

'Okay, Bashaar,' he said, still chuckling quietly, 'let's talk to your cousin the dope dealer.'

31

IT WAS almost three o'clock. The midday heat had drained the streets of people. Only armed men lounged in the shade of entrances, playing backgammon or listening to the tinny blare of radios. Dogs with infected eyes scavenged in the alleys between the buildings. Neither men nor dogs heeded the ear-shattering buzz of the moped.

The man rode with his knees drawn up, his feet resting on the frame over the crank. His body was thin and angular where the slipstream pressed the thin cotton clothes against his body. The flesh around his eyes was pinched, and deep crevices stretched from beside the narrow nostrils to the corners of the mouth. He rode fast, swerving around the broken patches in the asphalt with casual verve. A hundred metres from the gate of the camp he slowed and dismounted with a flourish, swinging himself off before he had fully stopped. He pulled two padlocks from the satchel across his chest and locked the machine to a decapitated street lamp. He probed briefly into the satchel as though checking over its contents and swaggered towards the thick mesh gate.

Between the man and the gate an emplacement of sandbags and cinder blocks barred half the roadway. Two armed men, wearing the distinctive armbands of Amal, detached themselves from the deep shadow of the blockhouse. He sauntered across to them, grinning. He raised a hand.

'Salaam aleikum.'

The men nodded and replied in bored voices, *'Aleikum salaam.'*

The rider made a joke. The men did not smile. He made as though to pass the barrier. One of the men called him back, an almost imperceptible stiffening in his voice.

The moped rider turned back to him. He reached into his satchel and, without taking his eyes from the other man's, produced a small slab of a brown, leathery substance, the size of a cigarette packet but much thinner. He placed it in the sentry's outstretched palm. He was still grinning as widely as before. Only the set of the creases around his eyes changed, as he mentally added an item to his catalogue of humiliations. The armed man closed his fist over the slab of hashish and waved the man away with a smirk.

The dealer's grin melted the moment he turned his back on the men. Like many of the Sunni Moslems of the city, he was contemptuous of the Amal people. They were a party of the poor, recruited among the least educated of the young Shi-ites of the south. He sniggered. It did not bother him if they and the Palestinians wanted to fight their private war to see who would be bottom of the heap and who would be one from the bottom. It was good for business.

Like the Amal men, the Palestinian guards also recognized the dealer. One of them let him through the small gate set into the larger one, greeting him with no particular show of friendliness. He followed the guard to the sentry post where three men sat smoking. This time he was prepared. He pulled from a pocket of his trousers three balls of the same brown substance, each the size of a marble, and handed one to each of the men. He was the only one smiling now. The men pocketed the resin with monosyllables of acknowledgment and watched him pick his way through the barbed-wire coils into the camp.

He strolled through the narrow streets with easy familiarity, staying off the wider alleys where families still sat eating. He kept to the mean back ways, alleys too narrow for people to gather convivially around their stoves. Several times he ducked into doorways, to emerge a few seconds later accompanied by an elderly man or woman or a gaunt young mother nursing a child.

The routine never varied. A few moments' whispered conversation followed by a furtive deal; a block of resin or a twist of foil. The furtiveness was a mannerism born of long habit, not of immediate danger. His presence was tolerated, even welcomed, by the Fatah militia who policed the camp. They were too shrewd to deprive their people of their drugs so long as they had neither food nor hope to put in their place.

At last, as though by chance, he reached the open space in front of the hospital. He loitered for a few seconds in the shadows, squinting around the open area in front of him. Most of the patients had been moved into the shade. Nurses, young men and women distinguishable only by their red-cross armbands, hurried among them. Others sat around the square in the sparse shade taking their midday break. The man let his eyes rest for a moment on one youth who sat alone on a heap of cement blocks. The young man was staring fixedly at the ground, fidgeting and chewing at the ends of his fingers. Smiling wolfishly, the dealer walked with his curious bouncing swagger towards him.

The youth started violently as the man leaned over him and spoke. Recovering himself, he eagerly signalled the man to sit beside him. Leaning close to the young man's face the dealer spoke in a soft, urgent voice. The youth answered agitatedly, gesticulating and nodding, his eyes still cast down. He half-turned to the smiling dealer, reaching out a hand to touch the man's shirt-front in a gesture of pleading. The dealer leaned away, as though the hand were repulsive to him. Behind them, a group of men and women in chequered headcloths and chadors emerged from the hospital, passing close by them as they hurried silently out of the square. The dealer let them get well out of earshot before speaking again, insistently, to the younger man. The young man muttered something and gestured towards the hospital. Nodding, the dealer opened his satchel, and withdrew a half-dozen screws of foil.

He was already on his feet as the boy opened the first of the tiny packages, dabbed a finger into the splash of white powder and pushed it to his nose. By the time the boy looked up the dealer was already several strides away, disappearing behind the end of the hospital building.

The street behind the hospital was narrow and dark. On the far side were the windowless backs of a row of crumbling houses. There was no one in sight except a tiny, naked child poking at the corpse of a small animal with a length of rusty wire. The only sound was the vexed hum of the cloud of circling flies. He set off at an ungainly lope along the alley, watching the small windows set in the hospital wall just above the height of his head. Approaching the last window, he thrust a hand into his satchel and pulled out a dark metal object that nestled neatly in the palm of his hand.

He arrived beneath the window. Glancing quickly up and down the alley he saw nobody except the filthy toddler, who prodded the tiny cadaver with solemn intensity. He ripped the pin from the grenade and began counting. At five he reached up and slapped his empty hand flat against the window. Glass fell clinking into the room. He lobbed the grenade after it and ran for the nearest alley.

The explosion tore away the end of the flimsy building and sent sheets from the corrugated-iron roof cartwheeling into the air. The tremor could be felt through the hard-packed ground for two hundred metres around.

'Holy shit! What was that?'

Ray looked back towards the square. His vivid blue eyes were the only part of his face visible behind the headcloth he wore wound around his face. All around them people were spilling from their houses and running towards the square.

Alice Carnegie let her chador fall from her face. She stopped and half turned. 'Some kind of explosion. I must go back. That was near the hospital.'

Another of the chador-clad figures stepped close to Alice and reached out to take her by the arm. The people running towards the square turned to stare in amazement as the cloth slipped from the figure's head, revealing the bandaged face of Michael. He looked into her eyes. 'No, Alice. What matters most is to get us out of here.' He held up his bandaged hand. 'We don't know yet just what the bastards who did this to me are planning, but you can be sure it'll mean much more useless killing.' His voice grew very soft. His smile was at once sad and determined. 'We *have* to get away from here and stop them.'

For a moment her gaze wavered between Michael and the direction of the square. Her shoulders heaved under the chador. 'You're right,' she sighed. 'And if you stay here you'll bring trouble. Plenty of people in here would sell you out.' She brushed Michael's hand away and set off, almost running, in the direction they had been heading.

Moments later, they turned a corner and were surprised to find themselves only thirty metres from the perimeter fence. For a virtual township of ten thousand people the camp was astoundingly small. Halfway along the block two young men squatted against the wall of a house, playing dominos. As the group approached they could hear clearly the quick clicks as they slapped the worn plaques onto the concrete block that served as a table.

They were within five metres of the two men when, at once, all hint of idleness fell away. One of the men rose to his feet with an easy, feline movement and let them see a gun which he held at his side. The other stayed on the ground. He held a short, Israeli-made machine gun aimed at the level of their bellies.

Alice motioned her companions to stop. Alone, she stepped forward and addressed the standing man, in loud and atrocious French. A head appeared at the door of the house. The face was a ruffian's face, broad and flat with a scar running from above one eyebrow through the grey-flecked ten-day stubble to the jawbone. Gold glinted in its huge grin.

'Dr Carnegie! Please come in.'

They followed her into the unlit interior. The man was huge, heavy-shouldered and larded with an inch-thick coating of fat that rounded his outline, disguising the immense power of his frame. His belly lay stacked in folds above a broad, worn leather belt. He wore a Hawaiian-print shirt, open over his chest and belly. A shoulder holster hung next to the skin under his left arm. He enclosed Alice in an embrace in which she all but disappeared. After some seconds he deposited her back on her feet.

'She fixed this,' he explained to the four watchers, touching two fingers affectionately to his scar. 'If it wasn't for Dr Carnegie I'd be . . .' He broke off, drawing a finger across his throat and making a croaking sound. 'What do you want?' His mouth still smiled at Alice. His eyes drilled into the others.

'I want you to let these people through the tunnel.'

The man's eyes studied Alice for a moment and then returned to the others. 'Why? You know this is the only secure one we have left. We permit its use for only the most essential items.'

She smiled up into the grim, brigand's face. 'They *are* essential items, Amir.'

32

MAJOR BRADMAN smiled and laid the binoculars on the window ledge. He flicked another glance at his watch. Seven minutes past three. In just under three hours the whole thing would be over. He could head south, into Israel, and go home. He realized for the first time that going home would be a disappointment for him. Lebanon had been the first posting since Vietnam where he had felt totally alive. He took up the binoculars again and watched the thin smudge of smoke over the camp disperse and merge with the haze.

Bashaar's cousin was a good man, like Bashaar himself. It was a pity, in a way. He turned from the window and took the tiny cup of coffee Bashaar proffered.

Fifteen minutes later the moped swooped around the corner, slalomed between the two burnt-out cars that lay in the road, the result of a stray shell that morning, and slid to a halt three floors below him. The rider vaulted from the machine, letting it fall unheeded into the road, and ran into the building. Seconds later the doorbell rang.

The dealer stood in front of Bradman, panting and pale. His sunken cheeks were even more pinched than before. His thin chest heaved as he fought for breath enough to speak. Bradman stood frowning but calm, finishing off a second coffee, waiting to hear what the man had to say.

'I'm sorry, sir. I'm really very sorry. They had left the hospital. Before I got there. I . . .' A stinging backhand blow from the big American sent him staggering. He sank to one knee, clutching at the side of his face. Bradman saw the man's frightened eyes slide to his cousin in a mute appeal. Bashaar ostentatiously busied himself with the coffee. Bradman's promises to Bashaar far outweighed the tenuous loyalty he might feel to this distant and untrustworthy 'cousin'.

'Where are they now?' Bradman asked coldly.

'I asked about that.' The man cringed, eager to regain Bradman's favour. 'It was very dangerous for me to stay, but I found out.' He paused, leaving a space for congratulations. Bradman offered none. 'They were taken out by the English woman, Dr Alice. By a tunnel on the north side. I don't know exactly where.'

Bradman stood for a moment, looking at the man without seeing him. Then, his face broke into a surprising smile and he stepped towards the kneeling figure. Shaking his head good-humouredly, he reached out a hand and helped the man to his feet. 'That's good work. You must have been running quite a risk.'

The man nodded vigorous agreement. 'I was. Many people saw me near the hospital. It was very dangerous. It still is.'

Bradman nodded. 'Would you be ready to do something else for me? It wouldn't be dangerous but it would be well paid.'

The man nodded eagerly. 'In dollars?'

'Of course.' Bradman turned to Bashaar. 'Bashaar, I want you to do something very quickly. We have to prevent them from getting word out. Go to the people at the sports centre. Get some explosives. Ten kilos, at least. Do you have money?'

Bashaar shook his head.

Bradman reached into a pocket in his overalls and pulled out his wallet, grateful for the reflex that had made him transfer it when he had left his clothes in the limousine. He passed five one-hundred-dollar bills to Bashaar. 'Go quickly. Meet me downstairs as soon as you can. And bring some good men. At least four.' He began to replace the wallet, then as if on an afterthought, he opened it up again and thumbed out two more hundreds. He pushed them into the hand of the drug dealer. 'Here's something in advance,' he said, smiling at the man. The dealer gave a quick lizard smile, licked his lips and pushed the money into a pocket.

Bradman watched Bashaar leave. He looked again at his watch. 'We've got about a half-hour before Bashaar gets back.' He plucked distastefully at the material of his overalls where dark patches of sweat showed on the chest and back. 'Mind if I take a shower before we talk? It's been a hard day. I feel like shit.' The man shrugged and shook his head. 'Help yourself to coffee.'

He turned on both taps, forced the reluctant plug into its seating and stripped off his clothes. He let the bath run deep before turning it off and wrapping a towel around his waist. He walked back into the living room and over to the coffee table. The man watched without curiosity, his eyes drawn to the scars puckering Bradman's left shoulder. Bradman picked up the simmering pot and poured himself a coffee. As he did so a few drops splashed onto his bare feet. He jumped aside, spilling his cup over the man.

The dealer was very nimble. He sprang to his left, his eyes intent on the falling coffee. Too intent to see Bradman swing the edge of his hand down in a scooping motion.

The blow caught the dealer below the left ear, sending him sprawling on the sofa. It was not quite low enough to get beneath the jawbone and strike cleanly at the jugular. Even as Bradman's weight slammed down on top of him the dealer's streetfighter reflexes had begun working. He jabbed and clawed at Bradman with desperate strength, until Bradman's fingers began to find the soft parts of his throat.

The dealer started to gasp. His struggle began to lose strength. Sensing it, Bradman shifted position, looking for more purchase on the man's throat. He was momentarily forced to slacken his grip. As he did so the man drew back his lips, as though to scream, and sank his teeth into the flesh of Bradman's naked shoulder. He did not ease the pressure as he felt bone but went on sinking his teeth deeper until he tasted the warm sweetness of blood.

Bradman gave a bellow of surprise and pain. Berserk with the pain, he reared abruptly, tearing his shoulder from the man's maw, and crashed a closed fist down into the exposed throat. The man gave a short gargling noise and was still.

Bradman hauled the man off the sofa and dragged him to the bathroom. The man's eyes were open. They stared imploringly at Bradman as he lifted him over the edge of the bath.

It took perhaps twenty seconds for the man to die. After five seconds more Bradman placed his hand flat on the man's chest and pressed down hard. The drowned man vomited a cloud of bubbles. They made pink eddies as blood from Bradman's shoulder wound ran into the water.

He stood up, took a last dispassionate look at the thin face, magnified by the water, that stared lifelessly back up at him, and began washing his wound at the washbasin, rubbing soapy water hard into the lesions as though he thought the man might be a rabies carrier. Satisfied, he began rooting quickly in the medicine cabinet, throwing tubes and vials aside until he found the lint and sticking plaster he wanted. He wadded some lint and dressed the wound.

He waited another quarter of an hour before putting his clothes back on. He had chosen the killing method expressly to avoid bloodstains. The last thing he needed was to arouse Bashaar's suspicions at this stage. He was disappointed that it had gone wrong, a sign of encroaching age, maybe. He shrugged himself into the overall. Before going downstairs to wait for Bashaar's return, he strode back into the bathroom and removed the two hundred dollars from the dead man's pocket.

They stood blinking in the light of a naked bulb. They were crowded into a windowless room with bare cement block walls. The young man who had guided them through the tunnel unlocked a door armoured with a heavy steel plate.

The door was concealed on the far side by a heavy brocade curtain. They pushed past it into the outer room. It was an open-fronted shop, filled to the ceiling with precarious piles of cloth. Festoons of samples formed a maze which effectively shielded the rear of the shop from the gaze of customers. Several impassive, heavily built 'salesmen' stood casually among the heaps of material, ready to bar the way to inquisitive browsers. Their guide led them between the displays and out to the street.

Selim turned and embraced the man quickly. 'Thank you. God be with you, cousin.' He turned back to his companions. 'Come.'

The four of them, Ray and Selim in headcloths, Michael and Julia in chadors, headed for the street.

They set off away from the shop, the two men leading, the two black-shrouded figures following at a few paces, in deference to the Moslem custom. Michael, in particular, was relieved to see that what women there were, in this predominantly Shi-ite southern suburb, were also enveloped in billowing black chadors. Even amid the tension and fear Michael had been chafing under a sense of absurdity. The others had not listened to his protests. Only the chador would fully hide the dressing on his head.

It was still too early in the afternoon for many people to be on the street. A few old men sat in the shade. Children played noisy games. Forty metres away a group of children hung around two slightly older boys on mopeds, admiring the coveted machines. Nobody was taking any notice of the four customers from the shop. At the first intersection they stopped. Julia and Michael drew closer.

'Habib's?' Julia murmured, addressing Ray, sure he would have had the same thought. He nodded.

They stepped to the edge of the kerb and hailed one of the few dusty taxis that crawled the empty street. Selim wedged himself next to the driver, pushing aside the scattering of tape cassettes, loose coins and other small objects that lay there. He gave the driver the address, wincing as the man bullied the reluctant gearbox into action.

The two boys on mopeds had lost interest in the childrens' admiration. They had been told to look for only one woman and three men. Two women and two men were not exactly that. But there were rumours about the textile shop.

They were very young, perhaps only twelve or thirteen, but they had lived those years in a city shredded by violence and treachery. It had left them with a shrewd, street-smart eye for the unusual. A good man could progress very fast in the militias. Some of the most senior people among Rachid's supporters were not more than twenty. One of them jerked his machine off its stand and set off in pursuit of the taxi.

The cab stopped in front of Habib's building. They had found new security guards, who looked up abstractedly at their approach. One of them rose sullenly to his feet. He ran the metal detector over Selim and Ray, ignoring the chador-wrapped figures. After a couple of cursory questions to Selim he waved them on.

Julia leaned on the bell push. It was some time before she heard the soft snick of the cover of the spyhole being lifted aside. She did not remember there having been a spyhole before. She let the veil fall from her face and ran her fingers through her hair, smiling at the lens of the judas. There was a pause of several seconds. The smile was becoming a strain when they heard the muffled crash of a security lock being opened. The muzzle of a gun showed in the crack of the door. Julia ignored the gun. She stared for a long time at the face behind it. Recognition came slowly.

'Christ,' she gasped. 'What the hell happened to you?'

The door opened wider. Habib's face and skull were swathed in bandages, leaving only small areas free around the mouth and eyes. He wore a pair of cotton slacks, above which the swaying belly and bearish shoulders were littered with rectangles of sticking plaster. Ray pushed back his own head covering and stared at Habib. The Lebanese looked back at him, his eyes scarcely even registering surprise, as though they were too tired to care any more, about anything. When Michael shrugged back the chador to reveal himself as a man, even Habib's pain-dulled look began to show a flicker of curiosity. He followed them into the living room.

Everything in the room was broken. Curtains and upholstery hung in ribbons. The pictures Habib had collected in London hung in streamers from shattered frames. The carpet was stained with food. Shards of broken glass and china lay in a heap in one corner. A broom lay nearby. Habib had evidently been clearing up.

The destruction shocked Julia almost more than Habib's physical appearance. She reached for Ray's hand as she stood dumbly surveying the wrecked room. With her other hand she reached over and caught Habib's.

'The bastards!' she said through clenched teeth. 'They did this to you for helping us?'

Habib shrugged gently. 'I was very lucky, Julia. I'm still alive. I didn't think I would be.'

'But who did it, Habib? Who even knew you'd helped us?'

He shrugged again. His eyes filled with gentle sadness. 'What does it matter, Julia? It's all an absurd game. What does it matter which of the players it happens to be?' He smiled gently. 'What brings you here now? What do you want from me?'

She outlined the events that had brought them back to him. He listened without comment, only raising his eyebrows when she reached the revelation of Bradman's role in Michael's kidnapping. Even that did not seem to surprise him too much.

'And what do you intend to do now?' he asked mildly.

'Try to phone the *Times*, if you'll let me.'

He spread his hands and gestured towards the telephone. 'Be my guest,' he murmured. 'If you'll all excuse me, I'm going back to bed. I've had a headache since I was attacked.'

He padded from the room as Julia pounced on the phone.

33

IT WAS EIGHT O'CLOCK in the morning. Dean Sutcliffe's head ached with a blinding intensity. He was too old for sleepless nights. At the sound of the buzzer on the Chief of Staff's desk he wheeled from the window.

'The President'll see you now, Dean.' Ed Seymour, the Chief of Staff, a longtime crony of Foreman's, had always irritated him. Right now he would have liked to drive a fist into his ingratiating smirk. Foreman had made him wait twenty minutes.

The President sat at his desk studying a typed sheet. He started as Sutcliffe entered, feigning surprise, and doing it badly. 'Dean,' he said, with uneasy good humour. 'What's it all about? Where's the fire?'

Sutcliffe was too angry for the sarcasm he would normally have used. He pulled a sheet of pink paper from an inside pocket and slapped it onto the desk.

'Here! It's the cable that came in from Tel Aviv!'

The President blinked and peered reluctantly at the paper,

not touching it. He cleared his throat noisily. 'Ah, er, this is the one you, er, mentioned, huh?'

'Oh, for Christ's sake, Jack!' Anger had made him cast aside the President's title. 'You know what it is! It's the one I've had Zimund pestering me about for half the fucking night!'

The President blinked, thrown off-balance by Sutcliffe's vehemence.

'The people in Tel Aviv want to know what the fuck's going on. Jesus, *I* want to know what's going on.' He leaned closer to the President, his fists on the desk. 'I don't like being made a horse's ass, Jack. I'm not supposed to find out about US foreign policy initiatives from the Israelis!'

'Maybe there's a mistake here, Dean. They must have some wires crossed.'

Sutcliffe reared away from the desk. 'There's no mistake. I've had Zimund on the phone four times. A fish can't fart in the Gulf without them getting it on tape. He read me the stuff they'd got. Messages from the carrier to the support group. *Our* navy's planning to hit a whole bunch of targets in Lebanon and *he's* telling *me* about it!'

The President gulped. 'You're taking this personally, Dean. Don't . . .'

The Secretary of State stared at him. '*I'm* taking it personally? Zimund's taking it personally. He told me he tried to talk to you half a dozen times. You refused to talk to him.'

The President's voice rose. He slammed a palm flat on the desk. 'That's right!' His voice had risen to a shout. 'He called up at five, refusing to tell Ed what it was about. It might have been different with Mayer. He's a man you can talk to. Zimund's an oily little shit. I wouldn't trust him an inch.'

Sutcliffe removed his glasses and pinched the bridge of his nose, waiting for the tantrum to blow over. He knew Jack Foreman's trick of turning embarrassment to anger too well to bother reacting.

'Okay, Jack,' he said finally, almost in a whisper. 'So you'll only talk to the top man. You're President. You have the right. Even if you know the top man's in intensive care and Zimund's got full authority. Here's what Zimund had to say, put simply. The Israelis, Mayer included, don't want us to hit Lebanon. They want us to leave the place strictly and absolutely alone.'

'So what's their angle?' Foreman cut in, heavily sarcastic. 'They hit the dump often enough themselves, don't they?'

Sutcliffe shrugged. 'I don't know. Zimund wouldn't tell me. He said he *couldn't*. He didn't even know. He just said Mayer was *begging* us to call it off.'

'So Mayer's fit enough to talk to him but not to talk to me, huh?'

Sutcliffe shook his head. 'That's all I know. Zimund promised Mayer would call you himself as soon as he was able. Meanwhile they're *imploring* us to cancel it.'

The President came around the desk and paced the room. He pawed at the loose wisps of grey hair with one big hand. Sutcliffe noticed the brown mottling among the thick hair on the back of the hand. Age. He and Jack Foreman were the same age. Maybe it was time they both called it a day.

When the President spoke, the bogus anger had gone from his voice, leaving it hoarse and almost inaudible. 'I can't do it, Dean. You've seen the polls. That bastard Wilton's taking it right out from under us.'

'So anything goes? Including slaughtering innocent people?'

The President looked at him as though Sutcliffe had just offered him rat poison. 'I just want to win this fucking election. I want another four years. And I've got forty-eight hours to make sure I get them. This Colter thing's going to do it for us. Tom and I have been over it a dozen times.'

Sutcliffe's anger flared at the mention of Jordan. 'This whole thing has Tom Jordan's name written all over it. Can't you see? He's playing soldier again. Christ, we don't even know who has the kid.'

'Of course we do. It's this, er, Revolutionary, er, thing.'

'The Islamic Revolutionary Faction? Even the Israelis have

never heard of them! Mossad's paying off somebody in every damned group there is out there. But they never heard of this one. We're dealing with a handful of mavericks.'

'A handful of mavericks that sends us pieces of one of our citizens! People have been seeing this in the papers. They're tired of seeing America kicked around. They want something done.'

'Regardless of whether it does any good?'

'Yeah!' The President's voice held a sneer. 'Look, *I* don't understand what the fuck's going on in that snakepit. I'm damned sure the voters don't. If Jimmy Carter had only had the balls to let the B-52s loose on Tehran instead of farting around when they held the hostages there, he'd have been re-elected.'

Sutcliffe stood up, sighing. 'Jesus, Jack, you really *like* being President, don't you?' He headed for the door.

'Damn right! And you like being Secretary of State!'

Sutcliffe looked over his shoulder and nodded. 'Air Force One beats lining up for the shuttle. By the way, there's one more thing in Zimund's message.'

'Huh? What?'

'If you go through with this the Israelis will declare in favour of Wilton.'

The President looked as though he had been slapped. 'They can't do that,' he said huskily. 'After all I've done for those bastards. They'll come begging.'

Sutcliffe shook his head. 'Not to you. They'll take New York off you. Without New York you've blown it for sure. You won't *be* President.'

34

BRADMAN had been waiting only six or seven minutes in front of the apartment block when Bashaar's car returned, shadowed by a pick-up with five men in it. He crossed the pavement in three fast strides and threw himself into the car.

'North,' he said at the driver's enquiring look. 'Fast! Take the corniche.' The car lurched away from the kerb. Bradman turned to Bashaar. 'Did you get the plastic?' Bashaar pointed to a torn airline bag on the seat between them. He opened it for inspection. Inside lay a dozen slabs of greyish explosive and a handful of detonators. 'Good. Get it ready.' Bashaar busied himself with the explosive, moulding the malleable material around the detonators with practised deftness.

Bradman chewed at a thumbnail with uncharacteristic edginess. His composure was strained to snapping point. Wherever the Colter group were, they would be trying to get a call out, to contact the outside world. A single phone call would be enough. He would be finished. Worse, he would have screwed up. The story would be all over the newspapers the next morning and on breakfast television an hour later. His picture would be staring out at a hundred million viewers from New York to California.

It would not take ten minutes to connect him to Tom Jordan. Their association was common knowledge to anyone who cared. It had been for twenty years. And Tom Jordan's office was in the heart of the White House. He saw the President every single day. The Commander-in-Chief's candidacy would go down the same chute as Bradman's own career. He snapped monosyllabic instructions to the driver, who responded silently, swinging the car through corners at speeds that threatened the final destruction of the dilapidated tyres.

'Stop! Pull in here!' They were in one of the wide streets leading to the circus where the main post office stood. The steps teemed with people. At the doors of the post office they could see the guards, Lebanese Army men, half-heartedly asserting the last shred of the official Government's authority. Bradman squinted at the distant figures of the soldiers.

'You're sure they can handle it?' He jerked a thumb over his shoulder at the pick-up.

'You asked me to bring only the best men, Major.'

Bashaar's voice held the faint whine of the congenitally deceptive sensing a slur on his integrity.

'Good,' Bradman said grimly. 'Get them to it.'

Bashaar looked surprised. 'But aren't we going with them?'

'We've got something else to attend to.'

Bashaar looked disappointed at the thought of missing some mayhem. 'What?'

'Habib. The bar owner. If they're still in the city that's the most likely place they'd hole up.'

Bashaar seemed cheered. Maybe there would yet be some killing to be done.

Ray lounged on the balcony, his thick forearms on the railing, watching the street below. In the headcloth he looked like any local idler watching the world go by. In fact his attention has been riveted for the past ten minutes on the youth tinkering with his motorbike a block away. The boy had been constantly looking at their building. He had been joined by a second young man. After a short conversation the second man had entered a café. Maybe to find a phone.

'For Christ's sake, Julia, forget the call. We've got to get out of here.'

Julia ignored him. She continued prowling the room, never moving far from the phone. Ray was about to speak again when the phone shrilled. Julia pounced on it at the first ring.

'Harry Moore, please. This is Julia Colter.'

The others stood watching in absolute silence. Michael was at Julia's elbow. Ray had returned to watching the street. A third man, armed, had sauntered by the boy with the bike. After a short exchange of conversation and a glance at the building, he had drifted across the street and disappeared into an alley. Now the rear of the building was covered.

'Oh, fuck his meeting! Interrupt him! It's a matter of life and death, literally!' Julia was almost screaming into the phone.

Ray stepped into the room. 'Give it to him in thirty words

and let's get the fucking hell out of here. Something weird's going on down there.'

She nodded, not really hearing. 'Harry!' she exploded, almost crying with relief. 'It's Julia.'

'Julia! For Christ's sake!' Harry took a great gulp of air. The twenty-five-yard dash to his office had left him breathless. 'Where are you?'

'Beirut. With Michael. And Ray Walker. We're all okay. Harry, Michael wasn't kidnapped by the Lebanese. It was all a set-up. It was our own people. Bradman. The security guy at the Embassy here.'

Moore held the phone away from his ear, scowling. He smacked the mouthpiece against his palm and put it back to his ear. 'Where are you?' He was shouting. He shrugged and scowled at Ron Watt who held an extension phone. Faces crowded at the office door, watching silently. From the phones the sound of static was loud in the room.

'Damn. Damn. Damn.' He slammed the phone down. 'We've lost the line.'

Julia went on speaking for some seconds before she became aware of the echo on the line. She broke off. 'Harry?' she called.

The hum continued. 'Harry!' She was almost weeping with anger and frustration. She called Harry's name one last time. She stood up and threw the telephone from her. Rage and bewilderment and frustration mingled in her face. Her voice came out in a howl. 'He didn't hear me! The line's gone! The bastards! They've cut the line. How did they *know*?'

Ray called from the balcony. 'Look!' They all moved to the window. A kilometre or more away a billow of black smoke drifted over the rooftops.

'The post office,' Habib said flatly. 'They've sabotaged the whole system.'

'The hell with that,' Ray murmured. 'Look down there!' As he spoke he hustled them from the balcony. Two more men had joined the youth. Ray shepherded them into the room. 'We have to get the hell out of here. Now!'

'Where will you go?' Habib spoke very softly.

There was a short silence. Ray broke it. 'Michael? You have anyone here you can trust?'

Michael gave a short laugh. He held up his maimed hand. 'The last time I trusted someone in this city, it was Bradman.' He shook his head. 'No. Not a soul. I wouldn't trust anyone at the University right now with my lunch box, let alone my life.'

Julia smiled wryly and looked at Ray. 'Ray?'

He shook his head. 'You've seen how it is, Julia. We're taboo.'

They fell silent again. Julia chewed at her lip. Abruptly, she seemed to make up her mind. 'Bcharré! We'll go back to Bcharré. To Mehdi.'

Ray stared at her incredulously. 'You're kidding! Without transport, with half the gunmen in this town after us? Forget it.'

She shook her head. 'There's no choice. If we stay in Beirut we're dead. Between Bradman and Rachid's clan they'll be watching every place we might go. Every embassy, every contact we have.'

Ray drifted back to the window. He cast anxious looks down at the street. 'Julia, there's no way we'll make it. We don't even know if Bahrawi's still there.'

Julia looked at Selim. He nodded.

'He is there,' he said quietly.

'Will you come with us?'

He smiled gravely at her. 'I promised Mehdi Bahrawi. I will try to help you.'

At the window Ray swore. Another man had joined the group below. One of them pointed openly up at their window. Ray spun to face the room.

'Okay. Bcharré. Let's move.' He was already on his way to the door.

Julia turned to Habib. 'Habib? Are you with us?'

He smiled his pained, gentle smile. 'God be with you all.' He gestured around the ruined flat. 'This is my home.' Julia leaned up and planted a kiss on his cheek. Ray and Michael were already calling her from the landing.

Ray reached the foot of the stairs first. A single security guard sat in the hall yawning, rousing himself from his torpor. As Ray moved to the door to check the street Selim drifted over to the guard, greeting him pleasantly. The guard's response emerged as a sigh as Selim rammed his fist into the bulge beneath the seated man's ribs. He scooped up the guard's rifle and ran to the door.

The four men had left their post at the end of the block. They were strolling towards the building, one staying on the far side of the street. They were still fifty metres away. Ray pointed to an alley across the street. 'Let's go!'

They burst from the building at a run. They heard a cry, almost a shriek, from one of the young men. They were halfway across the street when they heard the first shot. They kept running.

The young men were quick. They had drawn closer. With a shout to the others to go on, Selim spun to face them, dropping to one knee. As he raised the rifle the four youths threw themselves to the ground. With a whoop of pleasure Selim fired twice and then raced off in pursuit of the others.

He reached them in the mouth of the alley. He was grinning. 'They have only pistols. They're afraid.'

Another shot exploded, very close. Selim's grin turned to a grimace. He fell face-down in the dirt of the alley.

Ten metres ahead of them, where another alley intersected theirs, stood Bashaar. The wisp of smoke from the shot drifted across the grimed, sneering face. He jerked his head towards the alley from which he had emerged.

'Come,' he said, smirking. 'A representative of your government would like to speak to you.'

35

BASHAAR JABBED angrily at them with his gun muzzle, forcing them into the alley. Julia moved reluctantly, ignoring the blows, looking anxiously back at Selim. Blood from his new wound darkened the cloth of his trousers and turned the dust to a sticky brown paste. Selim clutched his thigh tightly with both hands and bit deeply into his lower lip, refusing to scream. A painful blow to the back of the neck sent Julia reeling after the others and out of sight of their wounded companion.

The alley was less than twenty metres long. Across the far end of it, blocking the exit, was the black bulk of the Embassy limousine. The rangy figure of Bradman sat upright in the front passenger seat chewing hard on a thumbnail. At the sight of them he started with relief, jerked his hand away from his mouth and clambered lithely from the car to wait for them. All the nervousness had evaporated now. He stood with his feet apart, his hands resting lightly on his hips. His lips curled in the small, tight smile of a gambler savouring success.

Bashaar herded the three prisoners towards the waiting figure. They shuffled through the rubbish that lay in banks along the narrow alley, sending clouds of huge blue flies swirling angrily. An emaciated dog moved grudgingly away from some unspeakable object at their approach, keeping its shoulders low to the ground, ready to dispute ownership. Beyond the dog, in a recess leading to a padlocked steel door, more rubbish had gathered in an unwholesome drift, a knee-high heap of rotting food remnants, bones, empty cans and broken plastic.

The sight of the snarling dog made Julia hesitate. A vicious blow to the kidneys made her gasp and stagger forwards. Angrily, Ray turned to protest. Bashaar swung the butt of the rifle at Ray's head. Ray took a step back to avoid the blow, stumbled and appeared to lose his footing. He staggered two steps and fell sprawling face down in the heap of garbage. The dog snarled and snapped around him. With a cry, Julia sprang to Ray's side. Michael, too, leapt forward, ignoring Bashaar's cries. As Julia knelt by Ray he drove the dog back with flailing kicks at the animal's head.

A thick mist of flies droned resentfully around them as Ray grovelled, up to his elbows in the loathsome filth.

'Get up! Move! Be quick!' Bashaar's voice was an angry hiss.

Keeping his eyes on the dog, Michael was moving to help Ray to his feet. 'Fuck you,' he said, conversationally.

A kick from Bashaar deep into his groin sent him to his knees. He rolled forward helplessly, clutching himself and retching.

White-faced, Julia sprang to her feet and, with a speed that surprised the Lebanese, raked her fingernails down his face. The Arab roared and snatched one of her wrists, wrenching it violently behind her back. He hurled her from him. She fell sprawling at Bradman's feet. With an easy careless grace, he pulled her up and pinioned her against him. The bone of his powerful forearm cut painfully into her throat.

She writhed ineffectually as Bashaar moved purposefully towards Michael, bent on venting his anger. The expression on the man's face was an obscene cocktail of hatred, cruelty and pleasure. He stood looking down at the bowed, helpless figure of Michael. He raised his weapon.

Julia tried to scream. Bradman watched impassively as Bashaar, with a slow, madman's relish, raised the gun high, the heavy stock aimed at Michael's unprotected head. With a soft cackle of insane glee, he began driving the weapon downwards. He was still giggling when he died.

In that instant of Bradman's shock, as Bashaar reared backwards, his mouth still twisted in a laugh and his eyes frowning in incomprehension, Julia tore herself away from him. Ray was on his knees facing the American. His face was dead white. The dark gun, made huge by the silencer screwed to its snout, shook in his hands. He watched Bradman's eyes flicker around him. The man was a soldier. Ray could almost read his thoughts as his training made him instinctively measure distances, weigh chances, seek escape routes. He saw the man's eyes slide from his face to the gun. He knew Ray was no expert, but the alley was narrow, Julia had moved too far for him to use her as cover, and the car hemmed him in from behind. And it was a big gun. Even a glancing blow from one of the bullets would fell a man. Bradman gave a slow grin, shrugged, and raised his hands.

'Against the wall, over here. Feet apart,' Ray ordered hoarsely, nodding at a spot several feet from the car.

Still wearing his slightly off-centre grin, Bradman moved to the spot Ray indicated. He walked with a loose, relaxed stride in which there was no fear, only a due respect for the gun.

Keeping his eyes on Bradman's back, Ray half turned to Julia and Michael, who was now on his feet. 'In the car. Fast.'

Julia looked at him for a moment, her eyes widening in disbelief. 'We're not leaving Selim?'

Ray licked his lips and shrugged. 'Christ,' he said in a voice that rasped in his parched throat. 'Just make it quick.'

Selim still lay in almost the same spot. He had dragged himself into the relative shelter of one wall of the alley and lay watching the street. With one hand he kept a weak grip on the gun, with the other he clutched at his damaged thigh. Great beads of sweat gathered on his forehead. A spreading stain darkened the dust beneath him from his waist to his knees.

Julia and Michael took an arm each and hoisted him unceremoniously to his feet. For the first time he allowed himself to groan. He smiled weakly. 'They are afraid of the rifle. They are waiting for help. It will be arriving very soon. You must go.'

Michael plucked the rifle from the ground. 'You're coming, too, Selim.'

Selim shook his head. 'It's impossible. I can't walk. You must hurry.'

Michael shook his head and smiled. 'You won't have to walk. We have a limo service.'

Ray stood exactly as they had left him, his eyes riveted on Bradman's tapering back. They dragged Selim to the car and pushed him roughly into the back seat. Michael clambered in beside him. Julia slid behind the wheel.

She called sharply to Ray, gunning the powerful motor. Without taking his eyes from Bradman he began backing towards the car. He was one step away from the vehicle when a group of men burst into view at the far end of the alley; the ones Selim had kept at bay plus another man, somewhat older, beefily built, in a faded olive-green uniform. He was puffing hard and carrying a short machine gun. A rocket-launcher was slung across his back.

Julia's scream alerted Ray. In the moment it took the newcomer to size up the situation he spun and dived headlong into the car. Julia's foot came off the brake. The car bounded forward.

The momentum swung the door closed as a spray of bullets clanged against the reinforced metalwork. Julia's last, fleeting impression was of Bradman straightening and watching them go. His lips were curled in an ugly little smile.

Julia held her foot to the floor as they barrelled through the short street and onto the main road. She swung the car north, leaving dark arcs of rubber on the hot asphalt.

They drove in silence for a few seconds. Julia caught Ray's eye. 'Where the hell did that come from?'

Ray waved the gun. He grinned. 'When we first came to Habib's. A couple of days ago. I told you. I buried the gun in the rubbish.'

She took a deep breath. 'Jesus,' she said softly. 'We're going to need luck like that.'

Several hundred yards behind them the beefy gunman was hauling the driver from a lavender-painted taxi.

•

The immaculate sentry guarding the Secretary of State's personal lift allowed one undisciplined eyebrow to lift in mild surprise as Dean Sutcliffe strode from the car that had ferried him the short distance from the White House. The Secretary's head was bowed as though he carried some great load of personal grief. Extraordinarily, he made no greeting to the soldier who opened the thick glass door for him, nor to the sentry, who stood at respectful attention by the lift. Instead he plunged into the lift and stabbed with an abstracted venom at the button that would take the machine non-stop to his suite of offices. The sentry waited until he heard the machinery begin to turn before grimacing at his companion.

'World War Three?' he mouthed, rolling his eyes cheerfully at the prospect.

Sutcliffe stepped into the carpeted hush of the Secretary's suite. He crossed the lobby, ignoring more sentries, and entered his own office. Lights glowed on the telephones on his desk. He sat down with slow care and remained for several moments with his chin resting on his hands, his eyes staring unfocused at the desktop. Then he shuddered and reached for the nearest of the phones.

'Susan?'

'Yes, Mr Secretary. Good morning.'

Susan Brand had been his secretary for over thirty years. He had nearly married her. And yet still she could not be convinced that he preferred his name and not his title. 'What's up?'

She listed a long series of calls that had come in and the appointments arranged for that morning. 'Oh, and Harry Moore's tried half a dozen times. I told him you were with the President.'

Automatically, Sutcliffe looked at his watch. 'If he calls again put him off. This is not a day I want to start with a conversation with the press.'

'Fine. I'll do that.' Susan's voice held a faint frosting of disappointment. She knew Harry Moore and liked him. 'He did say it was most urgent. That you'd want to talk to him. It's about the Colter kidnapping. He says he's got something new you'd be interested in.'

Sutcliffe's head snapped upright. 'Get him for me, will you?'

Less than half a minute later Moore's voice came on the line. 'Dean?'

'Harry, what is it you have on the Colter case?'

Harry Moore was in too much of a hurry to tell his story to be offended by Sutcliffe's brusque manner. 'We got a call from Beirut this morning. From Julia Colter.'

'And?'

'She had her brother with her.'

There was a long silence.

'Harry,' Sutcliffe said at length, slowly and warily, 'this couldn't be some kind of stunt?'

'Not ours. Somebody's. I'll give you her exact words. "Michael wasn't kidnapped by Lebanese. It was all a set-up. It was our own people." That's what she said, word for word, Dean. "Our own people." And she wasn't talking about us up here in New York City.' He stopped, letting the words sink in in the long silence that followed. 'What the hell's going on, Dean?' he said, at length. There was no reply from the other end of the line. 'Dean?' he called. 'Can you hear me?' He shook the phone and clicked the cradle several times. 'You there?'

'What a prick.' Sutcliffe's voice was suddenly older.

'Eh?'

'Tom Jordan! What a prick he is!'

'I don't follow you, Dean.'

'Jordan. He's the bastard behind this.' He sighed. 'He enjoyed his wars and he's never had as much fun since.'

Sutcliffe's voice had grown faint, as though he were addressing himself.

'You think Tom Jordan's involved in this somehow?'

'Eh?' Sutcliffe gave a start. 'God knows. Look, will you do me a favour?'

'Sure. What?'

'Call the President. Tell him what you've just told me.'

'But, Dean, I thought, well, it's the Secretary of State's responsibility, isn't it? That's why I called you. I . . .'

Sutcliffe cut him off with a short bark of laughter. 'Yeah, thanks, Harry. You're right, of course. It's the Secretary of State's responsibility. But I quit.'

This time it was Harry Moore's turn to pause. 'Jesus, Dean,' he said in a hushed voice, 'when?'

'Now.' As he spoke, Sutcliffe stood up, still holding the phone. 'See you around, Harry.'

'Hold it. Wait. Look, is this official? Can we print it? I mean . . .'

''Bye, Harry.'

'Hold it! Where are you going?'

'Out. To the park. I need some air. Call Foreman. You'd better do it right now.' He hung up.

36

JULIA DROVE fast and recklessly, pulling all the power from the car's huge engine. They screamed through corners, leaving more rubber on the road and scattering pedestrians. Behind her, Michael struggled to dress Selim's wound using strips cut from Bradman's jacket.

Twice, groups of armed men signalled them to stop. Both times Julia roared past them without slowing, wincing as bullets whanged against the toughened metalwork. In the relative safety of the limousine they were grateful for these armed groups. They obliged the taxi to stop for identification. Without the interruptions it would quickly have overhauled the powerful but ponderous car.

Julia raced towards another turn. The taxi was no more than seventy metres behind them, accelerating away from the last knot of armed men. The burly gunman was leaning from a near door gesticulating towards the limousine.

As Julia watched in her mirror one of the sentries dropped to one knee and began firing. Masonry flew from the building on their left. A black-swathed woman scurried from the path of the car for the safety of the narrow pavement. As she reached it more masonry flew. She toppled sideways to the ground. The cloth of her chador had ridden above her knee revealing loose folds of chalk-white flesh, obscene against the dark cloth. She lay absolutely still as a crimson stain spread from beneath her head.

Julia threw the car through the turn, fighting down bile.

The sight of the checkpoint on the Green Line drove the image of the woman from her mind. 'We've made it,' she murmured, as though dazed.

'Yeah. Great driving. Slow down.' Ray's eyes were on the checkpoint. He gripped his gun tightly, sweat beading his forehead. They drew closer to the barrier. It appeared to be unmanned. Ray had the door half open when a face appeared above a pile of sandbags. The man stood up. He wore the green uniform of Rachid's men.

With a shout of alarm Ray slammed the door shut. '*Go!*' he screamed.

A line of spider's web cracks stitched itself into the windscreen.

Julia stamped on the accelerator. The big car reared and leaped forward. The front bumper struck the concrete-filled oil drum that barred their way, smashing it aside. There was a deafening sound of grinding metal as the car gouged its way through the ruins of the barrier and then they were over the Green Line, racing into the Christian sector.

They swept past the University. Behind the chainlink fence topped with the ubiquitous, fearsome razor-wire, young men and women in sweaters and jeans strolled together, laughing and talking. The cheerful faces of the girls were framed by luxuriant dark hair. Ray took time to relish the sight after the oppressive, chador-clad uniformity of the Moslem suburbs.

His relief was short-lived. Julia gave a curse and gripped the wheel tighter. Ray twisted in his seat. The taxi had crossed the Green Line, using the gap they had created. It was a hundred and fifty metres behind them.

Julia flung the car into a tight turn. They raced north, following the eastern perimeter of the campus, making for the coast road. On the straight stretches of the corniche they would be able to put enough distance between them to shake off their pursuers.

The green, orderly campus fell behind them. Beyond it a whole block of houses had been destroyed. A shantytown of tents and packing-case shacks had sprung up in the gap. The teeming children stopped their games to watch the speeding limousine. Stones ricocheted off the bodywork. It was a game children played in the chaos of Beirut, until they were old enough for someone to give them guns.

Julia sent the car lurching into a right turn, into the broad Avenue General Fouad Chehab. A wry corner of her mind was wondering who General Chehab had been, or what he had done to have a street named after him, when the car was shaken by a sudden gust of wind. The sound came a moment later, a great clap of noise that numbed the senses.

'Shit,' Michael murmured. 'Artillery.'

Debris slammed into the metalwork and peppered the road in front of them. Instinctively, Julia braked, fearful of a chunk of masonry smashing through the toughened windscreen. Another shell struck a shop forty metres ahead of them. Bolts of bright cloth were catapulted into the air and then fell slowly back, unfurling as they fell. They lay in the road in a tangle of blues, reds and yellows, like the aftermath of some incongruous festivity.

'Left! Left! Turn left!' Ray was almost screaming at Julia, who stared ahead of her as though temporarily stunned by the bombardment. With a shake of her head she spun the wheel and jabbed her foot down hard. The car screamed into a narrow side road at the moment their pursuers turned onto the avenue. The gap had narrowed to no more than sixty metres.

Julia's knuckles showed dead white against the tan of her hands as she fought to control the car. They bounced and leapt over foot-deep potholes. The impacts on the edges of the holes made Selim cry out in pain. Julia was forced to slacken speed. The taxi slewed into the road behind them. The head of the burly gunman stuck out of a window, the face contorted as he shouted encouragement to his driver.

Julia threw the car into another right turn. The rear wheels broke away, sending a shower of dust and gravel into the midst of a group of women huddled at the corner of the narrow street. The women hardly noticed the car rebound off the kerb by their feet. They stood hunched in a tight group with their attention riveted on the scene thirty metres ahead of them.

A battered bus lay diagonally across the road, its snout thrust into the entrance of a narrow-fronted, unhygienic little supermarket. Most of the bus windows were shattered. Injured people struggled, screaming, from the wreckage as flames began to lick around them. Some wrestled with packages of belongings, impeding those behind, who fought hysterically to evade the flames. A woman in late middle age sat in the gutter, cradling the bloodied head of a much younger man. Her face was a grotesque mask of inexpressible grief.

Julia stamped on the brake and brought the car shuddering to a stop.

'Shit!' she said softly. With no other word she shoved the automatic shift into reverse and sent the car rocketing backwards.

The noise of the collision made the women turn their attention momentarily from the scene. The rear bumper of the car, with all the mastodon weight of the armour behind it, struck the onrushing taxi just as it turned into the street. The taxi, a lightly-built Toyota, spun away from them like a toy.

Julia fought to bring the car around. She threw the shift back into low drive and jammed her foot to the floor. The tyres screamed on the loose surface as they picked up momentum. The big gunman sprang lightly from the moving Toyota. The rocket-launcher was cradled in the crook of one arm.

Michael saw the man first. He gave a sharp shout. Instinctively, he reached out a hand to Julia's shoulder, pushing her down. It was his injured hand, but he did not even notice the pain. They hunched forward, crouching low in their seats. The street was too narrow for evasive action and, ahead, the wrecked bus blocked the road. For the first time in her life Julia felt the curious prickling sensation of the hair at the nape of her neck rising.

Her eyes were on the mirror, mesmerized by the slow wavering of the bulbous nose of the rocket as the gunman coolly sought his aim.

The next fraction of a second seemed to her to pass in slow motion.

The rocket-launcher appeared to be snatched upwards and away from the gunman. He followed it, rising onto his toes, an expression of wonderment on his face. He continued upwards, leaving the ground completely, arched as though a giant fist had struck him in the small of the back. His head snapped back, his expression changed to one of agony and he plunged face first to the ground, one arm bent under him in a position that left no doubt it had snapped.

Behind the man, the Toyota had reared onto its back wheels, fallen back, bounced and somersaulted to come to rest on its roof. The lavender paint was scorched so fiercely that bare metal showed through the sooty coating.

The world seemed to freeze for the tiny fraction of a second before the blast stove in their rear window. Julia cried out as stinging crystals of the thick laminated glass showered around her. Metal whanged into the roof, gouging six-inch slashes in the quilted fabric.

Ray snatched at the handbrake, bringing them slewing to a

stop. He pushed the short dark hair from the back of Julia's neck and wiped the blood away. Two tiny cubes of glass came away under his fingers.

'You okay? It just seems to be scratches.'

She nodded. 'Let's get out of here, before more shells come in.'

He leant and kissed the bloodied back of her neck. 'Sure. Just a second.' He turned to Michael. 'Can you handle Selim's gun?'

Michael nodded. 'I guess so. Why?'

'Come on. Just cover me.' Ray slid from the car. Shrugging off Julia's protest, Michael joined him, holding the rifle awkwardly at his waist.

Warily, with Michael three paces behind him, Ray approached the wrecked taxi. Women stood staring dumbly at the smoking wreckage, too stunned or curious even to flee the shelling. A scattering of ragged children lurked, already sensing a chance of spoils. The guns kept them at a respectful distance.

Ray stooped and snatched open the driver's door, burning himself on the hot metal. The body of the driver spilled onto the road. Ray turned away, one hand clutched to his stomach. He moved to the passenger side. A single body lay in the back, crumpled against the roof of the car. His eyes were wide open. Only the whites showed. Through the blasted aperture of the front window he could see the face of the man in the front passenger seat. It was a red mass of flesh, shredded to the bone. Retching, Ray reached in and pulled at a blood-soaked beret the corpse wore. The hair beneath was thin and frizzy. Ray turned away, still fighting the impulse to vomit.

He turned to face Michael. 'So where the hell's Bradman?' he murmured.

37

MAJOR BRADMAN had watched the four men crowd into the dilapidated taxi. He followed it with his eyes as it sped in pursuit of the limousine, a faint smile on his face. It was the smile of a man who has given someone a task knowing he would have done it better himself.

He walked perhaps three hundred yards through the crowded streets, moving with an easy stride, fast but unhurried. His eyes roved restlessly, sizing up escape routes and potential ambush points. It was a habit he had formed in war and which had served him well in Beirut.

Heads turned to watch the tall foreigner. A Westerner alone on the streets of Beirut was a rare sight, one with the conspicuous confidence of Bradman even rarer.

A taxi drew up opposite. Two men in dark business suits argued briefly about who would pay. Bradman was across the street in a few lithe strides. He brushed aside a woman carrying a child who already had her hand on the door handle. The two businessmen turned to add to the woman's protests. The look on Bradman's face checked them, sending the men scurrying away.

The cab stopped in front of a low villa enclosed by a wall a metre taller than Bradman. He thrust money at the driver and turned to the wide gate. Steel plates were riveted behind the intricately wrought iron, shielding the interior from outside eyes.

He jabbed at a small keyboard set in a wall beside the gate. It opened with a soft snicking sound. He pushed it open a foot and sidled through the gap, slamming it behind him. Anyone happening on the correct code could enter in the same way. Anyone but Bradman would have been shot down by the young man who sat, almost invisible in camouflage overalls, in the dappled shade of a vine. The young man held a gun in one hand and an accountancy textbook in the other. He was a gunman who planned to get ahead. Bradman ignored the man's greeting, striding past him into the villa. The man followed him into the hallway.

'Is something wrong, Major?' He was half smiling despite Bradman's brusqueness, eager to please.

'Start the Land-Rover. Bring it round here and stay with it.' He watched the man trot from the house, heading for the garage in the rear. He closed the door and flipped the latch, locking it.

Moving with orderly haste he walked into the clinically clean kitchen. He put his shoulder to the refrigerator and moved it away from the wall. He knelt, removed a short section of skirting board and picked up a key which lay in the cavity.

The biggest of the bedrooms had louvred shutters at all the windows. They threw the room into near darkness. And they made it impossible to see in from the garden. He flicked on a light and moved to a closet that covered a wall. The closet held only a single complete change of clothes, immaculately laundered and folded. He dropped to his knees, throwing aside the single pair of black brogues that stood there.

Gripping the edge of the carpet in both hands he yanked it hard. It came away with a ripping sound, exposing a steel plate the size of a coffin set in a concrete floor. He pushed the key into the sunburst-shaped keyhole in the edge of the plate. The lock opened with the soft thud of well-engineered metal. He heaved the plate aside.

From the cavity he pulled a dark-green canvas bag the size of a golf bag. He laid it carefully beside him. Next, he withdrew a khaki-painted metal box with webbing handles and laid it next to the bag. Then a pair of scratched binoculars. They were East German, the best he had ever owned. He had got them from a Soviet 'adviser' in Cambodia almost twenty years earlier, after knifing the man to death. The next item he took out was a Russian automatic rifle. It seemed almost unpatriotic but the fact was it was the most reliable weapon around. Lastly he dragged out an ammunition vest that gleamed with copper bullet casings.

He got to his feet and pulled on the vest, grimacing. He had forgotten how much the things weighed. He grabbed the bag, rifle and binoculars in one hand, the webbing straps of the box in the other and strode out to the waiting Land-Rover. He threw them inside without a word to the young man, who stood looking like a dog that has just retrieved a stick, and wheeled back into the house.

He knelt again at the cavity. This time he took out four packages, each the size of a shoebox, and a small canvas pouch. He emptied the pouch onto the carpet. Four cylinders of grey metal rolled onto the thick pile.

Deftly, he tore the protective polythene sheet from each of the packages and slotted a cylinder into a housing in the end of each one. He stacked the boxes on top of each other and aligned them carefully. On each box was a simple switch like a lightswitch. He ran his finger down the switches.

He stood up, carrying the boxes. He slid one beneath the bed, pushing it out of sight with his foot. Moving very fast now, he left one behind the sofa in the unused living room, another under the bed in another bedroom. The last one he placed, with a wry smile, in the oven.

He was on his way to the front door when the phone jangled. He faltered, half turned and then looked hard at his watch, calculating. 'Ah shit. The hell with it,' he muttered. He left the house. He had been inside less than six minutes.

The young man smiled eagerly, as if trying to compensate for some shortcoming he could not identify.

'Open the gate,' Bradman snapped, hauling himself into the driving seat.

The man scuttled to comply. 'When can I expect you back, Major?'

He shrugged, gunning the motor. 'A couple of days. Take care of things.'

The boy flicked his hand from his brow in an approximation of an American salute and swung the gate closed. He stooped to pick up his book. The phone was still ringing. He hesitated for a moment before running into the house.

'Bradman?'

The boy recognized the abrupt style. Nevertheless, he stuck to his instructions. 'Can I have the password, sir, please?'

'The landlord, you little prick. Get him on the line, fast.' Screwing around with stupid codewords had always been the aspect of clandestine operations that pissed Jordan off the most.

'He's just left, sir. I'm sorry.'

'Damn!' Jordan roared the word. Instantly, he softened his voice again, making it persuasive. 'Can you get him back? It's absolutely vital. The Major would be very grateful.'

'I'll try, sir. Please hold on.' He set down the phone and sprinted from the room.

At the other end of the line, on the aircraft carrier *Connecticut*, in the spacious day cabin of the Admiral commanding the task force, Jordan fumed silently. The little asshole spoke like the customer complaints department at a gourmet food store.

Bradman pushed the Land-Rover hard through the gears. The needle was hovering at around seventy when he checked the mirror. He let out an exclamation. The boy was in the middle of the road with one hand held to the side of his head, mimicking someone holding a phone. With his other hand he gesticulated to Bradman to turn around.

Bradman twisted his wrist and glanced at his watch. Eighty-two seconds had elapsed. Whatever Jordan wanted he would only find out when it was all over. He let two more seconds tick by and raised his eyes to the mirror again.

The boy had disappeared, engulfed by a fireball that filled the width of the street. A cloud of orange and black rose over the villa. Even two of the incendiaries would have been enough to reduce the place to a paste. It left only the Colter crowd to be dealt with.

38

TOM JORDAN stared out at the vivid blue waters of the Gulf. Forty-eight hours without sleep had left him red-eyed and irritable, in no shape to appreciate the molten gold of the sunset. He muttered impatiently as he waited for the boy to get Bradman to the phone.

The call from the President had not helped his frame of mind. All the preparation, the planning, the persuasion had gone down the drain. He had tried to argue, to make the half-witted blowhard understand. If the Colter boy was on the loose it was even *more* imperative that the operation go ahead. The coverage, the media applause, would drown out the Colter story completely. By the time anybody got around to focusing on it the election would be over.

A succession of tremendous crashes made him wince. He scowled at the phone. 'Bradman? You there?' The crackling of the line gave way to a wrenching sound and then a pinging emptiness. He slammed the instrument back on its cradle, unaware he had just heard the sound of a phone melting.

The line had been his last hope of talking to Bradman. The Embassy lines were already dead. It would simplify things if Bradman were dead, too. He turned to face the Admiral, who had entered the room as he replaced the phone. 'Go okay?'

Admiral Langston was a stocky red-faced man with the veined nose of a drunk. In fact he was an abstinent fighting sailor with the decorations and a silver plate in his skull to testify to it.

At Jordan's question he shrugged. 'I told them. They're disappointed. That's all.'

'Me too.'

The Admiral looked at Jordan as though about to speak and thought better of it. He knew Jordan's reputation. He was a welcome change from the theorists plucked from the university lecture circuit who usually got the job. Nevertheless, it surprised Langston to hear Jordan express disappointment. As far as he could see the whole operation would have no military justification whatever. Maybe with only six months to go he was losing his taste for action. Spite seemed a poor reason to use the Navy's power.

Julia accelerated hard away from the last checkpoint and onto the bridge. Seconds later they were across the Beirut River and clear of the city. They hit the highway that led east and then north, following the coast towards Tripoli. The road had been less of a target than the bridge during the years of indiscriminate artillery harassment so that she was able to hold a reasonable speed. Even so, the drumming of the damaged tyres sounded ominously loud through the broken rear window.

For a minute or two nobody spoke. Selim lay in a corner, his eyes closed. His face was deathly pale. He snored softly. He awoke and cursed as the wheel rim rebounded on the edge of a pothole.

Ray glanced around anxiously. 'We're not going to make it. We'll be lucky if the tyres hold out as far as Jouniah.' The town of Jouniah was only a few kilometres ahead of them.

Behind him Selim shook his head. 'Getting to Jouniah wouldn't be lucky at all. Not for *you*.' He smiled grimly. 'Jouniah has been in the hands of Rachid's men for a week.'

'Shit!'

'As you say. We could run into some of Rachid's people at any moment. We have to get off this road, avoid Jouniah.'

'Selim,' Ray said with exaggerated patience, 'there isn't any other road. There might be some tracks, but nothing we could risk in this.'

Selim nodded. It was hard for him to move. 'You're quite right. There's no other road. But there's another *way* to go.'

Julia shot a glance over her shoulder. 'How's that?'

He paused to shift his weight, easing his leg. 'Do you have money?'

'Some,' Julia said, frowning at Ray. 'Why?'

'How much?'

Julia patted the pocket of her shirt. 'Two, two and a half thousand dollars.'

'I've got around twelve hundred, plus a few hundred Lebanese pounds,' Ray added.

Michael went through the pockets of Bradman's suit. He produced a handful of Lebanese change. 'Army pay's still terrible,' he murmured, letting the money trickle to the floor of the car.

Selim grimaced. 'Let us hope what we have will be enough. Keep on this road until I tell you, another two or three kilometres.'

Bradman kept his foot to the floor. The Land-Rover whined and shook. He drove one-handed, threading his way between the worst of the ruts and craters. With his right hand he unzipped the long bag and shook the rocket-launcher free of its folds. Leaning down, he groped in the metal box and pulled out one of the swollen-nosed rockets. He placed it carefully on the seat beside him. His expression never changed. It was the serene half-smile of a person listening to a favourite piece of music.

The Christian militiamen at the last checkpoint before the bridge had told him the black car was only three or four minutes ahead of him. Their tyres had seemed to be damaged. With a caressing movement of his hand he checked the magazine of the rifle was in place. He whistled a snatch of tune to himself.

The road swung in a wide curve northward around Saint George's Bay. After three kilometres he passed the town of Antelias. From the road he could see the broken neon of the single cinema and the gaping hole in its roof. After Antelias the road, shadowed on the seaward side by the railway, ran straight to Zouk Mkayel and Jouniah, with scarcely a settlement between.

Before the war this road had been thronged with Mercedes

and American limousines. Now it was little used, abandoned to the paramilitary groups and the decrepit trucks of the tenacious local farmers. The owners of the Mercedes and the limos had long since left, with their cars, for Paris or California poolsides.

The militia trucks slowed him a little. He made sure they all got a friendly wave and a smile as he drew level. Suicidal drivers themselves, they shared a pathological hatred of being overtaken. They were quite likely to let him have a burst from a Kalashnikov just to show their annoyance.

He had just passed a convoy and was pushing his speed back up to the hundred and ten kilometre mark when he let out an involuntary exclamation and leaned closer to the windscreen. The broad dark shape ahead soon resolved itself into the familiar outline of the Embassy car. He was closing rapidly.

He eased up a little on the accelerator. There was no point in alerting them by approaching too fast. Damaged tyres or not, the damned car was still bulletproof. The Land-Rover was not. Walker and the Colters might not be too dangerous but the Arab could be. Anyway, they had been smart enough, or dangerous enough, to get Bashaar off their backs.

The distance was down to about six hundred metres. He let his hand slide over his weapons and allowed his foot to drop just a little harder on the accelerator. Not taking his eyes off his quarry he slid the rocket into the launcher.

He was no more than four hundred metres behind now. He smiled suddenly. A face had appeared at the rear window. There was *no glass* in it. In three minutes he would be able to put a rocket right in there. His own problem, Jordan's problem, the President's problem, would all be neatly settled.

'Fuckers!' His voice was almost a scream.

Without warning the limousine had swung to the left. It bucked over the central reservation and careered across the empty oncoming lane. Without slowing, it bounced over the sagging hard shoulder and ploughed into the thorny scrub that crowded along the roadside strip.

Bradman's face congealed into an expression of icy rage. It was impossible that they had recognized him. His own eyesight was exceptional, and he had been unable even to tell if the face at the window was that of a man or a woman. Maybe they had just taken fright at the approach of the Land-Rover. They had a lot to be afraid of.

Two hundred metres from where they had run off the road he too swung across the carriageway and into the scrub.

39

SELIM SANK his teeth into his lower lip in the effort not to scream. The pain as they bucked over the central reservation was almost intolerable. Perspiration welled from every pore of his face. The jagged leading edge of the pain passed.

'Go on until you reach the railway,' he gasped, his breath shortened by pain.

Julia nodded without speaking. They sped forward, weaving crazily between the scrubby olive trees, crashing through the thick scrub. They had gone three hundred metres when the undergrowth ended abruptly, revealing the twin tracks of a railway running parallel to the coast. Grass and weeds thrust up between the rails.

'Stop,' Selim breathed. 'We must leave the car.'

His companions scrambled to help him from the car. They spoke in whispers. Selim gave a short, rasping laugh. 'No,' he told them, 'don't be cautious. Be loud. As natural as you can. It would be very dangerous to be too quiet.'

Julia looked anxiously around her. 'How's that?' Her voice sounded unnaturally loud in the silence.

Selim dragged himself upright, using Ray and Michael for support. 'You'll see. Help me over the tracks.'

Their feet crunched noisily in the sharp clinker of the track bed. Their eyes flicked restlessly over the dense curtain of vegetation ahead of them. Julia felt the strange tingle of vulnerability at the nape of her neck. In the straight, bare corridor they offered a perfect target.

They reached the side of the track and almost threw themselves into the shelter of the undergrowth. For a moment, the distant mewing of a gull was the only sound. Julia was the first to speak.

'Paths.' She pointed to a spot close to them. Her face was a mixture of relief and apprehension.

Selim's streaked, contorted face lit up in a sudden grin. 'Yes. We go that way.' He nodded at the track forking to the right.

Their progress was slow. The track was wide enough for one person. Supporting Selim, Ray and Michael were forced to move in a painful sideways shuffle. Blood welled from dozens of lacerations on their arms inflicted by the vicious shrubs. Taking Selim's instruction to heart, Ray swore loudly and continuously.

After forty or fifty metres the path emerged into a clearing. Discarded cans and cigarette ends littered the trodden ground. Beyond the clearing the path split again into two. Julia turned to Selim.

'Which way?'

As she spoke Selim's arms slid from around the supporting shoulders. He crumpled and lay face down in the dust. His eyes, underscored by patches that showed bluish under the pale olive skin, were closed. The jowls seemed to have sunk, sculpted by pain. With a cry, Julia dropped down beside him. His breath was coming in raucous snores. The makeshift dressing on his leg wound had shifted. Blood ran into the red dirt. Working frantically, Michael snatched off the headcloth he still wore and tore it into strips. He passed the strips to Julia who was desperately trying to staunch the blood and redress the wound. Ray took up the rifle.

'I'll take a look ahead.' He had gone three paces when he heard the unmistakable sound of a weapon being primed. He whirled to face the noise.

'Please don't move,' a voice said equably from behind him. 'Or I'll shoot you.'

When Bradman stopped the Land-Rover he did not immediately leave it. Instead, he swung himself out of the cab and stood in the doorway. His head was well clear of the highest of the scrub, almost at the height of the dilapidated olive trees that grew tenaciously among the sea of thorn. Shielding his eyes from the glare of the setting sun, he scanned the expanse of dusty vegetation. The progress of the limousine was clearly flagged by a pennant of red dust that rose above the bushes and hung immobile in the still air.

He waited until the plume of dust stopped advancing. Voices carried indistinctly to him. He could not make out the words but the intonations told him they were speaking English. Lightly, he sprang to the ground and considered his armoury. The rocket-launcher would be useless. His quarry was out of the armour-plated car now. It was on foot in the undergrowth. Just the way he would have ordered it.

Moving with an easy speed that looked almost casual but was in reality meticulous, he checked over the rifle and slung it across his body. He passed the binoculars across the opposite shoulder and tugged the weight of the ammunition vest into place. He half turned to go and then, almost as an afterthought, reached into the cab and groped beneath the dashboard. His hand came out clutched around the hard rubber hilt of a double-edged dagger. The thin coating of oil on the blade dulled its glint as he slid the eight-inch length of it into a sheath sewn into the thigh of his overalls. He plunged into the undergrowth.

The faint track he was following petered out within twenty metres in an impenetrable tangle of branches. With a single soft curse he dropped to the earth. At ground level the way was much clearer. Staying flat on his belly he began hauling himself forward on his elbows and his knees. The skeins of branches interlocked a few inches above his head. Stray branches tore at his face and picked at the tough cloth of his overalls. Many years ago he had trained for this. Moving in this way he could still advance as fast as many people walked.

Every few metres the branches thinned enough to enable him to get to his feet and run. Alternately running and crawling it took him nearly five minutes to reach the car. He lay for some seconds in the shelter of the bushes. There was no movement. All four doors hung open. Drawing himself into a crouch, he sprinted the last few yards and threw himself into the car. He allowed himself to lie still for just a moment, a sour grin on his lips.

His breath was coming in gasps and he could feel the pulse in his neck as the blood pounded. He still had the skills; just the youth had gone. Gulping air, he ran his eyes over the interior of the car. When they settled on the bloodstains on the rear seat he gave a soft grunt of satisfaction. The Arab had bled badly. He would be seriously slowing them down. It would be helpful. If the Arab were handicapped, wiping out the reporters and the boy would be child's play. He pushed himself out of the car.

He found the first spot of blood exactly where he expected it, on the stony bed of the railway track. He loped across the rails, his eyes flickering from the ground to the way ahead, looking for blood and trouble with equal care. Two paths led into the bushes. It took only a second to find the telltale stain and scuffed earth that led him into the path cutting obliquely to his right.

He moved forward, placing his feet with care to avoid stepping on the brittle fragments of twig that littered the path. His feet made no sound on the dust that blanketed the ground to a finger's depth. Every few paces he paused to listen intently. The third time he stopped he heard a sound, a groan or a sigh. His eyes narrowed, he waited for further sounds. After a few seconds it came again. A long exhalation from somewhere only a few steps ahead.

He took three long breaths himself, exhaling slowly and silently, trying to still the excitement that raced in him, fuelled by the adrenaline that flooded his system. With intense care he moved forward to the edge of a small clearing. The sighing sound reached him for a third time and with it a familiar aroma. He stepped from cover.

In the centre of the littered clearing a young Arab in a checked headdress squatted on his haunches. A Kalashnikov lay in the dust beside him. Impervious to any threat, he was sucking with single-minded vigour on a cigarette. The marijuana smoke grated on Bradman's throat.

40

WHEN THE MAN said he would shoot his tone had left no room for the slightest doubt. His look left even less. He was a big, tan-skinned man around fifty, with the broken nose and the solid swelling belly of a retired heavyweight fighter. A dead-straight scar ran from one nostril diagonally across his mouth to his jawline. It gave his lips a curious kink, as though he were constantly smiling at some acrid inner joke. His clothes were in elegant, costly contrast to his rough-hewn physique. He wore a well-cut lightweight suit of pale tan, which he had somehow managed to keep clean. His shoes, although coated with dust, were tasselled moccasins polished to a rich mahogany sheen.

'Please put down your weapon. And you, if you have any,' he added, gesturing negligently with the handgun at Michael and Julia. Ray lowered the rifle gently to the ground. 'Search them,' he said quietly, looking past them.

They swivelled to follow his gaze. Two more Arabs, younger than the first, one in well-made casual clothes, the other in jeans and a stained singlet, had emerged silently from the thicket. The two men began frisking them with neat, one-handed efficiency. Keeping his gestures very slow and deliberate, Ray wryly pointed out the silenced pistol pushed into his belt. The man grunted softly, took away the gun and frisked him anyway. Then he nodded and gave Ray a sharp shove, sending him stumbling into the dust alongside Julia and Michael.

The same man turned his attention to Selim, who still lay motionless, his face pressed into the dust. The man put a hand under his chin and jerked his face roughly around. Selim's eyes opened. They stared out dully from the haggard, dust-caked face. He seemed at first to be on the verge of losing consciousness again. Then, very slowly, the caked lips parted in a fragile smile. The gunman stared incredulously back into the exhausted face.

'Selim!' He threw an arm under Selim's head. 'It's Selim!' he called in Arabic to the big man. His voice was cracking with surprise and emotion.

The older man frowned and threw a short, suspicious glance at the group who stood apprehensively watching, their own faces clouded with incomprehension. His eyes moved to the prone figure of Selim. Still wary, he moved sideways, craning for a better view. Abruptly, with a sharp cry, he stepped forward and fell to his knees next to Selim.

To the mute astonishment of the three Americans, he took Selim's head gently in his hands and kissed him tenderly on both cheeks. Even more astonishingly, a tear trickled down the big man's face.

The man continued looking down at the wanly smiling face of Selim for some moments before twisting to look at the three of them, standing silently under the threat of the young man's gun. He stared for several seconds. Julia's hand sought Ray's. There was murder in his eyes.

Abruptly, his face still filled with hatred, the man turned back to speak quickly to Selim. Selim's response came to them only as a rasping whisper. The man spoke again, his lips even closer to Selim's ear. Selim answered him, speaking with difficulty. One hand fluttered in an effort at a gesture. The big man turned once again to look at the Americans. Again he stared, this time for a full five seconds. His eyes were the hardest any of them had ever seen. He rose and strode across to them.

He smiled a brief, disfigured smile. 'You saved our cousin's life.'

'Oh God!' Julia's exclamation was almost a sob. She whirled and sank her head into Ray's chest.

He folded an arm around her and exhaled for the first time in quite a few seconds. 'Your cousin?' His voice rose as he almost laughed with relief.

The man nodded. He looked around at the youth who still knelt by Selim, examining his wound. 'All three of us. Through my grandfather's brother,' he added, by way of explanation.

Ray nodded. None of them was going to bother working it out. This was Arabia. Cousin was a loose term. They did not care if they were claiming common ancestry through Mohammed himself, as long as they were not going to shoot them. 'Did he tell you what's going on?'

The man nodded. 'Something. We must get help for him. He wants us to help you also. Come.'

Julia had recovered herself. She looked down at Selim. He was grinning up at them, the pride stronger than the pain. She gave him a smile in return. One of her very best ones.

The big man had returned to Selim's side. He pushed his gun into the waistband of his trousers, squatted, slid his arms beneath the injured man and lifted him as easily as though he had been a child. He turned to look at the Americans. 'Does anyone know you're here?'

They exchanged looks. Michael spoke. He was still crouched by Selim. 'We don't think so.'

'You sound hesitant.' His eyes flickered over Michael's bloodied dressings. 'Selim said you were the one kidnapped from the American University. Were you followed here?'

Michael pushed himself to his feet and lifted his shoulders in a shrug. 'There was a Land-Rover behind us. It didn't seem in any hurry, though. It looked like there was just the driver in it.'

The man nodded. 'Suleiman!' The boy in the singlet stepped forward eagerly. The man spoke a few short guttural phrases. He turned back to face the others. 'Follow us. Quickly.'

He strode past them into the opening of the right-hand path, taking care to hold Selim high, well clear of the thorns. Michael scooped up the rifle and the three of them followed at his heels. The better dressed man fell into step behind them, leaving the younger one alone in the clearing.

The youth watched them disappear into the thicket. Humming quietly, he drew out a buckled pack of Marlboro from his jeans, laid down his gun and squatted. He opened the packet and probed inside. The cigarette he pulled out was loosely made, tapering, with wisps of tobacco spilling from one end. Philip Morris would never have let it out of their factory. He found a disposable lighter rolled into the sleeve of his tee-shirt and lit the cigarette. He drew noisily on it, smacking his lips, and let the smoke drift slowly out through his nostrils.

The joint was half smoked when Bradman stepped from the bushes. For a split second the two men were absolutely still, surveying each other. Bradman was as surprised as the other man, but he had the advantage that he had not been smoking hashish. He took two rapid paces towards the gaping boy, drew back a booted foot and kicked the gun out of the Arab's reach.

The boy's eyes swivelled to watch the weapon spin away from him. They returned immediately to Bradman's face. He was coming down fast from the effects of the hashish. Bradman saw the boy shift his weight forward, bringing it onto the balls of his feet. He swore softly, almost reading the young man's thoughts. The boy had seen what Bradman had hoped he would not. Bradman's own rifle was no threat at all. He would not dare to use it.

Bradman's hand dropped to his thigh at the same instant as the other man launched himself. The Arab used his legs as pistons, propelling himself at Bradman's solar plexus. The American tried to side-step, knowing the boy had chosen his target well. The lower abdomen is the hardest part of the body to move. He had taught that to a lot of recruits in the past. The boy's shoulder, driven by the full weight of his powerful thrust, caught him just above the hip.

He hit the ground flat on his back, the last ounce of breath knocked from him. His right hand was still at his thigh, clasped around the knife he had not had time to unsheath. The boy's fingers closed around his wrist. They were disconcertingly strong. An elbow ground into his stomach just below the sternum, preventing him catching his breath. The boy was good.

Breathing in shallow gasps he groped with his left hand for the boy's head. He ran his hand down and, holding his fingers around the back of his assailant's neck, he drove his thumb as hard as he could up into the cavity just under and behind the socket of the jawbone. The boy cried out and twisted to beat his arm away.

The move forced him to take one hand from Bradman's right forearm. Bradman jerked the knife clear of its sheath. The boy still gripped his wrist in his powerful fingers, making it impossible to strike a blow with the knife. The boy's elbow smashed deep into his abdomen again. He made an ugly gagging sound between pain and nausea and his head dropped back into the dust. Helpless, he felt the boy writhing above him, changing position. A hand moved from his wrist and began probing at the cloth of his crutch.

Bradman gritted his teeth, bracing himself. What happened next was much worse, and more agonizing than he had anticipated. The boy simply bent his head and sank his teeth into a testicle.

If he had yet had the breath for it, Bradman would have screamed. The sound that came from his contorted mouth was a ghastly rasping gurgle that rose from deep in his throat. He clutched involuntarily at the crushed testicle.

The young Arab pushed himself to a kneeling position,

keeping his weight firmly on Bradman's wrist, and looked quickly into his opponent's agonized face. His face wore the vacant, almost bored, look of an expert tradesman doing the job he had been trained for. He read the anguish in the other man's face and pushed himself to his feet. Stepping across Bradman, he stooped to scoop up Bradman's gun.

Bradman had been a soldier for more than twenty-five years. Three times he had been wounded, twice by gunshot and once by a grenade fragment. He had lain on the forest floor while North Vietnamese soldiers filed by seven feet away, with red-hot metal lodged in his back, cooking the flesh around it. And he had not cried out. He had stayed cool through pain few men would have borne at all.

When the boy's teeth had sunk into his testicle the pain had been much greater than he would have thought possible. There had been an element of surprise which had caused him to cry out almost as much as the hurt itself. The surprise had passed now. The pain remained, as bad as anything he had known. He knew, though, that pain, any amount of it, could be ignored. Messages could be willed to the brain that would override the agonized warnings of simple nerve-endings. He opened his eyes. The Arab was stepping forward, bending as he went. Bradman's own knees were drawn up in almost a foetal position. He drove his left leg straight.

His foot caught the young Arab just as he transferred his weight forward. The boy stumbled. In a desperate lunge Bradman drove his knife at the boy. It caught him low down on the outside of his leg.

The boy gave a shout of outrage and shock and fell to his knees. His hands were on the rifle. He was bringing it to bear when his face drained abruptly of expression. He gave a single grunt and fell sideways to the ground.

Bradman climbed painfully to his feet, pulling the knife from where his second blow had driven it, just under the boy's diaphragm. He shook his head. It really was a shame. He had been the kind of man Bradman could have used working for him.

Moving stiff-legged in an effort to ease the pain, he set off towards the opening of the path the others had taken. Despite the time he had lost, he moved with even more caution than before. The boy had been a nasty surprise. He did not want any others.

41

WITH SELIM cradled easily in his arms the big man moved quickly along the path. A short way from the clearing the path widened. Julia drew abreast of the man. She looked anxiously into the face of Selim. It was ashen. His head lolled loosely at every step. He was asleep, or unconscious. Or dead.

'You think you can help him?'

The man made a noncommittal face. 'We'll try our best. We don't have much you could call medical facilities.'

Julia frowned. 'What *do* you have? Who *are* you?'

The man glanced briefly at her and smiled. She was not sure if the trace of malice in the smile was real or the effect of the scar. 'You'll see in a few moments.' His tone invited no further questions.

The undergrowth ended abruptly, giving way to a roughly semicircular clearing a hundred metres across. At the far edge of the clearing the land seemed to end abruptly, as though at a cliff. Beyond it lay the sea, gleaming gold in an exuberant prelude to the sunset. Ray drew level with Julia's shoulder.

'Keep to the path!' the big man snapped. In response to Ray's angry look, he added, in a friendlier tone, 'Mines.'

Ray leapt for the well-beaten track. Smiling at his sudden pallor, Julia gestured around the clearing. 'This whole area?'

The man nodded. 'We have interests to protect,' he said offhandedly.

They strode on, approaching a jumble of boulders at the cliff top. Twenty metres from the pile of rocks Julia glanced around at Ray and Michael. She jerked her head significantly at the cliff edge. They looked in the direction she indicated. They, too, saw what Julia had already noticed. The rocks were not a natural outcrop but a carefully arranged barricade. They formed a rampart with apertures that afforded a view, and a field of fire, covering the entire clearing. In the apertures heads moved against the brightness of the sky.

The big man led them through an opening in the rocky breastwork. Two men sat smoking and surveying the clearing. Between them lay the battered and dusty backgammon board with which they relieved the boredom. They looked up curiously at the figure the man carried in his arms. He spoke a single curt phrase. They began scanning the ground in front of them with new alertness.

Behind the rampart the path turned at a right-angle and led down the face of a low cliff of red sandstone. Below it lay a narrow strip of gravel beach, enclosed between two fingers of rock extending forty or fifty metres into the sea. The two promontories would shield the beach from most seas. They also meant the beach could be seen only from directly above, where the land had been so carefully cleared, or from directly out to sea.

Julia gave a low whistle and stopped short. Moored in an angle of the rocks, in deeper water some way from the beach, were two motorboats. They were each about ten metres long, low and sleek and very fast-looking. Above the boats they were astonished to see camouflage netting fastened onto metal supports driven into the rocks, placed to conceal the mooring from the air. Whatever it was they were looking at, somebody had invested a lot of money and effort in it.

On the beach itself several men worked quickly picking wooden trays from a neat stack and passing them from hand to hand out along the promontory to the nearer of the boats. Two more men stood in the open well of the boat stowing the trays. All of them stared briefly at the party descending the cliff path and then immediately turned their attention back to their work, not interrupting the smooth rhythm of their activity.

The big man strode quickly past the stacked trays. The others hurried at his heels. As they passed the stack Michael lifted a corner of the oiled paper that covered the top tray.

'Hey,' he whispered, grinning. 'You looking for a smoke?'

Julia gave another low, barely audible whistle. Beneath the paper the tray was completely filled with neat dark-brown briquettes, each of them the size of a cigarette packet. She guessed that each of the trays held about ten kilos of the stuff. She glanced back at the stack. It was about fifteen trays high. Each layer of the stack was a dozen trays.

Twelve times eight were ninety-six. Fifteen times ninety-six were fourteen hundred and forty kilos. One million, four hundred and forty thousand grammes. At a street price of a dollar a gramme . . . She abandoned the calculation.

'Jesus!' she whispered. 'No wonder they can invest in a set-up like this.'

The big man turned abruptly to his right and into the wide mouth of a recess in the cliff which was not quite deep enough to be called a cave. In the recess three men sat on canvas fishing stools around a folding camping table, smoking. A bottle half-full of a transparent, pale honey-coloured fluid stood on the table, alongside a ruined aluminium water canteen. Three glasses held drinks whose milky colour identified it as arak and water. The three men were studying a chart. They looked up sharply as the big man's shadow fell on them.

He spoke quickly in Arabic. Two of the listeners were around forty, sufficiently alike to be brothers. They murmured to each other as they listened, looking curiously at each of the Americans in turn. The third man, extremely old, sat quite still, listening intently, his face as tanned and wrinkled as a walnut. Only once as the big man spoke did his eyes leave the speaker's face. Without moving his head he flicked a glance at Michael. The faintest hint of a smile twitched at the corners of his mouth.

When the big one had finished the old man spoke in a voice that was smoky and fragile. With a nod, the big man laid Selim gently on the gravel floor. At a word from the old man, one of the other two drinkers ran to the boats.

A few seconds later he returned carrying an attaché case. He knelt beside Selim and threw open the case. It was a surprisingly comprehensive medical kit. He began working on Selim's leg.

Slowly, as though the friction in his joints were almost too much for him, the old man got to his feet. The other men were silent, as though waiting for him to speak. He hobbled painfully across and looked down at Selim's face, greasy with sweat and grime. Selim seemed to sense the man there. His eyes opened and he moved a hand in a feeble greeting.

With the same arthritic slowness the old man lowered himself to his knees and bent close to Selim. He placed his hands on the younger man's shoulders and kissed him lightly on both cheeks. Keeping his head very close he muttered into his ear. Selim breathed an inaudible response. The two continued whispering for some time. Several times the old man glanced around at the Americans, his face giving no clue to his thoughts. At length, he signalled the big man to help him to his feet. He shuffled over to stand looking up into their faces.

The man's eyes were bright and shrewd. Deposits of whitish mucus at the corners had dried into a gritty paving. The corners of his mouth, too, had cobwebs of white saliva that stretched and flexed with the movement of his thin lips. He looked into each of their faces in turn with the air of being about to examine their teeth.

'Do you want a drink?' he asked with abrupt irrelevance.

They all answered together. He waited until one of his companions had served them, using the same stained glasses.

'So you want to go north,' the old man said curtly.

Julia nodded, her breath cut by the powerful drink. 'Yes,' she said, dabbing at the corner of her eye. 'To Bcharré.'

'Or Cyprus,' Ray broke in, glancing out of the cave entrance towards the boats. 'Cyprus would be best.'

The old man looked pityingly at Ray. He shook his head. 'Our boats aren't built for that. I won't risk my boats, or my men, on two hundred kilometres of open sea.'

'We can pay!' Julia protested.

The man looked at her curiously and then glanced at the men outside, still passing the boxes of dope. 'Are you carrying so much money that I can cancel tonight's run for one of my boats?'

Julia thought again of her aborted calculation. She shrugged. 'Will you take us north?'

'How much money *do* you have?'

She looked at Ray. He nodded. 'About three and a half thousand dollars.'

The old man was looking at her with a mixture of contempt and incredulity. '*Three* and a half thousand,' he snorted. 'To risk a boat?' He turned away and hobbled a few steps. 'Do you know what you're asking?' He shook his head. 'Of course you don't. You have no idea what it means to take a boat out from here in daylight.'

Ray spoke. 'It's only a thirty-kilometre run up to Batroun. Half an hour in one of those.' He pointed towards the sleek boats. 'We could stay well inshore.'

The old man's exasperation grew. 'Inshore or offshore, it makes no difference. Why do you think that netting is in place? Why do you think we have to skulk in holes in the ground like this?'

Julia shrugged. 'The Army? This part of the coast is still controlled by the Lebanese Army, isn't it?'

'Look,' the old man said, drawing closer and waving a finger at Julia, 'don't talk to me of the Lebanese Army. I can buy and sell the Lebanese Army. Our problem is the Israelis. They are the danger. They respect nothing! Territorial waters! Private property! Nothing! They're pirates!' His reedy voice had risen until it cracked with the righteous anger of the honest citizen being denied his rights. An honest dope pedlar could hardly make a living any more. 'Count it,' he added, suddenly businesslike. He pointed imperiously at the table.

Hastily, before his mood could change again, they turned out their cash and travellers' cheques onto the table.

'Two thousand four,' Julia announced.

'Twelve hundred and seventy,' Ray added.

The man screwed up his mouth. Then he looked around at Selim. After a further hesitation he reached a hand inside his decrepit sports jacket and pulled out a pen. 'Sign them,' he said, pushing the pen at Julia.

She took the pen, cocking an eyebrow at Ray. It was a heavy gold Cartier. She began countersigning her cheques.

While she did so the old man shuffled up close to Michael. He circled him as though the boy were a work of art he was considering buying. His breath wheezed in Michael's ear as he leaned close to examine the wounds.

'So, you were the one that was kidnapped, hmm?'

Michael nodded, looking down into the old man's eyes. The man looked back at him. There was a mischievous, mocking glitter in his expression. To Michael's surprise the man reached out and patted him paternally on the shoulder. 'Hmm,' he said again, smiling to himself.

Julia had finished signing her cheques and handed the pen to Ray. Ray had begun signing when the old man turned suddenly to him and held up a hand.

'That's enough,' he said roughly. 'You'll need money up there. You'll need transport to Bcharré.' He took back his pen from the astonished Ray, and pushed two or three hundred dollars of cash back at Julia. He said something to the big scar-faced man and turned his attention to Selim. The big man left the cave at a run.

The old man knelt laboriously by Selim. Selim's face, ashen and pearled with sweat, was contorted into a grimace. His teeth were sunk deep into the flesh of his lower lip. The attendant made a whispered remark to the old man, who nodded, not taking his anxious eyes from Selim's face.

The attendant ran to the far side of the cave. He quickly pulled aside an oilskin wrapping to reveal a metal case the size of a shoebox. He lifted the lid, pulling hard against the suction resistance of a rubber seal that ran around the rim, like the seal on a refrigerator door.

Inside the steel box lay a tight-packed array of postage-stamp-sized envelopes each containing a pinch of white powder. Julia recognized it. A television producer she had known well, before he died, had been a user. It was heroin, already bagged up and ready for market. The man took two of the bags, resealed the box and ran back to Selim's side.

He took a roll of kitchen foil from his attaché case, tore off a piece, and spread it on the open top of the case. Carefully, he tore open the bags and shook the contents into two separate lines. He grabbed the banknote the old man proffered and rolled it into a tube as thin as a drinking straw.

The old man held Selim's head up with one hand and the rolled banknote close to a nostril with the other. The second man pulled a lighter from his pocket. He held the foil six inches beneath Selim's nose. The old man spoke quietly to Selim as the other man held the lighter close beneath the kitchen foil directly under the first line of white powder.

The powder trembled, bubbled and fused into a brown tar, which then volatilized, leaving a dark-brownish trace on the foil. The man moved the lighter until the line was completely vaporized. Selim breathed out noisily after sniffing the potent vapours of the makeshift straw. He lay panting while the old man moved the tube to Selim's other nostril. They repeated the routine. When it was over the old man laid Selim's head gently on the ground and rose to his feet.

'It will have its effect in a few moments. It's fortunate he had it. Cleaning the wound would have been very painful for him without it.'

'You deal in that shit, too?' Julia asked angrily.

The man looked puzzled. 'Heroin? Of course,' he said frankly. 'It's an excellent business. Although the competition nowadays is very fierce,' he added, with a trace of nostalgia. 'Those damned Pakistanis.'

Julia's fists bunched angrily. 'But that stuff's . . .' Her anger made her choke inarticulately. 'Okay. Hashish, I never heard of harming anybody. But heroin! That's something else again!'

The man looked at her, smiling his malicious smile again. 'Oh, really,' he said with exaggerated courtesy. 'Why?'

'For Christ's sake, it kills people.'

'Not if they're sensible. My merchandise is very pure. You can blame the overdosing on the people who adulterate it, not us. They are the killers.'

She shook her head in frustration and fury. 'But it, it . . . Children in America are dying with that shit!'

Wearily, with the air of a man who had rehearsed his justifications too often, he pointed to a stack of automatic rifles against one wall of the cave. They all recognized them as American M16s and Soviet-made Kalashnikovs. 'Can you imagine how many children those things have killed, here in Lebanon? Is that *your* fault?'

Julia started to answer, but Michael had moved to her side. He gave her arm a sharp squeeze, reminding her who owned the boats. She let her anger die.

'When can we leave?' Ray asked the old man.

'A few more minutes. As soon as Selim is ready to be moved. He insists on going with you,' he added. His tone made it plain he thought Selim was out of his mind.

Bradman trod very carefully. A few feet ahead of him the undergrowth had been cleared, leaving an expanse of open ground as far as the sea. He shouldered his way off the path and moved cautiously to the edge of the clearing. He unslung the binoculars and began slowly surveying the terrain in front of him.

The heads of the sentries were clearly outlined behind the gaps in the rampart. They would be easy targets for a marksman like Bradman, but the noise of gunshots would alert whomever else he had to contend with. He considered the sightlines. From certain angles, on his belly, he could probably reach them without being seen. He brushed the hilt of the knife briefly. The idea was appealing, until another sweep of the binoculars showed up a patch of broken ground between a cluster of protruding roots. A dark-grey disc protruded above the loose earth. He lowered the binoculars with a growl of annoyance and scrutinized the ground just in front of him, knowing what he would find.

The mines were sown closely together in an irregular pattern. They had been placed by pros. He threaded the binoculars back across his chest. There was nothing for it but to skirt the clearing.

It took him several painful minutes. Many times he was obliged to backtrack to find a route around a particularly dense coil of thorn, encumbered by the gun and bulky ammunition vest. Finally, badly scratched and worse tempered, he found the land suddenly fell away beneath his face, revealing the beach below him.

He lay staring in disbelief. He understood instantly what the men were doing, even though the boats were hidden in the lee of the promontory. He made a mental note. It might be useful to him to know about this beach. This whole caper could get him into a lot of shit with a Congressional hearing. Blowing a major dope shipper might do him a lot of good. Congress was very hot on the drug thing, just now. It gave the impression of concern without any accompanying scope for action, just the kind of problem politicians liked. He worked his rifle off his shoulder and wondered where the hell the Colters had gone.

As he fitted the rifle neatly into place, nestling the stock firmly against his shoulder, a burly man in a light suit ran out from behind the high rocky finger that jutted into the sea, and sprinted across the beach. Bradman gave a grunt of surprise as the man appeared to melt into the rock face. He smiled. Although he could not see the entrance from where he lay, there had to be a cave down there. They had a nice operation going. He adjusted the gun more comfortably and settled down to wait.

He did not have to wait long. No more than a minute later a stir close to the cliff made him shift his position in anticipation. He raised the binoculars. The broad back of the big man sprang into close-up. Bradman could see the cloth of the jacket straining around the armpits as the man stooped forward under the weight of a burden. He stepped further out of the cave. His arms were beneath the armpits of a slumped figure, his fingers locked over the inert man's chest. Bradman was unable to see the identity of the injured man. He guessed it was the wounded Arab. He smiled. It was going to be a waste of Christian charity. His smile congealed into a look of angry contempt as the person holding the injured Arab's legs moved into view. Michael Colter, the scratches and scabs on his bare torso visible in stark detail through the powerful glasses, was smiling and talking to the big man. At the sight of him, Bradman felt an icy rage take hold. He spat a single curse. The boy had made a fool of him.

He put the binoculars aside. His finger moved on the trigger as he tracked the half-naked figure across the beach. His tongue flicked over his lips. Adrenaline raced through his system. With half an eye he watched for Julia and Ray Walker. He needed all three of them. The Arab would not matter, he would never be believed.

Julia Colter and Walker emerged side by side into the open. The crunch of their footsteps in the gravel drifted to him in a sudden stillness. He waited, letting them get well clear of the shelter of the cave. Not one of the three could be allowed to escape. He waited still, letting them advance over the beach. In another three or four steps they would be midway between the cliff and the first outcrops of the rocky point. The rifle muzzle moved imperceptibly. The crosshairs of the sight settled on a spot just below Michael's shoulder. The range was no more than seventy yards. It would blow a hole in the boy the size of a fist . . .

Without warning Julia turned and began running back towards the cliff.

It had taken almost seven minutes from the time Selim inhaled the heroin fumes to the moment when the pain drained magically from his crucified face to be replaced by a faint, tranquil smile. The big man ran back into the cave, panting hard. 'The boat's ready.'

The old man nodded. 'Go quickly. Be very careful with Selim.' He made a sign to the big man, who bent to pick up the injured man. Michael ran to take hold of Selim's legs, brushing aside Ray's protests, claiming his hand was no longer giving him trouble. Together they carried Selim awkwardly from the cavern.

Ray and Julia turned to the old man. They shook hands solemnly. 'Thanks. For everything,' Julia said, glancing from the shrewd, lined face of the old man to take in the others who remained in the cave. They looked blankly back at her, not speaking. She gulped once, grabbed Ray's arm and led him quickly in pursuit of the others. They were halfway across the beach when a shout from behind made her jerk her head around. The old man was beckoning her to return to the cave. With a moan of exasperation, she turned and ran back.

The man who had treated Selim held out several of the tiny cellophane envelopes of heroin. She looked blankly from the envelopes to the old man. He was grinning maliciously, the spittle at the corners of his mouth stretched into tiny stalactites. 'Take them,' he said with a cackle, 'you might get to like it.' Julia tossed her head angrily and turned to rejoin her friends. The old man's voice arrested her. 'Stop, miss. Take it, for Selim.' He muttered to the man holding the heroin. The man nodded and bent and ripped some foil from the roll. He groped in his pocket and placed his lighter with the foil and the drug. Julia remained motionless. 'Take it,' the old man said, all the mocking impudence gone from his tone. He stepped closer and put a kindly arm around Julia's shoulders. 'Believe me, he'll need it. Long before you reach Bcharré. *If* you reach it.' He took the items from the other man's palm and pressed them into Julia's. He folded her reluctant fingers around them. 'Take them, miss.' He glanced down at himself. 'I know I'm an old man and I don't shave very often. If I were a doctor in New York in a neat white tunic, prescribing morphine, you would accept it without question.' He tapped her closed fist. She began to speak. He held up a hand. 'Believe me, I know. My son *is* a doctor in New York.' He smiled. He was not kidding. 'This is our morphine. But this is not New York. Take it for Selim,' he said, turning away as though dismissing her reservations, 'and if he needs it give it to him. Don't make *him* suffer for *your* scruples.'

Julia watched his back for a moment more as he walked over to the table and drank from one of the half-finished glasses of arak. With a lopsided smile she tightened her fist over the heroin, turned and ran.

The others were already clambering along the point towards the boat. Ray was helping Michael hold Selim's legs and casting anxious looks back in search of Julia. She saw his face split in a grin of sheer relief as she emerged from the shadow of the cliff and sprinted across the beach.

On the cliff top eighty metres away Bradman drummed his fist into the dust and swore a stream of obscenities. He had almost had them cold. The woman had taken him by surprise, turning to run like that. He had not been able to shift position fast enough. While he fretted, waiting for her to reappear, the others had reached the cover of the rocks.

He had had his chance and blown it. He could have taken Walker and the brother. But she would have stayed in the cave while her Arab friends came after him. He needed all of them. If any of them got out the shit would hit the fan. The President, the Commander-in-Chief, would be brought down.

He stopped cursing and started thinking. There was one

more thing he needed to know before his next move. He took up his binoculars.

He had to wait only a few seconds before he heard the cough of engines coming to life. He watched the sea beyond the promontories. He caught his breath at the beauty of the boat as it bounded into view, its nose high over the twin plumes of its bow wave, its wake gleaming white on the golden sea. Frustration spoiled his enjoyment. He could see clearly the heads of his quarry where they sat in the shallow well of the boat.

He lowered the binoculars and watched the boat, squinting in the glare. It was two hundred metres from the promontories before he got what he was waiting for. The launch turned in a long, sweeping arc to its right. They were heading north. They were not heading for Cyprus. They were going up the coast. His original surmise had been right. They were heading for Bcharré.

He looked at his watch. It would be a close-run thing. He turned and began squirming back through the scrub. After only a few metres he scrambled to his feet and began running hell-for-leather back to his vehicle.

42

THE F 16 was a beautiful machine. Its handling was docile as a lamb and yet, Gerry Greeley knew, it packed the power to kick him skyward in an almost vertical climb quicker than any other fighter aircraft in service. It could outrun, outmanoeuvre and outfight anything flying, and it could skim a hundred feet above the surface, as it was doing now, at just below the speed of sound, and give you a ride as smooth and silent as a Mercedes on a motorway.

Greeley whistled softly to himself, with a lot of skilful vibrato. He felt terrific. The early part of the day had been as boring as the one before, cooped up in the stifling hut, studying his route, watching Dhahran television, which made the average American station look as though it were catering to an audience of Nobel Prize-winners, and wishing he had a woman. Around noon, though, the familiar electricity had begun to tingle in his system.

He had eaten a very light lunch and then slept for a couple of hours. On waking, a little after two, he had done thirty minutes of yoga. A long, cold shower had left him feeling fresh, fit and razor-sharp.

At four he had drunk two cups of coffee, American style, not the strong Arabic brew which would have set his heart pounding, undoing the effects of the yoga. A few minutes later he was in the cockpit of the needle-nosed aircraft, running through the final checks with the posse of eager engineers. By four-fifteen he was airborne, keeping his speed down to conserve fuel. Even with the extra tanks that replaced some of the normal armament load, the fourteen-hundred-kilometre one-way trip was the extreme limit of the range he had available. He still carried enough armament to destroy a decent-sized village.

He watched the expanse of the north Arabian peninsula unfurl beneath him, astonished at the subtleties of the colours beneath the setting sun. By day, this terrain was an unrelieved sea of dull tan. In the evening, by the slanting rays of the disappearing sun, it was transformed into an extraordinary kaleidoscopic display of reds, oranges and ochres.

He was able to enjoy the spectacle. There was no need to navigate. He was simply following the dead-straight track of the northern Arabian pipeline which ran clear across northern Saudi Arabia, through Jordan, Syria and Lebanon, built to transport oil from Dhahran to the Mediterranean coast.

Occasionally, the arid, deserted landscape was punctuated by a tiny postage stamp of greenery marking the site of a well. Sometimes there would be a building or two. Mostly there was nothing. Off to his right, beyond an unmarked and disputed border, lay the desert of southern Iraq. In other circumstances he might have been feeling vulnerable. The Iraqi Air Force carried a reputation. But recent events in Syria and the smouldering, unstable peace with Iran meant that the Air Force, and the radar that served as its eyes, were concentrated on the frontiers further north.

No. What they expected, and got, from the Saudis was money, not trouble. The Iraqis were doing the policing but the whole Sunni community, from Kuwait in the east to Morocco in the west, was helping pay the bills and anxiously watching their performance.

He smiled at the irony of it. The common idea of the Middle East was of an area bristling with military hardware. And yet here he was, right in the heart of it, cruising undetected through a million square kilometres of unpeopled wasteland.

There were, of course, some watchers, even here. The crews of the Awacs surveillance aircraft that he knew patrolled ceaselessly, miles overhead. In normal circumstances they could scarcely fail to pick him up. But Tom Jordan's fat friend Saïd had been categoric. It had been arranged on the highest authority in the kingdom, the man's very words, that they had been told to be looking elsewhere.

He checked his watch and his instruments. He was right on schedule to hit the hotel at six. All he had to do for the next six hundred kilometres, until he would have to veer away from the pipeline, north-west across the desolate salt flats of the Syrian desert, was stay on course and enjoy the scenery. He settled back in the narrow seat and began whistling a new tune.

The helicopters came in from the sea, three in a line. The first and third were gunships, bristling with heavy machine guns and rapid-fire cannon. Young men with quick reflexes and excellent eyesight crouched in the open gunports, their thumbs resting lightly on the firing buttons of their weapons. The second helicopter in the formation, nestled between the two armed escorts, was a passenger machine, quite normal except for its conspicuous lack of markings. The men in it wore civilian clothes. In all but one case the clothes concealed weapons.

Their route had been meticulously planned to avoid passing close to any significant settlements. They sped inland on a south-easterly tack for just over sixteen kilometres, passing well south of the town of Amioun. Guided by the fork in the road where the route which follows the valley down from Bcharré divides, heading west towards Batroun or north towards Tripoli, they swung through thirty degrees to head directly west. They climbed over the thousand-metre shoulder of mountain that barred their way and rushed on up the valley for the last fifteen kilometres to Bcharré.

In front of the hotel a large part of the square had been cleared. It was ringed by armed troops. They were the best men from Mukhtar Hussein's very disparate forces. Fit men, who had been trained as soldiers, rather than boys who had graduated from the fragmented neighbourhood militias. They stood with their weight on the balls of their feet, scanning the crowd that stood gawping at the approaching helicopters, and observing closely the rooftops and nearby hillsides.

One of the gunships landed first. A group of men tumbled from the open doorways and ran to form a square, looking outwards at the ring of Mukhtar Hussein's men. The civilian machine landed in the middle of the square while the second gunship remained low overhead. The noise was dcafcning. Great eddies of dust blasted the eyes of the onlookers.

A group of men in slacks and light windbreakers stepped out of the helicopter. At the centre of the group, virtually hidden by them, was a small, neat man in a dark-blue three-piece suit, who smiled a lot and joked with the packed bodyguard. The man's hair was thick but quite white. It had been white since he was sixteen, when he had seen all of his family but himself selected for the gas chambers at Dachau. The face beneath the hair was a curious contrast, smooth and strangely youthful. It was the false youthfulness that comes from certain types of medical treatment, in this case for chronic heart disease. In fact, the man was in his early sixties. At a word from one of the bodyguards they moved in a close-knit body towards the hotel steps.

Two turbanned figures emerged from the gloom of the interior and stood at the top of the steps that led up to the entrance. They watched in poker-faced silence as the group of men approached. Sheik Mukhtar Hussein, with his ten-day stubble and bulbous, pitted nose, stood to the left of the steps. Mehdi Bahrawi, taller, younger, his beard carefully trimmed, stood to his left. The small man moved to the front of the group, without actually detaching himself from it. He took each of the two robed and turbanned men by the shoulders and kissed them on both cheeks. Some of the bodyguards could scarcely conceal their surprise.

He stood back and, for several seconds, the men surveyed each other. There was frank curiosity on both sides.

Mukhtar Hussein spoke first. 'Welcome to Lebanon. We are most happy you were able to accept our hospitality.'

English had from the beginning been the language of all their contacts. Hussein's, though stilted and heavily accented, was perfectly adequate. He was a man who knew quite clearly what he wanted to say, a characteristic that always made language less of a barrier.

The visitor smiled. 'Me, too. Frankly, a few weeks ago I wouldn't have put money on it.' The visitor's accent was closer to Boise, Idaho, than to Beirut, Lebanon. It was there, after all, that he had lived from the war's end until 1959.

Hussein nodded, not smiling. 'You would have been wise not to. Shall we go inside?'

He turned and led the way. The visitor spoke briefly to his bodyguard and stepped through the open door. The guards settled down on the steps to wait. The nearest of the armed Lebanese stared openly at the men. There was curiosity and hostility in their faces. Hostility generally had the upper hand.

Inside the hotel the lobby had been cleared. It no longer resembled a field hospital. Alert-eyed men stood in attitudes of relaxed readiness at each of the shuttered windows and closed doors.

The three men crossed the lobby to what had once been the hotel's bar. Posters of jubilant skiers amid perfect snow hung around the walls. A bare table with a water carafe and three glasses and three chairs around it stood like an island in the centre of the cigarette-scarred carpet. A single bulb burned in the damaged overhead light fitting, throwing a pool of light dramatically over the table. The edges of the shuttered room were almost lost in a twilit blur. There was just enough light for the newcomer to observe that sandbags were stacked in thick ranks all around the walls and over the windows.

The visitor gestured at the sandbags. 'You're very careful people.'

Hussein scowled. 'If we were not we would not have got as far as this meeting.' He looked at Bahrawi and waited for his nod before again meeting the visitor's eye.

'Now, Prime Minister,' he began, speaking very softly and leaning forward, his forearms flat on the table, 'why don't you begin by outlining the Israeli position for us?'

The Israeli premier looked at them both for a moment as though giving himself a last chance for second thoughts. Then, with a sigh, he drew a small sheet of paper with a few notes from his pocket, put on a pair of steel-rimmed glasses, and began to speak.

43

THE SEA was less docile than it had looked. The boat leapt and twisted, slamming down on the waves with sickening force. In the cramped cabin Julia pushed cushions under Selim's head, making him as comfortable as she could. Selim did not seem to care. The heroin had left him too drowsy to notice the pounding of the water on the thin hull beneath him. Julia watched his eyes close and pushed herself to her feet. The movement, the solvent smell from the new fibreglass of the hull and the sweet aroma of hashish were combining to make her feel violently sick. She climbed out of the cabin with sweat glistening on her face.

The big man had the wheel. Two other men sat silent and sullen-faced on the floor with heavy machine guns across their knees. Opposite them sat Ray and Michael. They were laughing and passing a cigarette between them. She refused their offer to share it with a look of half-serious disgust and turned to the big man.

'How long to Batroun?'

He glanced at his watch. It was nine minutes to five. They had been under way for seven or eight minutes. He squinted briefly at the flickering needle of the speedometer. 'Twenty minutes?' He made it into a question.

'*Insha'allah*,' Julia replied, smiling.

He took a long drag at the cigarette he held in a cupped palm. 'It's not Allah I'm afraid of. It's the Israelis.' As he spoke his eyes roved over the sea ahead of them. His face was strained. He was genuinely afraid.

She sat down next to Ray. Maybe it explained the other men's hostility. They accepted the dangers of night-time rendezvous with the drug-runners' ships. It was what they were paid for. This run, in daylight, at the mercy of the heavily armed Israeli gunboats that treated these waters as their own, was a stupid risk without any reward.

Silently she began to cry. Tears spilled down her cheeks, mingling with the salt spray. Ray passed the joint back to Michael and turned to her. Impervious to the stares of the two gunmen she twined her arms around him. He responded, holding her tight against him. He let her cry, his lips on her damp hair. When the first great sobs diminished, he raised her chin so that their faces were inches apart. Very tenderly he thumbed the tears away.

'It's all right. It's nearly over.'

'Oh, Jesus, Ray. I've been so *scared*.'

'Me too. Shitless.' He smiled and kissed her gently on the mouth. 'Another hour, it'll all be over. Bahrawi'll get us out of this.'

She nodded, gazing back at the coast. She felt that she had lived the last few hours in some hideous nightmare world where normal human thought had been replaced by a mad instinct for violence. Even as she watched, a cloud of smoke billowed from a line of cliffs. Another bomb, another shell. More futile destruction. She shuddered and pulled herself close to Ray.

Two kilometres away, on a headland overlooking the bay of Jouniah, Bradman watched through the powerful binoculars as the boat sped across the mouth of the bay. Although unable to make out their faces he could discern quite clearly the three figures that sat facing him, their heads above the gunwale of the low boat showing as dark silhouettes against the sun. He threw down the binoculars. From here on they would outrun him. It did not matter. He was absolutely sure now of their destination. He slammed the Land-Rover into gear.

The chunky tyres bit into the loose red dirt, throwing up the spurt of dust Julia had seen as smoke. The Land-Rover roared up the steep slope to rejoin the road.

He drove flat out on the almost empty highway, pushing the car to its limit as the road hugged the coast east and then northwards around the bay. At intervals the sea was visible through gaps in the thick scrub that bordered the road. Not once did he glance at it in an effort to get a further sight of the launch. His mind was made up now, his destination fixed. His only preoccupation was to stay clear of trouble on the way.

He passed a handful of other vehicles, mostly trucks returning from Beirut after making deliveries of produce from the farms that lay on the narrow coastal strip. Only once did he see anything that looked military, a truck parked haphazardly in the slow lane around which a crew of young men shouted instructions to each other on how to change a wheel.

A little beyond the truck, surrounded by a deep litter of drink cans and plastic cups, stood an open-fronted booth. A scattering of chairs stood in slovenly attitudes in front of it. The aroma of donner kebab reminded him he had not eaten since early that morning. He eased his foot off the throttle a little.

Two hundred metres beyond the hut he found the track he was looking for. It cut inland alongside the bed of a dry stream. It was little more than a ribbon of barer earth among the parched weeds and struggling grass. He swung the car off the metalled surface of the road, picking up speed again as he went.

The Land-Rover bucked and swayed over the rough ground, making the wheel writhe in his hands. He gripped harder and drove faster. The distance to Bcharré was nearly forty kilometres. The reporters would not have much less than that to do, wherever they landed. But they had protection. That meant they would be able to do it all by road. He would be crossing very hostile territory. It meant he would be forced to travel across country. It was going to be close.

In the time since he had arrived in Lebanon Bradman had made it his business to learn everything he could of the terrain. Many nights he had been out with men of Bashaar's faction, deep into territory held by rival groups, on missions to kidnap or assassinate. He had used this experience to put together a fair map of the tracks and goat-trails of the interior. It had already been useful for outsiders, such as the Dutchman they had used to bomb a Beirut cinema used by a certain Palestinian leader. It had allowed the man to walk out over the mountains, through the Beqaa into Syria. He had resumed his identity as a salesman for a chemical supplier and flown home while half the Lebanon was still looking for him.

Bradman pulled the map from the door pocket and spread it on the seat beside him.

The first half of the journey was familiar to him. He could have done it as easily by night as by day. His route would take him along the southern flank of the valley of the Ibrahim River towards the lake and the once-fashionable resort of Quartaba. Until then he would have the river and the road that ran north of it to guide him. After that he would have to strike east across the more rugged terrain of the mountains with only the map and compass for help and no time for error. Once night fell he would be totally lost. Everything would be.

For a half-dozen kilometres the terrain was barren, mostly covered with jagged stones among which only the toughest, spikiest vegetation managed to claim a foothold. He was grateful for the stones. They meant there was no plume of dust to flag his progress to any hostile watcher.

Close to the village of Ghbalé the land began to rise abruptly. The angular silhouette of a ski-lift showed starkly against the skyline. He began looking for the track that would lead him to the left, skirting the village. The defunct ski resorts were some of the most dangerous places in a dangerous country. The militia groups found the remote collections of hotels and apartment blocks precisely suited to their needs for barracks and training camps. They teemed with the youngest, most eager, most unstable elements, heavily armed and nervous of outsiders. He found the left-hand fork and swung onto it.

Racing along the narrow track which curved in a wide sweep among sparse pines, he checked his weapons. After no more than a kilometre the track would bring him to the road which led up to the village. Above the road the mountain rose in a sheer, impassable wall. For a short distance he would have no choice but to take it, winding through a series of knuckle-whitening hairpins before being able to regain the comparative safety of the rough country.

In another minute the road was in front of him. He could

see only a three-hundred-metre stretch before it was swallowed up by the first of the bends. Without slowing, he tightened his grip on the wheel and plunged down the steep embankment.

The tracks had been rough. The road was still rougher. Years of neglect through the hard, snowy winters and the spring thaws had taken their toll. The tarmac was buckled and pitted, with ragged holes big enough to swallow a wheel of the Land-Rover and smash the suspension. He wove skilfully between them. It made him think of New York City.

The wry grin the thought brought to his face was abruptly wiped out as he screamed through the first hairpin. An old man stood thirty feet in front of him. The man's seamed face, dark as earth, worked as he shouted at the onrushing Land-Rover. A gnarled hand waved furiously, signalling him to stop. Behind the man a herd of mud-coloured goats milled and pranced, completely blocking the road.

The road was very narrow. Two cars would not have passed. To his right the rock rose in a sheer wall for twenty feet. To the left it fell away in a precipitous chaos of boulders and broken trees. Standing on the brake he could probably stop a foot from the man. He pressed the accelerator the last two inches to the floor.

The vehicle surged forward. The brown face froze for a moment in incomprehension. Incomprehension melted into terror and the old man threw himself with astonishing nimbleness against the rock wall.

Bradman braced himself for the impact as the front of the Land-Rover scythed into the herd. Incredibly, he felt and heard nothing. Instead, he became aware of an extraordinary phenomenon. The Land-Rover seemed to be preceded by a kind of bow wave of panic. As it ploughed forward, the goats just ahead of it simply rose and spilled out of its path. Some went to the left, flowing unhesitatingly over the edge onto the almost sheer slope, others sprang to the right, finding footholds on the vertical rock that defied gravity. Bradman had just time to see the man scramble to his feet and begin screaming obscenities at the retreating vehicle before they were lost to sight as he swayed into the next bend.

He stayed on the road for another two kilometres through a tight series of switchbacks. He saw no one. Nonetheless, he gave a low whistle of relief when he saw the cluster of stunted oaks that marked the point where he could again leave the road.

The track was narrow but worn to a flat shelf by centuries of use by herds such as the one he had just encountered. It hugged the contour as it wound around the shoulder of the Jabal Moussa Mountain, leading him into the shelter of its thickly wooded northern slopes.

He relaxed his grip on the wheel and allowed some of the tension to flow out of him. Until Quartaba there was nothing for kilometres around, no villages and no road. For the next fifteen minutes he was safe.

44

THE PRESIDENT stared from the window of Air Force One. Below him, the northern tip of the Great Salt Lake showed as a dirty grey smudge. Beyond that, not too far to the northwest, lay Idaho. He had had a great boyhood up there. Weeklong fishing trips with his father. Big salmon, almost too big sometimes for the spindly boy that he had been before he began packing on muscle, to hold up for the proud photographs.

He remembered Larry, the huge-shouldered river guide, who looked like every boy's idea of a western hero; who knew every inch of the river and all there was to know of wildlife and the wilderness. And who also took quiet times to tell him of books to read and how to read them, while his own father, Big Jack to all the other men along on the trip, spent his time gulping scotch and bragging loudly.

Over the years he had used more of what he had learned

from his father than of what he had learned from Larry. The back-slapping, hard swearing, hard screwing stereotype did better in politics. You could never get to be President by impersonating Gary Cooper. Except maybe if you were Abraham Lincoln. His shoulders lifted beneath the white barber's shroud that he wore. He wondered if Larry were still alive. Maybe he would be looking him up soon. It was as sure as hell he was not going to be President much longer. He sighed.

'Ah, bullshit.'

'Sir?' Foreman's personal barber and make-up man paused and gazed at the President's face. His eyes wore an expectant shine, as though bullshit were the opening word of Hamlet's soliloquy.

'I said, bullshit,' the President snapped with sudden savagery.

The barber blinked. 'Yes, sir.' With the minutest stirring of a flounce he tipped a little more of the brown fluid onto a wad of cotton and continued touching up the President's tan.

He had been with Jack Foreman for a long time, since the Senate. Twice a week for ten years he had trimmed his hair and given him a manicure. With the hands the man had he might as well have been manicuring a werewolf. Whenever the President had a public appearance to make, or was to be on television, it was his job to make sure the tan was even, the shadows beneath the eyes masked. He was good at it. Anyone who did not know Jack Foreman's age would almost certainly have given him five years less than his passport showed. Until lately.

In the last few days the task had become impossible. The President's flesh seemed to have shrunk on his skull. His shirt collars were no longer snug. The hair had become somehow wilfully unruly, making it impossible to disguise its sparseness. He dabbed fastidiously at the pale spot where he had shortened the President's sideburn, leaning back from the waist and squinting appraisingly at the effect in a parody of a painter's posture. The President shoved his arm roughly aside.

'This is all bullshit, too,' Foreman said angrily, clawing the cape from his shoulders and pushing it into the arms of the startled barber. 'Get out of here, you creepy little prick!'

The barber bobbed in what was almost a curtsey and walked quickly from the President's private cabin, his shoulders pinioned erect by wounded dignity.

Jack Foreman let out a snort of exasperation and contempt. He had never completely mastered his dislike of homosexuals, no matter how great they were at cutting hair. He groaned and wiped a hand over his face. There would be plenty of them today. A rally in San Francisco seemed to attract hardly anyone else these days. Gays dressed as nuns, gays dressed as stormtroopers, gays in leather, gays in gingham. There would probably be that bunch of crazy dikes that had been cavorting in front of the cameras at the convention back in August, with giant dildos strapped around their waists. He wiped his face again, massaging the flesh that was grey beneath the bogus tan. Jesus Christ.

'Mr President?' A round-faced man with thick glasses and the bad shave of the campaign trail was looking diffidently around the door. 'We have a call for you, sir.'

Foreman groaned. 'Ah shit! Who is it?'

'Tel Aviv, sir. Zimund. He says he absolutely must talk to you.' The man raised an eyebrow like a trimming from a piece of dark carpet and left it raised.

The President's face showed a flash of irritation and distaste. He opened his mouth, intending to tell the man to divert the call to the Secretary of State. Then he remembered. 'Aw, what the fuck,' he said with a gesture of resignation. He walked heavily through into the adjoining cabin and picked up the phone.

'Mr President? We have a problem here.'

Foreman made a wry face at the young aide, who smirked knowingly back at him. 'Tell me about it, Rudi. You know we're always ready to help in any way we can.' The practised affability of his voice betrayed none of his dislike for the man. He could not have said why he felt it. It arose from a vague feeling that the man was somehow always outwitting him.

'We seem to have a warplane, an F16, heading our way. Our people picked it up out of Dhahran.'

The ironic expression fell from the President's face. 'A *Saudi* machine?' he asked, his voice high with disbelief.

'We don't know. That's why I'm calling. An F16 couldn't belong to many people, Mr President. We wondered first of all if it might be yours.'

Jack Foreman frowned at the Israeli's tone. It was blunt, untempered by the respect that protocol normally imposed, even in men who disliked each other personally. Zimund had been reading the opinion polls, too.

Foreman shook his head. 'Out of Dhahran? No. That can't be. We don't have planes operating out of Saudi, Rudi, you know that. God knows, we've been over it enough times, with them and with you.'

'Are you telling me you're absolutely certain of that, Mr President? Because anything coming our way out of an Arab country unannounced like this had better be very, very careful.'

'I'm telling you, it's not ours. I've given no such order. We don't have aircraft down there. I swear to that.' Even as he spoke, the President felt a worm of misgiving.

Zimund paused. 'Mr President, we might be heading for a major incident here. Will you do something very urgently for us? Will you speak to the Saudis? We need to know what's going on out there. Quickly!'

Foreman massaged the back of his neck with his free hand. 'Yeah,' he said, with a hint of hoarseness in his voice. 'I'll do that, Rudi. I'll get right back to you. Give me a few minutes, will you?' He handed the phone to the aide. 'Get me Riyadh.'

'Right, sir. Who do you want to talk to?'

'The man who cleans the toilets!' The man looked dumbly back at him. 'The King, you asshole! Who do you think?' He scowled at the cowed aide and then turned away abruptly to stare pensively from the window.

It took several minutes to get the King to the phone. He was a staunch defender of the local traditions. He still believed in sleeping away the afternoon's heat, even if the palace did have more air-conditioning than Los Angeles.

'Mr President?' The strangely reedy voice carried the traces of his abrupt awakening.

'Your Highness? How are you?' he asked warmly. The obscene racking cough at the other end of the line told him. The King felt the way everyone who smoked sixty Pall Mall a day would feel when they first got out of bed. 'We, ah, have a problem, ah, Your Highness. We're hoping you, er, might be able to help us out with it. It concerns the, ah, cousins.'

'Go on, Mr President.'

The chill in the King's voice at the use of the word they used as a code for the Israelis was unmistakable. They had adopted the word in the first place out of regard for his sensibilities. It was not terrifically successful. A pragmatic, easy-going man in most ways, he went into a cold rage at the very mention of Israel. He saw himself as the trustee of the holy places of Islam. These holy places, as Foreman had been told a thousand times, included Jerusalem. The King saw the Israelis as occupiers of Moslem shrines. His duty was to throw them back into the sea.

Foreman had never given much for his chances. He described the call from Zimund. The King was categoric. 'It's not ours,' he said flatly.

The President knew the King too well to argue. 'Thank you, Your Highness. Goodbye.' He turned to the waiting aide. 'Get me that prick Jordan,' he said, almost inaudibly.

Admiral Langston rested the phone carefully on the low mahogany table and turned to Tom Jordan. 'It's for you. The President.'

Jordan put down his glass of scotch and walked over to the phone, puzzled by a faint trace of amused malice in Langston's tone. He picked up the phone and turned his back to the admiral. 'Mr President?'

A few seconds earlier Tom Jordan had been fairly drunk. Now his eyes came suddenly into focus and his face tautened. His back straightened perceptibly. Like a soldier coming under fire he was abruptly alert. He listened to the President's words, inspecting every nuance with total, intense lucidity, looking for ways out of the trouble that was coming.

The options were simple. He could deny all knowledge of the plane. The Israelis would try to bring it down. He could tell the truth, or some of it. The President would *beg* them to bring it down. Either way, Gerry was going to have a bad day.

'Believe me, Mr President,' he said with all the quiet sincerity he could muster, 'I know nothing whatsoever about this.'

45

IT WAS NOT quite five minutes past five when the big man called out and pointed ahead of them. Michael and Ray clambered to their feet, their eyes probing the evening haze that lay on the sea. Michael was the first to discern the minaret of the principal mosque rising slightly out-of-true over the mist.

They continued speeding shoreward. The dirty tan blur of the shoreline resolved itself into a magnificent sweep of yellow beach. A few years earlier, when Batroun had been a major resort, the beach had been packed with parasols and deckchairs. Now it was crowded with rough hovels of driftwood and old packaging materials. The smoke of cooking fires thickened the haze.

The big man brought the launch slashing in a wide arc to within fifty metres of the beach and cut the engine. In the first seconds of sudden calm they could hear only the soft sucking of water against the hull as it rocked in the swell, just outside the line where waves broke and raced, boiling, for the beach.

Gradually, they became aware of the insistent blare of car horns and then a growing commotion from the beach. The scattering of children at play broke from their games. Others erupted from the shacks. As though at a signal, they ran in a group to the water's edge to stand chattering and pointing at the boat.

The big man spoke sharply to one of the Lebanese who still lounged, silent and resentful, in the well of the boat. Grumbling, the man stood up, stripped to a pair of nylon briefs and plunged over the side. They watched in silence as he swam in an unschooled crawl that carried him surprisingly quickly to the shore. He waded from the surf and after a brief hesitation selected the biggest of the children, a boy of about twelve.

Grinning with pride, the boy followed him a few paces away from the group. Under the envious eyes of the crowd he listened in silence, nodding twice as the man spoke briefly to him. When the man had finished, the boy turned and sprinted up the beach. The man waved to the boat, signalling the Americans to join him.

In the cabin Julia was finishing the administration of another dose of heroin smoke to Selim when the big man pushed his way through the narrow entrance. He pulled a life jacket and a square of oilskin from a locker. 'Leave him. Take this and wrap your money. You'll need all of it out there.' He handed Julia the oilskin and pushed her roughly from the cabin. As she looked back she saw him easing the life jacket around Selim's shoulders. Her own throat constricted as she saw tears slide down the big man's broad, battered face.

On deck Julia put all their money into a single thin wad and wrapped it in the oilskin, making a tight bundle. She unbuttoned her shirt and pushed it into her brassiere. The big man emerged awkwardly through the bulkhead with Selim cradled in his arms. Selim smiled up at them, anaesthetized by the heroin.

'Go over the side. Take great care with him.'

He waited until the three of them had slid into the water and then leant over and lowered Selim as tenderly as though he had been a baby. Michael and Ray each took Selim by an arm. With Julia ahead of them, they struck out for the shore.

By the time they struggled clear of the water the boy was back, grinning and gesticulating to the man in the nylon briefs, his words spilling out in a torrent between the heaves of his thin chest. Julia was relieved to see that Selim was not so doped that he did not watch the boy's face, listening intently to every word.

The boy finished speaking. The young man turned to them, his eyes still hostile. His brows knitted in concentration as he assembled his English. 'This boy has found car. To go with you to Bcharré. The owner will drive. Five hundred dollars.' He held up the spread fingers of one hand in emphasis. 'You have them?'

Julia nodded. The young man looked disappointed that he had not asked for more. 'And fifty dollars for him?' He nodded at the boy who stood kicking at the sand.

'You've got it.'

The boy beamed suddenly, understanding the words. He took Julia by the hand. 'Come.'

Ray and Michael hoisted Selim between them. With a final wave to the boat they turned to follow the boy.

The open Toyota pick-up the boy led them to was ancient, scabbed and dilapidated. So was the driver. He was a thin, unpleasant looking man with the dark, sour, prematurely aged face of a man who spent a lot of time in the open air resenting other people's luck. He lounged in the open doorway of the pick-up, probing at his back teeth with a match. At their approach he threw away the match and surveyed them with shrewd eyes. He spoke swiftly to the child. The boy nodded and turned to Julia.

'Dollars!' His English vocabulary was all a rising Lebanese adolescent needed.

Julia felt at her breast for the oilskin package. The old man moistened his lips several times with his tongue, staring at Julia with hooded, lizard eyes. He watched her unroll the package and pull out travellers' cheques. At Julia's questioning look he groped in the cab and produced a broken Bic biro. She handed the cheques to Ray. He signed while Julia counted out fifty dollars for the youth. As she closed up the package the man's eyes were shrouded, as though he, too, were regretting his error of judgment.

Julia brandished the package. 'All of it.' His frown deepened. *'Tout ça!'* Understanding came back into his eyes. *'Pour vous.'* She jabbed a finger at Selim, whose skin had taken on a yellowish tinge. *'Si nous arrivons à temps.'*

The man looked appraisingly at Selim, as though he were a shrewd judge of the time it took a person to die. He sniffed with startling force. *'Allez. Montez. Ya'aala.'*

Ray and Michael laid Selim carefully among the masonry debris in the rear. They leapt in next to him. Ray handed Julia up beside them.

Michael shivered, swept by a sudden chill. It was as though the fever of a couple of days earlier were returning. All at once, he was very tired. The whole thing was crazy. An American held hostage by his own people, seeking the protection of the very Shi-ite fanatics who had been the chief hostage-takers. The irony did not even make him smile. He just wanted it to be over. He rapped a fist on the roof of the cab.

'Let's go. To Bcharré!'

46

PRIME MINISTER MEYER thrust his cigarette end into the overfilled ashtray at his elbow, sending debris spilling onto the floor. He had been told by his doctors to stop smoking after his first heart attack. He had obeyed them, more or less, cutting from sixty a day to none. Now he only smoked in times of acute stress. For a Prime Minister of Israel that was most days. Since the beginning of the meeting he had chain-smoked through most of a pack.

'So there it is, gentlemen.' He pulled off his glasses and wiped his eyes. He leaned easily in his chair and smiled benevolently at the two men opposite, as though he had just proffered a valuable gift. 'Put in as few words as I am able.'

Mukhtar Hussein's eyes flashed angrily. 'No!' he cried, pushing himself noisily to his feet. 'Those are conditions we could never accept. I could never carry my people. I would never even put such a proposition to them. They would take me for a traitor!'

Mehdi Bahrawi sat staring at the map which lay open on the table before them, streaked with cigarette ash. He chewed slowly at the short hair on his lower lip, seeming not to hear Hussein's words.

'The whole of the Beqaa would be ours?' He stroked gently at the silky dark hair on his cheek.

Meyer nodded, the smile still on his lips. Behind the glasses his eyes were unblinking, fixed on Bahrawi's face. 'Absolutely.' Over the last weeks he had discussed that matter with Zimund and the military people to the point of exhaustion. In the end, they had all come around to his way of thinking. The heights of the Jabal el Barouk mountains would be the limit of the Israeli-run area. From there they could dominate the whole of the troublesome Beqaa valley while at the same time leaving it as a buffer between themselves and the Syrians. The lesson of the Golan Heights was one the Israelis had absorbed well.

The arrangement would give the Shi-ites free rein the length of the Lebanese border with Syria. Meyer allowed his eyes to join in the smile. It was beautiful. President Assad thought he had problems *now* with his Shi-ites . . .

He looked up suddenly at Mukhtar Hussein, who paced the room behind Bahrawi, protesting. 'What is it in our proposal you object to? It seems to us a fair one. By far the greater portion of the country would be yours.' He spoke expansively, his tone softly reasonable. 'The Beqaa, all of the north. I repeat what I've said so many times, we are interested in security, not territory.'

'Like on the West Bank? Like Golan?' Hussein's voice was choked with bitterness.

Meyer shrugged imperceptibly and gave him a gracious, forgiving smile. 'Those aren't the issues here,' he said smoothly.

Hussein approached and leaned over the table, scowling at the gently smiling Israeli. 'What *is* at issue, Mr Meyer, is Beirut. It's an impossible demand. Beirut in the hands of the Jews . . . of the Israelis?' He broke off, fighting to control his emotions. 'It's inconceivable. My people would take me for a madman.'

Meyer shook his head. 'I'm sorry, gentlemen. My colleagues sent me here with no mandate to even discuss the point. It's simply not negotiable.' He spoke with steely affability. 'The Palestinians, you see,' he added, almost apologetically.

Hussein's eyes blazed. The nostrils of his great nose flared, dark and uninviting. 'You're mad,' he seethed. 'My people would never accept it. For the camps to fall into Jewish hands . . . It's unthinkable! Impossible!' He reared angrily away from the table and resumed pacing the room, unable to continue speaking.

The Israeli Premier opened his mouth to speak. Bahrawi cut him short. 'We must have Beirut.'

Meyer stared at him, searching the Iranian's face for a clue, for a sign that somewhere there was a flexibility absent from the voice. 'It's out of the question,' he said, almost mechanically, his eyes still on Bahrawi's face.

The deep, brown, emotionless eyes stared back at him. 'We *must* have it.' His voice was still low but each word sounded quite distinct in the silent room. A few feet away Mukhtar Hussein stood silent and immobile, his intent eyes glancing from one to the other of the two expressionless faces in front of him.

Meyer shook his head. 'I can't. The camps. My colleagues regard it as crucial that we control them.' He lifted his hands and let them drop to the table again. 'You both know my position.'

Only the lips moved in Bahrawi's face. 'Without Beirut I can't deliver. I, too, have other opinions to consider.'

Meyer's voice rose. 'Without Beirut I can do nothing. Without neutralizing the Palestinian camps we might as well . . .'

Bahrawi interrupted, his own voice still cool and level. 'We can deal with the Palestinians.'

The silence in the room was complete. Meyer and Hussein stared at the Iranian, hardly daring to grasp what he was saying.

'It's like this, Mr Meyer.' Bahrawi leaned forward and placed a finger on the map in front of them. 'The northern limit of your zone will run from here.' He jabbed his finger at the point where Highway 2, the Beirut to Damascus road, passed through the mountains after leaving the Beqaa. He traced the road with his finger until a fork, where it traced a curve south-west, to the valley of the Danour River and to the coast. 'To here. You'll have more territory than your people ever dreamed of. We shall have Beirut. With such an agreement I'll have what I need. Our so-called President and his clique will be removed. My friends and I shall take their place.' He paused to let the implications strike home. 'I absolutely guarantee you, we will deal with the Palestinian problem.' He glanced up at the face of Hussein. 'Mukhtar Hussein will be the undisputed governor of our sector. You will run yours as you wish.'

Hussein nodded agreement. 'The Palestinians need not be an obstacle, Mr Meyer.' He grinned unpleasantly.

Meyer took off his glasses and cleaned them with studied languor, gaining time to collect his racing thoughts. It was a turn of events he had not foreseen. The Palestinian problem eliminated by the Arabs themselves, without Israel's participation. The Sabra and Chatila debacle had alienated opinion almost fatally. Especially the Americans. Avoiding a similar episode could only be helpful. Beirut in itself was useless to them. Israel did not lack deepwater ports. He sat back in his seat, pushing his glasses back on his nose.

'You're confident that you could carry it off, Mr Bahrawi? All our intelligence indicates that your President, at least, still commands great respect. As the Imam's legitimate heir.'

'It would scarcely have needed the Mossad to tell you that, Mr Meyer,' Bahrawi answered with a trace of mockery. 'However, they won't have failed to tell you that he's very old. Almost as old as the Imam, God bless him, would be if he had been spared.'

'But very well, apparently.'

Bahrawi moved a hand in a tiny dismissive gesture. 'Many things can happen to old men. Eating something, for example, something that disagrees with them.'

Meyer looked frankly startled at Bahrawi's words. He stared at him, wondering if he had correctly grasped the implications of the man's intonation. Bahrawi's next words removed his last shreds of doubt.

'He's not the problem. The problem is the succession. As you're well aware, I'm just one candidate among several. Some of the others are better placed than I.' Meyer nodded, almost transfixed by what Bahrawi was saying to him. 'That's my whole purpose in being at this meeting. If I *am* to be the one who replaces him. If I *am* to have the chance to restore Iran to its place in the world I need all the prestige of this agreement. That's why the Shi-ites and not the Jews must have Beirut.'

For several seconds the three men were quite silent. At length, the Israeli Premier spoke.

'One thing, Mr Bahrawi. How will your people accept your dealing with us?'

Bahrawi smiled. A sudden, bright, ironic smile. He knew

he had won. 'They'll accept it, believe me. When I bring them Beirut.'

'Even as a gift from the Israelis?' Meyer asked, smiling.

'That means nothing to us. You know it very well, Mr Meyer. Since antiquity Persian and Jew have seen their common interest. There's no hatred for you among us. I will go home from here as a patriot, not a traitor. It won't be difficult to show them how our agreement serves Iran's interests.'

Meyer nodded. 'Just how do you intend to do that?'

Bahrawi smiled again. 'You forget I'm a Shi-ite, not a secret democrat or a closet Christian. With a Shi-ite regime here in Lebanon the Sunni regimes of Saudi Arabia and the Gulf will be forced to take notice. We'll have over two hundred kilometres of frontier with Syria. We'll hound their regime from power. The Shi-ites in Bahrain, Saudi, even Egypt will all take heart from Mukhtar Hussein's example.'

Meyer watched Bahrawi's eyes as he spoke. He did not like what he saw. The man's own rhetoric kindled a light of fanaticism in his eyes. 'To come back to more concrete matters, Mr Bahrawi. As I've told you, my colleagues and I are very concerned about the Americans' reaction. They're going to come under a lot of pressure, especially from Riyadh.' He cleared his throat and readjusted his glasses. 'You mentioned your country's willingness to help us if they were to, er, cut off our aid. Could we talk about some specific numbers?'

As Gerry Greeley had flown almost directly west the sun had risen a little, so that the land had lost some of its evening splendour. He was on the edge of boredom. Below him was an unrelieved succession of pale-brown ridges and dry river beds, marked by an occasional smudge of dusty sage-green where vegetation clung to their parched banks. The wadis ran northeast, following the imperceptible tilt of the land towards the Mesopotamian basin three hundred kilometres away to his right. The point where Iran and Iraq came together. The cradle of civilization.

'Those were the days,' he muttered wryly.

He checked his position and re-calculated his schedule. The calculation told him what he already knew, that he was right on time.

Below him, on the highway that hugged the pipeline, a single vehicle moved. Above him the sky was completely empty. In other circumstances the dark-blue void would have been the perfect opportunity to put the aeroplane through its paces. Flying low and slow in a machine like an F16 gave him a terrible sense of deprivation. He made himself a promise to see what it could do, once out over the Mediterranean. After the job was done.

Five hundred kilometres to the west, in a narrow valley deep in the hills around Dimona, a group of pilots in shiny fireproof jumpsuits, their bulky flying helmets under their arms, stood listening to their officer as he traced on the big wall map the progress of the lone aircraft. Their casual poses gave no clue to the intensity with which they listened and absorbed what the officer was telling them. The aircraft was unidentified, coming out of an Arab country and heading for Israel. It would have to identify itself soon, or be brought down. Or both.

47

BRADMAN COULD almost taste the adrenaline. He was racing northeast, following the dry bed of a ravine. The lack of rain was a stroke of luck. Crossing the Ibrahim River above Quartaba had been easy. After rain it would have been impossible. The fast shallow stream he had driven through became a boiling torrent within minutes when rain poured off the impervious hillsides.

The ravine he was in now would have been impassable. As it was, he raced over the baked surface, weaving between the boulders and the bleached corpses of uprooted trees that lay like prehistoric bones.

He drove fast and recklessly, confident in the knowledge he was far from any road. The dense scrub that covered the steep banks gave cover enough. At worst he would meet a solitary hunter or shepherd. They would be wise to stay out of his way.

Abruptly, the ravine began to narrow further. Ahead of him the dry river bed rose sharply, cutting straight across the contours, carved out by the power of the spring thaw water crashing down from the heights.

The nose of the Land-Rover rose giddily in front of him. For the first time he was forced to slow down, picking a path among the rubble of rocks and trees. Progress became painfully slow. For several minutes he blundered on, looking for the trail his map said was there. All the while he murmured a soft stream of obscenities. He cursed his map, he cursed Bashaar, and he cursed himself. Especially himself, for depending on Bashaar.

He brought the vehicle roaring out of yet another rocky cul-de-sac. Shouting with rage, he jammed it into gear and rammed its nose at a thinner patch where two huge rosemary bushes met. Branches slapped and tore at the bodywork. The smell of the rosemary engulfed him. A dark shape launched itself at the windscreen.

With a yell Bradman ducked low in his seat. He was snatching for his gun when a second shape sprang at the bonnet and rebounded with tremendous clanging blows over the roof of the cab.

He stopped the Land-Rover. For several seconds he sat motionless except for the trembling of his hands. Abruptly he laughed aloud. His nerves were really going. The two deer had almost made him turn the thing over.

He thrust forward into a small clearing. To one side of the belt of vegetation that bounded it rose the steep flank of the hill. On the other side, beyond a patch of scrub, a growth of pines stretched away down the shoulder of the mountain.

With a low whistle of relief he ran the Land-Rover at the belt of bushes, forcing a way through.

Once in the open it took him only a moment to get his bearings. To his right the slope grew steeper until above the tree line it merged with the streaked sandstone cliffs of the summits. In the light of the setting sun the cliffs seemed to be aflame. In the distance snow gleamed on the ten-thousand-foot peaks of the Dahr el Quadib. The beauty of the scene was breathtaking. Bradman did not even see it, as he raced across the open ground for the shelter of the pines.

The going among the trees was easy. The thick carpet of pine needles stifled any undergrowth. The trees were widely spaced enough to enable him to drive fast. There was no longer any need of a trail, nor even of the map. By staying with the contour, keeping the mountain on his right, he would be in sight of Bcharré within twenty minutes.

It took him precisely eighteen minutes before he rounded the head of the valley and saw the cluster of neat buildings below him, each casting a shadow longer than itself as the sun dipped towards the horizon. A few vehicles, jeeps and military trucks, sped along the road below the village. Above it, where the road wound towards the Beqaa in a series of impossibly tight turns carved into the mountainside, nothing moved.

Driving very slowly, stopping every few seconds to listen intently, he drew closer to the village. A short distance ahead of him the trees came to an abrupt end, cleared in a dead straight line to form the limits of a ski-run. He switched off the ignition. For a few seconds he sat studying the scene beneath him. He could discern individual buildings grouped around a central square. In front of the biggest of the buildings, almost lost in its deep shadow, he could make out the spidery shapes of helicopters. Whistling low through pursed lips, a sound that could not be heard two metres away, he walked around to the passenger door. He settled the strap of the rifle over his shoulders and threaded the binoculars across his chest. In his right hand he took up the rocket-launcher, in the left the box of rockets. Moving with easy stealth, he began advancing to the edge of the trees.

The engine of the Toyota was missing badly. On the relatively gentle climb from the coastal plain into the foothills both the driver and the truck had performed better than they had looked capable of. They had made good time. Now, through the punishing steep hairpins and in the thinning air, the crumbling pick-up was faltering.

The air had got much colder as they climbed. Michael sat with his knees drawn up and his hands folded tight across his chest. Sweat from the fever glistened on his face and torso, cooling him further so that his body shook in convulsive spasms. His jaw muscles stood out in knots as he fought to keep his teeth from chattering. The driver had passed them a stained blanket from the cab. Michael had insisted it be used for Selim.

Even with the blanket across his chest Selim's teeth chattered audibly. At Michael's insistence Julia had abandoned him to concentrate her help on Selim. She crouched over him, trying to cushion his head as they slammed across the pitted surface. Despite her efforts he screamed with pain. The effect of the heroin had almost gone.

Ray leaned forward and touched Selim's arm. 'D'you want a snort?'

Selim stared up at him, his face glistening despite the bite of the air. He shook his head feebly. 'No,' he murmured, through tightly gritted teeth. 'We're very close. I must be conscious.' A stab of pain cut his breath, preventing him from saying more. His head fell back against Julia's cradling hand.

Ray leaned back against the wall of the truck. He looked at the fresh blood that stained the floor beneath Selim and then at Julia. He raised his eyebrows in a silent question.

Julia shrugged. She was about to mouth an answer when the driver braked abruptly. The rear wheels broke away. She was thrown sprawling in the filth of the truck floor as the wheels spun towards the void. Sounds came to her as in a dream, the hiss of the bald tyres over the dusty asphalt, the driver's curses and Ray's protesting obscenities.

She felt no fear, only the detachment, the feeling of being an observer, that often accompanies danger. She was still in that odd, slightly euphoric state when the truck stopped moving. She was conscious of men calling. She pushed herself upright and looked around her. The real fear began now.

Twenty metres ahead of them a roughly trimmed tree trunk lay across the road. Two lean gunmen stood by it. A third gunman had already reached the truck. He stood at the passenger door threatening the driver with a handgun. A fourth man stared at them over the side of the truck, angry and suspicious. Julia tried a smile. His anger and suspicion seemed to grow. He said something in the indecipherable dialect of the mountains.

They spread their hands and shrugged. Ray jabbed a thumb in the direction of their driver. The man ignored the gestures. He went on speaking, truculent and contemptuous. Julia tried to muster enough Arabic to make him understand. At the sound of Bahrawi's name his eyes narrowed. He scowled at each of them in turn, unsure how to react.

In her eagerness Julia moved towards the man. With a bray of protest he punched her with sudden viciousness in the stomach. She crumpled, gasping, to the floor of the pick-up.

Michael bellowed with rage. Fearful of what was coming, Ray tried to restrain him. Without a thought for his feverish state, Michael shook off Ray's restraining hand and launched himself at the man, his fists bunched angrily. The man saw him coming. A hand flashed at Michael's face. Michael groaned as the butt of a handgun cracked across the bridge of his nose. Clutching his face, Michael fell back, crashing onto Selim's outstretched leg.

Selim had been lying quite still, his face turned away from the man. Now his whole body contracted in a spasm of agony. He screamed once and raised his perspiration-soaked face to stare around him. His eyes were unfocused. Saliva dribbled from a corner of his mouth.

The man had not looked at Selim until then. Now his eyes fell on the tortured face. He began to frown. Confusion and fear seeped into his eyes. His gaze flicked over the Americans and then back to Selim. Without taking his eyes off Selim he called to one of the guards by the barricade. The guard sauntered towards them, smirking. He wore a beret, which might have been a sign of rank. The first man spoke to him in a low voice, his confused eyes still skittering from Selim to the Americans. The smirk on the face of the second man disappeared. He peered over the side of the truck at Selim. Swallowing, he spoke. Selim, who again seemed to have lost consciousness, made no response. The man in the beret took Selim by the shoulder, shook it tentatively and spoke again, louder and a little desperately.

Selim opened his eyes. He stared vacantly up at the speaker, his eyes as empty and unfocused as a blind man's. The man repeated his words a third time, leaning low over the wall of the truck. Understanding entered Selim's eyes. His lips moved weakly. The man thrust his face lower, straining to hear the faint, husky words. Selim continued speaking for some seconds, his voice growing fainter with each passing moment. As the guard listened his tongue flicked over his lips in rapid, nervous movements. His eyes, set deep in a rather handsome, angular face, moved repeatedly to those of his companion, who stood in an identical attitude, anxiously listening. Both of them from time to time looked over at the Americans. Ray stared sullenly back at them, his arm around Julia.

Selim finished speaking. His head fell back hard to the floor. His face, which had been grotesque with pain and effort, became suddenly peaceful as he again appeared to drop into unconsciousness. The two men conferred in urgent, soft voices. The one in the beret did appear to have some authority. He spoke to the man who was threatening the driver. The man withdrew his gun from the flesh of the driver's neck, still without lowering it completely. He stepped a pace back from the cab, his face still rigid with hostility.

The man in the beret called to the one who had remained by the log barrier. After a brief, shouted exchange the man left the barrier at a run, disappearing around the bend in the road ahead.

A motorcycle engine started with a clatter. A couple of seconds later the man who had run off came speeding towards them on a small shiny Suzuki. He laid the bike over and skidded through an ostentatious hundred-and-eighty-degree turn to come to a stop in front of them. The leader and one of his companions ran to drag the log aside. With a glance behind to make sure the driver was following, the motorcyclist gunned the engine hard and roared away. The truck droned laboriously in his wake.

They rounded the first bend, losing sight of the three men. Julia had recovered her breath. Michael sat against the wall of the truck, his face pale. Julia scrambled across to Selim and pressed two fingers to the side of his neck. After four or five seconds she turned to the others, her face grave.

'How long now?'

Ray shrugged. 'Five minutes? Ten, maybe.'

She made a wry face. 'He might just make it that far.'

48

IN THE WINDOWLESS briefing room at the Israeli Air Force's Dimona base the pilots' attitudes had lost all their casualness. The atmosphere was one of taut expectancy. The pilots were utterly silent, each of them absorbed in his own calculation. They needed ninety seconds to be airborne. Their modified Mirage fighters would head eastward at nearly two thousand kilometres an hour. If the aircraft heading out of the desert was a modern combat plane it would be capable of something very similar. They could be closing at four thousand kilometres an hour. If their commanders wanted to be absolutely sure of keeping the intruder out of Israeli airspace, to ensure any fighting was over the vast empty spaces of the Jordanian hills, the order to scramble had to come in less than five minutes.

Some of the pilots began to move restlessly, stealing glances at watches as complicated as their cockpits. All of them were seasoned fliers, veterans of a number of short, nasty wars. Nevertheless, the prospect of impending combat still made their pulses rise and their palms damp. They watched the officer with growing impatience.

He continued speaking in a low, emotionless voice, apparently untouched by the rising excitement in the room. He stood by a brightly lit map which took in the whole of Israel, Lebanon, Jordan, the northwestern sector of Saudi Arabia and tracts of Syria and Iraq. The map was projected onto a screen. With a hand-held control like a television remote control he could reduce or increase the area displayed. The path of the incoming plane showed as a green fluorescent line which crept slowly forward as he spoke.

The thickly padded headphones he wore were connected by a direct line to a very secret establishment even deeper in the Negev Desert than Dimona itself. Lodged deep in a bunker carved into the solid sandstone of a hill, it was the centre which received and processed information from a number of listening stations and small radar installations. The officer knew that information from this source had in the past proven extremely reliable and had given them warning extraordinarily early. He was unaware that the reason for the timeliness and precision of the information was that it was not gathered on Israeli territory at all.

The secret of this intelligence was known to only a handful of Israelis. It was collected by electronic listening posts and miniaturized radar, developed by the Israelis themselves and installed clandestinely in Jordan, Syria, and even as far east as Saudi Arabia and Iraq. The installation was carried out by specialist teams of engineer commandos who placed the booby-trapped equipment on the remote hilltops of the vast, arid, empty region.

The network gave the Israelis access to huge quantities of information, from potentially hostile military activity to the radio exchanges of Baghdad taxi drivers. It was from these latter, rather than from the breast-beating official communiqués, that the Israelis had been able to puzzle their American counterparts with such uncannily accurate assessments of the damage done to Baghdad by Iranian missile attacks. It was these same tracking stations that had picked up Gerry Greeley's aircraft almost as soon as it had taken off from its Dhahran base.

Although it was all laid out for him on the computer screen at his side the officer was unable to stop himself doing the same calculation as the men. His eyes went to a big clock on the wall. He watched it for several seconds, figuring his worst-case option: if the incoming aircraft suddenly slammed open his throttles and went hell-for-leather for Tel Aviv, or the Dimona nuclear power plant. In four minutes he would have to give his men the word. He turned his attention back to the screen.

He swore. A murmur ran around the group of pilots. It was a sound that held surprise, mystification, and just a suspicion of disappointment. The green fluorescent line had changed direction. It was now advancing, not towards Israel, but northwest, on a bearing that would take it across northeast Jordan, over the Syrian desert and towards Damascus.

The officer grabbed for the microphone that enabled him to speak to the tracker whose voice he had in his headphones. The pilots shuffled and grinned at each other, exchanging jokes, letting the tension go.

In Gerry Greeley the old excitement was beginning to rise. He had left the pipeline and the road just before the tiny, overblown village that was the town of Turayf. It was the point where the road and the pipeline parted company, the road curving southwest along the Saudi border while the pipeline, built by people who scorned national boundaries, sliced on across Jordanian territory towards the sea.

He had dropped even lower now. The aircraft skimmed across the drab, whitish-brown salt flats. Although technically Jordan, this was the Syrian desert. Such water as fell as rain in the area drained into the deep wadis which emptied into this featureless, land-locked depression. Over the millennia, the repeated annual arrival of these waters, laden with dissolved minerals leached out of the rocks, had left the land saline and utterly sterile. It was one of the emptiest, most desolate places in the world. One where he felt confident that a lone aircraft was most unlikely to be observed by a living soul.

Nevertheless, he flew as low as he dared, relying now on the aircraft's own systems, designed to permit it to skim at almost rooftop level over the roughest terrain. That was the manufacturer's story, anyway. Greeley was not yet ready to take them at their word once on the broken mountain landscape that lay ahead. For the next couple of hundred kilometres of billiard-table salt flat, he would trust them.

To the east, over his right shoulder, the sky was now a deep blue-black. In Dhahran it would already be night. Flying west had kept him up with the sun. Only now, flying at zero altitude, had he almost lost sight of the sun. It was just visible behind the ragged line of the mountains that ran almost unbroken down the Mediterranean coast. Above the mountains the sky was a smoky pink. The beaches of Lebanon were in for a great sunset, if anyone in that blighted country bothered to watch any more.

He checked his position on the navigation computer. In an old and redundant reflex he glanced at his watch and then settled his shoulders back easily against his seat. With a laugh of sheer enjoyment he pushed the throttle levers forward.

The flesh of his cheeks seemed to shrink back over the bones. His eyes pressed back in their sockets. The padded seatback slammed harder against him. He sat gripping the controls and grinning, relishing the feel of the monstrous power he had unleashed catapulting the aircraft forward. The speed indicator edged, shivering, towards the twelve hundred kilometre mark. He let it rest there, trembling in the faint vibration as the plane cut through the dense sea-level air.

Gerry watched the needle settle and gave a grunt of satisfaction. He was glad of the speed. Very soon he would be swinging in a wide arc around Damascus. It was a city that had been on a virtual war footing one way or another for years. Although their major air defence systems were still directed towards Israel, especially their SAM missiles, they had an air force that was well served by a lot of very smart combat pilots. Uninvited guests, if they hung around for it, could be made extremely unwelcome.

His route would take him past Damascus eighty kilometres to the east. He would then cross Highway 2, continue straight on until he hit Highway 5 and swing west.

In all, he would be in the Damascus area for no more than six minutes before climbing up over the mountains and into Lebanese airspace. Over the hills and far away. Even if they picked him up he would be out of Syria before they could get planes aloft. Provided they were not already on the alert for something else. He hoped the Israelis had not chosen that afternoon to do anything nasty to Syria. Five minutes after passing Damascus he would have zapped his target and be barrelling out over the sea, seeing what the machine could really do.

Bradman lay in the narrow wedge of shadow, breathing hard, his head cocked in an attitude of listening. Sounds rose from the village below him with astonishing clarity. Voices called, emphatic and harsh. An occasional bark of raucous laughter drifted upwards. Motors started and cut out again. Sharp metallic sounds of cooking utensils came from around the many fires, fires which had grown brighter in the last few minutes as the twilight in the valley had grown thicker.

Gradually, his breathing slowed. No cry came to him, no sudden uproar that would have told him he had been seen. He turned to look appraisingly at the ground he had covered.

From the treeline to where he lay was a distance of two hundred metres. Two hundred metres of broken rock and sparse scrub, all at a forty-five-degree slope. He was grateful to be wearing the camouflage overall. Even with it, and deploying all his jungle veteran's skills to move among the meagre cover, it was a miracle he had not been spotted. It had taken him seven minutes to cover the distance, worming his way down on his back, his weight on his heels and shoulders, to the comparative safety of the spot where he now lay.

It was not close enough. With infinite caution, he leaned out from behind the narrow rock, scanning the slope below. Fifty metres lower down, a little to his right, a jagged cluster of rocks thrust upwards, forming a rough semicircle. They would give him the cover he needed to get off several shots. Inch by inch, testing his ground at each movement, he began edging down the exposed face.

Beneath him he could see quite clearly the men crouched around cooking fires or moving to and fro, swathed in heavy woollen robes against the evening chill. Groups of men squatted around backgammon boards. The click of the dice reached him with crystal clarity, along with the shouted exclamations of the players and their supporters. Two young men walked across the centre of the square, picking a slow path among the parked jeeps and the groups around the fires. They walked hand in hand. None of the backgammon players paid them any attention as they drifted towards a dense clump of pines on the edge of the village. Everyone was free to choose his own form of entertainment.

The sound of an approaching vehicle made him stiffen. Very slowly, he set down the box and lifted the lid. He took out a rocket and fitted it to the launcher, taking great pains that there should be no noise of metal on metal. He began raising the weapon awkwardly to his shoulder.

The sound of the vehicle grew nearer. He ran his tongue over his lips and his eye over the terrain. The dying rays of the sun reddened the hillside above him. From where he sat to the safety of the trees would be a twenty-second run empty-handed on flat ground. On the loose, rocky slope it would take him most of a minute. There were a lot of rifles down there. He swallowed and squinted along the tube of the weapon.

In a crash of gears a pick-up truck bucketed off the main road into the square and skidded to a halt. A man in a checkered headcloth leaped out of the cab and ran over to a nearby campfire. He threw his arms around one of the men there, slapping him repeatedly on the back and kissing him several times on both cheeks. The flat back of the pick-up was empty. With a sigh Bradman lowered his weapon. He replaced the rocket in the box and continued making his way towards the outcrop of rock.

He was perhaps five metres from its shelter when he placed a foot carelessly. Before he could recover, a rock the size of his head was spinning down the hillside. He froze, pressed back into the rock face. The boulder gathered speed, bouncing and leaping over the scree, gathering more rocks in its wake until it was a small avalanche. He watched in helpless horror as the stones hurtled downward. At the foot of the rock wall lay a sloping grassy area, no more than five metres wide. At the far edge of it lay a parked lorry. Beyond the lorry five men squatted, arguing, around a leaping fire. The rocks hit the bottom with a sound like a splash, and formed a rocky delta reaching out onto the grass. A single stone bounced and struck the door of the cab with a clang that seemed to Bradman to resound through the valley.

The men around the fire instantly fell silent. Two of them snatched guns from the pile beside them and ran around the truck, one at each end. Their companions took up their own guns and stood ready to support them. The man at the front of the truck edged his way around the bonnet and then leapt clear of its shelter, dropping to one knee and sweeping the grassy area with the muzzle of his weapon. He stayed for several seconds in that posture. Then, Bradman heard a sudden bray of laughter. The man rose and called to his companion, walking to the door of the cab as he spoke. He pointed out the dent, stroking his fingers over the flaked paintwork, before stooping to take up the stone. Laughing with his companion, he walked back to the fire carrying the rock. He threw it playfully at one of the other men around the fire, making him drop his rifle, and pointed up at the hillside. All their heads turned to look directly at the spot where Bradman lay.

He had no time to avert his face. Any movement would have been fatal. He lay quite motionless, breathing in shallow, soundless gasps. He cursed himself silently for his casualness in not smearing mud on his face. He had been out of combat too long. A laugh rose from the group below him and they turned back to the fire.

For several seconds Bradman lay where he was, hardly daring to breathe. Very slowly, he made himself relax. Only then did he notice that the sun had dropped completely behind the mountain. The place where he lay was now in shadow. Only the trees above him were still bathed in the pink light. Letting out a long sigh he started moving once again, across the last few metres to the protection of the rocks.

For a long moment he lay back against the slope, basking in the safety of his eyrie and resting, easing the cramps in his thighs and back. Refreshed, he sat up and began laying out his equipment. Doing everything soundlessly, he checked the magazine of the rifle and laid it carefully to one side. He reloaded the rocket-launcher and placed that next to the rifle with a spare rocket alongside it. Shifting position slightly to give himself a clearer view through a cleft between two rocks he hauled the binoculars over his head and started scanning the encampment.

He took in the principal building, noting the guards who lounged outside, casual but alert. A short sweep of the ground in front of the building brought him to the helicopters. He examined them closely. They bore no markings and were painted in a particular dun colour that was characteristic of all armies, special to none. The circle of men posted around them told him where they came from. Something in their bearing. He had worked with the special forces of many countries. The Americans were bigger, on average, with a kind of rangy relaxation to them. The British SAS carried a touch of unnecessary bravado, the result, maybe, of making the newspapers too often. These men had the springy, contained look, the self-confident professionalism that marked out the Israelis. There were too many of them for his taste. He was going to be glad of the fading light.

The sound of a motor made him swivel to his left. He thumbed the knurled wheel on the binoculars, bringing into sharp focus a short section of the road some way below the village, where it rounded a hairpin before losing itself again in a fold of the hills. He stared at the patch of road. The engine noise grew louder, dropping suddenly in pitch as the driver was forced into second gear. Amid a snarl of heavy revving, a pick-up truck heaved out of the bend and into Bradman's view. It was preceded by a motorcycle.

The pick-up was nose-on to Bradman. A Toyota. Half the pick-ups in the country were Toyotas. The driver was alone in the cab. He watched it round the turn. Two people sat with their backs to him, only their heads visible over the side of the truck. One of the heads had reddish hair. Opposite those two, head bowed so that he could not make out her face, sat a woman. Abruptly, she raised her head. For just an instant he felt a desire to recoil, to duck into cover. He was staring straight into the face of Julia Colter.

He lowered the binoculars and carefully threaded them over his shoulders. When he ran for it he would dump his weapons, if he had to, but not these binoculars. Unhurriedly, he picked up the rocket-launcher and set it to his shoulder. He rested the nose of the weapon in a niche in the rock.

They would probably make straight for the hotel. Even if they did not, his vantage point covered the whole encampment. He settled himself comfortably, his eyes fixed on the point where the road came off the last bend and into the village.

49

JULIA SAT wedged between the inert form of Selim and the side of the truck. She clung on hard with her left hand, fighting for balance as the driver threw the pick-up through the turns. With her right hand she stroked sweat from Selim's forehead. For the past several minutes perspiration had been the only evidence that he was still alive. All the while, she screamed exhortations at the driver to push on faster, uncertain if he even heard her over the crashing of gears and the straining of the motor.

A shout from Ray made her look up suddenly. They were rounding a shoulder of the mountain. Ahead of them, beyond one more deep, rock-strewn ravine, the road disappeared into a steep basin scooped out of the rock. Beyond the narrow entrance to the canyon they could see the steeply gabled roofs of Bcharré.

Julia's cries to the driver became more urgent. Just once she heard him respond, a mournful, high-pitched wail that said he was trying and offered her in one short sound a panorama of a thousand years of tribal woes. She turned her attention fully back to Selim. The bleeding had been stemmed, though the floor for half a metre around him was sticky with a dirty cement of blood and dust. His clothes and Julia's were wet with it, their faces and hands smeared as though they were participants in some ghastly rite. The pulse in his neck was a faint fluttering, hardly detectable over the vibration of the vehicle. His skin had gone from greyish to a faint, papery yellow. She bent her head close to his ear and spoke, willing him, exhorting him, *ordering* him, to live.

They swayed round two more bends, grazing the rock face at one moment, inches from the sheer drop the next, as the driver grew more reckless. Even through the fever, Michael's relief at reaching the end of his ordeal bordered on euphoria. He grinned through the grime, the blood and the perspiration that caked his face, joining Julia and Ray in urging the driver to a final effort.

At last, the Toyota lurched off the final bend and into the entrance to the canyon. Ray and Michael gave a shout that was almost a cheer at the sight of the village laid out before them. The fires that studded the twilight gave it a festive air that fuelled their joy.

Their motorcycle escort, who had ridden ahead to announce their arrival, sat astride his machine waiting for them. As they came into view he set off again, beckoning them to follow. The guards watched them with slack-jawed curiosity as they passed, two shouting, laughing Europeans and a blood-smeared, haggard woman. Their escort sped through the crowded square, weaving between the campfires and the parked jeeps, shouting to the knots of men and gesticulating at the pick-up that ground along in his wake. He slid to a halt a few paces from the front steps of the hotel and signalled to the driver to do the same. A small group of men, one of them carrying a rolled stretcher, was already running hard towards the slowing Toyota.

Highway 2 flashed beneath the aircraft. Gerry Greeley was hardly aware of it. His attention was riveted on the terrain ahead and on listening in for the warning signal in the cockpit that would tell him Syrian radar had locked onto him. The cockpit stayed silent. He squinted ahead, looking for the distinctive ribbon of Highway 5 slicing north to south through the darkening landscape, hugging the foothills of the first of the ranges he had to cross.

According to the book he did not need to look, the aircraft's own systems would have done his looking for him. But then, according to the book, he should have had a navigator to take care of the systems for him. He preferred to trust his eyesight, the way he had first learned back in Korea.

Less than a minute after he crossed Highway 2 he picked up the headlights of a convoy heading south from Homs to Damascus. Fifty seconds more and he was over the wide dual carriageway, throwing the F16 into a tight westward turn and probably scaring the shit out of the drivers a hundred feet beneath him.

The land immediately began rising. In another thirty seconds he was leaving Syrian airspace, entering Lebanon. His relief was only momentary. The hills rose to nearly nine thousand feet. Then they fell again, steeply down into the Beqaa valley. God knew what kind of shit was down there. Everything from Russian SAMs to American-made Stingers bought retail in Pakistan. He pulled his speed back to subsonic. He would not need the speed again for three minutes, until he had hit this dump Bcharré with his bomb load and was barrelling out, before the half-trained dumbbells operating their anti-aircraft batteries knew he was there.

Relaxed behind the rocks Bradman watched the Toyota enter the village. He smiled grimly at the joy-filled faces of the two men. For a moment his smile dropped away. The woman had disappeared. It returned as Julia straightened from encouraging Selim and the back of her head appeared above the side of the pick-up. He let the binoculars hang and moved his shoulders, seeking the most comfortable position. Dropping his head so that one cheek lay on the cold metal of the rocket-launcher he squinted along it. The bulbous nose of the rocket swivelled slowly as he traversed the weapon, tracking the weaving pick-up. It skidded to a stop between the helicopters and the steps of the hotel. Bradman peered carefully along the sight as the Americans scrambled to their feet, making his target easier. He squeezed the trigger, wincing as the blazing gases of the rocket's propellant scorched his cheek.

Hugging Julia in the jubilation of their arrival, Ray's eye was caught by a metallic flash over the rim of the snow-covered crests. An aircraft streaked into view and came looping towards them, clinging low as it sped across first snow and then the bare red rock. Ray had been in a lot of air raids. After the minutest split second of stupefaction he simply crushed Julia tighter to him, snatched Michael by the wrist and dived over the tailboard.

The Toyota and the furthest helicopter exploded almost simultaneously. The helicopter was transformed instantly into a great orange fireball that pumped gorged coils of oily black smoke into the air above it. The impact on the pick-up was strangely muted. The rocket had torn through the passenger door and exploded inside the cab. A blinding white light, like a camera flashgun, shone through the windows in the instant before they shattered.

The three of them lay face-down in the dirt, too stunned immediately to understand what was happening. They felt the tremendous shock of a rapid series of explosions without grasping its significance. The screaming roar of the aircraft, which came only after the machine was already streaking away, up and over the mountain, made them cower again. Ray's thick arms stayed tight around Julia, pinioning her to the ground.

For a moment, after the plane's scream died, the silence seemed total. Then, slowly, they became aware of a growing background noise, like the sound of a waterfall. Painfully, Ray dragged himself to his feet, pulling Julia after him. He gave a choking cry at the sight of her. Blood covered the front of her shirt. She stood immobile, still too shocked to react, as he examined her. He discovered with relief that the blood was his. It still poured from his nose. Julia's left wrist was injured, probably sprained. She was still too shocked for it to have started hurting.

The helicopter that had been hit blazed fiercely. Explosions from within the heart of the fireball sent fragments in smoking arcs towards them. The machine nearest to it was beginning to blister and fume. In the cab of the Toyota the upholstery, and the driver, burned with a gentle blue flame.

The hotel was a solid mass of leaping fire. Flames spurted from windows and from holes in the roof. The whole of the outside of the building burned, as though it had been painted with flame. It was from there that the sound was coming that had seemed like rushing water. They stared speechlessly at the scene, their faces hollow with shock. Both recognized the effects of napalm.

Julia felt an arm on her shoulder. Michael stood next to her, staring at the blaze. In the flickering light, with his streaked, bloodied face, he looked like a wild man. The three of them, the two men with their arms around Julia's shoulders, stared silently at the destruction.

Bradman was cursing vilely. Not under his breath now, but aloud, spitting the words with bitter fury, knowing he would not be heard amid the furore below. A second rocket sat in the launcher. The brightness of the exploding helicopter had prevented him getting off the fast second shot. Now the fierce light of the burning chopper cast everything beyond it into deep shadow.

Raging at himself, he raised his head above the rocky parapet, straining to make sense of the swirl of figures and oily smoke around the fires. He gave a shout of triumph. In a momentary clearing in the smoke he saw the group of three figures, pressed close together, on the far side of the smouldering pick-up. They were only half hidden by the carcase of the truck.

He dropped back into a firing position. At the same moment a bullet struck the rock with a flat crack, inches from where his head had been. Splinters of stone slashed at his eyes. Cursing, he leaned forward again, keeping his head below the skyline now. He flicked tears from his eyes and swore again. A drift of smoke obscured his target. Shouts from below made him look down the hill. Four men were running hard for the foot of the slope.

He recognized them as some of the Israelis who had ringed

the helicopter. The bastards had seen the muzzle flash of the rocket-launcher.

'Fuck you,' he muttered softly. Raising his shoulder to tilt the weapon, he fired down the slope. The rocket struck the ground a foot from one of the running men. When the explosion cleared the man was no longer there. Bradman laughed a raucous, slightly hysterical bark. The other three men had thrown themselves into the sparse cover. Bullets began slapping into the rocks around him.

Grabbing the rifle, Bradman rose to his knees. With easy, unhurried movements, he found a position that was comfortable. A narrow aperture in the rocks gave him a clear view down the slope. Several more men were sprinting to join the others at the foot of the hill. Casually, he shot one. The others threw themselves flat among the scrub.

Squinting through the gap, he was in time to see flashes from beneath the nearest lorry. Instinctively, he leaned away from the gap just as the bullets bit into the rock. It was narrow, but not too narrow for a chance bullet to pass. He lay back against the slope and peered around the end of his rampart. One of the men was gathering himself for a dash at the slope. Bradman noted his position and pressed himself back into cover. He gave the man two seconds and then leaned out and snapped off a shot at the running man's legs.

His position was not bad. From where he lay he commanded the whole of the bare slope as it fell the two hundred yards or so down to the village. His cover was excellent and he had plenty of ammunition. It was true that he would have to cross two hundred yards of the same barren slope to get away. Also, given time, they could work their way up the slope off out of his sight and take him from above. He looked at the darkening sky. It was time they would not have. In another few minutes it would be dark enough to risk a move. He took up a handful of dust, spat into it and began smearing the dark red mud onto his face.

Julia began to cry. All the pent-up tensions of the last few days came out in immense gulping sobs. Without a word, Michael let his hand slip from her shoulders. She turned her face to Ray and buried it in his chest. Tenderly, taking great care not to hurt her injured arm, he enfolded her in his own arms. He kissed her hair and let her cry.

Around them the confusion began to gel into a pattern. Three tanker lorries had appeared from somewhere and men were rushing to unfurl hoses. A handful of men were struggling into fireproof overalls. The great cylindrical helmets with their smoked plexiglass windows gave them the incongruous air of astronauts.

The hoses began spouting. The crews wasted no time trying to douse the body of the fire. The meagre jets would have been useless against the ferocity of it. Instead, they concentrated on the entrance, attempting to restrain the blaze around the doors.

Gradually, the first ferocity of the inferno was tamed. The doors still burned, but with isolated tongues of flame that leapt and probed among hissing rivulets. The men in the fireproof suits stumbled awkwardly up the steaming steps and burst into the hotel. The doors hung open on broken hinges, revealing the lobby as a shell of flame. Great slow gobs of fire dropped from the ceiling as the materials melted. Only the marble-slab floor had saved the room from becoming totally impassable.

Around the three of them a crowd of young men had gathered. They watched in total silence as the men penetrated the lobby and disappeared, plunging into the flames.

They watched for two minutes before there was a stir among the men with the hoses nearest the door. Ray craned over the heads of the crowd. The first of the rescuers appeared at the door. Between them they supported a short figure who hung around their necks, barely conscious. The hair had gone, leaving the scorched and blistered skin of the scalp. The face was blackened. The eyebrows had evaporated, leaving two absurd crescent-shaped smudges. Ray stood for some seconds, his jaw slack with disbelief.

'Jesus Christ!' he said, under his breath. He looked across at Michael. 'Meyer!'

Michael stared incredulously at the seared face. Ray took Julia by the upper arms and gently shook her. 'Julia, look. For Christ's sake, look who it is.'

Slowly, as though coming out of a deep sleep, Julia turned to look towards the steps. As she did so another cluster of rescuers appeared. Between them, held in a sitting position, they carried a slumped figure. The figure was naked but for a few blackened wisps of clothing. Julia's eyes widened as they brought him down the steps. With an exclamation, she began fighting her way through the crowd. Ray and Michael elbowed through after her.

They came to the front of the watchers, close to the spot where the rescuers were handing over the fire victims to a group of frantic orderlies.

Julia scarcely looked at Meyer. For a second or two she stood transfixed, staring horror-stricken at the tortured face of the other man. With a choking cry, she ran to him and fell to her knees.

'Mehdi!' She cupped his cheek in her palm.

The eyelids flickered and opened. The deep brown eyes wavered, empty and unfocused for a second or two, as though they had forgotten how to look. Then, the brows came together. He seemed to become aware of Julia. The vacant eyes came gradually into focus.

'They shouldn't have, Julia. We were the best hope they had.' The voice was a grating whisper. His hand moved feebly, seeking Julia's. 'Can I have some water?'

Michael touched Julia's shoulder. 'I'll get it.' He pushed his way out of the crowd and ran for the nearest campfire.

Weakly, Bahrawi pressed her hand. The scorched lips twisted in an effort to smile. She held the hand tightly, fighting to stem fresh tears.

'The Ayatollah's way has won, Julia. Your people have

made it so. We were the best chance to fight it and they did this to us. Stupid, isn't it?'

For an instant his face glowed with the old, vigorous, teasing smile. Then, the eyes abruptly lost focus and the head lolled. He mumbled something softly in Farsi. And then he died.

Rough hands pushed Julia aside and began working feverishly at the limp form. Julia felt herself being pulled gently to her feet. Ray's arm was around her shoulders again. She could hear his voice, very gentle, in her ear as he coaxed her through the crowd.

Forty yards away Michael was running towards them. He shouted, holding the water canteen aloft for them to see. Julia clawed tears away from her eyes and made a gesture of hopelessness. Michael opened his mouth to say something. Before any sound came he was snatched off his feet. The canteen flew from his hand to land with a clatter a few yards from them. Michael flew five feet through the air, his arms thrown up in front of him. He hit the ground again, toes first, and pitched onto his face. He slid for a yard through the dust before coming to a halt.

Julia and Ray covered the few yards at a run. On Michael's bare back, six inches below the base of his neck, a hole the size of an egg pumped blood.

Julia opened her mouth and uttered an agonized scream that reverberated over the noise of the camp and echoed off the mountainside. She collapsed into the dust.

Bradman gave a single whoop of victory and rolled away from the aperture. He had been unable to believe his luck. It was almost dark. Any second now and the Israelis would be storming his eyrie. He had just been preparing to get the hell out when the boy had appeared in the light of the camp fire. A perfect target. Shouldering the gun, aiming and firing had taken him just two seconds.

A grenade exploded against the rocky buttress, showering him with rock splinters. Laughing out loud, he dropped the rifle next to the rocket-launcher and began crawling through the gathering darkness up the slope.

Gerry Greeley had thumbed the buttons that released the weight of the bomb load and felt the aircraft buck under its new freedom, as though it shared his own elation. He rammed the throttles to maximum thrust. He let out a full-blooded whoop at the sheer thrill of it as the awesome power of the engines pinioned him against the seat. His eyes felt as though they were filled with mercury as the massive g-forces rammed them back deep in their sockets.

Still whooping with excitement, he dragged at the controls, sending the fighter corkscrewing into an almost vertical climb, back up into the last sunlight. As the aircraft twisted skyward the deep blue of the darkened eastern sky alternated with the suffuse pink and gold of the sunset to the west. Glancing below and behind him he caught the gleam of the last light on the snows of the peaks and the faint pale line of the surf that marked the coast, stretching north to Syria and south to Israel.

At thirty thousand feet he eased out of the climb and turned northwest. Below him the sea was the same midnight blue as the sky at his back. He pursed his lips, began whistling a Cole Porter tune, and sat back finally to enjoy the sunset that had been before him almost since leaving Dhahran. He checked his watch. Right on time. The fuel gauge needle rested on its stop. He stretched out a hand and flipped the switch to start the flow from the reserve tanks.

The engines stopped. They did not cough or shudder. They simply stopped. Dead. He swore once and rocked the switch several times. Exasperated, he waggled the aircraft's wings, aiming to release any blockage in a fuel line. Nothing.

Already, he could feel the plane losing stability. A modern fighter was a very unstable shape. Without the necessary minimum airspeed it would soon start to tumble and spin, no more able to glide than a bucket. Murmuring to himself, he pushed the craft's nose down, putting it into a steep dive. The machine plummeted downward, giving him back manoeuvrability as it picked up speed. Several times he tried to restart the motors, using the plane's own speed. It failed each time.

At fifteen thousand feet he pulled out of the steep dive and into the shallowest one that would keep him airborne. He would get as close to the rendezvous point as he could.

At three thousand feet he decided to call it a day. Beneath him he could just make out the shimmer of whitecaps in the darkness. The water was going to be choppy. A night in the tiny self-inflating life raft was going to be very uncomfortable.

He let the plane drop another thousand feet. He was going to get seasick. He knew that. He had been down in the sea once before, many years earlier. The Yellow Sea, off South Korea. Towards the end of the fourteen hours spent clinging to wreckage before they winched him out he had felt so bad he had seriously considered letting the sea put him out of his misery. The dinghy could not be worse than that.

Settling well into the seat he reached down and felt for the red-painted lever that fired the explosive ejector charge. Bracing himself, he yanked at the lever.

Nothing happened. He yanked at it again, already knowing. 'Bastards!' he screamed.

Frantically, he began scrabbling to release the canopy. He was still fumbling at it when the white glint of foam flashed beneath him. The aircraft was on its side. Its wing tip had bitten into the crests.

'Fuck you, Tom,' he said conversationally, as the plane cartwheeled and crashed flat on its back into the sea.

Epilogue

SPRING HAD STRUCK Washington early and hard. For over a month, since early April, the temperatures had been hovering in the high seventies. In the streets outside, the trees were in full leaf and the banks of flowers that studded the trim government-maintained lawns were bursting with colour. Inside the room, deep in the Senate building where the hearings were being held, the television lights had pushed the temperature over the hundred mark.

Smoke hung in strata below the high ceiling, heaving lazily in the currents of hot air rising from the lamps. Everything else in the room was in uproar. After four weeks of hearings the Senate Committee investigating the affair had just delivered its informal verdict. Their report would not be complete for another six weeks or so. Meanwhile, Major Bradman could leave the room without a stain on his character.

Julia sat motionless at the table in the well of the room. Two lawyers, Ray, and Harry Moore leant over her protectively, attempting to shield her from the few photographers who hung back for pictures of her. Most of the press crowded around Major Bradman. He stood ramrod straight in an immaculate Marine uniform, his chest thick with medal ribbons, gravely accepting the congratulations of his own lawyers.

In the end the case had come down to Ray and Julia's word against Bradman's. As Bradman's lawyers had so plausibly presented it, the word of a distraught sister and her lover against that of a highly decorated, patriotic career officer. An officer who had given his best years to the service of his country; service that had seen him wounded in action three times.

Harry Moore had done his best. The *Times* had had people

combing Washington for any fact, any gossip or whisper that would link Bradman to the kidnapping. They had sent people to Lebanon and to Saudi Arabia trying to prise something loose. There had been nothing, except a threat that had kept the man in Lebanon holed up in his hotel in fear of his life.

Everybody knew Bradman was Tom Jordan's man. Nobody could show a shred of evidence of it. Jordan had stonewalled throughout the hearing. He had admitted to the planned raid. He had insisted it be cancelled as soon as the President had instructed. Admiral Langston's testimony supported that. It was true he had made some calls to a number in Beirut. They had been to a contact he had been nursing there for years. Unfortunately the villa where that phone was had been the subject of a fire-bomb attack. His contact was another casualty of his efforts to help obtain the Colter boy's release.

He understood Julia's grief. He was sorry she had felt it necessary to allow it to cloud her judgment, to accuse fine public servants like the Major.

The Saudis had sent a representative, a delicate-featured man with a Chester Barrie suit and exquisite hands. He was unable to explain how the aircraft that hit Bcharré had come out of Saudi territory. He accepted that the Israelis had tracked it, it was just that the Saudis knew no more about its origins than they did. He regretted it, very much. Since nobody was able to produce either the plane or the pilot, he was unfortunately unable to help elucidate matters. Perhaps one was obliged to question the sincerity of the Israelis, after all. It was yet another line of enquiry that led nowhere.

The room began to empty. Bradman's lawyers gathered in a protective knot around their client, forcing a path for him through the jostling crowd of pressmen and well-wishers. They piloted him slowly towards the door, to the eye of a storm of flashguns and calls for statements from the baying journalists.

They watched him go. Ray wore a faint, sardonic smile and

kept a hand on Julia's shoulder. Julia sat utterly still, her face pale from the many days in the airless room. Her jaw was clenched tight. In the weeks since the hearings began her face had grown thinner so that the strong overhead lights threw her cheeks into shadow.

The swarm of pressmen spilled out of the imposing double doors, leaving the room suddenly quiet. The quiet lasted only a matter of seconds before technicians began noisily dismantling the television equipment. Ray shrugged and shook his head.

'Shall we go?' he said softly. Julia did not respond. She sat, still staring blankly at the door through which Bradman's group had just passed. Ray squeezed her shoulder and spoke again, stooping closer. 'It's all over, Julia. It's time to go home.'

She looked up at him, staring for a second into his face as though she did not recognize him. Then her face softened and she laid her hand on his and gave him a startling, vivacious smile. 'Yeah. You're right. Let's go.'

They made their way to the door, ignoring the mild curiosity of the technicians. Ray kept his arm tight around Julia's shoulders. Something in her smile had troubled him. Throughout the hearings she had borne everything with unbelievable control. She had not shed a tear under the vicious and sneering questioning of Bradman's or the State Department's lawyers. Now, a glint of hysteria in her smile made him fear something was about to crack.

He guided her along the panelled corridor towards the stairs. Officials with files clamped under their arms and marshals with ostentatious side arms glanced at them furtively or greeted them sympathetically, depending on their own interpretation of the hearings. Ray nodded acknowledgment, Julia dispensed more over-bright, distracted smiles.

They made their way up the wide stairs to the lobby of the building. A few stragglers were retrieving bags or light coats from the cloakroom. Outside, through the immense glass doors, Bradman was posing for pictures for the milling photographers. Ray fished in a pocket for a plastic tab and handed it over in exchange for Julia's shoulder bag. Dumbly, she took it from him and slung it over her shoulder. Together, they walked out into the sunlight.

They paused, squinting, at the top of the broad sweep of steps. Bradman was reading a telegram to the assembled television crews and journalists. It was a message of congratulation from President Wilton. He finished reading amid a rattle of applause and folded the paper with studious care, making to stow it inside his tunic. At that moment he appeared to catch sight for the first time of Julia and Ray, who stood, two isolated figures, to his left. He turned and began walking purposefully towards them. His smile was a telegenic mixture of sympathy and modest pride, like the winner of a tennis tournament about to offer condolences to a brave loser.

Julia watched him approach, trailed by the eager television crews. Her face was bleak and empty. As he drew closer, tall and immaculate, a picture of rectitude and old-fashioned values, Julia's eyes focused on his. For just an instant, his face masked from the cameras, he let her see him gloat. The arrogance and contempt stayed in his eyes for only a fraction of a second before he extended a hand to her, smiling.

Julia stared into the open, tanned face. The gleaming, hypocrite's grin seemed to fill her vision. Her own hand slipped into the shoulder bag. She thought of Michael's mutilated hands. She saw him lying, broken, in the dirt of Bcharré, caked in mud and blood. She thought, too, of Rich Archer. Vain and pompous, and afraid, but kind and loving and, above all, utterly harmless. And of Mehdi Bahrawi. Their first strange encounter, many years before, and his appalling death. Her hand closed around the inlaid hilt of the knife Mehdi had given her that first time she had met him.

Bradman made no sound as he fell. He lay sprawled across the top four steps, his limbs spreadeagled, a foot from Julia. Blood had splashed onto her shoes.

For an instant the world was quite silent. The press corps,

the spectators, the lawyers, Julia, Ray, stood mute and immobile, unable immediately to take in what had happened. Then, everybody spoke at once. The crowd rushed forward to jostle around the lifeless Bradman. Two uniformed policemen pushed their way through and thrust back the crowd while a third shouted into a walkie-talkie. The babbling mob craned to stare down at the body. A hole the size of a penny just above his right cheekbone discharged a thin trickle of blood.

A uniformed doorman pushed his way breathlessly through the crowd and grabbed the arm of the policeman with the radio. He pointed to an office building four hundred yards away. 'Over there,' he bawled. 'I saw a flash. And smoke. From the roof.' The policeman turned to squint at the building, already yelling new instructions into the walkie-talkie.

Stiff with shock, Julia gradually relinquished her grip on the knife and withdrew her hand from the bag. She turned to Ray. 'Get me away from here, please. I need to be sick.'

At the back of the crowd a tall, bulky, sallow-skinned man, with a light silk suit and several gold rings, pushed his way forward, seeking a view of the body. His suit strained over his enormous belly as he leaned forward over the shoulders of the knot of people. Finally, satisfied, he turned away. Smiling thinly, he glanced up at the building where the doorman had pointed. With a nod to himself he set off down the steps, smiling broadly now and treading with a surprisingly light step to where a chauffeured Lincoln limousine waited for him.

Fontana Paperbacks: Fiction

Fontana is a leading paperback publisher of fiction. Below are some recent titles.

- ☐ ULTIMATE PRIZES Susan Howarth £3.99
- ☐ THE CLONING OF JOANNA MAY Fay Weldon £3.50
- ☐ HOME RUN Gerald Seymour £3.99
- ☐ HOT TYPE Kristy Daniels £3.99
- ☐ BLACK RAIN Masuji Ibuse £3.99
- ☐ HOSTAGE TOWER John Denis £2.99
- ☐ PHOTO FINISH Ngaio Marsh £2.99

You can buy Fontana paperbacks at your local bookshop or newsagent. Or you can order them from Fontana Paperbacks, Cash Sales Department, Box 29, Douglas, Isle of Man. Please send a cheque, postal or money order (not currency) worth the purchase price plus 22p per book for postage (maximum postage required is £3.00 for orders within the UK).

NAME (Block letters)_____

ADDRESS_____

_____

While every effort is made to keep prices low, it is sometimes necessary to increase them at short notice. Fontana Paperbacks reserve the right to show new retail prices on covers which may differ from those previously advertised in the text or elsewhere.